The Stories of
FANNIE HURST

T0162338

The Stories of
FANNIE HURST

CHOSEN AND WITH AN INTRODUCTION BY

SUSAN KOPPELMAN

The Helen Rose Scheuer Jewish Women's Series

The Feminist Press
at The City University of New York
New York

Published by the Feminist Press at the City University of New York
The Graduate Center, 365 Fifth Avenue, New York, NY 10016
feministpress.org

First Feminist Press edition, 2004

08 07 06 05 04   5 4 3 2 1

Compilation and introduction copyright © 2004 by Susan Koppelman.
The stories of Fannie Hurst are reprinted here by arrangement with Brandeis
University and Washington University, St. Louis. Copyright to individual stories is held
in the name of the author.
All rights reserved.

No part of this book may be reproduced or used, stored in any information retrieval
system or transmitted in any form or by any means, electronic, mechanical, photo-
copying, recording, or otherwise without prior written permission from The Feminist
Press at the City University of New York, except in the case of brief quotations embod-
ied in critical articles and reviews.

Library of Congress Cataloging-in-Publication Data

Hurst, Fannie, 1889-1968.
    [Short stories. Selections]
    The stories of Fannie Hurst / chosen and with an introduction by
Susan Koppelman.— 1st Feminist Press ed.
        p. cm. — (The Helen Rose Scheuer Jewish women's series)
    ISBN 1-55861-483-4 (pbk. : alk. paper) — ISBN 1-55861-488-5
(library cloth : alk. paper)
    1. Women—Fiction. 2. Domestic fiction, American. 3. Feminist fiction,
American. I. Koppelman, Susan. II. Title. III. Series.
    PS3515.U785A6 2004
    813'.52—dc22

                                                                        2004017137

Steven H. Scheuer, in memory of his mother and in celebration of her life and the
100th anniversary of her birth (1995), has been pleased to endow the Helen Rose
Scheuer Jewish Women's Series. *The Stories of Fannie Hurst* is the eleventh named book
in the series.

Text design by Dayna Navaro
Printed on acid-free paper by Transcontinental Printing
Printed in Canada

This book is dedicated to the fourteen women who participated in the Fannie Hurst Reading Project between 1985 and 1988:

Linda Knowlton Appel
Josey Briggs
Janet Cuenca
Susan Currier
Bernice Curry
Beth DaGue
Gail Mills
Nancy Movshin
Bertha Russ
Jeanne Ryan
Babette J. Sommer
Robin Mayer Stein
Mary Beth Wimp
Virginia Wise

They read all eight volumes of stories by Fannie Hurst (although none of the uncollected stories) and made recommendations of the ten stories they each thought most worthy of reprinting for contemporary audiences.

And to the ten women and two men who were in my class on mothers and daughters in the Oasis Program at Famous Barr in South St. Louis in 1985, who remembered the South St. Louis world in which many of Fannie Hurst's stories were set and who always read "beyond the endings."

And to Martha K. Baker and Betty Burnett, St. Louis authors who wrote with intelligence and kindness about Fannie Hurst as a home-town woman during the years when people weren't paying attention, who became my friends, and who inherited the responsibility of visiting Fannie Hurst's grave in the Shaare Emeth Cementary when I moved to Arizona.

CONTENTS

INTRODUCTION

Rediscovering Fannie Hurst

Until recently a Great American Writer had to be male, white, upper-class, Christian, apparently heterosexual, and preferably dead. And while the rules for who could be considered important began to shift over time, not so the rules about the language authors used: in order to be accepted as GAWs, they had to learn to write like WASPs, in "standard," "cultured" English—the same language that is still taught in schools, and the same language that is still a necessary passport to professional success in most sectors of American society.

In the last forty years—and only thanks to the efforts of writers, scholars, teachers, and activists who are outsiders—have we really begun to move toward a broader, more diverse, and more inclusive definition of what constitutes American culture, American language, and American literature. (And here I include women of all backgrounds among the outsiders who struggled to be heard.) Despite fierce and still lingering resistance, "Great Books" courses now include Toni Morrison and Richard Wright, and surveys of American literature include Kate Chopin, James Baldwin, Hisaye Yamamoto, N. Scott Momaday, Paula Gunn Allen, Americo Paredes, Sandra Cisneros, Bharati Mukherjee, and Zora Neale Hurston. We understand "greatness" as something that has been culturally determined and literary greatness as something that transcends the conventions of grammar and the boundaries of the dialect of the power elite.

Yet some writers who are great by our new understanding of greatness have not yet been included in this great awakening. One of these is Fannie Hurst. It is time to say, for the record, that Fannie Hurst is a Great American Writer.

Those of us who search the American twentieth century keep finding traces of Fannie Hurst (1885–1968). Literary scholars rediscover her novels and short stories, while historians and sociologists read these same works and realize they are important social documents. Historians of the New Deal discover her as a figure close to the highest levels of government and activism. Scholars of secular American Judaism notice her involvement with Jewish war relief efforts and, towards the end of her life, with Israeli causes, as well as the fact that her early short stories were among the first fictional representations of American Jewish ghetto life. Women's studies scholars recognize her as a committed feminist and a vital early chronicler of the lives and concerns of working women. Working-class studies scholars value her depictions of the working conditions of people whose labors were the most poorly paid and the least often documented. Film scholars are impressed by the numerous films made from her fiction and her connections with important figures in the world of early American cinema; media scholars note her participation in each new medium—radio, film, and television—as it developed; and popular culture scholars find imprints of her carefully managed celebrity in dozens of venues.

In the last dozen years we have begun to see explorations of her work in conjunction with the writings of Anzia Yezierska and Edna Ferber in some of the journals devoted to multi-ethnic American literature and Jewish literature. Hurst's achievements and influence are being recognized by the contemporary literary critical establishment and, as a result, by teachers, students, scholars, and general readers—but until the publication of this book, they have had little access to her work.

Hurst's novel *Imitation of Life* has been in and out of print but is not reliably available, and her other seventeen novels and all eight of her story collections are out of print. A dwindling number of copies exist in libraries and with book dealers (who tell me her work has little value in the used-book market, though it has begun to appear with some regularity on eBay and the online book markets). Only a handful of her stories can be found in contemporary anthologies (and almost all of these are my own collections). Film scholars know her name, but tend to ignore the books behind the movies. Even the fine biography of Hurst by Brooke Kroeger, *Fannie: The Talent for Success of Writer Fannie Hurst,* which appeared in 1999, seemed to do little to revive lasting critical, scholarly, or popular interest in Hurst's vast body of work. Those readers old enough to remember her from her peak years—which ended with the 1940s—grow fewer by the day.

Yet Fannie Hurst was once the most popular and highly paid writer in the United States, an acknowledged leader in social causes, and an international celebrity.

In the period between 1912 and the mid-1930s, Hurst's short stories were dearly loved, eagerly awaited, and avidly read. These were times when literacy was spreading to all classes, and writing still faced little competition from other mass media. The announcement on the cover of *Cosmopolitan* or the *Saturday Evening Post* of "A New Fannie Hurst Story Inside" (or an advertisement on the side of the city busses) could be counted on to sell out the entire issue. In all,

Hurst published more than three hundred short stories, sixty-three of which were collected in eight volumes that appeared during her lifetime.

Hurst's eighteen bestselling novels were translated into fourteen languages. She published work in every form except poetry: five plays, a full-length autobiography, an autobiographical memoir, many magazine articles and personal essays, plus the uncounted, often unsigned articles over five decades for the numerous organizations to which she devoted much of her life.

Hurst independently wrote several screenplays and wrote or collaborated on half a dozen more. In all, twenty-nine films were made from her fiction. Among the best-remembered are *Imitation of Life* (1934, 1959), *Humoresque* (1920, 1946), *Back Street* (1932, 1941, 1961), and *Young at Heart* (first filmed as *Four Daughters* in 1938 and then remade as the well-known musical in 1954). Such legendary directors as Frank Borzage, Frank Capra, and Douglas Sirk collaborated with such legendary scriptwriters as Frances Marion in their effort to bring Fannie Hurst's fiction to the screen. In their time, the films' origins in works by Fannie Hurst were considered major selling points (although each successive film version seemed farther removed from what she had actually written).

Hurst's work was also esteemed by reviewers and critics. Six of her stories were reprinted in the annual *The Best American Short Stories* annuals including "T. B." and "She Walks in Beauty"; more than a dozen others were listed in the BASS Index of significant stories for the year in which they were first published; and one of her stories, "Humoresque," was also included in *The O. Henry Prize Stories*. Edward O'Brien, writing in the 1916 volume of *The Best American Short Stories*, compared Hurst with Mark Twain and O. Henry, saying that she "interpret[ed] with fine democratic heart the heart of the American people as adequately as" they did and declared his conviction that "the most essential literary documents of our city life for the inquiring literary historian of another century" would be the stories of Fannie Hurst. Editors eagerly sought permission to include her stories in anthologies—both those designed for mass-market appeal and those intended for classroom purposes. Twenty-four of her stories have been reprinted at least once.

Fannie Hurst's writing career was so productive and so successful and so important that if she had done nothing else but write, we would be able to say *dayanu*—it was sufficient. But she was also an activist in the service of social justice causes. For more than forty years the name of Fannie Hurst appeared on letterheads of charitable organizations, lending them prestige and panache. Hurst donated money and time, doing the work she did best— writing articles. She also gave speeches and raised funds. However, I believe that the most important social justice advocacy and activities of Fannie Hurst were her short stories.

For instance, Hurst's 1915 story "T. B." humanizes the most feared and dangerous public health scourge of the period of her young womanhood—tuberculosis—and chronicles early public health attempts to teach people how to protect themselves from the disease. The story captures an historical reality: the 1905 educational traveling exhibit that was the first public activity of the National Association for the Study and Prevention of Tuberculosis (now The American Lung Association), founded the previous year. It also brings together many of Hurst's concerns: capitalist exploitation of workers, sexist exploitation of women, and the importance of education as a means of empowerment of the exploited. Here they are explored in a parable-like tale of the Innocent but Foolish Maiden, exploited equally and simultaneously by the Bad (Impersonal, Profits Over People) Corporation and the Selfish Cad, who is saved by the Good Man (who has himself been saved by) and the Public Health Service. The story teaches good health habits: getting the right nourishment and plenty of rest and fresh air and exercise. It also teaches recognition of The Wrong Man, i.e., the selfish man who cares more for his pleasure than for the well-being of the young woman who has become ill from the unhealthy circumstances of her work life and through his careless treatment of her.

Hurst played a part in Heterodoxy, the radical women's dining group that met in Greenwich Village between 1912 and 1940 for conversation, conviviality, consciousness raising, and organizing. It included women from all the professional and creative careers they were then pioneering—law, prison reform, social work, education, journalism, and so forth.[1] She supported sex education and reproductive rights with her membership in Planned Parenthood, which was then considered a radical organization. She worked for peace with the Women's International League for Peace and Freedom. She lobbied for civil rights in collaboration with the Urban League, the NAACP, the Mayor's Committee on Unity, and the American Committee for the Foreign Born. She participated in the struggle for the professionalization and unionization of writers through her militant participation in the Authors' Guild, PEN International, and the Writers War Board. She advocated on behalf of settlement houses and educational opportunities for the disadvantaged, on behalf of women's right to retain their name after marriage—as she did—and on behalf of the social and medical rights of homosexuals.

Hurst is listed as one of the members of the Conference for Progressive Political Action founded in Chicago in 1922. She also belonged to the Victor L. Berger National Foundation. The founding president of the organization was Clarence Darrow, and the vice presidents included Jane Addams, John Dewey, and Upton Sinclair. She worked against fascism and anti-Semitism, lobbied for early American entry into the Second World War, and supported many Jewish social service organizations in the United States, ranging from Hadassah to the Guild for the Jewish Blind and the Federation of Jewish Philanthropies. At the same time, she helped raise funds for the Children's Welfare Fund, the Salvation Army, the YWCA, and the American Cancer Society.

Hurst became a celebrity in a way that is today reserved for movie, music, and sports stars, but rarely applies to writers. For decades the *New York Times* reported on Hurst's comings and goings, from her habitual early morning walks in Central Park with her beloved Yorkies to her frequent departures via ocean liner for travels abroad, from the interior decoration of her legendary three-story apartment in the Hotel des Artistes on 67th Street just off of Central Park West to her stylish wardrobe, to her diets.

Born at her maternal grandparents' farm in Hamilton, Ohio, Fannie Hurst grew up in St. Louis, the daughter of first-generation German Jewish Americans Rose Koppel and Samuel Hurst. Her childhood was not the comfortable middle-class idyll she portrays in her 1958 autobiography *Anatomy of Me: A Wanderer in Search of Herself*. There were many crises: medical, financial, and emotional. When she was four years old, her older and only sister died during a diphtheria epidemic. Her father had a hard time earning a living, changing businesses at least four times during her girlhood, never achieving much financial success, and failing dismally at least once. The family is listed at eleven different addresses before she was sixteen, all of them boardinghouses. According to her autobiography, she shared a bedroom with her parents for much of her girlhood. She had absolutely no sex education but was no doubt exposed to some version of the primal scene. Her story "The Spangle That Could Be a Tear" offers eloquent illustration of the need for sex education and of the vulnerability to sexual abuse of children whose innocence endangers them. How much these themes related to her own childhood cannot be known at this date, but they were themes she explored with aching insight in other stories and, most dramatically, in the two novels that seem to have the most autobiographical overtones: *Star-Dust* and *Imitation of Life* (especially the first third of the book).

Unlike many girls of her generation, she insisted on completing her high school studies. She attended St. Louis's only public high school at the time, Central High School, and then was able to enroll at Washington University in St. Louis, just a streetcar ride away from her family's home. She received her degree in 1909 and published her first short story that same year in *Reedy's Mirror*.[2] Six more of her stories, including "The Joy of Living," which opens this collection, were published in *Reedy's*. Although she had been "scribbling" since early girlhood and her work had frequently appeared in student publications, this was her first recognition in the professional literary marketplace, and a highly esteemed recognition it was. At the time, *Reedy's* circulation surpassed that of *Atlantic Monthly*.

Fannie's graduation was followed by a year-long period of anguished discussion, argument, suffering, and despair in the Hurst household regarding her future. At the end of this period she moved to New York City, where she lived and wrote for the rest of her life. Although her earliest years there were characterized by the young writer's adventures wandering the city streets and sitting up late in the night courts of Lower Manhattan observing the defendants, struggles in grueling jobs such as waitressing and department store clerking, and rejections of her literary efforts, she achieved startling results from her many literary submissions in 1912 when she published twelve short stories in two leading mass-market magazines of the day, *Cavalier* and *Saturday Evening Post*. On the strength of "Summer Resources," editor Ray Long, who inaugurated the skyrocketing prices paid to authors who wrote for William Randolph Hearst–owned magazines, decided he wanted Hurst to write exclusively for his *Cosmopolitan Magazine*. By 1918, *Cosmopolitan* had successfully beaten out all the other magazines in negotiating an exclusive contract with Hurst for all of her short stories.

Through her writing she far surpassed any success her family managed to achieve, becoming a very wealthy woman and one of the most famous figures in a city of four million. She was a well-known and sought-after public speaker. She had one of the earliest radio advice shows and was a frequent guest host for her friend Mary Margaret McBride's radio talk show. And she also had her own television talk show in the 1940s and 1950s.

As an adult, Hurst had a rich personal life. Her only marriage, which lasted for thirty-seven years, was very happy, despite the unconventional way in which it was lived and the early objections made to her choice of husband by her parents; they disapproved of his immigrant status and his Russian Jewish rather than German Jewish origin. Jacques (born Jacob) Danielson was a music teacher and pianist mentored by the Hungarian-born and world-famous concert pianist, composer, and teacher, Raphael Joseffy. "Jack," as Fannie called him, toured the United States and Europe with Joseffy, and it was on one such tour that he and Fannie first met. He was phobic about public appearances, so the great concert career that had once been predicted for him never came about, though his career as an accompanist to and music teacher of some who did achieve public success was remembered by them with respect and gratitude. He also became his wife's business manager, and her great wealth was due not just to the extraordinary payments she received for her work but also to his competent management of her finances.

Hurst and Danielson were married in 1915, the year of Joseffy's death and while Jack was still not yet an American citizen. Their union remained a secret, however, until a reporter accidentally discovered their marriage records in a New Jersey courthouse and announced to the world in 1920 that they had been married but living separately for five years. The news created an explosion in the media, which resulted in the term "a Fannie Hurst marriage" to describe a modern marriage between two independent people who maintained separate lives and residences. Hurst and Danielson had divergent interests and social realms: he was not the political activist she was; she found the classical music world rather boring, though she profited from her association with it as a writer, incorporating references to and metaphors derived from music in many stories, and exploring the social and class tensions around the pursuit of music as a career in "Humoresque."

She never fully recovered from her husband's death in 1952, despite her full public and literary life and being courted by a number of prominent men.

Hurst had a great gift for enduring friendships. Ten of the women with whom she became friends in her girlhood remained close, visiting her and corresponding with her for the rest of their lives. When it came time for Fannie to write her autobiography, she asked them all to write their memories of her early years. Some of their words and stories found their way into *Anatomy of Me*. But not all of those memories were included. My favorite of the unpublished stories that languish in the archives of the Harry Ransom Humanities Research Center at the University of Texas at Austin is about the 1904 World's Fair in St. Louis. She and her best friend used to take the streetcar to the fair every day during that summer. It was their habit to find a spot on one of the thoroughfares that was empty of people at that moment. The two young women would then begin to look up, pointing, gasping, and making "oooooh"ing sounds until a crowd gathered and began to join them in their scrutiny of the sky. When the crowd got big enough to satisfy the jokers, they would edge their way to its outskirts, yell "What are you all looking at? There's nothing there," and run away.

Hurst's most famous friend was Eleanor Roosevelt. The two women met when they both became involved in the struggle for better wages and working conditions for domestic workers (conditions captured in Hurst's 1923 novel *Lummox*), and Roosevelt brought Hurst into the center of New Deal politics. In November 1936, the First Lady wanted only one friend by her side while she waited with her husband for the outcome of the vote on his second term: she waited with Fannie Hurst.

While her bonds with women friends were strong, Hurst had a relationship with her mother that was simultaneously devoted and suffocating.

According to Hurst's autobiography and some of her letters at Brandeis, Rose Koppel Hurst had an explosive and unpredictable temper which kept her husband and daughter off balance and on the defensive. The fact that sunshine always followed Rose's storms evidently kept them attached to her, but the emotional abuse she heaped on her husband and daughter during these outbreaks left scars on the young writer. Rose Koppel Hurst may have been the victim of a mood disorder. Hurst's 1921 story, "She Walks in Beauty," in describing the horror of drug addiction—the addiction of a lovely upper-middle-class "nice" woman and its impact on her daughter's life—may be an indirect record of her mother's mood swings. At the time of its publication, the editors of *Cosmopolitan* touted it as "A Great Masterpiece—and One of the Most Impressive Stories Published in Years."

"She Walks in Beauty" is only one of the many mother/daughter stories Hurst published. The relationship was a theme she explored repeatedly in her stories and novels. Her first novel, the 1921 *Star-Dust,* and her more famous novel, the 1933 *Imitation of Life,* have the mother/daughter relationship at their center as do "Forty-Five" and "The Hossie-Frossie" in this collection.

Among the people who occupied Hurst's brilliant social life, New York Mayor Fiorello LaGuardia was an important figure, as was legendary Reform Rabbi Stephen Wise. Leon Trotsky, whom she met on a summer 1924 trip to post-revolutionary Russia when he was still commissar of the Red Army and Lenin's right-hand man, proved that he had memorized one of her novels (*Lummox,* also Hurst's own personal favorite) by reciting long passages to her. She had friendships with the writers Rebecca West, Dorothy Canfield Fisher, and Zona Gale that included all of the best elements of women's bonds: gossip, encouragement, mutual reflections of their best selves, good food, and fun. And she was a friend, patron, and financial resource to Zora Neale Hurston, an important literary and personal connection which has become a center of controversy among scholars in recent years: the women left differing versions of their relationship in their writings, and while both were prone to being unreliable narrators of their own lives, there were clearly tensions emanating from their unequal statuses as white and black women, rich and poor, donor and recipient. Their relationship was further complicated by the fact that Fannie thought she was a lot older than Zora—because both women lied about their ages (and were, in fact, just about the same age)—and treated Zora as a protégée rather than a peer. Furthermore, Hurston didn't seem to notice or understand that Hurst, as a Jewish woman, was subject to some of the same forms of prejudice and exclusion that Hurston, as a black woman, was subject to. Therefore, Fannie's attempts to collaborate with her on defying conventional exclusionary practices were sometimes interpreted by Zora as exploitations.

Hurst continued to write and publish until the mid-1960s, although her audience declined steadily. When Abram Sacher, the founding president of Brandeis University, received a phone call in 1968 telling him of Fannie Hurst's death and her request that he deliver the eulogy at her funeral, he was both surprised and struck with pity for a woman once so famous and now apparently so forgotten that she had to invoke the kindness of a stranger to be remembered. Yet her request may have been a reflection of her instinct for public relations, her recognition of their shared St. Louis roots, and her wish to assert her sense of connection with the American Jewish community. Sacher and his wife had, in fact, met Hurst once, years earlier, when they had shared a table for a few days during a vacation. On that occasion he had spoken with his usual passionate enthusiasm about the soon-to-be-great Jewish university he was in the process of building. Now, years later, he was astonished to discover that Fannie Hurst had made Brandeis heir to half her considerable fortune. The other half went to Washington University in St. Louis, her hometown alma mater.

She seems to have wanted to position herself as a significant and committed participant in both the secular charitable and secular intellectual Jewish communities represented by Sacher and Brandeis. And to secure a place for herself in literary history, she chose the English departments of the two universities she thought most likely to respect her work: Brandeis because she was a Jew, Washington University because she was a distinguished graduate. At both universities, in the buildings that house the English departments, there are Hurst Lounges, where, standing at lecterns in front of her portrait, poets and critics, novelists and short story writers share their work with audiences of colleagues and students. Many in these audiences, I imagine, do not know or even wonder for whom the lounge was named or who the woman in the picture is. Most of those poets and critics, novelists and short story writers are there as Hurst Professors; she endowed a professorship in each of those English departments, which has accounted for the frequent exchanges and the close relationship between the two departments over the years.

In Fannie Hurst's peak years, her writing and the historical moment were perfectly matched. She had an enormous natural audience—the millions of recent immigrants and first-born generation of Americans about whom she wrote, struggling for economic survival and with the tensions between Old World traditions and assimilation into the American ethos of individualism. For these readers, the preparation for reading Fannie Hurst was their own lives. For others, it was sympathy with those lives or curiosity about them.

That "natural" audience of Eastern European immigrants and their first-generation American families that existed in Hurst's own time is gone. But we can learn to read her from a contemporary perspective as our nation resumes the struggle to incorporate huge waves of new immigrants from other lands. Meanwhile Hurst's work offers scholars from the fields of American literature, American studies, Jewish studies, African American studies, women's studies, family and labor history, film studies, and popular culture rare insights into what is now a lost world. General readers, too, can enter this world, while at the same time enjoying her remarkable gifts as a storyteller and her enormous sophistication and skill as a literary stylist.

Fannie Hurst's greatest literary achievements were her short stories. She knew how to tell a story; she created characters who breathed; she captured the reality of an oft-neglected segment of the American population with a seriousness and sympathy that has rarely been equaled. An important American writer, she transferred the meticulous artistry of the nineteenth-century regionalist realists—their emphasis on the telling details of domestic life, accessible language, and stories of common women and social injustice—to urban workers of the early twentieth century. She was an ironist, a humorist, and a modern tragedian.

Hurst is also one of America's inheritors of the emotionally and socially potent literary school founded by the great (mostly) European nineteenth-century naturalists to whom she refers in her autobiography: "I inclined toward authors who labored in the field of the common man: Tolstoy, Dostoevsky, Gorki, Dumas, Balzac, de Maupassant, Ibsen, Strindberg, Wedekind, Lagerlof, Undset, Arnold Bennett, O. Henry, Edwin Markham, Edgar Lee Masters."

Hurst took as her subject matter what she called "the common man" or "the common people." During her lifetime, she drew closer to these common people, leaving her family and hometown to live among them, sharing the material details of their lives—details judged distasteful and repugnant in the world of her childhood, details her family was gratified to have escaped, details about which nice people didn't talk and to which ladies paid no attention. (At the same time, once her work had brought in enough money for her to live comfortably and even luxuriously—although never carelessly— she seems to have felt no compunction about spending it and enjoying it. She was always generous with her wealth, but never so generous that she risked the continuation of its personal benefits to her.) Her stories draw vivid pictures of a slice of American society that previously had been largely ignored in literature. Her characters are the huddled masses—the polyglot, immigrant former peasants in the process of becoming urban Americans. Most often, they are Jewish immigrants from Eastern Europe. Usually they are working-class people, learning to survive in a new place, eager to assimilate into a new culture, but anxiously drawn to the old. Sometimes they are people who have become richer and more comfortable than they ever imagined they could become—but are not as happy as they thought they would be if they ever did.

The richness, variety, and authenticity of Fannie Hurst's early portrayals of urban Jewish life stand as one of her major achievements—and one of the reasons for us to read her work today. Hurst wrote about the conflicts between old and new cultures experienced within families of immigrants and exacerbated by the lure of assimilation for some and the impossibility of assimilation for others. She depicts the varying degrees of insistence by the parents on loyalty to old ways and old values, and the intergenerational turbulence and confusion that occurs when parents become the pupils of their children in "how to be American." She portrays the children's sometimes disrespectful and condescending assumption of authority over their parents based on the children's quick metamorphoses into "natives" at ease with local customs and the new language. Hurst also brings a nuanced attention to gender to the assimilation question. In her 1925 story, "The Gold in Fish," the disrespectful child and apparently successful assimilator is a son, and the loyal child upon whom assimilation is urged but who we, as readers, understand is incapable of and utterly resistant to the necessary changes, is a daughter.

Family resolutions about how to adapt to the New World often turned on two public manifestations of the self: one's name and one's appearance. Individual choices on these matters were complicated by differences among family members about which were right or wrong, acceptable and unacceptable, possible and impossible choices for them as individuals. Many Jewish Americans wanted to seem, or actually to become, as assimilated as possible in order to take advantage of the greater opportunities of all kinds available to those who are most "like" the members of the dominant culture, i.e., white[3] Christians. Then again, they may have wanted to become Americanized by changing their names because they thought of their history as that of a wandering people, a history of successive assimilations, and knew full well that there already had been successive name changes. They may, in fact, have seen the overarching "fact" of their tradition as change, adaptation for the sake of survival. "The Gold in Fish" is perhaps the most important presentation of this struggle in American literature. Film historian Patricia Erens notes in her 1984 book *The Jew in American Cinema* that the era of the Ghetto film begins and ends with Fannie Hurst films, both wonderfully true to the Hurst stories: "Humoresque," first filmed in 1920, and "The Gold in Fish," filmed in 1929 under the title *The Younger Generation*.

Hurst is again noteworthy as one of the very first literary chroniclers of American urban working women. She wrote about them with her feminist consciousness attuned to issues of sexual harassment and the careless disposal of women as they age beyond their youthful and commercially useful sexual appeal. She especially singled out and wrote about the lives and struggles of women laboring in the garment industry—the "rag trade"—whether clerking in department stores, modeling in wholesale clothing houses, designing, or sewing. She also portrayed the circumstances of women clerking for small businesses, laboring in private homes and large office buildings as domestic workers, and in other urban sex-segregated jobs.

In *Anatomy of Me,* Hurst includes her memories of Willie, an African American woman domestic worker Hurst encountered in her early years, either in one of the boardinghouses she and her family lived in or in the Hurst household in the days of Fannie's college years. Hurst had an acute and uncomfortable awareness of the fact that Willie worked too hard, was treated unfairly by her employer, whether that was the boardinghouse keeper or her mother, and worked under oppressive and unhealthy conditions—too many hours, too little warmth in winter, too few escapes from the oppressive heat and humidity of St. Louis summers, too few rewards, too little respect. She identifies this early awareness as influencing her adult dedication to social action and to socially conscious fiction. These early inclinations were reinforced when she herself took temporary jobs in factories in St. Louis and department stores and restaurants in New York and were informed by her undergraduate study of history, economics, and labor at Washington University[4] and experiences of social justice struggles familiar to her from her night court observations and the stories told by the women of Heterodoxy.

Hurst cared about working women; she clearly meant to be their advocate, as her involvement with a variety of related organizations demonstrates. But her most important means of advocacy was through the medium of her fiction. Social scientists found Hurst's portraits believable counterparts of the data they collected. But Hurst was not writing for them; she was writing for the working women themselves. Her stories provided her readers with a means of examining and reflecting on their own lives. She helped them to recognize that the problems of sexual harassment, unhealthy working conditions, inadequate benefits, age discrimination, and unequal pay were problems shared by millions of working women. She also, at times, provided a model of "good work"—work that was fairly compensated and performed in a safe and respectful environment. Even more, she created images of working women that encouraged their real-life models to take pride in the heroism of their daily working lives.

Hurst was among the earliest writers to write consistently about the conflicts women faced not only between various suitors but also between work and love. The Hurst stories most likely to end in suicide or defeat are those about a particular type of working women—the women whose only "commodity" is their bodies, and who allow themselves to be exploited sexually, for example, the main character in the 1916 story "Sob Sister." But Hurst didn't villainize men as a class or consider all men responsible for some women's exploitation.

Hurst often wrote about "good men." She went beyond her era's typical conception of a good man as a man who doesn't do bad things (doesn't cheat, drink, stay out late, squander money, hit his wife, ignore his children, or abandon his aging parents). For Hurst, a good man is someone who really loves his mother, who is a generous and fair and humane employer, who is interested in and supports civic life and the arts, who adores his wife and proves it in the most practical and endearing ways, and loves, cherishes, and really knows his children. He is a real mensch. His looks are irrelevant to his value and to his worthiness of being loved. Just as she provided models of "good work," Hurst, in creating her "good man" characters, provides her readers with a model for the kind of men women ought to marry, and ought to raise their sons to be. She never prescribes, never preaches—but by example, she lights the way.

The typical Fannie Hurst story has three parts. First comes an introductory meditation, often a kind of short essay, written in elaborately crafted, lush, elegiac language filled with allusions to the classical tales and heroic figures of ancient Greece and Rome—and usually highly ironic. Here, Hurst reveals most bitingly the hypocrisy of social conventions and pretensions, especially those which elevate some people above others on the basis of class, ethnicity, and gender. The second part—the longest part of the story—introduces the characters and tells the story, replete with all the traditional tragic elements of a naturalist tale à la Chekhov, de Maupassant, or Zola. But the third part of the Hurst story, the ending or the denouement, often violates the expectations of the reader educated in the tragic traditions of masculine naturalism: her endings are usually happy. These happy endings have been disdained by some critics as "unrealistic." But in fact they are often quite complex. Even when a story ends happily for the central character, there is always as a sort of memento mori, a grim reminder of reality, in the shape of another character—usually another woman—whose problems are unresolved and are clearly going to defeat her, if they haven't already. The happy endings work the way the endings in Shakespeare's dark comedies work: they provide the kind of resolution that enables their audience to leave the work with a sense of social order being restored, of being able to continue with daily life. Hurst clearly does not want to leave her readers so depressed that they don't want to read her work again. Yet there is often something melancholy lingering beneath the happiness, a hint of bitter flavor beneath the sweet, because the happy endings or solutions are individual and not societal.

Fannie Hurst's stories are remarkable not only for their content, structure, and tone, but also for their language. And in this area, hers is a uniquely American type of genius. In a sense she was completely cut off from her own ethnic literary roots. (How many Eastern European Jewish women writers were taught in universities a hundred years ago? How many were even in print in English, in the United States?) Her education would also have afforded her relatively little exposure to literature by any other women. But she was blessed with a restless sense that something was missing, and so she read ravenously, hungrily, randomly in the literature of the whole world, looking for what would feel right, what she instinctively knew was there and was hers. I do not think she ever really found it. Yet she did something quite remarkable: she managed to create a new kind of writing. The intensity of her characters' emotional lives is reminiscent of the great nineteenth-century Russian writers. Her wit is very Jewish, and her characters' language is often inflected with a Yiddish accent. And all of these elements are filtered through the experience and perspectives of women.

The diction of Fannie Hurst's writing is of two distinct kinds. When her characters speak, their speech is true to their ethnic and class backgrounds—which again, is most often Jewish, Eastern European, working class. They speak a language that is as separate, as internally consistent, and as capable of greatness as so-called black English, Spanglish, or any ethnic or regional dialect. And yet, because she intended to reach a huge non-Jewish audience often touched with anti-Semitism, as well as the Jewish audience, she usually avoids the vocabulary of Yiddish and "Yinglish," or Yiddish English. Thus she uses spellings like "goil" and "theayter" but very rarely includes words like *"schlemmil."*[5] Her characters often ate noodle pudding but never kugel. On the other hand, all of her expository passages are written in absolutely elegant, "standard," received English. Her stories are, in fact, bilingual, reflecting what several generations later Gloria Anzaldúa referred to as "code-switching" and labeled "borderlands language" in her book *Borderlands/La Frontera*. In this way, they reflect the linguistic realities of millions of Americans—the majority, perhaps—who are immigrants, children of immigrants, or members of other groups marginalized by race, class, or geography. These Americans are schooled in so-called standard English, but raised speaking a language with grammatical structures, vocabulary, a rhythm and a melody of its own.

In combining vivid description with authentic dialect, Hurst in many ways resembles writers who are usually described as regionalists, or "local colorists." Hurst grew up in an age when the New England regionalists Mary E. Wilkins Freeman and Sarah Orne Jewett and her fellow Mississippi Missourians Kate Chopin and Samuel Clemens were among the reigning national geniuses of the short story. In an unpublished draft of her autobiography, Hurst talks about her love of and admiration for the New England women regionalists. And in the published version, she suggests that it was *Spoon River Anthology,* Edgar Lee Masters's portrait in verse of small town life in the Midwest, that first startled her into knowing how she wanted to write.

Hurst's settings, of course, are New York City and St. Louis—not places usually identified with the local colorists. Even that ultimate New York sophisticate, Edith Wharton, writing her early regionalist-influenced short stories a generation before Hurst, set the works in small New England towns, missing the opportunity to make use of the rich material out her own front door. But Hurst's New York City was a world apart from the dominant culture, and its inhabitants spoke a language of their own. It is the city, and history—both of which in a sense are characters in her stories—upon which she bestowed her lush artistic eloquence. In the long introductory passages of her stories, in which she sets the scene and place in which the people will live out their moment on the stage, she speaks in the voice of a poet—a voice in which there is not only elegance, lyricism, richness of vocabulary, but also the sense of irony of someone who has studied human history and learned that, at least here on Earth, things are usually unfair. She senses the comic in human lives and travails, and her wit is cutting and revelatory. But what is perhaps most remarkable about Hurst's language is that she manages to bring as much richness and style to the conversations of working-class immigrants as she does to her elegant, poetic descriptions. It is through dialogue that her characters come to life. She never spoils her characterizations of people by speaking for them, by putting words in their mouths. She doesn't tell us how to judge the characters and their relationships. Everything emerges through their own actions, their own words. She just describes and transcribes and leaves it up to us to draw our own conclusions.

How did such a remarkable talent come to be forgotten? How has this writer, who so skillfully brought together artistry and entertainment, humor and profundity, been permitted to sink into obscurity?

The decline in Hurst's literary stock paralleled the resurgence of anti-Semitism and xenophobia that slowly crept into the United States' psyche following the disillusionment of those who fought WWI and culminating with the unfettered blossoming of these social attitudes on the edge of World War II. Her social vision would prove out of step when the New Deal liberalism began to wane in the shiny world of post-war prosperity amidst the social mobility engineered by the GI bill. And her literary reputation came under attack by a new generation of writers and critics, for whom her social criticism represented a risky enterprise in the age of McCarthyism. They simultaneously dismissed her for an excess of realism and a superfluity of sentimentality; "Sob Sister," the title of her famous 1916 story, became the contemptuous and dismissive sobriquet for Hurst herself. In fact, the epithet referred to the sex-worker whose story is told in "Sob Sister" and not to a particular literary style. When the story was first published, literary critics greeted it with praise. Writing six years after its publication, the author of the column "The Literary Spotlight" in the esteemed review periodical *The Bookman* said, "The position of Fannie Hurst in the world of letters cannot be properly estimated without taking into account this truly remarkable short story. It is as daring a literary achievement as we have in the language; perfect portraiture, a superb example of the art of writing and the conquest of a field almost untouched by English and American authors."[6] This story is one of a number in the Hurst oeuvre in which a woman's sexual attractiveness to a man is used, sometimes successfully, temporarily, sometimes not, by the woman to earn a living.

This subject of the function of a woman's sexuality as potential capital to be sold, bartered, stolen, or gossiped about was not new to writing women. During Hurst's time both Charlotte Perkins Gilman and Mary E. Wilkins Freeman wrote similar stories. And Dorothy Parker's famous story "Big Blonde," first published in 1929, surely owes something to Hurst's "Sob Sister." What is most interesting about Hurst's stories, however, is that she was able to tread a hitherto undrawn line: her "bad" women are the central consciousness in each story; they and their story are sympathetic and treated so—but without sentimentality (even if the female characters themselves are 'sentimental'); they are conscious of the "capital" nature of their sexual bodies; they make choices. Perhaps the radical stance of these characters (and their author) contributed to the reaction to Hurst and dismissal of her writing.

But her critics' very worst condemnation, it seemed, was that she was a "popular writer"—an accusation that she could hardly deny. Of course, with a new generation of college educated men now schooled in the Anglo patriarchal tradition that encouraged them to associate their upward class mobility with gender re-segregation, the U.S. government collusion in banishing women from the workplaces and re-relegating them to domesticity in order to create a job market for returning veterans, and the "re-masculinizing" of the literary marketplace now that all those returning GIs were flocking to the newly inaugurated university creative writing programs, "popular writer" was really a synonym for "woman writer"—because these new literary men certainly didn't eschew popularity for themselves.

Critics seldom impugned the accuracy of Hurst's portrayals; rather, they disparaged her subject matter and her approach to it. Her poor, vulgar, unattractive immigrants with their garlic breath and broken English, her shallowly cultured nouveau middle-class strivers think of their personal destinies in more grandiose terms than appear seemly to their social and intellectual "betters." People of small estate are not expected to deem their personal fates of more than modest interest, according to those who judge them from above. How can their lives—their little loves, their petty disappointments, their pathetic triumphs—be given such emotional weight, such social significance?

In fact, one of the great strengths of Fannie Hurst's fiction is its absolute conviction that the lives of her characters are just as important as that of any character created by Shakespeare: they are living close to the edge and making decisions that literally mean life or death. Its seems she was able to communicate this conviction to the millions of readers who resembled her characters—the immigrant community, the blue-collar community, the waitresses and models and department store clerks and domestic workers. They recognized that the characters in her stories were every bit as real, as compelling, as individualized, as their relatives, their neighbors, and their own selves. Her readers found her characters so real that they often wrote her, speculating as to whether or not she had meant someone they knew, asking if she had been looking over their shoulders, eavesdropping on their lives. And they loved her, perhaps, because her work—like the work of many of the great realist writers she admired—confirmed that their lives and their struggles were important, and even heroic. She offered them validation; she acknowledged their dignity.

Hurst clearly believed in what she was doing. She made deliberate choices about her subject matter and the way she wrote about it. But because she was a serious artist, she was hurt by the critical dismissals. She was hurt when writers declared that they would rather be a "real" writer than a popular writer, a critical success instead of just a popular success "like Fannie Hurst." These comments hurt her, but they did not stop her.

And they should not stop us. Times change and change again. Today, readers, writers, and scholars have come to recognize "popular" as an epithet that has been inequitably applied to the work of women writers, especially those whose audience, like Hurst's, was also mostly women. It has also been applied to the literature of working-class writers, as if "popular" must by necessity mean lowbrow (as if Henry James ever stopped dreaming about the bestseller list). Moreover, we have learned that the contempt for public taste that has emanated from the academy is a feat of self-empowering sleight of hand by the dominant culture.

It is time for us to open our minds to this unique genius, to appreciate her in new contexts, to experience the exquisite pleasure of reading her stories. It is time to rediscover Fannie Hurst.

Susan Koppelman
Tucson, Arizona
September 2004

NOTES

1. See *Radical Feminists of Heterodoxy: Greenich Village 1912–1940*, by Judith Schwarz. Norwich, VT: New Victoria, 1986 revised edition.

2. This journal of arts and opinion was published and mostly written by William Marion Reedy in St. Louis from 1891 to 1920, a time when St. Louis was a major cultural and intellectual center for the United States. Highly respected, *Reedy's Mirror* included political commentary, social gossip, and poetry and fiction. In the twenty years before WWI, Reedy published Emily Dickinson, Stephen Crane, Ezra Pound, Edward Arlington Robinson, Amy Lowell, Sara Teasdale, Carl Sandburg, Vachel Lindsay, and Edgar Lee Masters. For an in-depth history of Reedy and his publication see *The Man in the Mirror: William Marion Reedy and his Magazine* by Max Putzel, Cambridge, Mass: Harvard University Press, 1963.

3. The best exploration of this subject of "becoming white" that I have discovered is "Jews in the U.S.: The Rising Costs of Whiteness" by Melanie Kaye/Kantrowitz in *Names We Call Home: Essays in Racial Identity* edited by Becky Thompson and Tyagi Sangesta, New York: Routledge, 1995. She begins her essay with a quotation from an essay by James Baldwin, "On Being 'White' . . . and Other Lies," from *Essence* (April, 1984). His paragraph follows:

> It took generations, and a vast amount of coercion, before this became a white country. It is probable that it is the Jewish community—or more accurately, perhaps, its remnants—that in America has paid the highest and most extraordinary price for becoming white. For the Jews came here from countries where they were not white, and they came here in part because they were not white; and incontestably—in the eyes of Black Americans (and not only in those eyes)—American Jews have opted to become white.

Kaye/Kantrowitz continues,

> Everything I think about Jews, whiteness, racism and contemporary U.S. society begins with this passage. What does it mean: *Jews opted to become white*. Did we opt? Did it work? Was it an illusion? Could we have opted otherwise? Can we still?

This perspective on "whiteness" does not take into account any of the other factors, such as class, ethnicity, and regional origins, that have an impact on and are used to distinguish among and provide cause for discrimination between and among "white" people. Undifferentiated "whiteness" as a category only exists conceptually in contrast to non-whiteness.

4. See my article "The Educations of Fannie Hurst," *Women's Studies International Forum* 1987

10(05): 503-516.

5. The word is spelled here as Hurst spells it in "Humoresque."

6. Reprinted in *The Literary Spotlight* with a Preface by John Farrar, New York: George H. Doran Company, 1924, 268.

The Stories of
FANNIE HURST

The Joy of Living

First Published: *Reedy's Mirror*, May 27, 1909

The savor of frying ham wafted piquant and flavorous through the little flat, and the hissing and sparkling in the kitchen sent a bluish haze up over the gas-stove and a thin trail drifted through the open doors into the bedroom and parlor beyond; it dulled the mirror in the folding-bed, and a toddling child, playing on the floor in the front room, rubbed the haze out of his eyes with his small, digging fists.

Suddenly the sizzle ceased, and the little mother in the kitchen flopped the curled, steaming slice upon a plate, clattered it into the warming-oven and pressed a shiny tin lid closer on a skillet of grease-saturated potatoes. The fragrance of coffee began to wind gently through the spout of the coffee pot, and she lowered the flame beneath, and with her blue-checked apron for protection of her hand, pushed it somewhat back from the heat.

Her oldest child began to cry lustily in the front room, and she hurried to him, picking her baby up by one arm as she passed through the bright-papered bedroom. With a tired little gasp she dropped into a golden oak rocking chair, and drew both of her heavy, sleepy children into her lap.

The sultry air percolated through the Nottingham lace curtains and cooled her heated face and stirred her crimped hair. Her heavy-featured children drowsed into a deep breathing sleep, and one little thick-wristed hand clung damply to her cheek. She rocked them and patted a small arm rhythmically.

She heard her husband unlock the door below, and a second later he bounded into the room. She met him with a "Sh-h-h," and he tip-toed across and bent over and kissed her and the sleeping children. Then he pulled off his coat and pinned back one of the Nottingham curtains to admit more air.

"Phew!" he said, "it's hot." She rocked softly on.

He came over and drew up a chair beside her.

"Say, Mayme," he whispered, and his dapper face sparkled above his red necktie, "what-a you think?"

"I dunno," she smiled back.

"Guess," he insisted, smiling broader.

"Aw, quit your kiddin', Charley." She poked him playfully with her foot.

"Go on, give a guess," he pleaded.

"We're goin' to Strake's Park Sunday?" she queried, a hope in her voice. Her husband leaned closer to her, his small face anticipating her joy.

"I'm promoted to the ribbons and laces—the floor-walker told me to-night."

She gave a little shriek that woke her babies to a duet of howls, and flew into his arms, her disturbed children trailing at her skirts.

Then she pulled him with her into the kitchen, and while she scraped the greasy potatoes into the serving dish and poured the coffee, she radiated her joy.

After the beaming father had tied the babies into their high chairs and knotted the bibs about their necks, she went over and sat on his lap before the little table and put her arms caressingly around him.

"Ain't we lucky, Charley?" she breathed.

Summer Resources

First Published: *Saturday Evening Post*, September 7, 1912
Reprinted: *Every Soul Hath Its Song*, Harper & Bros., 1916

At seven o'clock the Seaside Hotel struggled into full dress—ladies emerged from siestas and curl-papers, dowagers wormed into straight fronts and spread the spousal vestments of boiled shirt, U-shaped waistcoat *et al.* across the bed. Slim young men in the swelter of their inside two-fifty-a-day rooms carefully extracted their braided-at-the-seams trousers from beneath the mattresses and removed trees from patent-leather pumps.

At seven-thirty young girls fluttered in and out from the dining-room like brilliant night moths, the straight-front dowagers, U-vested spouses, and slim young men in braided trousers seams crowded about the desk for the influx of mail, and read their tailor and modiste duns with the rapt and misleading expression that suggested a love rune rather than a "Please remit." Interested mothers elbowed for the most desirable veranda rockers; the blather of voices, the emph-umph-umph of the three-nights-a-week orchestra and the remote pound of the ocean joined in united effort.

At eight o'clock Miss Myra Sternberger yawned in her wicker rocker and raised two round and bare-to-the-elbow arms high above her head.

"Gee!" she said. "This place is so slow it gets on my nerves—it does!"

Mrs. Blondheim, who carried toast away from the breakfast-table concealed beneath a napkin for her daughter who remained abed until noon, paused in her Irish crochet, spread a lace wheel upon her ample knee, and regarded it approvingly.

"What you got to kick about, Miss Sternberger? Didn't I see you in the surf this morning with that shirtwaist drummer from Cincinnati?"

"Mr. Eckstein—oh, I been meetin' him down here in July for two years. He's a nice fellow an' makes a good livin'—but he ain't my style."

"Girls are too particular nowadays. Take my Bella—why that girl's had chances you wouldn't believe! But she always says to me, she says, 'Mamma, I ain't goin' to marry till Mr. Right comes along.'"

"That's just the same way with me."

"My Bella's had chances—not one, but six. You can ask anybody who knows us in New York the chances that goil has had."

"I ain't in a hurry to take the first man that asks me, neither."

Mrs. Blondheim wrapped the forefinger of her left hands with mercerized cotton thread, and her needle flashed deftly.

"What about the little Baltimore fellow that went away yesterday? I seen he was keepin' you pretty busy."

"Aw, Mrs. Blondheim, can't a girl have a good time with a fellow without gettin' serious?"

But she giggled in pleased self-consciousness and pushed her combs into place—Miss Sternberger wore her hair oval about her face like Mona Lisa; her cheeks were pink-tinted, like the lining of a conch-shell.

"My Bella always says a goil can't be too careful at these here summer resorts—that's why she ain't out every night like some of these goils. She won't go out with a young man till she knows he comes from nice people."

Miss Sternberger patted the back of her hand against her mouth and stifled a yawn.

"One thing I must say for my Bella—no matter where I take that goil, everybody says what a nice, retirin' goil she is!"

"Bella does retire rather early," agreed Miss Sternberger in tones drippingly sweet.

"I try to make her rest up in summer," pursued Mrs. Blondheim, unpunctured. "You goils wear yourselves out—nothin' but beaus, beaus all the time. There ain't a night in New York that my Bella ain't out with some young man. I always say to her, 'Bella, the theayters ought to give you a commission.'"

Miss Sternberger rocked.

"Where did you say you live in New York, Miss Sternberger?"

"West One Hundred and Eleventh Street."

"Oh yes—are you related to the Morris Sternbergers in the boys'-pants business?"

"I think—on my father's side."

"Honest, now! Carrie Sternberger married my brother-in-law; and they're doin' grand, too! He's built up a fine business there. Ain't this a small woild after all!"

"It is that," agreed Miss Sternberger. "Why, last summer I was eatin' three meals a day next to my first cousin and didn't kow it."

"Look!" said Mrs. Blondheim. "There's those made-up Rosenstein goils comin' out of the dinin'-room. Look at the agony they put on, would you! I knew 'em when they were livin' over their hair-store on Twenty-thoid Street. I wonder where my Bella is!"

"That's a stylish messaline the second one's got on, all right. I think them beaded tunics are swell."

"If it hadn't been for the false-hair craze old man Rosenstein wouldn't—"

Mrs. Blondheim leaned forward in her chair; her little flowered-silk work-bag dropped to the floor. "There's Bella now! Honest, that Mr. Arnheim 'ain't left her once to-day, and he only got here this morning, too! Such a fine young man, the clerk says; he's been abroad six months and just landed yesterday—and been with her all day. When I think of the chances that goil had. Why, Marcus Finberg, who was down here last week, was crazy about her!"

"Did you say that fellow's name was Arnheim?"

"Yes. 'Ain't you heard of the Arnheim models? He's a grand boy, the clerk says, and the swellest importer of ladies' wear in New York."

Miss Sternberger leaned forward in her chair. "Is that Simon Arnheim?"

"Sure. He's the one that introduced the hobble skoit. My Bella was one of the foist to wear one. There ain't a fad that he don't go over to Europe and get. He made a fortune off the hobble skoit alone."

"Is that so?"

"Believe me, if he wasn't all right my Bella wouldn't let him hang on that way."

"I've heard of him."

"I wish you could see that Babette Dreyfous eying my Bella! She's just green because Bella's got him."

"Do you use the double stitch in your crochet, Mrs. Blondheim? That's a pretty pattern you're workin' on."

"Yes. I've just finished a set of doilies you'd pay twenty-five dollars for any-where."

Miss Sternberger rose languidly to her feet. "Well," she said, "I guess I'll take a stroll and go up to bed."

"Don't be so fidgety, Miss Sternberger; sit down by me and talk."

Miss Sternberger smiled. "I'll see you later, Mrs. Blondheim; and don't forget that preparation I was tellin' you about—Sloand's Mosquito Skit. Just rub the bottle stopper over your pillow and see if it don't work."

She moved away with the dignity of an emperor moth, slim and supple-hipped in a tight-wrapped gown.

The Seaside Hotel lobby leaned forward in its chairs; young men moved their feet from the veranda rail and gazed after her; pleasantries fell in her pathway as roses before a queen.

A splay-mouthed youth, his face and neck sun-burnt to a beefy red, tugged at her gold-colored scarf as she passed.

"Oh, you Myra!" he sang.

"Quit your kiddin', Izzy!" she parried back. "Who was that blonde I seen you with down at the beach this mornin'?"

A voluptuous brunette in a rose-pink dress and diamonds dragged her down to the arm of her rocker.

"I got a trade-last for you, Myra."

"For me?"

"Yes."

"Give it to me, Clara."

"No, I said a trade—and a dandy, too!"

"Who from—man?"

"Yes."

"Well, I got one for you, too—Leon Eckstein says he thinks you're an awfully sweet girl and will make some man a grand wife."

Clara giggled and fingered the gold-fringe edging of Miss Sternberger's sleeve. She spoke slowly and stressed each word alike.

"Well, there's a fellow just got here from Paris yesterday—says you sure know how to dress and that you got a swell figure."

"Who said it?"

"Guess."

"I should know!"

"That fellow over there with Bella Blondheim—the one with the smooth face and grayish hair. I hear he's a swell New York fellow in the importin' business."

"How'd Bella grab him?"

"She's been holdin' on to him like a crawfish all day. She won't let anybody get near him—neither will her mother."

"Here comes Izzy over here after me! If there's one fellow I can't stand it's him."

Miss Sternberger moved away with her chin tilted at a sharp angle. At a turn in the veranda she came suddenly upon Miss Bella Blondheim and a sleek, well-dressed young man with grayish hair. Miss Blondheim's hand was hooked with a deadlock clutch to the arm of her companion.

Miss Sternberger threw herself before them like a melodrama queen flagging a train. "Hello, Bella!" she said in a voice as low as a 'cello.

Miss Blondheim, who had once sold the greatest number of aprons at a charity bazar, turned cold eyes upon the intruder.

"Hello, Myra!" she said in cool tones of dismissal.

There was a pause; the color swept up and surged over Miss Blondheim's face.

"Are you finished with *Love in a Cottage*, Bella? I promised it to Mrs. Weiss when you're finished with it."

"Yes," said Bella. "I'll bring it down to-night."

There was another pause; the young man with the grayish hair coughed.

"Mr. Arnheim, let me introduce you to my friend, Miss Sternberger."

Miss Sternberger extended a highly groomed hand. "Pleased to meet you," she said.

"Howdy-do, Miss Sternberger?" His arm squirmed free from the deadlock clutch. "Won't you join us?"

"Thanks," said Myra, smiling until an amazing quantity of small white teeth showed; "but I just stopped by to tell Bella that Mrs. Blondheim was askin' for her."

There was a third pause.

"Won't you come along, Mr. Arnheim? Mamma's always so worried about me; and I'd like for you to meet mamma," said Bella, anxiously.

With a heroic jerk Mr. Arnheim managed to free himself entirely. "Thanks," he said; "but I think I'll stay out and have a smoke."

Miss Blondheim's lips drooped at the corners. She entered the bright, gabbling lobby, threading her way to her mother's stronghold. The maternal glance that greeted her was cold and withering.

"I knew if I couldn't hold her she'd get him away. That's why I didn't go and play lotto with the ladies."

"Well, I couldn't help it, could I? You're always nosin' after me so—anybody could say you want me and not be lyin'."

"That's the thanks I get for tryin' to do the right thing by my children. When I was your age I had more gumption in my little finger than you got in your whole hand! I'd like to see a little piece like her get ahead of me. No wonder you ain't got no luck!"

Miss Blondheim sat down wearily beside her mother. "I wish I knew how she does it."

"Nerve! That's how. 'Ain't I been preachin' nerve to you since you could talk? You'd be married to Marcus Finberg now if you'd 'a' worked it right and listened to your mother."

"Aw, maw, lemme alone. I couldn't make him pop, could I? I don't see other girls' mothers always buttin' in."

Out in the cool of the veranda Miss Sternberger strolled over to the railing and leaned her back against a white wooden column. Her eyes, upslanting and full of languor, looked out over the toiling, moiling ocean. She was outlined as gently as a Rembrandt.

"A penny for your thoughts, Miss Sternberger."

Mr. Arnheim, the glowing end of a newly lighted cigar in one corner of his mouth, peered his head over her shoulder.

"Oh, Mr. Arnheim, how you scared me!" Miss Sternberger placed the well-groomed left hand, with a seal ring on the third finger, upon the thread-lace bosom of her gown. "How you frightened me!"

"It's a nice night, Miss Sternberger. Want to walk on the beach?"

"Don't mind if I do," she said.

They strolled the length of the veranda, down the steps to the boardwalk and the beach beyond.

Mrs. Blondheim rolled her crochet into a tight ball and stuck her needle upright. "Come on, Bella; let's go to bed."

They trailed past the desk like birds with damp feathers.

"Send up some ice-water to three-hundred-and-eighteen," said Miss Bella over the counter, her eyes straining meanwhile past the veranda to the beach below.

Without, a moon low and heavy and red came out from the horizon; it cast a copper-gold band across the water.

"Let's go down to the edge, kiddo."

Mr. Arnheim helped Miss Sternberger plow daintily through the sand.

"If I get sand in my shoes I'll blame you, Mr. Arnheim."

"Little slippers like yours can't hold much."

She giggled.

They seated themselves like small dunes on the white expanse of beach; he drew his knees up under his chin and nursed them.

In the eery light they might have been a fay and a faun in evening dress.

"Well," said Mr. Arnheim, exhaling loudly, "this is something like it."

"Ain't that a grand moon, though, Mr. Arnheim?"

"The moon 'ain't got a show when you're round, little one."

"I'll bet you say that to every girl you meet."

"Nix I do; but I know when a girl looks good to me."

"I wish I knew if you was jollyin' me or not."

He tossed his cigar into the surf that curled at their very feet, leaving a rim of foam and scum. The red end died with a fizz. Then he turned his dark eyes full upon her with a steady focus.

"If you knew me better you'd know that I ain't that sort of a fellow. When I say a thing I mean it."

His hand lay outstretched; she poured rivulets of white sand between the fingers. They watched the little mounds of sand which she patted into shape.

"I'll bet you're a New York girl."

"Why?"

"I can tell them every time—style and all."

"I'll bet you're a New York fellow, too."

"Little New York is good enough for me. I've been over in Paris four months, now, and, believe me, it looked good yesterday to see the old girlie holdin' her lamp over the harbor."

Miss Sternberger ran her hand over the smooth sheen of her dress; her gown was chaste, even stern, in its simplicity—the expensive simplicity that is artful rather than artless.

"That's a neat little model you're wearin'."

"Aw, Mr. Arnheim, what do you know about clothes?"

Mr. Arnheim threw back his head and laughed long and loud. "What do I know about clothes? I only been in the biz for eight years. What I don't know about ladies' wear ain't in the dictionary."

"Well," said Miss Sternberger, "that's so; I did hear you was in the business."

"I'm in the importin' line, I am. Why, girl, I've put through every fad that's taken hold in the last five years—brought them over myself, too. I've dressed Broadway and Fifth Avenue in everything from rainy-day to harem skirts."

"Honest?"

"Sure! I've imported more good sellers than any dealer in New York. I got a new model now passin' customs that's to be a bigger hit than the sheath was. Say, when I brought over the hobble every house on the Avenue laughed in my face; and when I finally dumped a consignment on to one of them, the firm was scared stiff and wanted to countermand; but I had 'em and they couldn't jump me."

"Just think!"

"By Jove! It wasn't two weeks before that very model was the talk of New York and Lillian Russell was wearin' one in the second act of her show; and when she wears a model it's as good as made."

"Gee!" she said. "I could just sit and listen to you talk and talk."

He hunched close. "I sold the first dozen pannier dresses for a sum that would give you the blind staggers. I was just as scared as she was, too, but all you got to do with women is to get a few good-lookin' bell-sheep to lead and the others will follow fast."

She regarded him in the wan moonlight. "If there's anything I admire," she said, "it's a smart man."

"Oh, I don't know," he said. "I've just got a little better judgment than the next fellow. Those things come natural, that's all. In my line a fellow's got to know human nature. If I'd sprung the hobble on the Avenue five years ago I'd gone broke on the gamble; but I sprung the idea on 'em at just the right time."

Her hand, long and slim, lay like a bit of carved ivory on the sand; he leaned forward and covered it with his.

"I want to see a great deal of you while I'm down here."

She did not reply, but drew her hand away with a shy diffidence.

"I'll bet I could show you some things that would warm you up all right. I'm goin' into New York with the swellest bunch of French novelties you ever seen. I've got a peach-colored Piquette model I've brought over that's goin' to be the talk of the town."

"A Piquette?"

He laughed delightedly. "Sure! You never heard of the firm? Wait till you see 'em on show at the openin'. It's got the new butterfly back; and, believe me, it wasn't no cinch to grab that pattern, neither. I laid low in Paris two months before I even got a smell at it."

"You talk just like a story-book," she said.

He stretched himself full length on the sand and looked up into her face. "I'll show you a thing or two when we get back to New York, little one."

"You ain't like most of the boys I know, Mr. Arnheim. You got something different about you."

"And you got a face like the kind you see painted on fans—on the order of a Japanese dame. I got some swell Japanese imports, too."

"Everybody says that about me. I take after paw."

"Say, little one, I want your telephone number when I get back to New York."

"I'll be pleased to have you call me up, Mr. Arnheim."

"Will I call you up? Well, rather!"

"I know some nice girls I'll introduce you to."

He looked at her insinuatingly. "I know one nice girl, and that's enough," he said.

"Aw, Mr. Arnheim, of all the jolliers I ever knew you got 'em beat." She rose to her feet like a gold-colored phoenix from a mound of white sand. "When I meet a fellow I like I don't want him to tell me nothin' but the truth."

"That's just the way with me—when I meet a girl that looks good I want to treat her white, and I want her to do the same by me."

They strolled along the edge of the beach. Once the foaming surf threatened to lap over her slippers; he caught her deftly and raised her high above the swirl.

"Oh," she cried, a little breathlessly, "ain't you strong!" Then she laughed in a high-pitched voice.

They dallied until the moon hardened from a soft, low ball to a high, yellow disk and the night damp seeped into their clothes. Miss Sternberger's yellow scarf lay like a limp rag on her shoulders.

"You're a perfect thirty-six, ain't you, little one?"

"That's what they say when I try on ready-mades," she replied, with sweet reticence.

"Gee!" he said. "Wouldn't I like you in some of my models! Maybe if you ain't no snitch I'll show you the colored plates some day."

"I ain't no snitch," she said. Her voice was like a far-away echo.

They climbed the wooden steps to their hotel like glorified children who had been caught in a silver weft of enchantment.

The lobby was semi-dark; they asked for their keys in whispers and exchanged good-nights in long-drawn undertones.

"Until to-morrow, little one."

"Until to-morrow."

She entered the elevator with a smile on her lips and in her eyes. They regarded each other through the iron framework until she shot from sight.

At breakfast next morning Mrs. Blondheim drew up before her "small steak, French-fried potatoes, jelly omelet, buttered toast, buckwheat cakes, and coffee."

"Well, of all the nerve!" she exclaimed to her vis-à-vis, Mrs. Epstein. "If there ain't Myra Sternberger eatin' breakfast with that Mr. Arnheim!"

Mrs. Epstein opened a steaming muffin, inserted a lump of butter, and pressed the halves together. "I said to my husband last night," she remarked, "'I'm glad we 'ain't got no daughters'; till they're married off and all, it ain't no fun. With my Louie, now, it's different. When he came out of the business school my husband put him in business, and now I 'ain't got no worry."

"My Bella 'ain't never given me a day's worry, neither. I ain't in no hurry to marry her off. She always says to me, 'Mamma,' she says, 'I ain't in no hurry to marry till Mr. Right comes along.'"

"My Louie is comin' down to-day or to-morrow on his vacation if he can get away from business. Louie's a good boy—if I do say so myself."

"I don't want to talk—but I often say what my Bella gets when she marries is enough to give any young man a fine start in a good business."

"I must have my Louie meet Miss Bella. The notes and letters Louie gets from girls you wouldn't believe; he don't pay no attention to 'em. He's an awful mamma-boy, Mrs. Blondheim."

"It will be grand for them to meet," said Mrs. Blondheim. "If I do say it, my Bella's had proposals you wouldn't believe! Look at Simon Arnheim over there—he only met her yesterday, and do you think he would leave her side all day? No, siree. Honest, it makes me mad sometimes. A grand young man comes along and Bella introduces him to every one, but she won't have nothin' to do with him."

"Try some of this liver and onions, Mrs. Blondheim; it's delicious."

Mrs. Blondheim partook and nibbled between her front teeth. "I got a grand recipe for süss und sauer liver. When we're at home my Bella always says, 'Mamma, let's have some liver and *gedämftes fleisch* for lunch.'"

"Do you soak your liver first?" inquired Mrs. Epstein. "My Louie won't eat nothin' süss und sauer. It makes me so mad. I got to cook different for every one in the family. Louie won't eat this and his father won't eat that!"

"I'll give you the recipe when I give you the one for the noodles. Bella says it's the best she ever ate. My husband gets so mad when I go down in the kitchen—me with two grand girls and washer-woman two days a week! But the girls can't cook to suit me."

"Excuse me, too, from American cookin'."

Mrs. Blondheim's interest and gaze wandered down the dining-hall. "I wish you'd look at that Sternberger girl actin' up! Ain't it disgusting?"

"Please pass the salt, Mrs. Blondheim. That's the trouble with hotel cooking—they don't season. At home we like plenty of it, too. I season and season, and then at the table my husband has to have more."

"She wouldn't have met him at all if it hadn't been for Bella," pursued Mrs. Blondheim.

The object of Mrs. Blondheim's solicitude, fresh as spring in crisp white linen, turned her long eyes upon Mr. Arnheim.

"You ought to feel flattered, Mr. Arnheim, that I let you come over to my table."

Mr. Arnheim regarded her through a mist of fragrant coffee steam. "You betcher life I feel flattered. I'd get up earlier than this to have breakfast with a little queen."

"Ain't you ever goin' to quit jollyin'?"

He leaned across the table. "That ain't a bad linen model you're wearin'—it's domestic goods, too. Where'd you get it?"

"At Lipman's."

"I sold them a consignment last year; but, say, if you want to see real classy white goods you ought to see some ratine cutaways I'm bringing over. I've brought a model I'm goin' to call the Phoebe Snow. It's the niftiest thing for early fall you ever saw."

"Ratine?"

"You never heard of it? That's where I get my work in—it's the new lines, the novelty stuff, that gets the money."

"Are you goin' in the surf this morning, Mr. Arnheim?"

"I'm goin' where you go, little one." He dropped two lumps of sugar into her coffee-cup. "Sweets to the sweet," he said.

"Silly!" But she giggled under her breath.

They pushed back their chairs and strolled down the aisle between the tables. She smiled brightly to her right and left.

"Good morning, Mrs. Blondheim. Is it warm enough for you?"

"Good morning," replied Mrs. Blondheim, stabbing a bit of omelet with vindictive fork.

Mrs. Epstein looked after the pair with warming eyes. "She is a stylish dresser, ain't she?"

"I wish you'd see the white linen my Bella's got. It's got sixteen yards of Cluny lace in the waist alone—and such Cluny, too! I paid a dollar and a half a yard wholesale."

"Just look at this waist I'm wearin', Mrs. Blondheim. You wouldn't think I paid three and a half for the lace, would you?"

"Oh, yes; I can always tell good stuff when I see it, and I always say it pays best in the end," said Mrs. Blondheim, feeling the heavy lace edge of Mrs. Epstein's sleeve between discriminating thumb and forefinger.

Suddenly Mrs. Epstein's eyes widened; she rose to her feet, drawing a corner of the table-cloth awry. "If it ain't my Louie!"

Mr. Louis Epstein, a faithful replica of his mother, with close black hair that curled on his head like the nap of a Persian lamb, imprinted a large, moist kiss upon the maternal lips.

"Hello, maw! Didn't you expect me?"

"Not till the ten-o'clock train, Louie. How's papa?"

"He'th fine. I left him billing thom goods to Thpokane."

"How's business, Louie?"

"Not tho bad, but pa can't get away yet for a week. The fall goods ain't all out yet."

"Ain't it awful, the way that man is all for business, Mrs. Blondheim? This is my son Louie."

"Well, well, Mr. Epstein. I've heard a lot about you. I want you to meet my daughter Bella. You ought to make friends."

"Yeth'm," said Mr. Epstein.

Out on the clean-washed beach the sun glinted on the water and sent points of light dancing on the wavelets like bits of glass. Children in blue rompers burrowed and jangled their painted spades and pails; nursemaids planted umbrellas in the sand and watched their charges romp; parasols flashed past like gay-colored meteors.

In the white-capped surf bathers bobbed and shouted, and all along the shore-line the tide ran gently up the beach and down again, leaving a smooth, damp stretch of sand which soughed and sucked beneath the steps of the bathers.

Far out, where the waters were highest and the whitecaps maddest, Mr. Arnheim held Miss Sternberger about her slim waist and raised her high over each rushing breaker. They caught the swells and lay back against the heavy tow, letting the wavelets lap up to their chins.

Mr. Arnheim, with little rivulets running down his cheeks, shook the water out of his grayish hair and looked at her with salt-bitten, red-rimmed eyes.

"Gee!" he wheezed. "You're a spunky little devil! Excuse me from the beach-walkers; I like 'em when they're game like you."

She danced about like an Amphitrite. "Who would be afraid of the water with a dandy swimmer like you?"

"This ain't nothin'," said Mr. Arnheim. "You ought to see me in still water. At Arverne last summer I was the talk of the place."

They emerged from the water, dripping and heavy-footed. She wrung out her brief little skirts and stamped her feet on the sand. Mr. Arnheim hopped on one foot and then on the other, holding his head aslant. Then they stretched out on the white, sun-baked beach. Miss Sternberger loosened her hair and it showered about her.

"Gee! 'Ain't you got a swell bunch of hair!"

She shook and fluffed it. "You ought to seen it before I had typhoid. I could sit on it then."

"That Phoebe Snow model that I got in mind for Lillian Russell would make you look like a queen, with that hair of yourn!"

She buried his arm in the sand and patted the mound. "Now," she said, "I got you, and you can't do anything without askin' me."

"You got me, anyway," he said, with an expressive glance.

"Yes," she purred, "that's what you say now; but when you get back to New York you'll forget all about the little girl you met down at the shore."

"That's all you know about me. I don't take up with every girl."

"I'm glad you don't," she said.

"But I'll bet you got a different fellow for every day when you're in New York."

"Nothin' like that," she said; "but, anyway, there's always room for one more."

Two young men without hats passed. Miss Sternberger called out her greeting.

"Hello, Manny! Wasn't the water grand? What? Well, you tell Leo he don't know nothin'. No, we don't want to have our pictures taken! Mr. Arnheim, I want to introduce you to Mr. Landauer, a neckwear man out of Baltimore, and Mr. Manny Sinai, also neckwear, out of New York."

They posed, with the white sunlight in their eyes.

"I hope we won't break the camera," said Arnheim.

The remark was greeted with laughter. The little machine clicked, the new-comers departed, and then Miss Sternberger and Mr. Arnheim turned to each other again.

"You ain't tired, are you—Myra?"

"No—Simon"—she danced to her feet and tossed the hair back from her face—"I ain't tired."

They walked down the beach toward the bath-house, humming softly to themselves.

"I'll be out in ten minutes," she said, pausing at the door of her locker.

"Me too," he said.

When they met again they were regroomed and full of verve. She was as cool as a rose. They laughed at their crinkly finger-tips—wrinkled by the water like parchment; and his neck, where it rose above the soft high collar, was branded by the sun a flaming red.

"Gee!" she cried. "Ain't you sunburnt!"

"I always tan red," he said.

"And me, I always tan tan."

They exchanged these pithy and inspired bits of autobiography in warm, intimate tones. At their hotel steps she sighed with a delicious weariness.

"I wish I could do everything for you, little one—even walk up-stairs."

"I ain't tired, Simon; only—only—Oh, I don't know."

"Little one," he said, softly.

In the lobby Miss Bella Blondheim leaned an elbow on the clerk's desk and talked to a stout young man with a gold-mounted elk's tooth on his watch-fob, and black hair that curled close to his head.

They made a group of four for a moment, Miss Blondheim regarding the arrivals with bright, triumphant eyes.

"My friend, Mr. Louis Epstein," she said.

The men shook hands.

"Related to the Epstein & Son Millinery Company, Broadway and Spring?"

"Thertainly am. I happen to be the thon mythelf."

"Was you in the surf this mornin', Bella? It was grand!"

"No, Myra," replied her friend. "Mr. Epstein and me took a trip to Ocean View."

"You missed the water this mornin'. It was fine and dandy!" volunteered Mr. Arnheim.

"Me and Mr. Epstein are goin' this afternoon—ain't we?"

"We thertainly are," agreed Mr. Epstein, regarding Miss Blondheim with small, admiring eyes.

Miss Sternberger edged away. "Pleased to have met you, Mr. Epstein."

Mr. Arnheim edged with her and they moved on their way toward the dining-room.

Mrs. Blondheim from her point of vantage—the wicker rocker—leaned toward her sister-in-law.

"Look, Hanna! That's Louie Epstein, of the Epstein & Son Millinery

Company, with Bella. He's a grand boy. I meet his mother at Doctor Bergenthal's lecture every Saturday morning. Epstein & Son have got a grand business, and Bella could do a whole lot worse."

"Well, I wish her luck," said Mrs. Blondheim's sister-in-law.

"I smell fried smelts. Let's go in to lunch."

Mrs. Blondheim stabbed her crochet needle into her spool. "I usually dip my smelts in bread crumbs. Have you ever tried them that way, Hanna?"

"Julius don't eat smelts."

They moved toward the dining-room.

Late that afternoon Miss Sternberger and Mr. Arnheim returned from a sail. Their faces were flushed and full of shy, sweet mystery.

"I can't show you the models the way I'd like to, dearie, but I got 'em in colors just like the real thing."

"Oh, Simon, you're doin' a thing like this for me without me even askin' you!"

His hold of her arm tightened. "I wouldn't show these here to my own sister before the twenty-fifth of the month. Now you know how you stand with me, little one."

"Oh," she cried, "I'm so excited! It's just like lookin' behind the scenes in a theayter."

He left her and returned a few moments later with a flat, red-covered portfolio. They sought out an unmolested spot and snuggled in a corner of a plush divan in one of the deserted parlors. He drew back the cover and their heads bent low.

At each turn of the pages she breathed her ecstasy and gave out shrills and calls of admiration.

"Oh, Simon, ain't that pink one a beauty! Ain't that skirt the swellest thing you ever seen!"

"That's the Piquette model, girlie. You and all New York will be buyin' it in another month. Ain't it the selectest little thing ever?"

Her face was rapt. "It's the swellest thing I've ever seen!" she declared.

He turned to another plate.

"Oh-h-h-h-h!" she cried.

"Ain't that a beauty! That there is going to be the biggest hit I've had yet. Watch out for the Phoebe Snow! I've got the original model in my trunks. That cutaway effect can't be beat."

"Oh-h-h-h-h!" she repeated.

They passed slowly over the gay-colored plates.

"There's that flame-colored one I'd like to see you in."

"Gee!" she said. "There's some class to that."

After a while the book was laid aside and they talked in low, serious tones;

occasionally his hand stroked hers.

The afternoon waned; the lobby thinned; the dowagers and their daughters asked for room keys and disappeared for siestas and more mysterious processes; children trailed off to rest; the hot land-breezes, dry and listless, stirred the lace curtains of the parlor—but they remained on the plush divan, rapt as might have been Paolo and Francesca in their romance-imbued arbor.

"How long will you be down here?" she asked.

"As long as you," he replied, not taking his eyes from her face.

"Honest?"

"Sure. I don't have to go in to New York for a week or ten days yet. My season ain't on yet."

She leaned her head against the back of the divan. "All nice things must end," she said, with the 'cello note in her voice.

"Oh, I don't know!" he replied, with what might have been triple significance.

They finally walked toward the elevator, loath to part for the interim of dressing.

That evening they strolled together on the beach until the last lights of the hotel were blinking out. Then they stole into the semi-dark lobby like thieves—but soft-voiced, joyous thieves. A few straggling couples like themselves came in with the same sheepish but bright-eyed hesitancy. At the elevator Miss Blondheim and Mr. Epstein were lingering over good-nights.

The quartette rode up to their respective floors together—the girls regarding each other with shy, happy eyes; the men covering up their self-consciousness with sallies.

"Ain't you ashamed to keep such late hours, Miss Blondheim?" said Mr. Arnheim.

"I don't see no early-to-bed-early-to-rise medals on none of us," she said, diffidently.

"These thummer rethorts sure ain't no plathe for a minither's thon," said Mr. Epstein.

Laughter.

"Remember, Mr. Arnheim, whoever's up first wait in the leather chair opposite the elevator."

"Sure thing, Miss Sternberger."

Her last glance, full of significance, was for Mr. Arnheim. The floor above he also left the elevator, the smile still on his lips.

Left alone, Mr. Epstein turned to Miss Blondheim.

"Good night, dearie," he whispered. "Thweet dreamth."

"Good night, Louie," she replied. "Same to you."

Mr. Arnheim awoke to a scudding rain; his oceanward window-sill dripping and a great patch of carpet beneath the window dark and soggy. Downstairs the lobby buzzed with restrained energies; a few venturesome ones in oils and turned-up collars paced the veranda without.

Mr. Arnheim, in his invariable soft collar and shadow-checked suit, skirted the edge of the crowd in matinal ill humor and deposited his room key at the desk. The clerk gave him in return a folded newspaper and his morning mail.

Mr. Arnheim's morning aspect was undeniable. He suggested too generous use of soap and bay rum, and his eyes had not lost the swollen heaviness that comes with too much or too little sleep. He yawned and seated himself in the heavy leather chair opposite the elevator.

His first letter was unstamped and addressed to him on hotel stationery; the handwriting was an unfamiliar backhand and the inclosure brief:

> DEAR MR. ARNHEIM:
>   I am very sorry we could not keep our date, but I got a message and I got to go in on the 7:10 train. Hope to see you when I come back.
> Sincerely, MYRA STERNBERGER.

Mr. Arnheim replaced the letter slowly in the envelope. There were two remaining—a communication from a cloak-manufacturing firm and a check from a banking-house. He read them and placed them in his inside coat pocket. Then he settled the back of his neck against the rim of the chair, crossed one leg over the other, rattled his newspaper open, and turned to the stock-market reports.

One week later Mr. Simon Arnheim, a red portfolio under one arm, walked into the mahogany, green-carpeted, soft-lighted establishment of an importing house on Fifth Avenue.

Mrs. S. S. Schlimberg, senior member, greeted him in her third-floor office behind the fitting-rooms.

"Well, well! *Wie geht's*, Arnheim? I thought it was gettin' time for you."

Mr. Arnheim shook hands and settled himself in a chair beside the desk. "You know you can always depend on me, madame, to look you up the minnit I get back. Don't I always give you first choice?"

Mrs. Schlimberg weighed a crystal paper-weight up and down in her pudgy, ringed hands. "None of your fancy prices for me this season, Arnheim. There's too many good things lyin' loose. That's why I got my openin' a month sooner. I got a designer came in special off her vacation with some good things."

Mr. Arnheim winked. "Schlim, I got some models here to show you that you can't beat. When you see 'em you'll pay any price."

"I can't pay your fancy prices no more. I paid you too much for that plush fad last winter, and it never was a go."

Mr. Arnheim chuckled. "When you see a couple of the designs I brought over this trip you'll be willin' to pay me twice as much as for the hobble. Come on—own up, Schlim; you can't beat my styles. Why, you can copy them for your import-room and make ninety per cent. on any one of 'em!"

"They won't pay the prices, I tell you. Some of my best customers have gone over to other houses for the cheaper goods."

"You can't put over domestic stuff on your trade, Schlim. You might as well admit it. You gotta sting your class of trade in order to have 'em appreciate you."

"Now, just to show you that I know what I'm talking about, Arnheim, I got the best lines of new models for this season I've had since I'm in business—every one of them domestics too. I'm puttin' some made-in-America models in the import-room to-day that will open your eyes."

Mr. Arnheim laughed and opened his portfolio. "I'll show you these till my trunks come up," he said.

"Just a minute, Arnheim. I want to show you some stuff—Miss Sternberger!" Mrs. Schlimberg raised her voice slightly, "Miss Sternberger!"

Almost immediately a svelte, black-gowned figure appeared in the doorway; she wore her hair oval about her face, like a Mona Lisa, and her hands were long and the dusky white of ivory.

"Mr. Arnheim, I want to introduce you to a designer we've got since you went away. Mr. Arnheim—Miss Sternberger."

The whir of sewing-machines from the work-rooms cut the silence.

"How do you do?" said Miss Sternberger.

"How do you do?" said Mr. Arnheim.

"Miss Sternberger is like you, Mr. Arnheim—she's always out after novelties; and I will say for her she don't miss out! She put out a line of uncut velvets last winter that was the best sellers we had."

Mr. Arnheim bowed. Mrs. Schlimberg turned to Miss Sternberger.

"Miss Sternberger, will you bring in some of those new models that are going like hot cakes? Just on the forms will do."

"Certainly." She disappeared from the doorway.

Mrs. Schlimberg tapped her forefinger on the desk. "There's the finest little designer we've ever had! I got her off a Philadelphia house, and I 'ain't never regretted the money I'm payin' her. She's done more for the house in eight months than Miss Isaacs did in ten years!"

Miss Sternberger returned; a stock-boy wheeled in the new models on wooden figures while Mrs. Schlimberg and her new designer arranged them for display. Miss Schlimberg turned to Mr. Arnheim.

"How's the wife and boys, Arnheim? I 'ain't seen 'em since you brought 'em in to see the Labor Day parade from the store windows last fall. Them's fine boys you got there, Arnheim!"

"Thanks," said Arnheim.

"Now, Arnheim, I'm here to ask you if you can beat these. Look at that there peach-bloom Piquette—look! Can you beat it? That there's the new butterfly skirt—just one year ahead of anything that's being shown this season." Mrs. Schlimberg turned to a second model. "Look at this here ratine cutaway. If the Phoebe Snow ain't the talk of New York before next week, then I don't know my own name. Ain't it so, Miss Sternberger?"

Miss Sternberger ran her smooth hand over the lace shoulder of the gown. "This is a great seller," she replied, smiling at Mr. Arnheim. "Lillian Russell is going to wear it in the second act of her new play when she opens to-morrow night."

"I guess we're slow in here," chuckled Mrs. Schlimberg, nudging Mr. Arnheim with the point of her elbow.

Miss Sternberger spread the square train of a flame-colored robe full length on the green carpet and drew back a corner of the hem to display the lacy avalanche beneath. Then she bowed slightly and turned toward the door.

Mrs. Schlimberg laid a detaining hand on her sleeve. "Just a minute, Miss Sternberger. Mr. Arnheim's brought in some models he wants us to look at."

The Other Cheek

First Published: *Saturday Evening Post*, April 11, 1914
Reprinted: *Just Around the Corner*, Harper & Bros., 1914

Romance has more lives than a cat. Crushed to earth beneath the double-tube, non-skiddable tires of a sixty-horse-power limousine, she allows her prancing steed to die in the dust of yesterday and elopes with the chauffeur.

Love has transferred his activities from the garden to the electric-heated taxi-cab and suffers fewer colds in the head. No, romance is not dead—only reincarnated; she rode away in divided skirt and side-saddle, and motored back in goggles. The tree-bark messages of the lovers of Arden are the fifty-word night letters of to-day.

The first editions of the Iliad were writ in the tenderest flesh parts of men's hearts, and truly enough did Moses blast his sublime messages out of the marble of all time; but why bury romance with the typewriter as a headstone?

Why, indeed—when up in the ninth-floor offices of A. L. Gregory, stenographers and expert typewriters—Miss Goldie Flint, with hair the color of heat-lightning, and wrists that jangled to the rolled-gold music of three bracelets, could tick-tack a hundred-word-a-minute love scene that was destined, after her neat carbon copies were distributed, to wring tears, laughter, and two dollars each from a tired-business-man audience.

Why, indeed, when the same slow fires that burned in Giaconda's upslanted eyes and made the world her lover lay deep in Goldie's own and invariably won her a seat in the six-o'clock Subway rush, and a bold, bad, flirtatious stare if she ventured to look above the third button of a man's coat.

Goldie Flint, beneath whose too-openwork shirtwaist fluttered a heart the tempo of which was love of life—and love of life on eight dollars a week and ninety per cent. impure food, and a hall-room, more specifically a standing room, is like a pink rose-bush that grows in a slack heap and begs its warmth from ashes.

Goldie, however, up in her ninth-floor offices, and bent to an angle of forty-five degrees over the dénouement of white-slave drama that promised a standing-room-only run and the free advertising of censorship, had little time or concern for her various atrophies.

It was nearly six o'clock, and she wanted half a yard of pink tulle before the shops closed. Besides, hers were the problems of the six-million-dollar incorporateds, who hire girls for six dollars a week; for the small-eyed, large-diamoned birds of prey who haunt the glove-counters and lace departments of the six-million-dollar incorporateds with invitations to dinner; and for the night courts, which are struggling to stanch the open gap of the social wound with medicated gauze instead of a tight tourniquet.

A yard of pink tulle cut to advantage would make a fresh yoke that would brighten even a three-year-old, gasolene-cleaned blouse. Harry Trimp liked pink tulle. Most Harry Trimps do.

At twenty minutes before six the lead-colored dusk of January crowded into the Gregory typewriting office so thick that the two figures before the two typewriters faded into the veil of gloom like a Corot landscape faints into its own mist.

Miss Flint ripped the final sheet of her second act from the roll of her machine, reached out a dim arm that was noisy with bracelets, and clicked on the lights. The two figures at the typewriters, the stationary wash-stand in the corner, a roll-top desk, and the heat-lightning tints in Miss Flint's hair sprang out in the jaundiced low candle-power.

"I'm done the second act, Miss Gregory. May I go now?"

Miss Flint's eyes were shining with the love-of-life lamps, the mica powder of romance, and a brilliant anticipation of Harry Trimp. Miss Gregory's were twenty years older and dulled like glass when you breathed on it.

"Yes; if you got to go I guess you can."

"Ain't it a swell play, Miss Gregory? Ain't it grand where he pushes her to the edge of the bridge and she throws herself down and hugs his knees?"

"Did you red ink your stage directions in, with the margin wide, like he wants? He was fussy about the first act."

"Yes'm; and say, ain't it a swell name for a show—'The Last of the Dee-Moolans'? Give me a show to do every time, and you can have all your contracts and statements and multigraph letters. Those love stories that long, narrow fellow brings in are swell to do, too, if he wa'n't such an old grouch about punctuation. Give me stuff that has some reading in it every time!"

Miss Gregory sniffed—the realistic, acidulated sniff of unloved forty and a thin nose.

"The sooner you quit curlin' your side-hair and begin to learn that life's made up of statements and multigraphs, instead of love scenes on papier-mâché bridges and flashy fellows in checked suits and get-rich-quick schemes, the better off you're going to be."

The light in Goldie's face died out as suddenly as a Jack-o'-lantern when you blow on the taper.

"Aw, Miss Grego-or-ee!" Her voice was the downscale wail of an oboe. "Whatta you always picking on Harry Trimp for? He ain't ever done anything to you—and you said yourself when he brought them circular letters in that he was one handsome kid."

"Just the same, I knew when he came in here the second time hanging round you with them blue eyes and black lashes, and that batch of get-rich-quick letters, he was as phony as his scarf-pin."

"I glory in a fellow's spunk that can give up a clerking job and strike out for hisself—that's what I do!"

"He was fired—that's how he started out for himself. Ask Mae Pope; she knows a thing or two about him."

"Aw, Miss—"

"Wait until you have been dealing with them as long as I have! Once get a line on a man's correspondence, and you can see through him as easy as through a looking-glass with the mercury rubbed off."

The walls of Jericho fell at the blast of a ram's horn. Not so Miss Flint's frailer fortifications.

"The minute a fellow that doesn't belong to the society of pikers and gets a three-figure salary comes along, and can take a girl to a restaurant where they begin with horse-doovries instead of wiping your cutlery on the table-cloth and deciding whether you want the 'and' with your ham fried or scrambled—the minute a fellow like that comes along and learns one of us girls that taxi-cabs was made for something besides dodging, and pink roses for something besides florist windows—that minute they put on another white-slave play, and your friends begin to recite the doxology to music. Gee! It's fierce!"

"Gimme that second act, Goldie. Thank Gawd I can say that in all my years of experience I've never been made a fool of: and, if I do say it, I had chances in my time!"

"You—you're the safest girl I know, Miss Gregory!"

"What?"

"You're safe if you know the ropes, Miss Gregory."

"What did you do with the Rheinhardt statement, Goldie? He'll be in for it any minute."

"It's in your left-hand drawer, along with those contracts, Miss Gregory. I made two carbons."

Miss Flint slid into her pressed-plush fourteen-dollar-and-a-half copy of a fourteen-hundred-fifty-dollar unborn-lamb coat, pulled her curls out from under the brim of her tight hat, and clasped a dyed-rat tippet about her neck so that her face flowered above it like a small rose out of its calyx.

The Bacon-Shakespeare controversy, the Fifth Dimension, and the

American Shopgirl and How She Does Not Look It on Six Dollars a Week, and Milk-Chocolate Lunches are still the subjects that are flung like serpentine confetti across the pink candle-shades of four-fork dinners, and are wound like red tape round Uplift Societies and Ladies' Culture Clubs.

Yet Goldie flourished on milk-chocolate lunches like the baby-food infants on the backs of magazines flourish on an add-hot-water-and-serve, twenty-five-cents-a-can substitute for motherhood.

"Good night, Miss Gregory."

"Night!"

Goldie closed the door softly behind her as though tiptoeing away from the buzzing gnats of an eight-hour day. Simultaneously across the hall the ground-glass door of the Underwriters' Realty Company swung open with a gust, and Mr. Eddie Bopp, clerk, celibate, and aspirant for the beyond of each state, bowed himself directly in Goldie's path.

"Ed-die! Ain't you early to-night, though! Since when are you keeping board-of-directors hours?"

"I been watching for you, Goldie."

Eddie needs no introduction. He solicits coffee orders at your door. The shipping-clerks and dustless-broom agents and lottery-ticket buyers of the world are made of his stuff. Bronx apartment houses, with perambulators and imitation marble columns in the down-stairs foyer, are built for his destiny. He sells you a yard of silk; he travels to Coney Island on hot Sunday afternoons; he bleaches on the bleachers; he bookkeeps; he belongs to a building association and wears polka-dot neckties. He is not above the pink evening edition. Ibsen and eugenics and post impressionism have never darkened the door of his consciousness. He is the safe-and-sane strata in the social mountain; not of the base or of the rarefied heights that carry dizziness.

Yet when Eddie regarded Goldie there was that in his eyes which transported him far above the safe-and-sane strata to the only communal ground that men and socialists admit—the Arcadia of lovers.

"I wasn't going to let you get by me to-night, Goldie. I ain't walked home with you for so long I haven't a rag of an excuse left to give Addie."

Miss Flint colored the faint pink of dawn's first moment.

"I—I got to do some shopping to-night, Eddie. That's why I quit early. Believe me, Gregory'll make me pay up to-morrow."

"It won't be the first time I shopped with you, Goldie."

"No."

"Remember the time we went down in Tracy's basement for a little alcohol-stove you wanted for your breakfasts? The girl at the counter thought we—we were spliced."

"Yeh!" Miss Flint's voice was faint as the thud of a nut to the ground.

They shot down fifteen fireproof stories in a breathtaking elevator, and then out on the whitest, brightest Broadway in the world, where the dreary trilogy of Wine, Woman, and Song is played from noon to dawn, with woman the cheapest of the three.

"How's Addie?"

"She don't complain, but she gets whiter and whiter—poor kid! I got her some new crutches, Goldie—swell mahogany ones with silver tips. You ought to see her get round on them!"

"I—I been so busy—night-work and—and—"

"She's been asking about you every night, Goldie. It ain't like you to stay away like this."

Their breaths clouded before them in the stinging air, and down the length of the enchanted highway lights sprang out of the gloom and winked at them like naughty eyes.

"What's the matter, Goldie? You ain't mad at me—us—are you?"

Eddie took her pressed-plush elbow in the cup of his hand and looked down at her, trying in vain to capture the bright flame of her glance.

"Nothing's the matter, Eddie. Why should I be mad? I been busy—that's all."

The tide of home-going New York caught them in its six-o'clock vortex. Shops emptied and streetcars filled. A newsboy fell beneath a car, and Broadway parted like a Red Sea for an overworked ambulance, the mission of which was futile. A lady in a fourteen-hundred-fifty-dollar unborn-lamb coat and a notorious dog-collar of pearls stepped out of a wine-colored limousine into the gold-leaf foyer of a hotel. A ten-story emporium ran an iron grating across its entrance, and ten watchmen reported for night duty.

"Aw, gee! They're closed! Ain't that the limit now! Ain't that the limit! I wanted some pink tulle."

"Poor kid! Don't you care! You can get it to-morrow—you can work Gregory."

"I—I wanted it for to-night."

"What?"

"I wanted it for my yoke."

They turned into the dark aisle of a side street; the wind lurked around the corner to leap at them.

"Oh-h-h-h!"

He held tight to her arm.

"It's some night—ain't it, girlie?"

"I should say so!"

"Poor little kid!"

Eddie's voice was suddenly the lover's, full of that quality which is like unto the ting of a silver bell after the clapper is quiet.

"You're coming home to a good hot supper with me, Goldie—ain't you, Goldie? Addie'll like it."

She withdrew her hand from the curve of his elbow.

"I can't, Eddie—not to-night. I—tell her I'm coming over real soon."

"Oh!"

"It's sure cold, ain't it?"

"Goldie, can't you tell a fellow what's the matter? Can't you tell me why you been dodging me—us—for two weeks? Can't you tell a fellow—huh, Goldie?"

"Geewhillikins, Eddie! Ain't I told you it's nothing? There ain't a girl could be a better friend to Addie than me."

"I know that, Goldie; but—"

"Didn't we work in the same office thick as peas for two whole years before her—accident—even before I knew she had a brother? Ain't I stuck to her right through—ain't I?"

"You know that ain't what I mean, Goldie. You been a swell friend to poor Addie, stayin' with her Sundays when you could be havin' a swell time and all; but it's me I'm talking about, Goldie. Sometimes—sometimes I—"

"Aw!"

"I've never talked straight out about it before, Goldie; but you—you remember the night—the night I rigged up like a Christmas tree, and you said I was all the ice-cream in my white pants—the night Addie was run over and they sent for me?"

"Will I ever forget it!"

"I was tuning up that evening to tell you, Goldie—while we were sitting there on your stoop, with the street-light in our eyes, and you screechin' every time a June-bug bumbled in your face!"

"Gawd, how I hate bugs! There was one in Miss Gregory's—"

"I was going to tell you that night, Goldie, that there was only one girl—one girl for me—and—"

"Yeh; and while we were sittin' there gigglin' and screechin' at June-bugs poor Addie was provin' that a street-car fender has got it all over a mangling-machine."

"Yes; it's like she says about herself—she was payin' her initiation fee for life membership into the Society of Cripples with a perfectly good hip and a bit of spine."

"Poor Addie! Gawd, how she loved to dance! She used to spend every noon-hour eatin' marshmallows and learning me new steps."

The wind soughed in their ears, and Goldie's skirts blew backward like sails.

"You haven't got a better friend than Addie right now, girlie! She always says our little flat is yours. The three of us, Goldie—the three of us could—"

"It's swell for a girl that ain't got none of her own blood to have a friend like that. Swell, lemme tell you!"

"Goldie!"

"Yes."

"It's like I said—I've never talked right out before, but I got a feelin' you're slippin' away from me like a eel, girlie. You know—aw, you know I ain't much on the elocution stuff; but if it wasn't for Addie and her accident right now—I'd ask you outright—I would. You know what I mean!"

"I don't know about anything, Eddie; I'm no mind-reader!"

"Aw, cut it out, Goldie! You know I'm tied up right now and can't say some of the things I was going to say that night on the stoop. You know what I mean—with Addie's doctor's bills and chair and crutches, and all."

"Sure I do, Eddie. You've got no right to think of anything."

She turned from him so that her profile was like a white cameo mounted on black velvet.

"You just give me a little time, Goldie, and I'll be on my feet, all righty. I just want some kind of understanding between us—that's all."

"Oh—you—I—"

"I got Joe's job cinched if he goes over to the other firm in March; and by that time, Goldie, you and me and Addie, on eighty per, could—why, we—"

She swayed back from his close glance and ran up the first three steps of her rooming-house. Her face was struck with fear suddenly, as with a white flame out of the sky.

"'Sh-h-h-h-h-h!" she said. "You mustn't!"

He reached for her hand, caught it and held it—but like a man who feels the rope sliding through his fingers and sees his schooner slipping out to sea—slipping out to sea.

"Lemme go, Eddie! I gotta go—it's late!"

"I *know*, Goldie. They been guyin' me at the office about you passin' me up; and it's right—ain't it? It's—It's him—" She shook her head and tugged for the freedom of her hand. Tears crowded into her eyes like water to the surface of a tumbler just before the overflow. "It's *him*—ain't it, Goldie?"

"Well, you won't give—give a girl a chance to say anything. If you'd have given me time I was comin' over and tell you, and—and tell—"

"Goldie!"

"I was—I was—"

"It's none of my business, girlie, but—but he ain't fit for you. He—"

"There you go! The whole crowd of you make me—"

"He ain't fit for no girl, Goldie! Listen to me, girlie! He's just a regular ladykiller! He can't keep a job no more'n a week for the life of him! I used to know him when I worked at Delaney's. Listen to me, Goldie! This here new minin' scheme he's in ain't even on the level! It ain't none of my business; but, good God, Goldie, just because a guy's good-lookin' and a swell dresser and—"

She sprang from his grasp and up the three remaining steps. In the sooty flare of the street lamp she was like Jeanne d'Arc heeding the vision or a suffragette declaiming on a soap-box and equal rights.

"You—the whole crowd of you make me sick! The minute a fellow graduates out of the sixty-dollar-clerk class, and can afford a twenty-dollar suit, without an extra pair of pants thrown in, the whole pack of you begin to yowl and yap at his heels like—"

"Goldie! Goldie, listen—"

"Yes, you do! But I ain't caring. I know him, and I know what I want. We're goin' to get married when we're good and ready, and we ain't apologizing to no one! I don't care what the whole pack of you have to say, except Addie and you; and—and—I—oh—"

Goldie turned and fled into the house, slamming the front door after her so that the stained-glass panels rattled—then up four flights, with the breath soughing in her throat and the fever of agitation racing through her veins.

Her oblong box of a room at the top of the long flights was cold with a cavern damp and musty with the must that is as indigenous to rooming-houses as chorus-girls to the English peerage or insomnia to black coffee.

Even before she lighted her short-armed gas-jet, however, a sweet, insidious, hothouse fragrance greeted her faintly through the must, as the memory of mignonette clings to old lace. Goldie's face softened as if a choir invisible was singing her ragtime from above her skylight. She lighted her fan of gas with fingers that trembled in a pleasant frenzy of anticipation, and the tears dried on her face and left little paths down her cheeks.

A fan of pink roses, fretted with maidenhair fern and caught with a sash of pink tulle, lay on her coarse cot coverlet, as though one of her dreams had ventured out of its long night.

What a witch is love!

Pink leaped into Goldie's cheeks, and into her eyes the light that passeth understanding. Life dropped its dun-colored cloak and stood suddenly garlanded in pink, wire-stemmed roses.

She buried her face in their fragrance. She kissed a cool bud, the heart of which was closed. She unwrapped the pink tulle sash with fingers that were addled—like a child's at the gold cord of a candy-box—and held the filmy streamer against her bosom in the outline of a yoke.

In Mrs. McCasky's boarding-house the onward march of night was as regular as a Swiss watch with an American movement.

At nine o'clock Mr. McCasky's tin bucket grated along the hall wall, down two flights of banisters, across the street, and through the knee-high swinging-doors of Joe's place.

At ten o'clock the Polinis, on the third-floor back, let down their folding-bed and shivered the chandelier in Major Florida's second-floor back.

At eleven o'clock Mr. McCasky's tin bucket grated unevenly along the hall wall, down two flights of banisters, across the street, and through the knee-high swinging-doors of Joe's place.

At twelve o'clock the electric piano in Joe's place ceased to clatter through the night like coal pouring into an empty steel bin, and Mrs. McCasky lowered the hall light from a blob the size of a cranberry to a French pea.

At one o'clock the next to the youngest Polini infant lifted its voice to the skylight, and Mr. Trimp's night-key waltzed round the front-door lock, scratch-scratching for its hole.

In the dim-lit first-floor front Mrs. Trimp started from her light doze like a deer in a park, which vibrates to the fall of a lady's feather fan. The criss-cross from the cane chair-back was imprinted on one sleep-flushed cheek, and her eyes, dim with the weariness of the night-watch, flew to the white-china door-knob.

Reader, rest undismayed. Mr. Trimp entered on the banking-hour legs of a scholar and a gentleman. With a white carnation in his buttonhole, his hat unbattered in the curve of his arm, and his blue eyes behind their curtain of black lashes, but slightly watery, like a thawing ice-pond with a film atop.

"Hello, my little Goldie-eyes!"

Mr. Trimp flashed his double deck of girlish-pearlish teeth. When Mr. Trimp smiled Greuze might have wanted to paint his lips for a child-study. Women tightened up about the throat and dared to wonder whether he wore a chest-protector and asafetida bag. Old ladies in street-cars regarded him through the mist of memories, and as if their motherly fingers itched to run through the heavy yellow hemp of his hair. There was that in his smile which seemed to provoke hand-painted sofa-pillows and baby-ribboned coat-hangers, knitted neckties, and cross-stitch slippers. Once he had posed for an Adonis underwear advertisement.

"Hello, baby! Did you wait up for your old man?"

Goldie regarded her husband with eyes that ten months of marriage had dimmed slightly. Her lips were thinner and tighter and silent.

"I think we landed a sucker to-night for fifty shares, kiddo. Ain't so bad, is it? And so you waited up for your tired old man, baby?"

"No!" she said, the words sparking from her lips like the hiss of a hot iron when you test it with a moist forefinger. "No; I didn't wait up. I been out with you—painting the town."

"I couldn't get home for supper, hon. Me and Cutty—"

"You and Cutty! I wasn't born yesterday!"

"Me and Cutty had a sucker out, baby. He'll bite for fifty shares sure!"

"Gee!" she flamed at him, backing round the rocker from his amorous advances. "Gee! If I was low enough to be a crook—if I was low enough to try and make a livin' sellin' dead dirt for pay dirt—I'd be a successful crook, anyway; I'd—"

"Now, Goldie, hon! Don't—"

"I wouldn't leave my wife havin' heart failure every time McCasky passes the door—I wouldn't!"

"Now, don't fuss at me, Goldie. I'm tired—dog-tired. I got some money comin' in to-morrow that'll—"

"That don't go with me any more!"

"Sure I have."

"I been set out on the street too many times before on promises like that; and it was always after a week of one of these here slow jags. I know them and how they begin. I know them!"

"'Tain't so this time, honey. I been—"

"I know them and how they begin, with your sweet, silky ways. I'd rather have you come staggering home than like this—with your claws hid. I—I'm afraid of you, I tell you. I ain't forgot the night up at Hinkey's. You haven't been out with Cutty no more than I have. You been up to the Crescent, where the Red Slipper is dancing this week, you—"

Mr. Trimp swayed ever so slightly—slightly as a silver reed in the lightest breeze that blows—and regained his balance immediately. His breath, redolent as a garden of spice and cloves, was close to his wife's neck.

"Baby," he said, "you better believe your old man. I been out with Cutty, Goldie. We had a sucker out!"

She sprang back from his touch, hot tears in her eyes.

"Believe you! I did till I learnt better. I believed you for four months, sittin' round waiting for you and your goings-on. You ain't been out with Cutty—you ain't been out with him one night this week. You been—you—"

Mrs. Trimp's voice rose to a hysterical crescendo. Her hair, yellow as cornsilk, and caught in a low chignon at her back, escaped its restraint of pins and fell in a whorl down her shirt-waist. She was like a young immortal eaten by the corroding acids of earlier experiences—raw with the vitriol of her deathless destiny.

"You ain't been out with Cutty. You been—"

The piano-salesman on the first-floor back knocked against the closed folding-door for the stilly night that should have been his by right. A distant night-stick struck the asphalt, and across Harry Trimp's features, like filmy clouds across the moon, floated a composite death-mask of Henry the Eighth and Othello, and all their alimony-paying kith. His mouth curved into an expression that did not coincide with pale hair and light eyes.

He slid from his greatcoat, a black one with an astrakan collar and bought in three payments, and inclined closer to his wife, a contumelious quirk on his lips.

"Well, whatta you going to do about it, kiddo—huh?"

"I—I'm going to—quit!"

He laughed and let her squirm from his hold, strolled over to the dresser mirror, pulled his red four-in-hand upward from its knot and tugged his collar open.

"You're not going to quit, kiddo! You ain't got the nerve!"

He leaned to the mirror and examined the even rows of teeth, and grinned at himself like a Hallowe'en pumpkin to flash whiter their whiteness.

"Ain't I! Which takes the most nerve, I'd like to know, stickin' to you and your devilishness or strikin' out for myself like I been raised to do? I was born a worm, and I ain't never found the cocoon that would change me into a butterfly. I—I had as swell a job up at Gregory's as a girl ever had. I'm an expert stenographer, I am! I got a diploma from—"

"Why don't you get your job back, baby? You been up there twice to my knowin'; maybe the third time'll be a charm. Don't let me keep you, kiddo."

The sluice-gates of her fear and anger opened suddenly, and tears rained down her cheeks. She wiped them away with her bare palm.

"It's because you took the life and soul out of me! They don't want me back because I ain't nothin' but a rag any more. I guess they're ashamed to take me back cause I'm in—in your class. Ten months of standing for your funny business and dodging landladies, and waitin' up nights, and watchin' you and your crooked starvation game would take the life out of any girl. It would! It would!"

"Don't fuss at me any more, Goldie-eyes. It's getting' hard for me to keep down; and I don't want—want to begin gettin' ugly."

Mr. Trimp advanced toward his wife gently—gently.

"Don't come near me! I know what's coming; but you ain't going to get me this time with your oily ways. You're the kind that walks on a girl with spiked heels and tries to kiss the sores away. I'm going to quit!"

Mr. Trimp plucked at the faint hirsute adornment of his upper lip and folded his black-and-white waistcoat over the back of a chair. He fumbled it a bit.

"Stay where you're put, you—you bloomin' vest, you!"

"I—I got friends that'll help me, I have—even if I ain't ever laid eyes on 'em since the day I married you. I got friends—*real* friends! Addie'll take me in any minute, day or night. Eddie Bopp could get me a job in his firm to-morrow if—if I ask him. I got friends! You've kept me from 'em; but I ain't afraid to look 'em up. I'm not!"

He advanced to where she stood beneath the waving gas-flame, a pet phrase clung to his lips, and he stumbled over it.

"My—my little—pussy-cat!"

"You're drunk!"

"No, I ain't, baby—only dog-tired. Dog-tired! Don't fuss at me! You just don't know how much I love you, baby!"

"Who wouldn't fuss, I'd like to know?"

Her voice was like ice crackling with thaw. He took her lax waist in his embrace and kissed her on the brow.

"Don't, honey—don't! Me and Cutty had a sucker out, I tell you."

"You—you always get your way with me. You treat me like a dog; but you know you can wind me round—wind me round."

"Baby! Baby!"

He smoothed her hair away from her salt-bitten eyes, laid his cheek pat against hers, and murmured to her through the scratch in his throat, like a parakeet croons to its mate.

"Pussy-cat! Pussy!"

The river of difference between them dried in the warm sun of her for-giveness, and she sobbed on his shoulder with the exhaustion of a child after a tantrum.

"You won't leave me alone nights no more, Harry?"

"Thu—thu—thu—such a little Goldie-eyes!"

"I can't stand for the worry of the board no more, Harry. McCaskys are gettin' ugly. I ain't got a decent rag to my back, neither."

"I'm going to take a shipping-room job next week, honey, and get back in harness. Bill's going to fix me up. There ain't nothin' in this rotten game, and I'm going to get out."

"Sure?"

"Sure, Goldie."

"You ain't been drinking, Harry?"

"Sure I ain't. Me and Cutty had a rube out, I tell you."

"You'll keep straight, won't you, Harry? You're killin' me, boy, you are."

"Come, dry your face, baby."

He reached to his hip-pocket for his handkerchief, and with it a sparse shower of red and green and pink and white and blue confetti showered to the floor like snow through a spectrum. Goldie slid from his embrace and laughed—a laugh frappéd with the ice of scorn and chilled as her own chilled heart.

"Liar!" she said, and trembled as she stood.

His lips curled again into the expression that so ill-fitted his albinism.

"You little cat! You can bluff me!"

"I knew you was up at the Crescent Cotillon! I felt it in my bones. I knew you was up there when I read on the bill-boards that the Red Slipper was dancing there. I knew where you was every night while I been sittin' here waitin'! I knew—I knew—"

The piano-salesman rapped against the folding-doors thrice, with distemper and the head of a cane. At that instant the lower half of Mr. Trimp's face protruded suddenly into a lantern-jawed facsimile of a blue-ribbon English bull; his hand shot out and hurled the chair that stood between them half-way across the room, where it fell on its side against the wash-stand and split a rung.

"You—you little devil, you!"

The second-floor front beat a tattoo of remonstrance; but there was a sudden howling as of boiling surf in Mr. Trimp's ears, and the hot ember of an oath dropped from his lips.

"You little devil! You been hounding me with the quit game for eight months. Now you gotta quit!"

"I—I—"

"There ain't a man livin' would stand for your long face and naggin'! If you don't like my banking-hours and my game and the company I keep you quit, kiddo! Quit! Do you hear?"

"Will—I—quit? Well—"

"Yeh; I been up to the Crescent Confetti—every night this week, just like you say! I been round live wires, where there ain't no long, white faces shoving board bills and whining the daylights out of me."

"Oh, you—you ain't nothing but—"

"Sure, I been up there! I can get two laughs for every long face you pull on me. You quit if you want to, kiddo—there ain't no strings to you. Quit—and the sooner the better!" Mr. Trimp grasped his wife by her taut wrists and jerked her to him until her head fell backward and the breath jumped out of her throat in a choke. "Quit—and the sooner the better!"

"Lemme go! Lem-me-go!"

He tightened his hold and inclined toward her, so close that their faces almost touched. With his hot clutches on her wrists and his hot breath in her face it seemed to her that his eyes fused into one huge Cyclopean circle that spun and spun in the center of his forehead, like a fiery Catharine-Wheel against a night sky.

"Bah! You little whiteface, you! You played a snide trick on me, anyway—lost your looks the second month and went dead like a punctured tire! Quit when you want to—there ain't no strings. Quit now!"

He flung her from him, so that she staggered backward four steps and struck her right cheek sharply against the mantel corner. A blue-glass vase fell to the hearth and was shattered. With the salt of fray on his lips, he kicked at the overturned chair and slammed a closet door so that the windows rattled. A carpet-covered hassock lay in his path, and he hurled it across the floor. Goldie edged toward the wardrobe, hugging the wall like one who gropes in the dark.

"If you're right bright, kiddo, you'll keep out of my way. You got me crazy to-night—crazy! Do you hear me, you little—"

"My hat!"

He flung it to her from its peg, with her jacket, so that they fell crumpled at her feet.

"You're called on your bluff this time, little one. This is one night it's quits for you—and I ain't drunk, neither!"

She crowded her rampant hair, flowing as Ophelia's, into her cheap little boyish hat and fumbled into her jacket. A red welt, shaped like a tongue of flame, burned diagonally down her right cheek.

"Keep out of my way—you! You got me crazy to-night—crazy to-night!"

He watched her from the opposite side of the room with lowered head, like a bull lunging for onslaught.

She moved toward the door with the rigidity of an automaton doll, her magnetized eyes never leaving his reddening face and her hands groping ahead. Her mouth was moist and no older than a child's; but her skin dead, as if coated over with tallow. She opened the door slowly, fearing to break the spell—then suddenly slipped through the aperture and slammed it after her. Then the slam of another door; the scurrying of feet down cold stone steps that sprung echoes in the deserted street.

The douse of cold air stung her flaming cheek; a policeman glanced after her; a drunken sailor staggered out of a black doorway, and her trembling limbs sped faster—a labyrinth of city streets and rows of blank-faced houses; an occasional pedestrian, who glanced after her because she wheezed in her throat, and ever so often gathered her strength and broke into a run; then a close, ill-smelling apartment house, with a tipsy gas-light mewling in the hall, and a dull-brown door that remained blank to her knocks and rings. The sobs were rising in her throat, and the trembling in her limbs shook her as with ague.

A knock that was more of a pound and a frenzied rattling of the knob! Finally from the inside of the door a thump-thump down a long hallway—

and the door creaked open cautiously, suspiciously!

In its frame a pale figure, in the rumpled clothes of one always sitting down and hunched on a pair of silver-mounted mahogany crutches that slanted from her sides like props.

"Goldie! Little Goldie!"

"Oh, Addie! Addie!"

Youth has rebound like a rubber ball. Batted up against the back fence, she bounces back into the heart of a rose-bush or into the carefully weeded, radishless radish-bed of the kitchen garden.

Mrs. Trimp rose from the couch-bed davenport of the Bopp sitting-dining-sleeping-room, with something of the old lamps burning in her eyes and a full-lipped mouth to which clung the memory of smiles. Even Psyche, abandoned by love, smiled a specious smile when she posed for the scalpel.

Eddie Bopp reached out a protective arm and drew Goldie by the sleeve of her shirt-waist down to the couch-bed davenport again.

"Take it easy there, Goldie. Don't get yourself all excited again."

"But it's just like you say, Eddie—I got the law on my side. I got him on the grounds of cruelty if—if I show nothin' but—but this cheek."

"Sure you have, Goldie; but you just sit quiet. Addie, come in here and make Goldie behave her little self."

"I'm all right, Eddie. Gee! With Addie treating me like I was a queen in a gilt crown, and you skidding round me like a tire, I feel like cream!"

Eddie regarded her with eyes that were soft as rose-colored lamps at dusk.

"You poor little kid!"

Addie hobbled in from the kitchen.

"I got something you'll like, Goldie. It's hot and good for you, too."

God alone knew the secret of Addie. He had fashioned her in clay and water, even as you and me—from the same earthy compound from which is sprung ward politicians and magic-throated divas, editors and plumbers, poet laureates and Polish immigrants, kings and French ballet dancers, propagandists and piece-workers, single-taxers and suffragettes.

He fashioned her in clay; and it was as if she came from under the teeth of a Ninth Avenue streetcar fender—broken, but remolded in alabaster, and with the white light of her stanch spirit shining through—Addie, whose side, up as high as her ribs, was a flaming furnace and whose smile was sunshine on dew.

"You wouldn't eat no supper; so I made you some chicken broth, Goldie. You remember when we was studying shorthand at night school how we used to send Jimmie over to White's lunch-room for chickenette broth and a slab of milk chocolate?"

"Do I? Gee! You were the greatest kid, Addie!"

"Eat, Goldie—gwan."

"I ain't hungry—honest!"

"Quit standing over her, Eddie; you make her nervous. Let me feed you, Goldie."

"Gee! Ain't you swell to me!" Ready tears sprang to her eyes.

"Like you ain't my old chum, Goldie! It don't seem so long since we were working in the same office and going to Recreation Pier dances together, does it?"

"Addie! Addie!"

"Do you remember how you and me and Ed and Charley Snuggs used to walk up and down Ninth Avenue summer evenings eating ice-cream cones?"

"Do I? Oh, Addie, do I?"

"I'm glad we had them ice-cream days, Goldie. They're melted, but the flavor ain't all gone." Addie's face was large and white and calm-featured, like a Botticelli head.

"You two girls sure was cut-ups! Remember the night Addie first introduced us, Goldie? You came over to call for her, and us three went to the waxworks show on Twenty-third Street. Lordy, how we cut up!"

"And I started to ask the wax policeman if we was allowed to go past the rail!" They laughed low in their throats, as if they feared to raise an echo in a vale of tears. "It's like old times for me to be staying all night with you again, Addie. It's been so long! He—he used to get mad like anything if I wanted to see any of the old crowd. He knew they didn't know any good of him. He was always for the sporty, all-night bunch."

"Poor kid!"

"Don't get her to talking about it, Eddie; it gets her all excited."

"He could have turned me against my own mother, I was that crazy over him."

"That," said Addie softly, "was *love!* And only women can love like that; and women who do love like that are cursed—and blessed."

"I'm out of it now, Addie. You won't never send me back to him—you won't ever?"

"There now, dearie, you're gettin' worked up again. Ain't you right here, safe with us?"

"That night at Hinkey's was the worst, Goldie," said Eddie. "It makes my blood boil! Why didn't you quit then; why?"

"I ain't told you all, neither, Eddie. One night he came home about two o'clock, and I had been—"

"Just quit thinking and talking about him, Goldie. You're right here, safe with me and Eddie; and he's going to get you a job when you're feeling stronger. And then, when you're free—when you're free—"

Addie regarded her brother with the tender aura of a smile on her lips and a tender implication in her eyes that scurried like a frightened mouse back into its hole. Eddie flamed red; and his ears, by a curious physiological process, seemed to take fire and contemplate instant flight from his head.

"Oh, look, Ad. We got to get a new back for your chair. The stuffin's all poking through the velvet."

"So it is, Eddie. It's a good thing you got your raise, with all these new-fangled dangles we need."

"To-night's his lodge night. He never came home till three—till three o'clock, lodge nights."

"There you go, Goldie—back on the subject, makin' yourself sick."

"Gee!"

"What's the matter, Goldie?"

"To-night's his lodge. I could go now and get my things while he ain't there—couldn't I?"

"Swell! I'll take you, Goldie, and wait outside for you."

"Eddie, can't you see she ain't in any condition to go running round nights? There's plenty time yet, Goldie. You can wear my shirt-waists and things. Wait till—"

"I got to get it over with, Addie; and daytimes Eddie's working, and I'd have to go alone. I—I don't want to go alone."

"Sure; she can't go alone, Addie; and she's got to have her things."

Eddie was on his feet and beside Goldie's palpitating figure, as though he would lay his heart, a living stepping-stone, at her feet.

"We better go now, Addie; honest we had! Eddie'll wait outside for me."

"You poor kid! You want to get it over with, don't you? Get her coat, Eddie, and bring her my sweater to wear underneath. It's getting colder every minute."

"I ain't scared a bit, Addie. I'll just go in and pack my things together and hustle out again."

"Here's a sweater, Goldie, and your coat and hat."

"Take care, children; and, Goldie, don't forget all the things you need. Just take your time and get your things together—warm clothes and all."

"I'll be waiting right outside for you, Goldie."

"I'm ready, Eddie."

"Don't let her get excited and worked up, Eddie."

"I ain't scared a bit, Addie."

"Sure you ain't?"

"Not a bit!"

"Good-by, Addie. Gee, but you're swell to me!"

"Don't forget to bring your rubbers, Goldie; going to work on wet mornings you'll need them."

"I—I ain't got none."

"You can have mine. I—I don't need them any more."

"Good-by, Ad—leave the dishes till we come back. I can do 'em swell myself after you two girls have gone to bed."

"Yes. I'll be waiting, Goldie; and we'll talk in bed like old times."

"Yes, yes!" It was as if Addie's frail hands were gripping Goldie's heart and clogging her speech.

"Good-by, children!"

"Good-by."

"S'long!"

The night air met them with a whoop and tugged and pulled at Goldie's hat.

"Take my arm, Goldie. It's some howler, ain't it?"

Their feet clacked on the cold, dry pavement, and passers-by leaned into the wind.

"He was a great one for hating the cold, Eddie. Gee, how he hated winter!"

"That's why he wears a fur-collared coat and you go freezing along in a cheese-cloth jacket, I guess."

"It always kind of got on his chest and gave him fever."

"What about you? You just shivered along and dassent say anything!"

"And I used to fix him antiphlogistin plasters half the night. When he wasn't mad or drunk he was just like a kid with the measles! It used to make me laugh so—he'd—"

"Humph!"

"But one night—one night I got the antiphlogistin too hot while I was straightening up—'cause he never liked a messy-looking room when he was sick—and he was down and out from one of his bad nights; and it—and it got too hot, and—" She turned away and finished her sentence in the teeth of the wind; but Eddie's arm tightened on hers until she could feel each distinct finger.

"God!" he said.

"I ain't scared a bit, Eddie."

"For what, I'd like to know! Ain't I going to be waiting right here across the street?"

"See! That's the room over there—the dark one, with the shade half-way up. Gee, how I hate it!"

"I'll be waiting right here in front of Joe's place, Goldie. If you need me just shoot the shade all the way up."

"I won't need you."

"Well, then, light the gas, pull the shade all the way down, and that'll mean all's well."

"Swell!" she said. "Down comes the shade—and all's well!"

"Good!"

They smiled, and their breaths clouded between them; and down through the high-walled street the wind shot javelin-like and stung red into their cheeks, and in Eddie's ears and round his heart the blood buzzed.

Goldie crossed the street and went up the steps lightly, her feet grating the brown stone like fine-grained sandpaper. When she unlocked the front door the cave-like mustiness and the cold smell of unsunned hallways and the conglomerate of food smells met her at the threshold. Memories like needle-tongued insects stung her.

The first-floor front she opened slowly, pausing after every creak of the door; and the gas she fumbled because her hand trembled, and the match burned close to her fingers before she found the tip.

She turned up the flame until it sang, and glanced about her fearfully, with one hand on her bruised cheek and her underlip caught in by her teeth.

Mr. Trimp's room was as expressive as a lady's glove still warm from her hand. He might have slipped out of it and let it lie crumpled, but in his own image.

The fumes of bay-rum and stale beer struggled for supremacy. The center-table, with a sickening litter of empty bottles and dead ashes, was dreary as cold mutton in its grease, or a woman's painted face at crack o' dawn, or the moment when the flavor of love becomes as tansy.

A red-satin slipper, an unhygienic drinking-goblet, which has leaked and slopped over full many a non-waterproof romance, lay on the floor, with its red run into many pinks and its rosette limp as a wad of paper. Goldie picked her careful way round it. Fear and nausea and sickness at the heart made her dizzy.

The dresser, with its wavy mirror, was strewn with her husband's neckties; an uncorked bottle of bay-rum gave out its last faint fumes.

She opened the first long drawer with a quivering intake of breath and pulled out a shirt-waist, another, and yet another, and a coarse white petti-coat with a large-holed embroidery flounce. Then she dragged a suit-case, which was wavy like the mirror, through the blur of her tears, out from under the bed; and while she fumbled with the lock the door behind her opened, and her heart rose in her throat with the sudden velocity of an express elevator shooting up a ten-story shaft.

In the dresser mirror, and without turning her head or gaining her feet, she looked into the eyes of her husband.

"Pussy-cat!" he said, and came toward her with his teeth flashing like

Carrara marble in sunlight.

She sprang to her feet and backed against the dresser.

"Don't! Don't you come near me!"

"You don't mean that, Goldie."

She shivered in her scorn.

"Don't you come near me! I came—to get my things."

"Oh!" he said, and tossed his hat on the bed and peeled off his coat. "Help yourself, kiddo. Go as far as you like."

She fell to tearing at the contents of her drawer without discrimination, cramming them into her bag and breathing furiously, like a hare in the torture of the chase. The color sprang out in her cheeks, and her eyes took fire.

Her husband threw himself, in his shirt-sleeves and waistcoat, across the bed and watched her idly. Only her fumbling movements and the sing of the too-high gas broke the silence. He rose, lowered the flame, and lay down again.

Her little box of poor trinkets spilled its contents as she packed it; her hair-brush fell from her trembling fingers and clattered to the floor.

"Can I help you, Goldie-eyes?"

Silence. He coughed rather deep in his chest, and she almost brushed his hand as she passed to the clothes wardrobe. He reached out and caught her wrist.

"Now, Goldie, you—"

"Don't—don't you touch me! Let go!"

He drew her down to the bed beside him.

"Can't you give a fellow another chance, baby? Can't you?" She tugged for her freedom, but his clasp was tight as steel and tender as love. "Can't you, baby?"

"You!" she said, kicking at the sloppy satin slipper at her feet, as if it were a loathsome thing that crawled. "I—I don't ever want to see you again, you—you—"

"You drove me to it, pussy; honest you did!"

"You didn't need no driving. You take to it like a fish to water—nobody can drive you. You just ain't—no—good!"

"You drove me to it. When you quit I just went crazy mad. I kicked the skylight—I tore things wide open. I was that sore for you—honest, baby!"

"I've heard that line of talk before. I ain't forgotten the night at Hinkey's. I ain't forgot nothing. You or horses can't hold me here!" She wrenched at her wrists.

"I got a job yesterday, baby. Bill made good. Eighty dollars, honey! Me and Cutty are quits for good. Ain't that something—now, ain't it?"

"Let me go!"

"Pussy-cat!"

"Let me go, I say!"

He coughed and turned on his side toward her.

"You don't mean it."

"I do! I do! Let go! Let go!"

She tore herself free and darted to the wardrobe door. He closed his eyes and his lashes lay low on his cheeks.

"Before you go, Goldie, where's the antiphlogistin? I got a chest on me like an ice-wagon."

"Sure, you have. That's the only time you ever show up before crack of dawn."

He reached out and touched her wrist.

"I'm hot, ain't I?"

She placed a reluctant hand on his brow.

"Fever?"

"It ain't nothing much. I'll be all right."

"It's just one of your spells. Stay in bed a couple of days, and you'll soon be ready for another jamboree!"

"Don't fuss at me, baby."

"It's in the wash-stand drawer in a little tin can. Don't make the plaster too hot."

"Sure, I won't. I'll get along all righty."

She threw a shabby cloth skirt over her arm and a pressed-plush coat that was gray at the elbows and frayed at the hem. He reached out for the dangling empty sleeve as she passed.

"You was married in that coat, wasn't you, hon?"

"Yes," she said, and her lips curled like burning paper; "I was married in that coat."

"Goldie-eyes, you know I can't get along without my petsie; you know it. There ain't no one can hold a candle to you, baby!"

"Yes, yes!"

"There ain't! I wish I was feelin' well enough to tell you how sorry, baby—how sorry a fellow like me can get. I just wish it, baby—baby—"

She surrendered like a reed to the curve of a scythe and crumpled in a contortional heap beside the bed.

"You—you always get me!"

He gathered her up and laid her head backward on his shoulder, so that her face was foreshortened and close to his.

"Goldie-eyes," he said, "I'll make it up to you! I'll make it up to you!" And he made a motion as though to kiss her where the curls lay on her face, but drew back as if sickened.

"Good God!" he said. "Poor little baby!"

Quick as a throb of a heart she turned her left cheek, smooth as a lily petal, to his lips.

"It's all right, Harry!" she said, in a voice that was tight. "I'm crazy, I guess; but, gee, it's great to be crazy!"

"I'll make it up to you, baby. See if I don't! I'll make it up to you."

She kissed him, and his lips were hot and dry.

"Lemme fix your plaster, dearie; you got one of your colds."

"Don't get it too hot, hon."

"Gee! Lemme straighten up. Say, ain't you a messer, though! Look at this here wash-stand and those neckties! Ain't you a messer, though, dearie!"

She crammed the ties into a dresser drawer, dragged a chair into place, removed a small tin can from the wash-stand drawer, hung her hat and jacket on their peg, and lowered the shade.

T. B.

First Published: *Saturday Evening Post,* January 9, 1915
Reprinted: *Every Soul Hath Its Song,* Harper & Bros., 1916
The Best Short Stories of 1915, ed. Edward J. O'Brien, Small, Maynard & Co., 1916

The figurative underworld of a great city has no ventilation, housing or lighting problems. Rooks and crooks who live in the putrid air of crime are not denied the light of day, even though they loathe it. Cadets, social skunks, whose carnivorous eyes love darkness, walk in God's sunshine and breathe God's air. Scarlet women turn over in wide beds and draw closer velvet curtains to shut out the morning. Gamblers curse the dawn.

But what of the literal underworld of the great city? What of the babes who cry in fetid cellars for the light and are denied it? What of the Subway track-walker, purblind from gloom; the coal-stoker, whose fiery tomb is the boiler-room of a skyscraper; sweatshop workers, a flight below the sidewalk level, whose faces are the color of the dead Chinese; six-dollar-a-week salesgirls in the arc-lighted subcellars of six-million-dollar corporations?

This is the literal underworld of the great city, and its sunless streets run literal blood—the blood of the babes who cried in vain; the blood from the lungs of the sweatshop workers whose faces are the color of dead Chinese; the blood from the cheeks of the six-dollar-a-week salesgirls in the arc-lighted subcellars. But these are your problems and my problems and the problems of the men who have found the strength or the fear not to die rich. The babe's mother, who had never known else, could not know that her cellar was fetid; she only cried out in her anguish and hated vaguely in her heart.

Sara Juke, in the bargain basement of the Titanic Department Store, did not know that lint from white goods clogs the lungs, and that the air she breathed was putrefied as from a noxious swamp. Sometimes a pain, sharp as a hat-pin, entered between her shoulder-blades. But what of that? When the heart is young the heart is bold, and Sara could laugh upward with the musical glee of a bird.

There were no seasons, except the spring and fall openings and semi-annual clearing-sales, in the bargain basement of the Titanic Store. On a morning when the white-goods counter was placing long-sleeve, high-necked nightgowns in its bargain bins, and knit underwear was supplanting the reduced muslins, Sara Juke drew her little pink-knitted jacket closer about her narrow shoulders and shivered—shivered, but smiled. "Br-r-r! October never used to get under my skin like this."

Hattie Krakow, room-mate and co-worker, shrugged her bony shoulders and laughed; but not with the upward glee of a bird—downward, rather, until it died in a croak in her throat. But then Hattie Krakow was ten years older than Sara Juke; and ten years in the arc-lighted subcellar of the Titanic Department Store can do much to muffle the ring in a laugh.

"Gee! You're as funny as your own funeral, you are! You keep up the express pace you're going and there won't be another October left on your calendar."

"That's right; cheer me up a bit, dearie. What's the latest style in under-taking?"

"You'll know sooner'n me if—"

"Aw, Hat, cut it! Wasn't I home in bed last night by eleven?"

"I ain't much on higher mathematics."

"Sure I was. I had to shove you over on your side of the bed; that's how hard you was sleeping."

"A girl can't gad round dancing and rough-housing every night and work eight hours on her feet, and put her lunch money on her back, and not pay up for it. I've seen too many blue-eyed dolls like you get broken. I—"

"Amen!"

Sara Juke rolled her blue eyes upward, and they were full of points of light, as though stars were shining in them; and always her lips trembled to laugh.

"There ain't nothing funny, Sara."

"Oh, Hat, with you like a owl!"

"If I was a girl and had a cough like I've seen enough in this basement get; if I was a girl and my skirtband was getting two inches too big, and I had to lie on my left side to breathe right, and my nightie was all soaked round the neck when I got up in the morning—I wouldn't just laugh and laugh. I'd cry a little—I would."

"That's right, Hat; step on the joy bug like it was a spider. Squash it!"

"I wouldn't just laugh and laugh, and put my lunch money on my back instead of eggs and milk inside of me, and run round all hours to dance-halls with every sporty Charley-boy that comes along."

"You leave him alone! You just cut that! Don't you begin on him!"

"I wouldn't get overheated, and not sleep enough; and—"

"For Pete's sake, Hat! Hire a hall!"

"I should worry! It ain't my grave you're digging."

"Aw, Hat!"

"I ain't got your dolly face and your dolly ways with the boys; but I got enough sense to live along decent."

"You're right pretty, I think, Hat."

"Oh, I could daub up, too, and gad with some of that fast gang if I didn't know it don't lead nowheres. It ain't no cinch for a girl to keep her health down here, even when she does live along decent like me, eating regular and sleeping regular, and spending quiet evenings in the room, washing out and mending and pressing and all. It ain't no cinch even then, lemme tell you. Do you think I'd have ever asked a gay bird like you to come over and room with me if I hadn't seen you to begin to fade like a piece of calico, just like my sister Lizzie did?"

"I'm taking that iron-tonic stuff like you want and spoiling my teeth, ain't I, Hat? I know you been swell to me and all."

"You ain't going to let up until somebody whispers T. B. in your shell-pink ear; and maybe them two letters will bring you to your senses."

"T. B.?"

"Yes, T. B."

"Who's he?"

"Gee! You're as smart as a fish on a hook! You oughtta bought a velvet dunce-cap with your lunch money instead of that brown poke-bonnet. T. B. was what I said—T. B."

"Honest, Hat, I dun'no'—"

"For Heaven's sake! *Too Berculosis* is the way the exhibits and the newspapers say it. L-u-n-g-s is another way to spell it. T. B."

"Too Berculosis!" Sara Juke's hand flew to her little breast. "Too Berculosis! Hat, you—you don't—"

"Sure I don't. I ain't saying it's that—only I wanna scare you up a little. I ain't saying it's that; but a girl that lets a cold hang on like you do and runs round half the night, and don't eat right, can make friends with almost anything, from measles to T. B."

Stars came out once more in Sara Juke's eyes, and her lips warmed and curved to their smile. She moistened with her forefinger a yellow spit-curl that lay like a caress on her cheek. "Gee! You oughtta be writing scare heads for the *Evening Gazette!*"

Hattie Krakow ran her hand over her smooth salt-and-pepper hair and sold a marked-down flannelette petticoat.

"I can't throw no scare into you so long as you got him on your mind. Oh, lud! There he starts now—that quickstep dance again!"

A quick red ran up into Miss Juke's hair, and she inclined forward into the attitude of listening.

"The silly! Honest, ain't he the silly? He said he was going to play that for me the first thing this morning. We dance it so swell together and all. Aw, I thought he'd forget. Ain't he the silly—remembering me?"

The red flowed persistently higher.

"Silly ain't no name for him, with his square, Charley-boy face and polished hair; and—"

"You let him alone, Hattie Krakow! What's it to you if—"

"Nothing—except I always say October is my unlucky month, because it was just a year ago that they moved him and the sheet music down to the basement. Honest, I'm going to buy me a pair of earmuffs! I'd hate to tell you how unpopular popular music is with me."

"Huh! You couldn't play on a side-comb, much less play on the piano like Charley does. If I didn't have no more brains than some people—honest, I'd go out and kill a calf for some!"

"You oughtta talk! A girl that 'ain't got no more brains than to gad round every night and every Sunday in foul-smelling, low-ceilinged dance-halls, and wear paper-soled slippers when she oughtta be wearing galoshes, and cheese-cloth waists that ain't even decent, instead of wool undershirts! You oughtta talk about brains—you and Charley Chubb!"

"Yes, I oughtta talk! If you don't like my doings, Hattie Krakow, there ain't no law says we gotta room together. I been shifting for myself ever since I was cash-girl down at Tracy's, and I ain't going to begin being bossed now. If you don't like my keeping steady with Charley Chubb—if you don't like his sheet-music playing—you gotta lump it! I'm a good girl, I am; and if you got anything to in-sinuate, if—"

"Sara Juke, ain't you ashamed!"

"I'm a good girl, I am; and there ain't nobody can cast a reflect on—on—"

Tears trembled in her voice, and she coughed from the deep recesses of her chest, and turned her head away, so that her profile was quivering and her throat swelling with sobs.

"I—I'm a good girl, I am."

"Aw, Sara, don't I know it? Ain't that just where the rub comes? Don't I know it? If you wasn't a good girl would I be caring?"

"I'm a good girl, I am!"

"It's your health, Sara, I'm kicking about. You're getting as pale and skinny as a goop; and for a month already you've been coughing, and never a single evening home to stick your feet in hot water and a mustard plaster on your chest."

"Didn't I take the iron tonic and spoil my teeth?"

"My sister Lizzie—that's the way she started, Sara; right down here in this basement. There never was a prettier little queen down here. Ask any of the old girls. Like you in looks and all; full of vim, too. That's the way she started, Sara. She wouldn't get out in the country on Sundays or get any air in her lungs walking with me evenings. She was all for dance-halls, too, Sara. She— she— 'Ain't I told you about her over and over again? 'Ain't I?"

"'Sh-h-h! Don't cry, Hat. Yes, yes; I know. She was a swell little kid; all the old girls say so. 'Sh-h-h!"

"The—the night she died I—I died, too; I—"

"'Sh-h-h, dearie!"

"I ain't crying, only—only I can't help rememebering."

"Listen! That's the new hit Charley's playing— 'Up to Snuff!' Say, 'ain't that got some little swing to it? Dum-dum-tum-tee-tum-m-m! Some little quickstep, ain't it? How that boy reads off by sight! Looka, will you? They got them left-over ribbed undervests we sold last season for forty-nine cents out on the grab table for seventy-four. Looka the mob fighting for 'em! Dum-dum-tum-tee-tum-m-m!"

The day's tide came in. Slowly at first, but toward noon surging through aisles and around bins, up-stairs and down-stairs—in, around, and out. Voices straining to be heard; feet shuffling in an agglomeration of discords— the indescribable roar of humanity, which is like an army that approaches but never arrives. And above it all, insistent as a bugle-note, reaching the basement's breadth, from hardware to candy, from human hair to white goods, the tinny voice of the piano—gay, rollicking.

At five o'clock the patch of daylight above the red-lighted exit door turned taupe, as though a gray curtain had been flung across it; and the girls, with shooting pains in their limbs, braced themselves for the last hour. Shoppers, their bags bulging and their shawls awry, fumbled in bins for a last remnant; hatless, sway-backed women, carrying children, fought for mill ends. Sara Juke stood first on one foot and then on the other to alternate the strain; her hands were hot and dry as flannel, but her cheeks were pink—very pink.

At six o'clock Hattie Krakow untied her black alpaca apron, pinned a hat as nondescript as a bird's nest at an unrakish angle, and slid into a warm, gray jacket.

"Ready, Sara?"

"Yes, Hat." But her voice came vaguely, as through fog.

"I'm going to fix us some stew to-night with them onions Lettie brought up to the room when she moved—mutton stew, with a broth for you, Sara."

"Yes, Hat."

Sara's eyes darted out over the emptying aisles; and, even as she pinned on her velveteen poke-bonnet at a too-swagger angle, and fluffed out a few carefully provided curls across her brow, she kept watch and with obvious subterfuge slid into her little unlined silk coat with a deliberation not her own.

"Coming, Sara?"

"Wait, can't you? My—my hat ain't on right."

"Come on; you're dolled up enough."

"My—my gloves—I—I forgot 'em. You—you can go on, Hat." And she burrowed back beneath the counter.

Miss Krakow let out a snort, as fiery with scorn as though flames were curling on her lips. "Hanging round to see whether he's coming, ain't you? To think they shot Lincoln and let him live! Before I'd run after any man living, much less the excuse of a man like him! A shiny-haired, square-faced little rat like him!"

"I ain't, neither, waiting. I guess I have a right to find my gloves. I—I guess I gotta right. He's as good as you are, and better. I—I guess I gotta right." But the raspberry red of confusion dyed her face.

"No, you ain't waiting! No, no; you ain't waiting," mimicked Miss Krakow, and her voice was like autumn leaves that crackle underfoot. "Well, then, if you ain't waiting here he comes now. I dare you to come on home with me now, like you ought to."

"I—You go on! I gotta tell him something. I guess I'm my own boss. I have to tell him something."

Miss Krakow folded her well-worn hand-bag under one arm and fastened her black cotton gloves.

"Pf-f-f! What's the use of wasting breath?"

She slipped into the flux of the aisle, and the tide swallowed her and carried her out into the bigger tide of the street and the swifter tide of the city—a flower on the current, her blush withered under the arc-light substitution for sunlight, the petals of her youth thrown to the muddy corners of the city streets.

Sara Juke breathed inward, and under her cheaply pretentious lace blouse a heart, as rebellious as the pink in her cheeks and the stars in her eyes, beat a rapid fantasia; and, try, as she would, her lips would quiver into a smile.

"Hello, Charley!"

"Hello yourself, Sweetness!" And, draping himself across the white-goods counter in an attitude as intricate as the letter S, behold Mr. Charley Chubb! Sleek, soap-scented, slim—a satire on the satyr and the haberdasher's latest dash. "Hello, Sweetness!"

"How are you, Charley?"

"Here, gimme your little hand. Shake."

She placed her palm in his, quivering.

You of the classes, peering through lorgnettes into the strange world of the masses, spare that shrug. True, when Charley Chubb's hand closed over Sara

Juke's she experienced a flash of goose flesh; but, you of the classes, what of
the Van Ness ball last night? Your gown was low, so that your neck rose out
from it like white ivory. The conservatory, where trained clematis vines met
over your heads, were like a bower of stars; music, his hand, the white glove
off, over yours; the suffocating sweetness of clematis blossoms; a fountain
throwing fine spray; your neck white as ivory, and—what of the Van Ness
ball last night?

Only Sara Juke played her poor little game frankly, and the cards of her
heart lay on the counter.

"Charley!" Her voice lay in a veil.

"Was you getting sore, Sweetness?"

"All day you didn't come over."

"Couldn't, Sweetness. Did you hear me let up on the new hit for a
minute?"

"It's swell, though, Charley; all the girls was humming it. You play it like
lightning, too."

"It must have been written for you, Sweetness. That's what you are, Up to
Snuff, eh, Queenie?" He leaned closer, and above his tall, narrow collar dull
red flowed beneath the sallow, and his long, white teeth and slick-brushed
hair shone in the arc-light. "Eh, Queenie?"

"I gotta go now, Charley. Hattie's waiting home for me." She attempted to
pass him and to slip into the outgoing stream of the store, but with a hesita-
tion that belied her. "I—I gotta go, Charley."

He laughed, clapped his hat slightly askew on his polished hair, and slid
his arm into hers.

"Forget it! But I had you going, didn't I, sister? Thought I'd forgot about
to-night, didn't you, and didn't have the nerve to pipe up? Like fun I forgot!"

"I didn't know, Charley; you not coming over all day and all. I thought
maybe your friend didn't give you the tickets like he promised."

"Didn't he? Look! See if he didn't!"

He produced a square of pink cardboard from his waistcoat pocket, and
she read it, with a sudden lightness underlying her voice:

HIBERNIAN MASQUE AND HOP
SUPPER   WARDROBE FREE
ADMIT GENT AND LADY   FIFTY CENTS

"Oh, gee, Charley! And me such a sight in this old waist and all. I didn't
know there was supper, too."

"Sure! Hurry, Sweetness, and we'll catch a Sixth Avenue car. We wanna get
in on it while the tamales are hot."

She grasped his arm closer, and straightening her velveteen poke-bonnet so that the curls lay pat, together they wormed through the sidewalk crush; once or twice she coughed, with the hollow resonance of a chain drawn upward from a deep well.

"Gee! I bet there'll be a jam!"

"Sure! There's some live crowd down there."

They were in the street-car, swaying, swinging, clutching; hemmed in by frantic, home-going New York, nose to nose, eye to eye, tooth to tooth. Around Sara Juke's slim waist lay Charley Chubb's saving arm, and with each lurch they laughed immoderately, except when she coughed.

"Gee! ain't it the limit? It's a wonder they wouldn't open a window in this car!"

"Nix on that. Whatta you wanna do—freeze a fellow out?"

Her eyes would betray her. "Any old time I could freeze you, Charley."

"Honest?"

"You're the one that freezes me all the time. You're the one that keeps me guessing and guessing where I stand with you."

A sudden lurch and he caught her as she swayed.

"Come, Sweetness, this is our corner. Quit your coughing, there, hon; this ain't no T. B. hop we're going to."

"No what?"

"Come along; hurry! Look at the crowd already."

"This ain't no—what did you say, Charley?"

But they were pushing, shoving, worming into the great lighted entrance of the hall. More lurching, crowding, jamming.

"I'll meet you inside, kiddo, in five minutes. Pick out a red domino; red's my color."

"A red one? Gee! Looka; mine's got black pompons on it. Five minutes, Charley; five minutes!"

Flags of all nations and all sizes made a galaxy of the Sixth Avenue hall. An orchestra played beneath an arch of them. Supper, consisting of three-inch-thick sandwiches, tamales, steaming and smelling in their buckets, bottles of beer and soda-water, was spread on a long picnic-table running the entire length of the balcony.

The main floor, big as an armory, airless as a tomb, swarmed with dancers.

After supper a red sateen Pierrette, quivering, teeth flashing beneath a sucy half-mask, bowed to a sateen Pierrot, whose face was as slim as a satyr's and whose smile was as upturned as the eye-slits in his mask.

"Gee! Charley, you look just like a devil in that costume—all red, and your mouth squinted like that!"

"And you look just like a little red cherry, ready to burst."

And they were off in the whirl of the dance, except that the close-packed dancers hemmed them in a swaying mob; and once she fell back against his shoulder, faint.

"Ain't there a—a up-stairs somewheres, Charley, where they got air? All this jam and no windows open! Gee! ain't it hot? Let's go outside where it's cool—let's."

"There you go again! No wonder you got a cold on you—always wanting air on you! Come, Sweetness; this ain't hot. Here, lemme show you the dip I get the girls crazy with. One, two, three—dip! One, two, three—dip! Ugh!"

"Gee! ain't it a jam, though?"

"One, two, three!"

"That's swell, Charley! Quit! You mustn't squeeze me like that till—till you've asked me to be engaged, Charley. We—we ain't engaged yet, are we, Charley?"

"Aw, what difference does that make? You girls make me sick—always wanting to know that."

"It—it makes a lot of difference, Charley."

"There you go on that Amen talk again. All right, then; I won't squeeze you no more, stingy!"

Her step was suddenly less elastic and she lagged on his arm. "I—I never said you couldn't, Charley. Gee! ain't you a great one to get mad so quick! Touchy! I only said not till we're engaged."

He skirted the crowd, guiding her skilfully. "Stingy! Stingy! I know 'em that ain't so stingy as you."

"Charley!"

"What?"

"Aw, I'm ashamed to say it."

"Listen! The're playing the new one—'Up to Snuff!' Faster! Don't make me drag you, kiddo. Faster!"

They were suddenly in the center of the maze, as tight-packed as though an army had conspired to close round them. She coughed, and in her effort of repression, coughed again.

"Charley, I—honest, I—I'm going to keel. I—I can't stand it packed in here—like this."

She leaned to him, with the color drained out of her face; and the crowd of black and pink and red dominoes, gnomes gone mad, pressed, batted, surged.

"Look out, Sweetness! Don't you give out in here! They'll crush us out. 'Ain't you got no nerve? Here; don't give out now! Gee! Watch out, there! The lady's sick. Watch out! Here; now sit down a minute and get your wind."

He pressed her shoulders downward and she dropped whitely on a little camp-chair hidden underneath the balcony.

"I gotta get out, Charley; I gotta get out and get air. I feel like I'm going to suffocate in here. It's this old cough takes the breath out of me."

In the foyer she revived a bit and drank gratefully of the water he brought; but the color remained out of her cheeks and the cough would rack her.

"I guess I oughtta go home, Charley."

"Aw, cut it! You ain't the only girl I've seen give out. Sit here and rest a minute and you'll be all right. Great Scott! I came here to dance."

She rose to her feet a bit unsteadily, but smiling. "Fussy! Who said I didn't?"

"That's more like it."

And they were off again to the lilt of the music, but, struggle as she would, the coughing and the dizziness and the heat took hold of her, and at the close of the dance she fainted quietly against his shoulder.

When she finally caught at consciousness, as it passed and repassed her befuddled mind, she was on the floor of the cloak-room, her head pillowed on the skirt of a pink domino.

"There, there, dearie; your young man's waiting outside to take you home."

"I—I'm all right!"

"Certainly you are. The heat done it. Here; lemme help you out of your domino."

"It was the heat done it."

"There; you're all right now. I gotta get back to my dance. You fainted right up against him, dearie; and I seen you keel."

"Gee! ain't I the limit!"

"Here; lemme help on with your coat. Right there he is, waiting."

In the foyer Sara Juke met Charley Chubb shamefacedly. "I spoilt everything, didn't I?"

"I guess you couldn't help it. All right?"

"Yes, Charley." She met the air gratefully, worming her little hand into the curve of his elbow. "Gee! I feel fine now."

"Come; here's a car."

"Let's walk up Sixth Avenue, Charley; the air feels fine."

"All right."

"You ain't sore, are you, Charley? It was so jammed dancing, anyway."

"I ain't sore."

"It was the heat done it."

"Yeh."

"Honest, it's grand to be outdoors, ain't it? The stars and—and chilliness and—and—all!"

"Listen to the garden stuff!"

"Silly!" She squeezed his arm, and drew back, shamefaced.

His spirits rose. "You're a right loving little thing when you wanna be."

They laughed in duet; and before the plate-glass window of a furniture emporium they paused to regard a monthly-payment display, designed to represent the $49.50 completely furnished sitting-room, parlor, and dining-room of the home felicitous—a golden-oak room, with an incandescent fire glowing right merrily in the grate; a lamp redly diffusing the light of home; a plaster-of-Paris Cupid shooting a dart from the mantelpiece; and last, two figures of connubial bliss, smiling and waxen, in rocking-chairs, their waxen infant, block-building on the floor, completing the picture.

"Gee! It looks as snug as a bug in a rug! Looka what it says too: 'You Get the Girl; We'll Do the Rest!' Some little advertisement, ain't it? I got the girl all right—'ain't I, hon?"

"Aw!"

"Look at the papa—slippers and all! And the kid! Look at the kid, Sweetness."

Her confusion nearly choked her and her rapid breath clouded the window-glass. "Yeh, Charley! Looka the little kid! Ain't he cute?"

An Elevated train crashed over their heads, drowning out her words; but her smile, which flickered like light over her face, persisted and her arm crept back into his. At each shop window they lingered, but the glow of the first one remained with her.

"Look, Sweetness—'Red Swag, the Train King! Performance going on now.' Wanna go in?"

"Not to-night. Let's stay outside."

"Anything your little heart de-sires."

They bought hot chestnuts, city harbingers of autumn, from a vender, and let fall the hulls as they walked. They drank strawberry ice-cream soda, pink with foam. Her resuscitation was complete; his spirits did not wane.

"I gotta like a queen pretty much not to get sore at a busted evening like this. It's a good thing the ticket didn't cost me nothing."

"Ain't it, though?"

"Look! What's in there—a exhibit?"

They paused before a white-lighted store-front, and read, laboriously:

FREE TUBERCULOSIS EXHIBIT
TO EDUCATE THE PEOPLE HOW TO PREVENT CONSUMPTION

"Oh!" She dragged at his arm.

"Aw, come on, Sweetness; nothing but a lot of T. B.'s."

"Let's—let's go in. See, it's free. Looka! It's all lit up and all; see, pictures and all."

"Say, ain't I enough of a dead one without dragging me in there? Free! I bet they pinch you for something before you get out."

"Come on, Charley. I never did see a place like this."

"Aw, they're all over town."

He followed her in surlily enough and then, with a morbid interest, round a room hung with photographs of victims in various emaciated stages of the white plague.

"Oh! Oh! Ain't it awful? Ain't it awful? Read them symptoms. Almost with nothing it—it begins. Night-sweats and losing weight and coughing, and—oh—"

"Look! Little kids and all! Thin as matches."

"Aw, see, a poor little shaver like that! Look! It says sleeping in that dirty room without a window gave it to him. Ugh! that old man! 'Self-indulgence and intemperance.' Looka that girl in the tobacco-factory. Oh! Oh! Ain't it awful! Dirty shops and stores, it says; dirty saloons and dance-halls—weak lungs can't stand them."

"Let's get out of here."

"Aw, look! How pretty she is in this first picture; and look at her here—nothing but a stack of bones on a stretcher. Aw! Aw!"

"Come on!"

"Courage is very important, it says. Consumptives can be helped and many are cured. Courage is—"

"Come on; let's get out of this dump. Say, it's a swell night for a funeral."

She grasped at his coat sleeve, pinching the flesh with it, and he drew away half angrily.

"Come on, I said."

"All right!"

A thin line filed past them, grim-faced, silent. At the far end of the room, statistics in red inch-high type ran columnwise down the wall's length. She read, with a gasp in her throat:

1. Ten thousand people died from tuberculosis in the city of New York last year.
2. Two hundred thousand people died from tuberculosis in the United States last year.
3. Records of the Health Department show 31,631 living cases of tuberculosis in the city of New York.
4. Every three minutes some one in the United States dies from consumption.

"Oh, Charley, ain't it awful!"

At a desk a young man, with skin as pink as though a strong wind had whipped it into color, distributed pamphlets to the outgoing visitors—a thin streamlet of them; some cautious, some curious, some afraid.

"Come on; let's hurry out of here, Sweetness. My lung's hurting this minute."

They hurried past the desk; but the young man with the clear, pink skin reached over the heads of an intervening group, waving a long printed booklet toward the pair.

"Circular, missy?"

Sara Juke straightened, with every nerve in her body twanging like a plucked violin-string, and her eyes met the clear eyes of the young clerk.

Like a doll automaton she accepted the booklet from him; like a doll automaton she followed Charley Chubb out into the street, and her limbs were trembling so she could scarcely stand.

"Gotta hand it to you, Sweetness. Even made a hit on the fellow in the lung-shop! He didn't hand me no literachure. Some little hit!"

"I gotta go home now, Charley."

"It's only ten."

"I better go, Charley. It ain't Saturday night."

At the stoop of her rooming-house they lingered. A honey-colored moon hung like a lantern over the block-long row of shabby-fronted houses. On her steps and to her fermenting fancy the shadow of an ash-can sprawled like a prostrate human being.

"Charley!" She clutched his arm.

"Whatcha scared about, Sweetness?"

"Oh, Charley, I—I feel creepy to-night."

"That visit to the morgue was enough to give anybody the blind staggers."

Her pamphlet was tight in her hand. "You ain't mad at me, Charley?"

He stroked her arm, and the taste of tears found its way to her mouth.

"I'm feeling so silly-like to-night, Charley."

"You're all in, kiddo." In the shadow he kissed her.

"Charley, you—you mustn't, unless we're—engaged." But she could not find the strength to unfold herself from his arms. "You mustn't, Charley!"

"Great little girl you are, Sweetness—one great little girl!"

"Aw, Charley!"

"And, to show you that I like you, I'm going to make up for this to-morrow night. A real little Saturday-night blow! And don't forget Sunday afternoon—two o'clock for us, down at Crissey's Hall. Two o'clock."

"Two o'clock."

"Good!"

"Oh, Charley, I—"

"What, Sweetness?"

"Oh, nothing; I—I'm just silly to-night."

Her hand lay on his arm, white in the moonlight and light as a leaf; and he kissed her again, scorching her lips.

"Good night, Sweetness."

"Good night, Charley."

Then up three flights of stairs, through musty halls and past closed doors, their white china knobs showing through the darkness, and then up to the fourth-floor rear, and then on tiptoe into a long, narrow room, with the moonlight flowing in.

Clothing lay about in grotesque heaps—a woman's blouse was flung across the back of a chair and hung limply; a pair of shoes stood beside the bed in the attitude of walking—tired-looking shoes, run down at the heels and skinned at the toes. And on the far side of the three-quarter bed the hump of an outstretched figure, face turned from the light, with sparse gray-and-black hair flowing over the pillow.

Carefully, to save the slightest squeak, Sara Juke undressed, folded her little mound of clothing across the room's second chair, groping carefully by the stream of moonlight. Severe as a sibyl in her straight-falling nightdress, her hair spreading over her shoulders, her bare feet pattered on the cool matting. Then she slid into bed lightly, scarcely raising the covers. From the mantelpiece the alarm-clock ticked with emphasis.

An hour she lay there. Once she coughed, and smothered it in her pillow. Two hours. She slipped from under the covers and over to the littered dresser. The pamphlet lay on top of her gloves; she carried it to the window and, with her limbs trembling and sending ripples down her nightrobe, read it. Then again, standing there by the window in the moonlight, she quivered so that her knees bent under her.

After a while she raised the window slowly and without a creak, and a current of cool air rushed in and over her before she could reach the bedside.

On her pillow Hattie Krakow stirred reluctantly, her weary senses battling with the pleasant lethargy of sleep; but a sudden nip in the air stung her nose and found out the warm crevices of the bed. She stirred and half opened her eyes.

"For Gawd's sake, Sara, are you crazy? Put that window down! Tryin' to freeze us out? Opening a window with her cough and all! Put it down! Put—it—down!"

Sara Juke rose and slammed it shut, slipping back into the cold bed with teeth that clicked. After a while she slept; but lightly, with her mouth open and her face upturned. And after a while she woke to full consciousness all at once, and with a cough on her lips. Her gown at the yoke was wet; and her neck, where she felt it, was damp with cold perspiration.

"Oh—oh—Hattie! Oh—oh!"

She burrowed under her pillow to ease the trembling that seized her. The moon had passed on, and darkness, which is allied to fear, closed her in—the fear of unthinking youth who knows not that the grave is full of peace; the fear of abundant life for senile death; the cold agony that comes in the night-watches, when the business of the day is but a dream and Reality visits the couch.

Deeper burrowed Sara Juke, trembling with chill and night-sweat.

Drowsily Hattie Krakow turned on her pillow, but her senses were too weary to follow her mind's dictate.

"Sara! 'Smatter, Sara? 'Smat-ter?" Hattie's tired hand crept toward her friend; but her volition would not carry it across and it fell inert across the coverlet. "'Smatter, dearie?"

"N-nothing."

"'Smat-ter, dear-ie?"

"N-nothing."

In the watches of the night a towel flung across the bedpost becomes a gorilla crouching to spring; a tree-branch tapping at the window an armless hand, beckoning. In the watches of the night fear is a panther across the chest, sucking the breath; but his eyes cannot bear the light of day, and by dawn he has shrunk to cat size. The ghastly dreams of Orestes perished with the light; phosphorus is yellowish and waxlike by day.

So Sara Juke found new courage with the day, and in the subbasement of the Titanic Store, the morning following, her laughter was ready enough. But when the midday hour arrived she slipped into her jacket, past the importunities of Hattie Krakow, and out into the sun-lashed noonday swarm of Sixth Avenue.

Down one block—two, three; then a sudden pause before a narrow store-front liberally placarded with invitatory signs to the public, and with a red cross blazoning above the doorway. And Sara Juke, whose heart was full of fear, faltered, entered.

The same thin file passed round the room, halting, sauntering, like grim visitors in a grim gallery. At a front desk a sleek young interne, tiptilted in a swivel chair, read a pink sheet through horn-rimmed glasses.

Toward the rear the young man whose skin was the wind-lashed pink sorted pamphlets and circulars in tall, even piles on his desk.

Round and round the gallery walked Sara Juke; twice she read over the list of symptoms printed in inch-high type; her heart lay within her as though icy dead, and her eyes would blur over with tears. Once, when she passed the rear desk, the young man paused in his stacking and regarded her with a warming glance of recognition.

"Hello!" he said. "You back?"

"Yes." Her voice was the thin cry of quail.

"You must like our little picture-gallery, eh?"

"Oh! Oh!" She caught at the edge of the desk, and tears lay heavy in her eyes.

"Eh?"

"Yes; I—I like it. I wanna buy it for my yacht." Her ghastly simulacrum of a jest died in her throat; and he said, quickly, a big blush suffusing his face:

"I was only fooling, missy. You 'ain't got the scare, have you?"

"The scare?"

"Yes; the bug? You ain't afraid you've ate the germ, are you?"

"I—I dun'no'."

"Pshaw! There's a lot of 'em comes in here more scared than hurt, missy. Never throw a scare till you've had an examination. For all you know, you got hay fever, eh! Hay fever!" And he laughed as though to salve his words.

"I—I got all them things on the red-printed list, I tell you. I—I got 'em all, night-sweats and all. I—I got 'em."

"Sure you got 'em, missy; but that don't need to mean nothing much."

"I got 'em, I tell you."

"Losing weight?"

"Feel."

He inserted two fingers in her waistband. "Huh!"

"You a doctor?"

He performed a great flourish. "I ain't in the profesh, missy. I'm only chief clerk and bottle-washer round here; but—"

"Where is the doctor? That him reading down there? Can I ask him? I—Oh! Ain't I scared!"

He placed his big, cool hand over her wrist and his face had none of its smile. "I know you are, little missy. I seen it in you last night when you and—and—"

"My—my friend."

"—your friend was in here. There's thousands come in here with the scare on, and most of 'em with a reason; but I picked you out last night from the gang. Funny thing, but right away I picked you. 'A pretty little thing like her'—if you'll excuse me for saying it—'a pretty little thing like her,' I says to myself. 'And I bet she 'ain't got nobody to steer her!'"

"Honest, did you?"

"Gee! it ain't none of my put-in; but when I seen you last night—funny thing—but when I seen you, why, you just kinda hit me in the eye; and, with all that gang round me, I says to myself: 'Gee! A pretty little thing like her, scared as a gazelle, and so pretty and all; and no one to give her the right steer!'"

"Aw, you seen me?"

"Sure! Wasn't it me reached out the pamphlet to you? You had on that there same cutey little hat and jacket and all."

"Does it cost anything to talk to the doctor down there?"

"Forget it! Go right down and he'll give you a card to the Victoria Clinic. I know them all over there and they'll look you over right, little missy, and steer you. Aw, don't be scared; there ain't nothing much wrong with you—maybe a sore spot, that's all. That cough ain't a double-lunger. You run over to the clinic."

"I gotta go back to the store now."

"After store, then?"

"Free?"

"Sure! Old Doc Strauss is on after five, too. If I ain't too nervy I'm off after six myself. I could meet you after and we could talk over what he tells you—if I ain't too nervy?"

"I—"

"Blaney's my name—Eddie Blaney. Ask anybody round here about me. I—I could meet you, little missy, and—"

"I can't to-night, Mr. Blaney. I gotta go somewheres."

"Aw!"

"I gotta."

"To-morrow? To-morrow's Sunday, little missy. There's a swell lot of country I bet you 'ain't never seen, and Old Doc Strauss is going to tell you to get acquainted with it pretty soon."

"Country?"

"Yes. That's what you need—outdoors; that's what you need. You got a color like all indoors—pretty, but putty."

"You—you don't think there's nothing much the matter with me, do you, Mr. Blaney?"

"Sure I don't. Why, I got a bunch of Don'ts for you up my sleeve that'll color you up like drug-store daub."

Tears and laughter trembled in her voice. "You mean that the outdoor stuff will do it, Mr. Blaney?"

"That's the talk!"

"But you—you ain't the doctor."

"I ain't, but I 'ain't been deaf and dumb and blind round here for three years. I can pick 'em every time. You're taking your stitch in time. You 'ain't even got a wheeze in you. Why, I bet you 'ain't never seen red!"

"No!" she cried, with quick comprehension.

"Sure you 'ain't!"

More tears and laughter in her voice. "I'm going to-night, then—at six, Mr. Blaney."

"Good! And to-morrow? There's a lot of swell country and breathing-space round here I'd like to introduce you to. I bet you don't know whether Ingleside Woods is kindling or a breakfast food. Now do you?"

"No."

"Ever had a chigger on you?"

"Huh?"

"Ever sleep outdoors in a bag?"

"Say, whatta you think I am?"

"Ever seen the sun rise, or took the time to look up and see several dozen or a couple of thousand or so stars glittering all at once?"

"Aw, come off! We ain't doing team-work in vaudeville."

"Gee! Wouldn't I like to take you out and be the first one to make you acquainted with a few of the things that are happening beyond Sixth Avenue—if I ain't too nervy, little missy?"

"I gotta go somewhere at two o'clock to-morrow afternoon, Mr.—Mr. Blaney; but I can go in the morning—if it ain't going to look like I'm a freshie."

"In the morning! Swell! But where—who—" She scribbled on a slip of paper and fluttered it into his hand. "Sara Juke! Some little name. Gee! I know right where you live. I know a lot of cases that come from round there. I used to live near there myself, round on Third Avenue. I'll call round at nine, little missy. I'm going to introduce you to the country, eh?"

"They won't hurt at the clinic, will they, Mr. Blaney? I'm losing my nerve again."

"Shame on a pretty little thing like you losing her nerve! Gee! I've seen 'em come in here all pale round the gills and with nothing but the whooping-cough. There was a little girl in here last week who thought she was ready for Arizona on a canvas bed; and it wasn't nothing but her rubber skirtband had stretched. Shame on you, little missy! Don't you get scared! Wait till you see what I'm going to show you in the country to-morrow—leaves turning red and all. We're going to have a heart-to-heart talk out there—eh? A regular lung-to-lung talk!"

"Aw, Mr. Blaney! Ain't you killing!" She hurried down the room, laughing.

At Sharkey's on Saturday night the entire basement café and dance-hall assumed a hebdomadal air of expectancy; extra marble-topped tables were crowded about the polished square of dancing-space; the odor of hops and sawdust and cookery hung in visible mists over the bar.

Girls, with white faces and red lips and bare throats, sat alone at tables or tête-à-tête with men too old or too young, and ate; but drank with keener appetite.

A self-playing piano performed beneath a large painting of an undraped Psyche; a youth with yellow fingers sang of Love. A woman whose shame was gone acquired a sudden hysteria at her lone table over her milky-green drink, and a waiter hustled her out none too gently.

In the foyer at seven o'clock Sara Juke met Charley Chubb, and he slid up quite frankly behind her and kissed her on the lips. At Sharkey's a miss is as good as her kiss!

"You—you quit! You mustn't!"

She sprang back, quivering, her face cold-looking and blue; and he regarded her with his mouth quirking.

"Huh! Hoity-toity, ain't you? Hoity-toity and white-faced and late, all at once, ain't you? Say, them airs don't get across with me. Come on! I'm hungry."

"I didn't mean to yell, Charley—only you scared me. I thought maybe it was one of them fresh guys that hang round here; all of 'em look so dopey and all. I—You know I never was strong for this place, Charley."

"Beginning to nag, are you?"

"No, no, Charley. No, no!"

They drew up at a small table.

"No fancy keeling act to-night, kiddo. I ain't taking out a hospital ward, you know. Gad! I like you, though, when you're white-looking like this! Why'd you dodge me at noon to-day and to-night after closing? New guy? I won't stand for it, you know, you little white-faced Sweetness, you!"

"I hadda go somewheres, Charley. I came near not coming to-night, neither, Charley."

"What'll you eat?"

"I ain't hungry."

"Thirsty, eh?"

"No."

He regarded her over the rim of the smirchy bill of fare. "What are you, then, you little white-faced, big-eyed devil?"

"Charley, I—I got something to—to tell you. I—"

"Bring me a lamb stew and a beer, light. What'll you have, little white-face?"

"Some milk and—"

"She means with suds on, waiter."

"No—no; milk, I said—milk over toast. Milk toast—I gotta eat it. Why don't you lemme talk, Charley? I gotta tell you."

He was suddenly sober. "What's hurting you? One milk toast, waiter. Tell them in the kitchen the lady's teeth hurt her. What's up, Sweetness?" And he leaned across the table to imprint a fresh kiss on her lips.

"Don't—don't—don't! For Gawd's sake, don't!" She covered her face with her hands; and such a trembling seized her that they fell pitifully away again and showed her features, each distorted. "You mustn't, Charley! Mustn't do that again, not—not for three months—you—you mustn't."

He leaned across the table; his voice was like sleet—cold, thin, cutting: "What's the matter—going to quit?"

"No—no—no!"

"Got another guy you like better?"

"Oh! Oh!"

"A queenie can't quit me first and get away with it, kiddo. I may be a soft-fingered sort of fellow, but a queenie can't quit me first and get away with it. Ask 'em about me round here; they know me. If anybody in this little duet is going to do the quitting act first it ain't going to be you. What's the matter? Out with it!"

"Charley, it ain't that—I swear it ain't that!"

"What's hurting you, then?"

"I gotta tell you. We gotta go easy for a little while. We gotta quit doing the rounds for a while till—only for a little while. Three months he said would fix me. A grand old doc he was!

"I been to the clinic, Charley. I hadda go. The cough—the cough was cutting me in two. It ain't like me to go keeling like I did. I never said much about it; but, nights and all, the sweats and the cough and the shooting pains were cutting me in two. We gotta go easy for a while, Charley; just—"

"You sick, Sara?" His fatty-white face lost a shade of its animation. "Sick?"

"But it ain't, Charley. On his word he promised it ain't! A grand old doc, with whiskers—he promised me that. I—I am just beginning; but the stitch was in time. It ain't a real case yet, Charley. I swear on my mother's curl of hair it ain't."

"Ain't what? Ain't what?"

"It ain't! Air, he said, right living—early hours and all. I gotta get out of the basement. He'll get me a job. A grand old man! Windows open; right living. No—no dancing and all, for a while, Charley. Three months only, Charley; and then—"

"What, I say—"

"It ain't, Charley! I swear it ain't. Just one—the left one—a little sore down at the base—the bottom. Charley, quit looking at me like that! It ain't a real case—it ain't; it ain't!"

"It ain't what?"

"The—the T. B. Just the left one; down at—"

"You—you—" An oath as hot as a live coal dropped from his lips, and he drew back, strangling. "You—you got it, and you're letting me down easy. You got it, and it's catching as hell! You got it, you white devil, and—and you're trying to lie out of it—you—you—"

"Charley! Charley!"

"You got it, and you been letting me eat it off your lips! You devil, you! You devil, you! You devil, you!"

"Charley, I—"

"I could kill you! Lemme wash my mouth! You got it; and if you got it I got it! I got it! I got it! I—I—"

He rushed from the table, strangling, stuttering, staggering; and his face was twisted with fear.

For an hour she sat there, waiting, her hands folded in her lap and her eyes growing larger in her face. The dish of stew took on a thin coating of grease and the beer died in the glass. The waiter snickered. After a while she paid for the meal out of her newly opened wage-envelope and walked out into the air.

Once on the street, she moaned audibly into her handkerchief. There is relief in articulation. Her way lay through dark streets where figures love to slink in the shadows. One threw a taunt at her and she ran. At the stoop of her rooming-house she faltered, half fainting and breathing deep from exhaustion, her head thrown back and her eyes gazing upward.

Over the narrow street stars glittered, dozens and myriads of them.

Literature has little enough to say of the heartaches and the heartburns of the Sara Jukes and the Hattie Krakows and the Eddie Blaneys. Medical science concedes them a hollow organ for keeping up the circulation. Yet Mrs. Van Ness's heartbreak over the death of her Chinese terrier, Wang, claims a first-page column in the morning edition; her heartburn—a complication of midnight terrapin and the strain of her most recent rôle of corespondent—obtains her a *suite de luxe* in a private sanitarium.

Vivisectionists believe the dog is less sensitive to pain than man; so the social vivisectionists, in problem plays and best sellers, are more concerned with the heartaches and heartburns of the classes. But analysis would show that the sediment of salt in Sara Juke's and Mrs. Van Ness's tears is equal.

Indeed, when Sara Juke stepped out of the streetcar on a golden Sunday morning in October, her heart beat higher and more full of emotion than Mrs. Van Ness could find at that breakfast hour, reclining on her fine linen pillows, an electric massage and a four-dollars-an-hour masseuse forcing her sluggish blood to flow.

Eddie Blaney gently helped Sara to alight, cupping the point of her elbow in his hand; and they stood huddled for a moment by the roadway while the car whizzed past, leaving them in the yellow and ocher, saffron and crimson, countryside.

"Gee! Gee whiz!"

"See! I told you. And you not wanting to come when I called for you this morning—you trying to dodge me and the swellest Indian-summer Sunday on the calendar!"

"Looka!"

"Wait! We 'ain't started yet, if you think this is swell."

"Oh! Let's go over in them woods. Let's." Her lips were apart and pink crept into her cheeks, effacing the dark rims of pain beneath her eyes. "Let's hurry."

"Sure; that's where we're going—right over in there, where the woods look like they're on fire; but, gee! this ain't nothing to the country places I know round here. This ain't nothing. Wait!"

The ardor of the inspired guide was his, and with each exclamation from her the joy of his task doubled itself.

"If you think this is great, wait—just you wait. Gee! if you like this, what would you have said to the farm? Wait till we get to the top of the hill."

Fallen leaves, crisp as paper, crackled pleasantly under their feet; and through the haze that is October's veil glowed a reddish sun, vague as an opal. A footpath crawled like a serpent through the woods and they followed it, kicking up the leaves before them, pausing, darting, exclaiming.

"I—Honest, Mr. Blaney, I—"

"Eddie!"

"Eddie, I—I never did feel so—I never was so—so—Aw, I can't say it." Tears sprang to her eyes.

"Sure you never was. I never was, neither, before—before—"

"Before what?"

"Before I had to."

"Had to?"

"Yeh; both of them. Bleeding all the time. Didn't see nothing but red for 'leven months."

"You!"

"Yeh; three years ago. Looked like Arizona on a stretcher for me."

"You—so big and strong and all!"

He smiled at her and his teeth flashed. "Gad! little girl, if you got a right to be scared, whatta you think I had? I seen your card over at the clinic last night, and you 'ain't got no right to have that down-and-out look on you had this morning. If you think you got something to be scared at you looka my old card at the clinic some day; they keep it for show. You oughtta seen me the day I quit the shipping-room, right over at the Titanic, too, and then see whether you got something to be scared at."

"You—you used to work there?"

"Six years."

"I—I ain't scared no more, Eddie; honest, I ain't!"

"Gee! I should say not! They ain't even sending you up to the farm."

"No, no! They're going to get me a job. A regular outdoor, on-the-level kind of a job. A grand old doc, with whiskers! I ain't a regular one, Eddie; just the bottom of one lung don't make a regular one."

"Well, I guess not, poor little missy. Well, I guess not."

"Three months, he said, Eddie. Three months of right living like this, and air and all, and I'll be as round as a peach, he said. Said it hisself, without me asking—that's how scared I was. Round as a peach!"

"You can't beat that gang over there at the clinic, little missy. They took me out of the department when all the spring-water I knew about ran out of a keg. Even when they got me out on the farm—a grown-up guy like me— for a week I thought the crow in the rooster was a sidewalk faker. You can't beat that, little missy."

"He's a grand old man, with whiskers, that's going to get me the job. Then in three months I—"

"Three months nothing! That gang won't let you slip back after the three months. They took a extra shine to me because I did the prize-pupil stunt; but they won't let anybody slip back if they give 'em half a chance. When they got me sound again, did they ship me back to the shipping department in the subbasement? Not muchy! Looka me now, little missy! Clerk in their biggest display; in three months a raise to ninety dollars. Can you beat it? Ninety dollars would send all the shipping-clerks of the world off in a faint."

"Gee! it—it's swell!"

"And—"

"Look! Look!"

"Persimmons!" A golden mound of them lay at the base of a tree, piled up against the bole, bursting, brown. "Persimmons! Here; taste one. They're fine."

"Eat 'em?"

"Sure!"

She bit into one gently; then with appetite. "M-m-m! Good!"

"Want another?"

"M-m-m—my mouth! Ouch! My m-mouth!"

"Gee! you cute little thing, you! See, my mouth's the same way, too. Feels like a knot. Gee! you cute little thing, you—all puckered up and all."

And linking her arm in his they crunch-crunched over the brittle leaves and up a hillside to a plateau of rock overlooking the flaming country; and from the valley below smoke from burning mounds of leaves wound in spirals, its pungency drifting to them.

"See that tree there? It's an oak. Look; from a little acorn like this it grew. See, this is a acorn, and in the start that tree wasn't no bigger than this little thing."

"Quit your kidding!" But she smiled and her lips were parted sweetly; and always unformed tears would gloze her eyes.

"Here, sit here, little lady. Wait till I spread this newspaper out. Gee! Don't I wish you didn't have to go back to the city by two o'clock, little lady! We could make a great day of it here, out in the country; lunch at a farm and see the sun set and all. Some day of it we could make if—"

"I—I don't have to go back, Eddie."

His face expanded into his widest smile. "Gee! that's great! That's just great!"

Silence.

"What you thinking of, little lady, sitting there so pretty and all?"

"N-nothing."

"Nothing? Aw, surely something!"

A tear formed and zigzagged down her cheek. "Nothing, honest; only I—I feel right happy."

"That's just how you oughtta feel, little lady."

"In three months, if—Aw, ain't I the nut?"

"It'll be a big Christmas, won't it, little missy, for both of us? A big Christmas for both of us; you as sound and round as a peach again, and me shooting up like a skyrocket on the pay-roll."

A laugh bubbled to her lips before the tear was dry. "In three months I won't be a T. B., not even a little bit."

"Sh-h-h! On the farm we wasn't allowed to say even that. We wasn't supposed to even know what them letters mean."

"Don't you know what they mean, Eddie?"

"Sure I do!" He leaned toward her and placed his hand lightly over hers. "T. B.—True Blue—that's what they mean, little lady."

She could feel the veins in his palm throbbing.

White Goods

First Published: *Metropolitan Magazine*, July 1915
Reprinted: *Humoresque and Other Stories*, Harper & Bros., 1919

On a slope a white sprinkling of wood anemones lay spread like a patch of linen bleaching in the sun. From a valley a lark cut a swift diagonal upward with a coloratura burst of song. A stream slipped its ice and took up its murmur where it had left off. A truant squelched his toes in the warm mud and let it ooze luxuriantly over and between them.

A mole stirred in its hole, and because spring will find a way, even down in the bargain basement of the Titanic Store, which is far below the level of the mole, Sadie Barnet, who had never seen a wood anemone and never sniffed of thaw or the wet wild smell of violets, felt the blood rise in her veins like sap, and across the aisle behind the white-goods counter Max Meltzer writhed in his woolens, and Sadie Barnet, presiding over a bin of specially priced mill-ends out mid-aisle between the white goods and the muslin underwear, leaned toward him, and her smile was as vivid as her lips.

"Say, Max, guess why I think you're like a rubber band."

Classic Delphi was never more ready with ambiguous retort.

Behind a stack of Joy-of-the-Loom bed-sheets, Max Meltzer groped for oracular divination, and his heart-beats fluttered in his voice.

"Like a rubber band?"

"Yeh."

"Give up."

"Aw, give a guess."

"Well, I don't know, Miss Sadie, unless—unless it's because I'm stuck on you."

Do not, ascetic reader, gag at the unsocratic plane. True, Max Meltzer had neither the grain nor the leisure of a sophist, a capacity for tenses or an appreciation of Kant. He had never built a bridge, led a Bible class, or attempted the first inch of the five-foot bookshelf. But on a two-figure salary he subscribed an annual donation to a skin-and-cancer hospital, wore non-reversible collars, and maintained a smile that turned upward like the corners of a cycle moon. Remember, then, ascetic reader, that a rich man once kicked a leper; Kant's own heart, that it might turn the world's heart outward, burst of pain; and in the granite cañon of Wall Street, one smile in every three-score and ten turns upward.

Sadie Barnet met Max Meltzer's cycle-moon smile with the blazing eyes of scorn, and her lips, quivering to a smile, met in a straight line that almost ironed out the curves.

"'Cause you're stuck on me! That's a swell guess. Gee! you're as funny as a sob, you are."

The words scuttered from her lips like sharp hailstones and she glanced at him sidewise over a lump of uplifted shoulder and down the length of one akimbo arm.

"'Cause you're stuck on me! Huh!"

Max Meltzer leaned across a counter display of fringed breakfast napkins.

"Ain't that a good reason, Miss Sadie? It's a true one."

"You're one swell little guesser, you are *not*. You couldn't get inside a riddle with a can-opener. 'Cause you're stuck on me! Gee!"

"Well, I am."

"I didn't ask you why you was like a bottle of glue. I asked you why you was like a rubber band."

"Aw, I give up, Miss Sadie."

"'Cause you're so stretchy, see? 'Cause you're so stretchy you'll yawn your arm off if you don't watch it."

Max Meltzer collapsed in an attitude of mock prostration against a stock-shelf.

"Gee! that must have been cracked before the first nut."

"Smarty!"

Across the specially priced mill-ends she flashed the full line of her teeth, and with an intensity his features ill concealed he noted how sweet her throat as it arched.

"It's the spring fever gets inside of me and makes me so stretchy, Miss Sadie. It's a good thing trade is slow down here in the basement to-day, because it's the same with me every year; the Saturday before spring-opening week I just get to feeling like all outdoors."

"Wait till you see me with a new red-satin bow stuck on my last summer's shape. Dee Dee's got to lend me the price for two yards of three-inch red-satin ribbon for my spring opening."

His breath rose in his throat.

"I bet you look swell in red, Miss Sadie. But a girl like you looks swell in anything."

"Red's my color. Dee Dee says my mamma was a gay one, too, when it came to color. Had to have a red bow pinned somewheres around all the months she was in bed and—and up to the very night she died. Gimme red every time. Dee Dee's the one that's always kicking against red; she says I got too flashy taste."

"Say, if she keeps bossing and bossing at you, what do you keep on living with her for?"

"Wouldn't you live with your own mother's sister if she raised you from a kid? What am I going to do, put her in cold storage, now that her eyes are going back on her? Up in the ribbons she can't hardly keep her colors graduated no more, that's how blind she's getting. Only yesterday a dame brought back some lavender ribbon and wiped up the whole department with Dee Dee for putting it over on her as blue. What am I going to do?"

"Honest, Miss Sadie, I didn't know that she was your aunt and that her eyes was bad. I've seen you two together a lot and noticed her thick lenses, but I just didn't think."

"Well, now I'm telling you."

"I just thought she was some old girl up in the ribbons you was living with for company. Honest, I didn't know she had bad eyes. Gee!"

"No, they ain't bad. Only she's so blind she reads her paper upside down and gets sore if you tell her about it."

"And me thinking she was nothing but a near-sighted old grouch with a name like a sparrow."

Miss Barnet laughed with an upward trill.

"Dee Dee ain't her real name. When I was a kid and she took me to raise, that's the way I used to pronounce Aunt Edith. Gee! you don't think Dee Dee was the name they sprinkled on her when they christened her, did you?"

Max Meltzer leaned to the breath of her laughter as if he would fill his lungs with it.

"Gee! but you're a cute little lady when you laugh like that."

"Say, and ain't you the freshie! Just because you're going to be promoted to buyer for your department won't get your picture in the Sunday supplement. No white-goods buyer I know of ever had to build white marble libraries or present a bread-line to the city to get rid of his pin-money."

"I bet you was a cute little black-eyed, red-cheeked little youngster, alrighty."

"I wasn't so worse. Like I tell Dee Dee, the way she's held me down and indoors evenings, it's a wonder a kid like me grew up with any pep at all."

"Poor little lady!"

"It's like Dee Dee says, though. I never was cut out for life behind the counter. Gee! I'd soak my pillow in gasolene every night in the week if it would make me dream I'm automobiling."

"Poor little lady!"

"Say, ain't it hot? With the Opening on Monday, they better get the fans working. Last year three girls keeled. Honest, sometimes I think I'd rather spend the summer under the daisies out on the hill than down here in this basement."

"Don't I wish I had an auto to take you spinning in to-night."

"You ought to see the flier a friend of mine has got. A Mercury Six with a limousine top like a grand-opera box."

"Your—your—friend?"

"Yes. He's that slick-looking, little fat fellow that's a cousin to Mamie Grant up in the ready-to-wears. He was down here talking to me the other day."

"I seen him."

"Gee! you ought to feel yourself in his Mercury Six. 'Lemme die,' I says to him the last time I was in it. 'Just lemme close my eyes right in here and die happy,' I says, cuddled up in the red-leather seat with a cornucopia of daffodils tickling my nose and a street-car full of strap-hangers riding alongside of us."

"I—I guess if you got swell friends like that, a boat excursion down the river 'ain't got much of a sound for you."

"He says he's got a launch in summer—"

"Honest, Miss Sadie, I—I just been trying for the better part of two weeks to ask permission if I could come and call on you some evening, Miss Sadie, but—"

"Whoops! ain't he the daredevil!"

"The first boat of the season, Miss Sadie, a swell new one they call the *White Gull,* goes down to Coney to-night, and, it being real springtime, and you feeling kind of full of it, I thought maybe, it being the first boat of the season, maybe you would take a river ride this grand April night, Miss Sadie."

Her glance slanted toward him, full of quirks.

"My aunt Dee Dee, Mr. Meltzer, she's right strict with me. She don't think I ought to keep company with any boys that don't come to see me first at my house."

"I know it, Miss Sadie; that's the right way to do it, but I think I can get around her all right. Wasn't she down here in the basement the day I first heard about my promotion, and didn't she give me the glad hand and seem right friendly to me? I can get around her all right, Miss Sadie. I can always tell if a person likes me or not."

"Anyways, if her eyes ain't too bad, Mr. Meltzer, I got a date with my friend if his car is out of the shop from having the limousine top taken off. We—we're going for a little spin."

A quick red belied her insouciance and she made a little foray into the bin of mill-ends.

"Gee! if I've made three sales this livelong day I don't know nothing about two of them."

Max Meltzer met her dancing gaze, pinioning it with his own quiet eyes.

"You're right to pick out the lucky fellows who can buy a good time. A little girl like you ought to have every enjoyment there is. If I could give it to you, do you think I would let the other fellows beat me to it? The best ain't none too good for a little lady like you."

"Aw, Mr. Meltzer!" Her bosom filled and waned. "Aw, Mr. Meltzer!"

"I mean it."

An electric bell grilled through his words. Miss Barnet sprang reflexly from the harness of an eight-hour day.

"Aw, looka, and I wanted to sneak up before closing and get Dee Dee to snip me two yards of red satin, and she won't cut an inch after the bell. Ain't that luck for you? Ain't that luck?"

Her lips drew to a pout.

"Lemme get it for you, Miss Sadie. I know a girl up in the ribbons—"

"No, no, Mr. Meltzer. I—I gotta charge it to Dee Dee, and, anyways, she gets mad like anything if I keep her waiting. I gotta go. 'Night, Mr. Meltzer! 'Night!"

She was off through the maze of the emptying store, in the very act of pinning on her little hat with its jaunty imitation fur pompon, and he breathed in as she passed, as if of the perfume of her personality.

At the ribbon counter on the main floor the last of a streamlet of outgoing women detached herself from the file as Miss Barnet ascended the staircase.

"Hurry up, Sadie."

"Dee Dee! How'd you girls up here get on your duds so soon? I thought maybe if I'd hurry upstairs you—you'd find time to cut me a two-yard piece of three-inch red satin for my hat, Dee Dee—to-morrow being Sunday. Two yards, Dee Dee, and that'll make two-sixty-nine I owe you. Aw, Dee Dee, it won't take a minute, to-morrow Sunday and all! Aw, Dee Dee!"

Miss Barnet slid ingratiating fingers into the curve of the older woman's arm; her voice was smooth as salve.

"Aw, Dee Dee, who ever heard of wearing fur on a hat in April? I gotta stick a red bow on my last summer's sailor, Dee Dee."

Miss Edith Worte stiffened so that the muscles sprang out in the crook of her arm and the cords in her long, yellowing neck. Years had dried on her face, leaving ravages, and through her high-power spectacles her pale eyes might have been staring through film and straining to see.

"Please, Dee Dee!"

Miss Barnet held backward, a little singsong note of appeal running through her voice.

Miss Worte jerked forward toward the open door. April dusk, the color of cold dish-water, showed through it. Dusk in the city comes sadly, crowding into narrow streets and riddled with an immediate quick-shot of electric bulbs.

"'Ain't you got no sense a-tall? 'Ain't you got no sense in that curly head of yourn but ruination notions?"

"Aw, Dee Dee!"

They were in the flood tide which bursts through the dam at six o'clock like a human torrent flooding the streets, then spreading, thinning, and finally seeping into homes, hall bedrooms, and Harlem flats.

Miss Edith Worte turned her sparse face toward the down-town tide and against a light wind that tasted of rain and flapped her skirts around her thin legs.

"Watch out, Dee Dee! Step down; there's a curb."

"I don't need you. It's lots you care if I go blind on the spot."

"Dee Dee!"

"God! if I didn't have nothing to worry me but red ribbons! I told the doctor to-day while he was putting the drops in my eyes, that if he'd let me go blind I—I—"

"Now, now, Dee Dee! Ain't you seeing better these last few days?"

"If you had heard what the doctor told me to-day when he put the drops in my eyes you'd have something to think about besides red ribbon, alrighty."

"I forgot, Dee Dee, to-day was your eye-doctor day. He's always scarin' you up. Just don't pay no attention. I forgot it was your day."

"Sure you forgot. But you won't forget if I wake up alone in the dark some day."

"Dee Dee!"

"You won't forget then. You won't forget to nag me even then for duds to go automobiling with fly men that can't bring you no good."

"Dee Dee, I 'ain't been but one night this week. I been saving up all my nights for—for to-night."

"To-night. Say, I can't keep you from going to the devil on skates if—"

"It's only the second time this week, Dee Dee, and I—I promised. He'll have the limousine top off to-night—and feel, it is just like summer. A girl's gotta have a little something once in a while."

"What do I gotta have? What do I gotta have but slave and work?"

"It's different with you, Dee Dee. You're older even than my mamma was, and didn't you say when you and her was girls together there wasn't a livelier two sisters? Now didn't you, Dee Dee?"

"In a respectable way, yes. But there wasn't the oily-mouthed, bald-headed divorced man alive, with little rat eyes and ugly lips, who could have took me or your mamma out auto-riding before or after dark. We was working-girls, too, but there wasn't a man didn't take off his hat to us, even if he was bald-headed and it was twenty below zero."

"Aw!"

"Yes, 'aw'! You keep running around with the kind of men that don't look at a girl unless she's served up with rum-sauce and see where it lands you. Just keep running if you want to, but my money don't buy you no red ribbons to help to drive you to the devil!"

"The way you keep fussing at me, when I don't even go to dances like the other girls! I—sometimes I just wish I was dead. The way I got to watch the clock like it was a taximeter the whole time I'm out anywhere. It's the limit. Even Max Meltzer gimme the laugh to-day."

"You'd never hear me say watch the clock if you'd keep company with a boy like Max Meltzer. A straight, clean boy with honest intentions by a girl lookin' right out of his face. You let a boy like Max Meltzer begin to keep steady with you and see what I say. You don't see no yellow streak in his face; he's as white as the goods he sells."

"I know. I know. You think now because he's going to be made buyer for the white goods in September he's the whole show. Gee! nowadays that ain't so muchy much for a fellow to be."

"No, I think the kind of fellows that fresh Mamie Grant gets you acquainted with are muchy much. I'm strong for the old rat-eyed sports like Jerry Beck, that 'ain't got an honest thought in his head. I bet he gives you the creeps, too, only you're the kind of girl, God help you, that's so crazy for luxury you could forget the devil had horns if he hid 'em under a automobile cap."

"Sure I am. I 'ain't seen nothing but slaving and drudging and pinching all my life, while other girls are strutting the Avenue in their furs and sleeping mornings as long as they want under eider-down quilts. Sure, when a man like Jerry Beck comes along with a carriage-check instead of a Subway-ticket I can thaw up to him like a water-ice, and I ain't ashamed of it, neither."

They turned into a narrow aisle of street lined with unbroken rows of steep, narrow-faced houses. Miss Worte withdrew her arm sharply and plunged ahead, her lips wry and on the verge of trembling.

"When a girl gets twenty, like you, it ain't none of my put-in no more. Only I hope to God your mother up there is witness that if ever a woman slaved to keep a girl straight and done her duty by her it was me. That man 'ain't got no good intentions by—"

"On, ain't you—ain't you a mean-thinking thing, ain't you? What kind of girl do you think I am? If he didn't have the right intentions by me do you think—"

"Oh, I guess he'll marry you if he can't get you no other way. Them kind always do if they can't help themselves. A divorced old guy like him, with a couple of kids and his mean little eyes, knows he's got to pay up if he wants a young girl like you. Oh, I— Ouch—oh—oh!"

"Dee Dee, take my arm. That was only an ashcan you bumped into. It's the drops he puts in your eyes makes 'em so bad to-night, I guess. Go on, take my arm, Dee Dee. Here we are home. Lemme lead you up-stairs. It's nothing but the drops, Dee Dee."

They turned in and up and through a foggy length of long hallway. Spring had not entered here. At the top of a second flight of stairs a slavey sat back on her heels and twisted a dribble of gray water from her cloth into her bucket. At the last and third landing an empty coal-scuttle stood just outside a door as if nosing for entrance.

"Watch out, Dee Dee, the scuttle. Lemme go in first. Gee! it's cold indoors and warm out, ain't it? Wait till I light up. There!"

"Lemme alone. I can see."

An immemorial federation of landladies has combined against Hestia to preserve the musty traditions of the furnished room. Love in a cottage is fostered by subdivision promoters and practised by commuters on a five-hundred-dollars-down, monthly-payment basis. Marble halls have been celebrated in song, but the furnished room we have with us always at three cents per agate line.

You with your feet on your library fender, stupefied with contentment and your soles scorching, your heart is not black; it is only fat. How can it know the lean formality of the furnished room? Your little stenographer, who must wear a smile and fluted collars on eight dollars a week, knows it; the book agent at your door, who earns eighteen cents on each *Life of Lincoln,* knows it. Chambermaids know it when they knock thrice and only the faint and nauseous fumes of escaping gas answer them through the plugged keyhole. Coroners know it.

Sadie Barnet and Edith Worte knew it, too, and put out a hand here and there to allay it. A comforting spread of gay chintz covered the sag in their white iron bed; a photograph or two stuck upright between the dresser mirror and its frame, and tacked full flare against the wall was a Japanese fan, autographed many times over with the gay personnel of the Titanic Store's annual picnic.

"Gee! Dee Dee, six-twenty already! I got to hurry. Unhook me while I sew in this ruching."

"Going for supper?"

"Yeh. He invited me. This is cottage-pudding night; tell old lady Finch when I ain't home for supper you got two desserts coming to you."

"I don't want no supper."

"Aw, now, Dee Dee!"

Miss Worte dropped her dark cape from her shoulders, hung it with her hat on a door peg, and sat heavily on the edge of the bed.

"God! my feet!"

"Soak 'em."

Miss Barnet peeled off her shirt-waist. Her bosom, strong and flat as a boy's, rose white from her cheaply dainty under-bodice; at her shoulders the flesh began to deepen, and her arms were round and full of curves.

"Here, Dee Dee, I'm so nervous when I hurry. You sew in this ruche; you got time before the supper-bell. See, right along the edge like that."

Miss Worte aimed for the eye of the needle, moistening the end of the thread with her tongue and her fluttering fingers close to her eyes.

"God! I—I just 'ain't got the eyes no more. I can't see, Sadie; I can't find the needle."

Sadie Barnet paused in the act of brushing out the cloud of her dark hair, and with a strong young gesture ran the thread through the needle, knotting its end with a quirk of thumb and forefinger.

"It's the drops, Dee Dee, and this gaslight, all blurry from the curling-iron in the flame, makes you see bad."

Miss Worte nodded and closed her eyes as if she would press back the tears and let them drip inward.

"Ych, I know. I know."

"Sure! Here, lemme do it, Dee Dee. I won't stay out late, dearie, if your eyes are bad. We're only going out for a little spin."

Miss Worte lay back on the chintz bedspread and turned her face to the wall.

"I should worry if you come home or if you don't—all the comfort you are to me."

"You say that to me many more times and you watch and see what I do; you watch and see."

"The sooner the better."

In the act of fluting the soft ruche about her neck, so that her fresh little face rose like a bud from its calyx, Miss Barnet turned to the full length of back which faced her from the bed.

"That's just the way I feel about it—the sooner the better."

"Then we think alike."

"You 'ain't been such a holy saint to me that I got to pay up to you for it all my life."

"That's the thanks I get."

"You only raised me because you had to. I been working for my own living ever since I was so little I had to lie to the inspectors about my age."

"Except what you begged out of my wages."

"I been as much to you as you been to me and—and I don't have to stand this no longer. Sure I can get out and—and the sooner the better. I'm sick of getting down on my knees to you every time I wanna squeeze a little good time out of life. I'm tired paying up for the few dollars you gimme out of your envelop. If I had any sense I—I wouldn't never take it from you, nohow, the way you throw it up to me all the time. The sooner the better is what I say, too; the sooner the better."

"That's the thanks I get; that's the—"

"Aw, I know all that line of talk by heart, so you don't need to ram it down me. You gotta quit insinuating about my ways to me. I'm as straight as you are and—"

"You—you—take off that ivory-hand breast-pin; that ain't yours."

"Sure I'll take it off, and this ruche you gimme the money to buy, and this red bracelet you gimme, and—and every old thing you ever gimme. Sure I'll take 'em all off. I wish I could take off these gray-top shoes you paid a dollar toward, and I would, too, if I didn't have to go barefoot. It's the last time I borrow from—"

"Aw, you commenced that line of talk when you was ten."

"I mean it."

"Well, if you do, take off them gloves that I bought for myself and you begged right off my hands. Just take 'em off and go barehanded with your little-headed friend; maybe he can buy—"

"You— Oh, I—I wish I was dead! I—I'll go barehanded to a snowball feast rather than wear your duds. There's your old gloves—there!"

Tears were streaming and leaving their ravages on the smooth surfaces of her cheeks.

"I just wish I—I was dead."

"Aw, no, you don't! There's him now, with a horn on his auto that makes a noise like the devil yelling! There's your little rat-eyed, low-lived fellow, now. You don't wish you was dead now, do you? Go to him and his two divorces and his little round head. That's where you belong; that's where girls on the road to the devil belong—with them kind. There he is now, waiting to ride you to the devil. He don't need to honk-honk so loud; he knows you're ready and waiting for him."

Miss Barnet fastened on her little hat with fingers that fumbled.

"Gimme—the key."

"Aw, no, you don't. When you come home to-night you knock; no more tiptoe, night-key business like last time. I knew you was lying to me about the clock."

"You gimme that key. I don't want you to have to get up, with all your kicking, to open the door for me. You gimme the key."

"If you wanna get in this room when you come home to-night, you knock like any self-respecting girl ain't afraid to do."

"You—oh—you!" With a shivering intake of breath Miss Barnet flung wide the door, slamming it after her until the windows and the blue-glass vase on the mantelpiece and Miss Worte, stretched full length on the bed, shivered.

Two flights down she flung open the front door. There came from the curb the blast of a siren, wild for speed.

Stars had come out, a fine powdering of them, and the moist evening atmosphere was sweet, even heavy. She stood for a moment in the embrasure of the door, scenting.

"Do I need my heavy coat, Jerry?"

The dim figure in the tonneau, with his arms flung out their length across the back of the seat, moved from the center to the side.

"No, you don't. Hurry up! I'll keep you warm if you need a coat. Climb in here right next to me, Peachy. Gimme that robe from the front there, George.

"Now didn't I say I was going to keep you warm? Quit your squirming, Touchy. I won't bite. Ready, George. Up to the Palisade Inn, and let out some miles there."

"Gee! Jerry, you got the limousine top off. Ain't this swell for summer?"

Mr. Jerome Beck settled back in the roomy embrasure of the seat and exhaled loudly, his shoulder and shoe touching hers.

She settled herself out of their range.

"Now, now, snuggle up a little, Peachy."

She shifted back to her first position.

"That's better."

"Ain't it a swell night?"

"Now we're comfy—eh?"

They were nosing through a snarl of traffic and over streets wet and slimy with thaw. Men with overcoats flung over their arms side-stepped the snout of the car. Delicatessen and candy-shop doors stood wide open. Children shrilled in the grim shadows of thousand-tenant tenement-houses.

"Well, Peachy, how are you? Peachy is just the name for you, eh? 'Cause I'd like to take a bite right out of you—eh, Peachy? How are you?"

"Fine and—and dandy."

"Look at me."

"Aw!"

"Look at me, I say, you pretty little peach, with them devilish black eyes of yours and them lips that's got a cherry on 'em."

She met his gaze with an uncertain smile trembling on her lips.

"Honest, you're the limit."

"What's your eyes red for?"

"They—they ain't."

"Cryin'?"

"Like fun."

"You know what I'd do if I thought you'd been crying? I'd just kiss them tears right away."

"Yes, you would *not*."

"Little devil!"

"Quit calling me that." But she colored as if his tribute had been a sheath of lilies.

They veered a corner sharply, skidding on the wet asphalt and all but grazing the rear wheels of a recreant taxicab.

"Gad, George! you black devil you, why don't you watch out what you're doing?"

"But, suh, I—"

"None of your black back-talk."

"Jerry!" She was shivering, and a veil of tears formed over her hot, mortified eyes. "Gee! what are you made of? You seen he couldn't help it when that taxi turned into us so sudden."

He relaxed against her. "Aw, did I scare the little Peachy? That's the way they gotta be handled. I ain't ready by a long shot to let a black devil spill my brains."

"'Shh-h. He couldn't—"

"Sure he could, if he watched. He's a bargain I picked up cheap, anyways, 'cause he's lame and can't hold down heavy work. And bargains don't always pay. But I'll break his black back for him if— Aw, now, now, did I scare the little peach? Gee! I couldn't do nothing but kill *you* with kindness if you was driving for me. I'd just let you run me right off this road into the Hudson Ocean if you was driving for me."

They were out toward the frayed edge of the city, where great stretches of sign-plastered vacant lots began to yawn between isolated patches of buildings and the river ran close enough alongside of them to reflect their leftward lights. She smiled, but as if her lips were bruised.

"It ain't none of my put-in, but he couldn't help it, and I hate for you to yell at anybody like that, Jerry."

"Aw, aw, did I scare the little Peachy? Watch me show the little Tootsie how nice I can be when I want to— Aw—aw!"

"Quit."

She blinked back the ever-recurring tears.

"All tired out, too; all tired out. Wait till you see what I'm going to buy you to-night. A great big beefsteak with mushrooms as big as dollars and piping-hot German fried potatoes and onions. M-m-m-m! And more bubbles than you can wink your eye at. Aw—aw, such poor cold little hands, and no gloves for such cold little hands! Here, lemme warm 'em. Wouldn't I just love to wrap a little Peachy like you up in a great big fur coat and put them little cold hands in a great big muff and hang some great big headlight earrings in them little bittsie ears. Wouldn't I, though. M-m-m-m! Poor cold little hands!"

Her wraith of a smile dissolved in a spurt of hot tears which flowed over her words.

"Gee! Ain't I the nut to—to cry? I—I'll be all right in a minute."

"I knew when I seen them red eyes the little Peachy wasn't up to snuff, and her cute little devilishlike ways. What's hurting you, Tootsie? Been bounced? You should worry. I'm going to steal you out of that cellar, anyways. Been bounced?"

"N-no."

"The old hag 'ain't been making it hot for you, has she?"

"Sh-she—"

"Gad! that old hag gets my fur up. I had a mother-in-law once tried them tricks on me till I learned her they wouldn't work. But the old hag of yourn—"

"It's her eyes; the doctor must have scared her up again to-day. When she gets scared like that about 'em she acts up so, honest, sometimes I—I just wish I was dead. She don't think a girl oughtta have no life."

"Forget it. Just you wait. She's going to wake up some morning soon and find a little surprise party for herself. I know just how to handle an old bird like her."

"Sometimes she's just so good to me, and then again, when she gets sore like to-night, and with her nagging and fussing at me, I don't care if she is my aunt, I just *hate* her."

"We're going to give her a little surprise party." Beneath the lap robe his hand slid toward hers. She could feel the movement of the arm that directed it and her own shrank away.

"But ain't I the limit, Jerry, airing my troubles to you, like you was a policeman."

"Now, now—"

"Quit! Leggo my hand."

They were spinning noiselessly along a road that curved for the moment away from the river into the velvet shadows of trees. He leaned forward suddenly, enveloping her.

"I got it. Why don't you lemme kidnap you, kiddo?"

"What—"

"Lemme kidnap you to-night and give the old hag the surprise of her life when she wakes up and finds you stolen. I'm some little kidnapper when it comes to kidnapping, I am, kiddo. Say, wouldn't I like to take you riding all wrapped up in a fur coat with nothing but your cute little face sticking out."

"Aw, you're just fooling me."

"Fooling! Lemme prove it, to-night. Lemme kidnap you this very night. I—"

She withdrew stiff-backed against his embrace.

"Is—is that what you mean by—by kidnapping me?"

"Sure. There ain't nothing I'd rather do. Are you on, Peaches? A sensible little queen like you knows which side her bread is buttered on. There ain't nothing I want more than to see you all bundled up in a fur coat with— headlights in your little bittsie pink ears."

She sprang the width of the seat from him.

"You— What kind of a girl do you think I am? O God! What kind of a girl does he think I am? Take me home—take me— What kind of a girl do you think I am?"

He leaned toward her with a quick readjustment of tone.

"Just what I said, Peachy. What I meant was I'd marry you to-night if we could get a license. I'd just kidnap you to-night if—if we could get one."

"You—you didn't mean that."

"Sure I did, Peachy. Say, with a little girl of my own I ain't one of them guys that you think I am. Ain't you ashamed of yourself, Peachy—now ain't you?"

The color flowed back into her face and her lips parted.

"Jerry— Only a girl like me's got to be careful—that was all I meant, Jerry. Jerry!"

He scooped her in his short arms and kissed her lips, with her small face crumpled up against his shoulder, and she lay quiescent enough in his embrace. Wind sang in her ears as they rushed swiftly and surely along the oiled road, but the two small fists she pressed against his coat lapels did not relax.

"Aw, now, Peachy, you mustn't treat a fellow cold no more! Ain't I going to marry you? Ain't I going to set you up right in my house out in Newton Heights? Ain't I going to give you a swell ten-room house? Ain't you going to live right in the house with my girl, and ain't she going to have you for a little stepmother?"

"Jerry, the—the little girl. I wonder if she wants—"

"Sure she does. Her mother gets her every other month. I'd let her go for good if you don't want her, except it would do her mother too much good. The courts give her to me every other month and I'll have her down to the last minute of the last hour or bust."

"Jerry!"

"That's what I gotta keep up the house out there for. The court says I gotta give her a home, and that's why I want a little queen like you in it. Gad! Won't her mother throw a red-headed fit when she sees the little queen I picked! Gad!"

"Oh, Jerry, her your first wife and all! Won't it seem funny my going in her house and—and living with her kid."

"Funny nothing. Cloonan won't think it's funny when I tell her she's finished running my house for me. Funny nothing. To-morrow's Sunday and I'm going to take you out in the afternoon and show you the place, and Monday, instead of going to your bargain bin, we're going down for a license, and you kiss the old hag good-by for me, too. Eh, how's that for one day's work?"

"Gee! and—and—Monday the spring opening and me not there! Jerry, I—I can't get over me being a lady in my own house. Me! Me that hates ugliness and ugly clothes and ugly living so. Me that hates street-cars and always even hated boat excursions 'cause they was poor folks' pleasures. Me a lady in my own house. Oh, Jerry!"

She quivered in his arms and he kissed her again with his moist lips pressed flat against hers.

"Ten rooms, Peachy—that's the way I do things."

They were curving up a gravel way, and through the lacy foliage of spring lights gleamed, and there came the remoter strains of syncopated music.

She sat up and brushed back her hair.

"Is this the place?"

"Right-o! Now for that steak smothered in mushrooms, and, gad! I could manage a sweetbread salad on the side if you asked me right hard."

They drew up in the flood-light of the entrance.

"'Ain't I told you not to open the door for me, George? I don't need no black hand reaching back here to turn the handle for me. That don't make up for bad driving. Black hands off."

"Jerry!"

They alighted with an uncramping and unbending of limbs.

"How'd some Lynnhavens taste to you for a starter, Peachy?"

"Fine, whatever they are."

A liveried attendant bowed them up the steps.

A woman in blue velvet, her white arms bare to the shoulder and stars in her hair, paused in the doorway to drop her cloak. Her heavy perfume drifted out to meet them.

Sadie Barnet's clutch of her companion's arm quickened and her thoughts ran forward.

"Jerry—gee! wouldn't I look swell in—in a dress like that? Gee! Jerry, stars and all!"

The cords in the muscles of his arm rose under her fingers.

"Them ain't one-two-three-six to the duds I'm going to hang on you. I know her; she's an old-timer. Them duds ain't one-two-three-six."

"Gee—Jerry!"

In the heart of a silence as deep as a bottomless pool, with the black hours that tiptoe on the heels of midnight shrouding her like a nun's wimple, limbs trembling and her hands reluctant, Sadie Barnet knocked lightly at her door once, twice, thrice, and between each rap her heart beat with twice its tempo against her breast.

Then her stealthy hand turned the white china knob and released it so that it sprang backward with a click.

"Who's that?"

"Me, Dee Dee."

Her voice was swathed in a whisper.

She could hear the plong of the bedspring, the patter of bare feet across the floor; feel the slight aperture of the opening door. She oozed through the slit.

"All right, Dee Dee."

"God! I—I must have been sound asleep. What time is it?"

"It isn't late, Dee Dee."

"Light the gas."

"I—I can undress in the dark."

"Light the gas."

"I—"

"Light it, I say."

"It's lit, Dee Dee."

The figure in the center of the room, in her high-necked long-sleeved nightdress, her sparse hair drawn with unpleasant tension from her brow, her pale eyes wide, moved forward a step, one bare foot, calloused even across the instep, extended.

"Lit?"

"Dee Dee, what's the matter?"

"Gimme—my glasses."

She took them from Miss Barnet's trembling fingers and curved them about her ears.

"Quit your nonsense now and light the gas. I ain't in no humor for foolin'. Quit waving that little spark in front of me. Light the gas. I ain't going to look at the clock. I'm done worrying about your carryings-on. I'm done. Light the gas, Sadie, there's a good girl. Light the gas."

"Dee Dee! My God! Dee Dee, I—I tell you it's lit—big."

"There's a good girl, Sadie. Don't fool your old aunt."

"See, dearie, I ain't fooling. See, the gas-jet here beside the dresser. Look—I can't turn it no higher. Hear it sing and splutter. You ain't awake good yet, Dee Dee."

Silence—the ear-splitting silence that all in its brief moment is crammed with years and years upon years. A cold gray wash seemed suddenly to flow over Miss Worte's face.

"Put my finger next to the gas flame. You—you're lying to me to—to fool your old aunt. Lemme feel my finger get burnt."

They moved, these two, across the floor, their blanched faces straining ahead. With the sudden sting of heat finally across her palm, reddening it, Miss Worte flung wide her arms and her head backward, and her voice tore out without restraint.

"God! God! God!" And she fell to trembling so that her knees gave way under her and she crouched on the floor with her face bared to the ceiling, rocking herself back and forth, beating her fists against her flat breasts.

"God! God! God!"

"Dee Dee!—Dee Dee! my darling! my darling!"

"O God! O God! O God!"

"Dee Dee darling, it ain't nothing! A little too much strain, that's all. 'Shh-h-h! Lemme bathe them. 'Shh-h-h, my darling. Oh, my God! darling! 'Shh-h-h!"

"Lemme go! Lemme go! He told me to-day it would come like this! Only he didn't say how soon. Not how soon. I'm done for, I tell you! I'm done! Kill me, Sadie; if you love me, kill me! He told me and I wouldn't believe it! Kill me, girl, and put me out of it! I can't breathe in the dark! I can't! I can't! I can't live in the dark with my eyes open! Kill me, girl, and put me out of it—kill me! Kill me!"

"Dee Dee, my darling, ain't I right here with you? Didn't you always say, darling, when it came you—you'd face it?"

Like St. Cecilia, who could not die, she crouched, and the curve of her back rose and fell.

"O God! Oh—"

"Dee Dee darling, try not to holler out so! Maybe it ain't for—for good. Aw, darling, keep your head down here next to me! Feel how close I am, Dee Dee, right here next to you. 'Shh-h-h! O God! Dee Dee darling, you'll kill yourself going on like that! Don't pull at your hair, darling—don't! Oh, my God, don't!"

"I'm done! Kill me! Kill me! Don't make me live in the dark with my eyes open—don't! There's a good girl, Sadie. Don't! Don't! Don't!"

From the room adjoining came a rattling at the barred door between.

"Cut it, in there! This ain't no barroom. Go tell your D. T.'s to a policeman."

They crouched closer and trembling.

"'Shh-h-h! Dee Dee, darling, try to be easy and not raise the house—try!"

Miss Worte lay back exhausted against Miss Barnet's engulfing arms. Her passion ebbed suddenly and her words came scant, incoherent, and full of breath.

"No use. No use. He told me to-day he wouldn't operate. He told me. No, no, all the colors so pale—even the reds—so pale! Lavender and blue I—I just couldn't tell. I couldn't. So pale. Two yards she brought back next day, kicking at— Oh, my God! Oh, my God!"

"'Shh-h-h, darling! Don't take on so! Wait till morning and we'll get new drops from him. 'Shh-h-h! Maybe it's only strain."

"I know. I'm in the dark for good, Sadie. Oh, my God! I'm in the dark!"

Except that her face was withered, she was like Iphigenia praying for death.

"Lemme die! Lemme die!"

"'Shh-h-h—darling— That's it, rest quiet."

Suddenly Miss Worte flung up one arm about Sadie Barnet's neck, pressing her head downward until their faces touched.

"Dee Dee darling, you—you hurt."

"You won't never leave me, Sadie, like you said you would? You won't leave me alone in the dark, Sadie?"

"No, no, my darling; you know I won't, never, never."

"You'll keep me with you always, promise me that, Sadie. Promise me *that* on the curl of your mother's hair you wear in your locket. Promise me, little Sadie, you won't leave your aunt Dee Dee alone in the dark. My poor little girl, don't leave me alone in the dark. I can't see; Sadie, I can't see no more. Promise me, Sadie, promise me, promise me!"

From Sadie Barnet's heart, weakening her like loss of blood, flowed her tears. She kissed the heart of Edith Worte where it beat like a clock beneath the high-necked nightdress; she made of her bosom a pillow of mercy and drew the head up to its warmth.

"I—I promise, Dee Dee, on her curl of hair. Sure I promise. Always will I keep you with me, darling, always, always, so help me, always."

Along the road to Newton Heights Spring and her firstlings crept out tenderly. Even close up to the rim of the oiled highway itself, an occasional colony of wood violets dared to show their heads for the brief moment before they suffocated. The threat of rain still lay on the air, but the Sunday rank and file of motors threw back tops, lowered windshields, and turned shining noses toward the greening fields.

In the red-leather tonneau, with her little face wind-blown and bared to the kiss in the air, Sadie Barnet turned to her companion and peered under the visor of his checked cap and up into his small inset eyes.

"Is—is that the house up on the hill there, Jerry?"

"Not yet. It's right around the next bend."

"Gee! My—my hands are like ice, I—I'm that nervous."

"Lemme feel."

"No."

"That's a swell way to treat a fellow who's promised to marry you."

"You—you must excuse me to-day, Jerry. Honest, without a wink of sleep last night—you must excuse me to-day. I—I'm so upset with poor Dee Dee, and on top of that so nervous about—your little girl and the house and everything. And, Dee Dee—when I think of Dee Dee."

"Don't think, Peachy; that's the way to get around that."

"I—I can't help it. You ought to seen her at the doctor's this morning, how—how the poor thing lost her nerve when he told her that there—there wasn't no hope."

"Aw, now, cut the sob stuff, Peachy! You can't help it. Nobody can, that's the trouble. Say, what kind of a little queen will they think you are if I bring you home all soppy with crying?"

"I ought not to have come, Jerry. I'm no kind of company to-day, only all of a sudden she's got so—so soft with me and she made me come while she—she tried to take a nap. Poor old Dee Dee!"

"Yeh, and poor old devil. Maybe she's just getting what's due to her."

"Jerry!"

"Sure, I believe every one of us gets what's coming to us."

"She—"

"Here we are, Tootsie. See, Peachy, that's the house I bought her and her mother, and they was kicking at it before the plaster was dry."

"Oh! Oh!"

"That's a concrete front. Neat, ain't it? That's a mosaic-floor porch, too, I built on a year after her and her mother vamoosed."

"It's a beau-tiful house, Jerry."

"You're the kind of kid that knows how to appreciate a home when she gets it. But her with her she-devil of a mother, they no sooner got in than they began to side with each other against me—her and her old mother trying to learn me how to run my own shebang."

"Where—"

"Gad! they're living in a dirty Harlem flat now and tryin' to put it over on me that they're better off in it. Bah! if I had to double up on alimony, I wouldn't give her a smell at this house, not a smell."

"Say, but ain't it pretty, Jerry, right up over the river, and country all around, and right over there in back the street-cars for the city when you want them?"

"This is going to be your street-car, Peachy, a six-cylinder one."

She colored like a wild rose.

"Oh, Jerry, I—I keep forgetting."

"By Gad! it's a good thing I'm going to give up my city rooms and come out here to watch my p's and q's. Gosh darn her neck! I told her to quit cluttering up that side-yard turf with her gosh darn little flower-beds! Gosh darn her neck! There never was a servant worth her hide."

"Jerry, why, they're beautiful! They just look beautiful, those pansies, and is that the little girl sitting up there on the porch steps? Is—is that Maisie?"

They drew to a stop before the box-shaped ornate house, its rough concrete front pretentiously inlaid over the doors and windows with a design of pebbles stuck like dates on a cake, and perched primly on the topmost step of the square veranda the inert figure of a small girl.

"Aw, ain't she cute?"

Miss Barnet sprang lightly to the sidewalk, and beside her Mr. Jerome Beck flecked the dust of travel from the bay of his waistcoat, shaking his trousers knees into place.

"This has got your Twenty-third Street dump beat a mile, and then some, 'ain't it, Peachy?"

"Jerry, call her here, the little girl. You tell her who—who I am. Tell her gently, Jerry, and—and how good I'm going to be to her and—Aw, ain't I the silly, though, to feel so trembly?"

The child on the step regarded their approach with unsmiling eyes, nor did she move except to draw aside her dark stuff skirts and close her knees until they touched.

"Hello there! Moping again, eh? Get up! Didn't I tell you not to let me catch you not out playing or helping Cloonan around? Say howdy to this lady. She's coming out here to live. Come here and say howdy to her."

The child shrank to the newel-post, her narrow little face overtaken with an agony of shyness.

"Cat got your tongue? Say howdy. Quit breathing through your mouth like a fish. Say howdy, that's a good girl."

"Don't force her, Jerry. She's bashful. Ain't you, dearie? Ain't you, Maisie?"

"Moping, you mean. If it was her month in the dirty Harlem flat she'd be spry enough. She knows what I mean when I say that, and she knows she better cut out this pouting. Quit breathing through your mouth or I'll stick a cork in it."

"Aw, Jerry, she can't help that!"

"Cat got your tongue? Where's Cloonan?"

The child's little face quivered and screwed, each feature drawing itself into position for tears. Her eyes disappeared, her nostrils distended, her mouth opened to a quivering rectangle, and she fell into silent weeping.

"Aw, Jerry—you—you scared her! Come here, darling; come here to me, Maisie; come, dearie."

But the child slid past the extended arms, down the wooden steps, and around a corner of the house, her arm held up across her eyes.

"Aw, Jerry, honest, you can be awful mean!"

"I'll get that out of her or know the reason why. They've poisoned her against me, that's about how it is in a nutshell. I'll get that pouting to be in that dirty Harlem hole with her mother and grandmother out of her or know the reason why."

"She—"

"Look, this is the front hall. Guess this 'ain't got that sty in Twenty-third Street beat some. Look! How do you like it? This way to the parlor and dining-room."

Sadie Barnet smiled through the shadows in her eyes.

"Jerry! Say, ain't this beau-tiful! A upright piano and gold chairs and— Why, Jerry! why, Jerry!"

"And look in here, the dining-room. Her and her mother shopped three weeks to get this oak set, and see this fancy cabinet full of china. Slick, ain't it?"

Her fingers curled in a soft clutch around her throat as if her breath came too fast.

"Jerry, it—it's just grand."

He marshaled her in all the pride of ownership.

"Look, butler's pantry, exposed plumbing."

"Oh! Oh!"

"Kitchen."

"Oh! Oh!"

"Here, Cloonan. I told you I was going to bring somebody out to take hold and sit on you and your bills, didn't I? This lady's coming out here to-morrow, bag and baggage. Hand over your account-book to her and I bet she does better with it. See that you fix us up in honeymoon style, too. Bag and baggage we're coming. Savvy?"

The figure beside the ill-kept stove, bowl in lap and paring potatoes with the long fleshless hands of a bird, raised a still more fleshless face.

"Howdy!"

"Cloonan's been running this shebang for two years now, Peachy, and there ain't nothing much she can't learn you about my ways. They ain't hard. Look! Porcelain-lined sink. It's got Twenty-third Street beat some, 'ain't it?"

"Yes, Jerry."

"Fix us a beefsteak supper, Cloonan, and lemme weigh up them groceries I sent out and lemme see your books afterward. Come, Peachy, here, up these stairs. This is the second floor. Pretty neat, ain't it? Her and her mother shopped three more weeks on this oak bed-set. Some little move out here from Twenty-third Street for a little rooming-house queen like you, eh? Neat little bedroom, eh, Peachy? Eh?"

His face was close to her and claret red with an expression she did not dare to face.

"And what's this next room here, Jerry? Ain't it sweet and quiet-looking! Spare room? Ain't it pretty with them little white curtains? Quit, quit, Jerry! You mustn't—you mustn't."

She broke from his embrace, confusion muddling her movements.

"Is this the—the spare room?"

"It is, now. It used to be the old woman's till I laid down on the mother-in-law game and squealed. Yeh, I used to have a little mother-in-law in our house that was some mother-in-law. Believe me, she makes that old devil of yourn look like a prize angel."

"I— This'll be just the room for Dee Dee, Jerry, where she can feel the morning sun and hear the street-cars over there when she gets lonesome. She ought to have the sunniest room, because it's something she can feel without seeing—poor thing. This will be a swell room for poor old blind Dee Dee, won't it, Jerry? Won't it, Jerry dear?"

"Cut the comedy, Peachy. There's a neat free ward waiting for her just the other direction from the city than Newton Heights. Cut the comedy, Peachy."

"Jerry, I—I gotta have her with me. I— Now that she—she's in the dark. She couldn't stand an institution, Jerry, she—she just couldn't."

"That's what they all say, but they get over it. I know a—"

"She couldn't, Jerry. She 'ain't had much in her life, but she's always had a roof over her head that wasn't charity, and she always said, Jerry, that she couldn't never stand a—a institution. She can take any other room you say,

Jerry. Maybe there's a little one up-stairs in the third story we could fix up comfy for her; but she's in the dark now, Jerry, and, my God! Jerry, she just couldn't stand an institution!"

He patted her shoulder and drew her arm through his.

"You lemme take care of that. She don't need to know nothing about it. We'll tell her we're sending her for a visit to the country for a while. After the second day she'll be as snug as a bug in a rug. They're good to 'em in those places; good as gold."

"No, no, Jerry! No, no! I gotta have her with me! She raised me from a kid and—and she couldn't stand it, Jerry! I gotta have her, I gotta! I want her!"

His mouth sagged downward suddenly and on an oblique.

"Say, somebody must have given you a few lessons in nagging, yourself. Them's the lines she used to recite to me about her she-devil of a mother, too. Gad! she used to hang on her mother's apron-strings like she was tied."

"Jerry, I—"

"Come, Peachy, don't get me sore. Come, let's talk about to-morrow. We gotta get the license first and—"

"Jerry, I— Promise me I can have her with me first. I— Just a little yes is all I want—Jerry dear—just a little yes."

A frown gathered in a triple furrow on his brow.

"Now, kiddo, you got to cut that with me, and cut it quick. If there's two things I can't stand it's nagging and pouting. Cloonan can tell you what pouting can drive me to. I'll beat it out of that girl of mine before she's through with me, and I won't stand it from no one else. Now cut it, Peachy, that's a nice girl."

He paced the carpeted space of floor between the dresser and bed, his mouth still on the oblique.

"Now cut it, Peachy, I said, and cut it quick."

She stood palpitating beside the window, her eyes flashing to his face and fastening there.

"God! I—I wanna go."

"Where?"

Her glance flashed past him out of the window and across the patch of rear lawn. A street-car bobbed across the country; she followed it with eager eyes.

"I wanna go."

He advanced now, conciliatory. "Aw, now, Peachy, a row just the day before we are married. You don't want to start out making me train you just like you was a little kid. If you was a little girl I could beat your little ways out of you, but I wanna be on the level with you and show you how nice I can be. All the things I'm going to give you, all—"

"Quit, you! I wanna go! I wanna go!"

"You can go to hell, for my part. I'm going to get a steak inside of me before we budge. Quit your fooling. See, you nearly got me sore there. Come, the car won't be back for us until six. Come, Peachy, come."

She was past him and panting down the stairs, out across the patch of rear lawn, and toward the bobbing street-car, the streamer of ribbon at her throat flying backward over her shoulder.

In the bargain basement of the Titanic Store the first day of the spring opening dragged to its close. In a meadow beside a round pond a tree dripped apple blossoms, each so frail a thing that it fluttered out and away, too light to anchor.

In careless similitude the bargain basement of the Titanic Store resuscitated from its storerooms, and from spring openings long gone by, dusty garlands of cotton May blossoms, festooning them between the great white supporting pillars of the basement and intertwining them.

Over the white-goods counter and over Sunday, as it were, a papier-mâché pergola of green lattice-work and more cotton-back May blossoms had sprung up as if the great god Wotan had built it with a word. Cascades of summer linens, the apple green and the butter yellow, flowed from counters and improvised tables. Sadie Barnet's own mid-aisle bin had blossomed into a sacrificial sale of lawn remnants, and toward the close of the day her stock lay low, depleted.

Max Meltzer leaned out of his bower, and how muted his voice, as if it came from an inner throat that only spoke when the heart bade it.

"Little one, them remnants went like hot cakes, didn't they?"

"Hot cakes! Well, I guess. You'd have thought there was a mill-end sale on postage stamps."

"And if you don't look all tired out! If you just don't!"

The ready tears swam in her voice.

"It's—it's been awful—me away from her all day like this. But, anyways, I got news for her when I go home to-night about her five weeks' benefit money. Old Criggs was grand. He's going to send the committee to see her. Anyways, that's some good news for her."

"I just can't get her out of my mind, neither. Seems like I—I just can see her poor blind face all the time."

"M-me, too."

"They say the girls up in the ribbons been crying all day. She was no love-bird, but they say she wasn't bad underneath."

"God knows she—she wasn't."

"That's the way with some folks; they're hard on top, but everybody knows hard-shell crabs have got sweeter meat than soft."

"Nobody knows that she was a rough diamond better than me. I got sore at her sometimes, but I—I know she was always there when I—I needed her, alrighty."

"Now, now, little girl, don't cry! You're all worn out."

"She—she was always there to stand by me in—in a pinch."

"Honest, Miss Sadie, you look just like a pretty little ghost. What you need is some spring air, girlie, some spring air for a tonic. Wouldn't I just love to take you all by your little self down the river to-night on one of them new Coney boats, where we could be—right quiet. Say, wouldn't I?"

"No—no!"

"I wanna talk to you, Miss Sadie. Can't you guess? I wanna get you all by yourself and talk to you right in your little ear."

"'Shh-h-h! You mustn't talk like that."

"That's the only way I have of trying to tell you how—how I feel, Miss Sadie—dearie."

"'Shh-h-h!"

"When I call you that it means—well, you know, dearie, you know. That's why I wanna take you to-night, dearie, all by your little self and—"

"No, no, Mr. Meltzer! I can't leave her alone like that. I promised I would never leave her alone in the dark if—if I could help it."

"Ain't I the dub? Sure you can't leave her. We gotta stick by her now, dearie. 'Ain't we? 'Ain't we?"

A red seepage of blood surged across his face and under his hair. Beneath his little hedge of mustache his lips quivered as if at their own daring.

"We gotta stick by her, dearie."

All her senses swam, nor could she control the fluttering of her hands.

"Oh—Mr. Meltzer—Max!"

"What you and poor old Dee Dee need is some of this spring air. Gee! Wouldn't I love to take you—and her down the river to-night on one of them new Coney boats? Gee! would I? Just you and—and her."

"Max—oh, Max dearie!"

Sob Sister

First Published: *Metropolitan Magazine*, February 1916
Reprinted: *Every Soul Hath Its Song*, Harper & Bros., 1916

Physics can answer whence goes the candle-flame when it vanishes into blackness and what becomes of sound when the great maw of silence digests it. But what science can know the destiny of the pins and pins and pins, and what is the oblivion which swallows that great army of street-walking women whose cheeks are too pink and who dwell outside the barbed-wire fence of respectability?

Let the pins go, unless one lies on the sidewalk point toward you, and let this be the story of Mae Munroe, herself one of the pink-cheeked grenadiers of that great army whose destiny is as vague as the destiny of pins, and who in more than one vain attempt to climb had snagged her imitation French embroidery petticoats on the outward side of that barbed-wire fence.

Then, too, in the years that lead up to this moment Mae Munroe had taken on weight—the fair, flabby flesh of lack of exercise and no lack of chocolate bonbons. And a miss is as good as a mile, or a barbed-wire fence, only so long as she keeps her figure down and her diet up. When Mae Munroe ran for a street-car she breathed through her mouth for the first six blocks after she caught it. The top button of her shoe was no longer equal to the span. But her eyes were still blue, rather like sky when you look straight up; her hair yellow to the roots; and who can gainsay that a dimple in the chin is not worth two in the cheeks?

In the florid disorder of a red velvet sitting-room cluttered with morning sunshine and unframed, unsigned photographs of stage favorites, empty bottles and dented-in cushions, Mae Munroe stirred on her high mound of red sateen sofa-pillows; placed her paper-bound book face down on the tabouret beside her; yawned; made a foray into an uncovered box of chocolate bonbons; sank her small teeth into a creamy oozing heart and dropped a particle of the sweet into the sniffling, upturned snout of a white wool dog cuddled in the curve of her arm; yawned again.

"No more tandy! Make ittsie Snookie Ookie sick! Make muvver's ittsie bittsie bow-wow sick! No! No!"

Each admonition she accompanied with a slight pat designed to intimidate further display of appetite. The small bunch in her arms raised his head and regarded her with pink, sick little eyes, his tongue darting this way and that in an aftermath of relish; then fell to licking her bare forearm with swift, dry strokes.

"Muvver's ittsie bittsie Snookie! Him love him poor muvver! Him poor, poor muvver!"

A cold tear oozed through one of Miss Munroe's closed eyes, zigzagged down her face, and she laid her cheek pat against the white wool.

"Muvver just wishes she was dead, Snookie. God! Don't she just!"

An hour she lay so. The morning sunshine receded, leaving a certain grayness in the cluttered room. From the rear of the flat came the clatter of dishes and the harsh sing of water plunging from a faucet. The book slid from its incline on the pillow to the floor and lay with its leaves crumpled under. The dog fell to snoring. Another while ticked past—loudly. And as if the ticking were against her brain like drops of water, she rose to a half-sitting posture, reached for the small onyx clock on the mantelpiece and smothered it beneath one of the red sateen sofa-pillows. When she relaxed again two fresh tears waggled heavily down her cream-colored cheeks. Then for a while she slept, with her mouth ever so slightly open and revealing the white line of her teeth. The tears slid off her cheeks to the mussed frills of her negligée and dried there.

The little dog emerged from his sleep gaping and stretching backward his hind legs. Mae Munroe yawned, extending her arms at full length before her; regarded her fair ringed fingers and the four dimples across the back of each hand; reached for a cigarette and with the wry face of nausea tossed it back into its box; swung to a sitting posture on the side of the sofa, the dog springing from the curve of her arm to the floor, shaking himself.

Her blowsy hair, burned at the ends but the color of corn-silk, came unloosed of its morning plait and she braided it over one shoulder, her blue eyes fixed on space. Tears would come.

Then she rose and crossed to the golden-oak piano between the windows, her negligée open its full length and revealing her nightdress; crossed with a slight limp and the dog yapping at the soiled and lacy train; fell to manipulating the self-playing attachment, peddling out a metallic avalanche of popular music.

At its conclusion she swung around on the bench, her back drooping as if under pressure of indolence; yawned; crossed to the window and between the parted lace curtains stood regarding the street two stories beneath, and, beyond the patches of intervening roofs, a limited view of the Hudson River, a barge of coal passing leisurely up center stream, a tug suckling at its side.

From the hallway and in the act of mopping a margin of floor, a maid-of-all-work swung back from all-fours and sat upright on her heels, inserting a head of curl-papers through the open doorway.

"Play that over again, Miss Mae. That 'Mustard Glide' sure does tickle my soles."

Miss Munroe turned to the room with the palm of her hand placed pat against her brow. "God!" said she, "my head!"

"Aw, Miss Mae, can't you get yourself in a humor? What's the matter with you and me going to a movie this afternoon, eh?"

"Movie! The way every damn thing gets on my nerves, I'd be a hit at a movie, wouldn't I? I'd be a hit anywheres!"

"I tell you, Miss Mae, all this worry ain't going to get you nowheres. He'll come around again all right if you only give him time. And if he don't, you should worry! I tell you there ain't one of 'em breathes is worth more than his bank-book."

"God! my head!"

The figure on all-fours rose to full height, drying each forearm on her apron.

"Lay down, dearie, and just don't you worry. I've seen 'em get spells or get holy and stay away for two months on a stretch, and the checks not coming in regular as clockwork like yours, neither. Two months at a time I've seen 'em stick away. Whey, when I worked on the lower West Side they used to stick away two or three months like that and then come loafing in one night just like nothing hadn't happened. You ain't got no kick coming, Miss Mae."

A layer of tears rose immediately to Miss Munroe's eyes, dimming them. She wiped them away with one of her sleeve frills.

"Max ain't like that and you know it. You've seen for yourself how he 'ain't missed his every other night in three years. You seen for yourself."

"They're all alike, I tell you, Miss Mae. The best way to handle 'em is to leave 'em alone."

"How he's been falling off. Loo, all—"

"'Sh-h-h, now, Miss Mae, don't begin getting excited—all last night while I was rubbing your head that's what you kept mumbling and mumbling even after you fell asleep. That—don't help none."

"All last month so irregular and now only once last week, and—and not at all this week. Good heavens! I just wonder, I—just wonder."

"Now, just whatta you bet he'll be up to supper to-night, Miss Mae? If I was you, dearie, I wouldn't be scared, I'd just go right to the telephone and—"

"He gets so sore, Loo. You remember that time I telephoned him about that case of wine he sent up and it came busted, and his mother—his old woman was in the office. He raises hell if I try to telephone him during business."

"Just the same, I got a hunch he'll be up to supper to-night, and when I get a hunch things happen."

"It's his old woman, I tell you. It's his old woman is sniffing things again. Say, if he'd ever let me clap eyes on that old hag, wouldn't I learn her how to keep her nose out of his business alrighty. Wouldn't I just learn her! God! my head!"

"Lay down on the sofa, dearie, and rest up your red eyes. Take my tip he'll be up to supper to-night. I'm going to order him a double sirloin and a can of them imported—"

"Ugh! For Pete's sake cut it, Loo! If anybody mentions bill of fare to me I'll yell. Take them empty bottles out of here, Loo, and choke that damn clock with another pillow. My head'll just bust if I don't get some sleep."

"There, there, dearie! Here, lemme pull down the shades. Just try to remember there ain't one of them is worth more than his bank-book. I ain't going down to the dance with Sharkey to-night; I'm going to stay right here and—"

"No, no, Loo. You go. You can have that blue silk waist I promised you and wear them red satin roses he—he brought me that time from Hot Springs. Wear 'em, but be careful of 'em."

"Aw, Miss Mae, with you here like a wet rag, and if he comes who'll fix—"

"He—he ain't coming, Loo, and if he does I'm the one he likes to fix his things, anyway. I wanna be alone, Loo. I—I just wanna be alone."

"That's just it, Miss Mae, you're too much alone; you—"

"For Pete's sake, Loo, cut it or I'll holler. Cut the conversation, dearie!"

"I'll fix the candied sweet-potatoes this morning, anyway, Miss Mae, so if he does come—"

"I tell you I'm going to yell, Loo, if you mention bill of fare to me. Cover up my feet, like a good girl, and take them bottles out and lemme sleep. My head'll bust if I don't get some sleep."

"I tell you, Miss Mae, there ain't one of 'em is worth more than his bank-book. You're always giving away everything you got, Miss Mae. Honest, you'd give your best blue silk coat off your back if—"

"If that's what you're hinting for, Loo, for pity's sake take it! I don't want it. It's too tight for me in the arms. Take it, Loo. I don't want it. I don't want anything but to be let alone."

"Aw, now, Miss Mae, I didn't mean—"

"Get out, I tell you! Get out!"

"Yes, Miss Mae." With a final pat to the rug across Mae Munroe's feet she scooped the litter of empty bottles under one arm and hurried out smiling and closing the door softly behind her and tiptoeing down the hallway to the kitchen.

On the couch Mae Munroe lay huddled with her face to the wall, her cheeks crumpled against the white wool of the dog in her arms, her lips dry, each breath puffing them outward. Easy tears would flow, enhancing her lacy disorder. Noon slipped into afternoon.

The dusk of the city which is so immediately peppered with lights came gradually to press against the drawn blinds. On the very crest of her unrest, as if her mental travail had stimulated a cocaine courage, Mae Munroe kicked aside the rug from her feet; rose and advanced to the wall telephone; unhooked the receiver; hooked it up again; unhooked it this time with a resolution that tightened and whitened her lips and sent the color high into her face; placed her mouth close to the transmitter.

"Broad three-six." And tapped with one foot as she stood.

"Zincas Importing Company? I want to speak to Mr. Max Zincas."

Wrinkles crawled about her uncertain lips.

"This is his—his mother. Yes, Mrs. Zincas."

She closed her eyes as she waited.

"Hello, Max? That you, Max?"

She grasped at the snout of the instrument, tiptoeing up to it.

"It's me, dear. But—I had to get you to the 'phone somehow. I—I— No, no, don't hang up, Max! Don't hang up, dear, I—I got to tell you something; I got to, dear."

She raised herself closer to the mouthpiece for a tighter clutch of it.

"I'm sick, dearie. I—I'm dog sick, dearie. 'Ain't been about in a week. The limp is bad and I'm sick all over. I am, dear. Come up to supper to-night, dearie. You 'ain't been near for—for a week. I got to see you about something. Just a quiet talk, dearie. I—I just got to see you, Max. I—I'm sick, dog sick."

Her voice slipped up and away for the moment, and she crammed the lacy fribble of a handkerchief tight against her lips, tiptoeing closer to the transmitter.

"No, no, Max, I swear to God I won't! Just quiet and no rough stuff. For my sake come home to supper to-night, dearie! I swear. It's my thigh, and I got a fever, dearie, that's eating me. What? Eight! No, that ain't too late. Any time you can come ain't too late. I'll wait. Sure? Good-by, dearie. At eight sharp. Good-by, dearie."

When she replaced the receiver on its hook, points of light had come out in her eyes like water-lilies opening on a lake. The ashen sheaf of anxiety folded back from her, color ran up into her face, and she flung open the door, calling down the length of hallway.

"Loo! Oh, Loo!"

"Huh?"

"Put a couple of bottles of everything on ice before you go, dearie; order a double porterhouse; open a can of them imported sausages he sent up last month, and peel some sweet-potatoes. Hurry, Loo, I wanna candy 'em myself. Hurry, dearie!"

She snatched up her furry trifle of a dog, burying her warming face in his fleece.

"M-m-muvver loves her bow-wow. Muvver loves whole world. Muvver just loves whole world. M-m-m-m, chocolate? Just one ittsie bittsie piece and muvver eat half—m-m-m! La-la! Bow-wow! La! La!"

Along that end of Riverside Drive which is so far up that rents begin to come down, night takes on the aspect of an American Venetian carnival. Steamboats outlined in electric lights pass like phosphorescent phantoms up and down the Hudson River, which reflects with the blurry infidelity of moving waters light for light, deck for deck. Running strings of incandescent bulbs draped up into festoons every so often by equidistant arc-lights follow the course of the well-oiled driveway, which in turn follows the course of the river as truly as a path made by a canal horse. A ledge of park, narrow as a terrace, slants to the water's edge, and of summer nights lovers drag their benches into the shadow of trees and turn their backs to the lamp-posts and to the world.

From the far side of the river, against the night sky and like an ablutionary message let slip from heaven, a soap-factory spells out its product in terms of electric bulbs, and atop that same industrial palisade rises the dim outline of stack and kiln. Street-cars, reduced by distance to miniature, bob through the blackness. At nine o'clock of October evenings the Knickerbocker River Queen, spangled with light and full of pride, moves up-stream with her bow toward Albany. And from her window and over the waves of intervening roofs Mae Munroe cupped her hands blinker fashion about her eyes and followed its gay excursional passage, even caught a drift of music from its decks.

Motionless she stood there, bare-necked and bare-armed, against the cold window-pane, inclosed from behind with lace curtains and watching with large-pupiled eyes the steamer slip along into the night; the black-topped trees swaying in the ledge of park which slanted to the water's edge; the well-oiled driveway and its darting traffic of two low-sliding lines of motor-cars with acetylene eyes.

At five minutes past eight Max Zincas fitted his key into the door and entered immediately into the front room. On that first click of the lock Mae Munroe stepped out from between the lace curtains, her face carefully powdered and bleached of all its morning inaccuracies, her lips thrust upward and forward.

"Max!"

"Whew!"

He tossed his black derby hat to the red velvet couch and dropped down beside it, his knees far apart and straining his well-pressed trousers to capacity; placed a hand on each well-spread knee, then ran five fingers through his thinning hair; thrust his head well forward, foreshortening his face, and regarded her.

"Well, girl," he said, "here I am."

"I—I—"

"Lied to me, eh? Pretty spry for a sick one, eh? Pretty slick! I knew you was lying, girl."

"I been sick as a dog, Max. Loo can tell you."

"What's got you? Thigh?"

"God! I dun'no'! I dun'no'!"

She paused in the center of the room, her lips trembling and the light from the chandelier raining full upon her. High-hipped and full-busted as Titian loved to paint them, she stood there in a black lace gown draped loosely over a tight foundation of white silk, and trying to compose her lips and her throat, which arched and flexed, revealing the heart-beats of her and the shortness of her breath.

"Is this the way to say hello to—to your Maizie, Max? Is—is this the way?" Then she crossed and leaned to him, printing a kiss on his brow between the eyes. "I been sick as a dog, Max. Ain't you going to—to kiss me?"

"Come, come, now, just cut that, Mae. Let's have supper and get down to brass tacks. What's eating you?"

"Max!"

"Come, come, now, I'm tired, girl, and got to stop off at Lenox Avenue to-night after I leave here. Where's your clock around here, anyways, so a fellow knows where he's at?"

"There it is under the pillow next to you, Max. I smothered it because it gets on my nerves all day. Tick-tock, tick-tock, tick-tock, right into my head like it was saying all the time: 'Oh-Mae! Oh-Mae! Oh-Mae!' till I nearly go crazy, Max. Tick-tock—God! It—it just gets me!"

He reached for the small onyx clock, placing it upright on the mantel, and shrugged his shoulders loosely.

"Gad!" he said, "you wimmin! Crazy as loons, all of you and your kind. Come, come, get down to brass tacks, girl. I'm tired and gotta get home."

"Home, Max?"

"Yes, home!"

"Max, ain't—ain't this home no more, ain't it?"

He leaned forward, an elbow on each knee and striking his left hand solidly into his right palm. "Now if that's the line of talk you got me up here for, girl, you can cut it and cut it quick!"

"No, no, Max, it ain't my line of talk. Here, sit down, dearie, in your own chair and I'll go and dish up."

"Where's Loo?"

"Her night off, poor girl. Four nights straight she's rubbed my head and—"

"Where's my—"

"Right here, dearie, is your box of pills, underneath your napkin. There, dearie! See? Just like always."

She was full of small movements that were quick as grace notes: pinning the black lace train up and about her hips; drawing out his chair; darting with the scarcely perceptible limp down the narrow hall, back with dishes that exuded aromatic steam; placing them with deft, sure fingers. Once she paused in her haste, edged up to where he stood with one arm resting on the mantelpiece, placed an arm on each of his shoulders and let her hands dangle loose-wristed down his back.

"Tired boy, to-night? Huh? Maizie's poor tired boy!"

"Now, now!"

He removed her hands, but gently, and strolled over to where the table lay spread beside the cold, gilded radiator, a potted geranium in its center, a liberal display of showy imitation pearl-handled cutlery carefully laid out, and at each place a long-stemmed wineglass, gold-edged and the color of amber.

"Come," he said, "let's eat and get it over."

She made no sign, but with the corners of her lips propped bravely upward in her too red smile made a last hurried foray into the kitchen, returning with a covered vegetable-dish held outright from her.

"Guess!" she cried.

"Can't," he said, and seated himself.

"Gowan, guess like you used to, dearie."

He fell immediately to sampling with short, quick stabs of his fork the dish of carmine-red pickled beets beside his plate.

"Aw, gowan, Max, give a guess. What did you used to pay for with six big kisses every time I candied them for you? Guess, Max."

"Sit down," he said, and with his foot shoved a small stool before her chair.

"Lordy!" she said, drawing up en tête-à-tête, unpinning and spreading her lacy train in glory about her, "but you're some little sunbeam to have around the house."

"What these beets need is a little sugar."

She passed him the bowl; elevated her left foot in its slightly soiled white slipper to the footstool; fastened her napkin to her florid bosom with one of her numerous display of breastpins; poured some opaque wine into his glass, coming back to flood her own to the brim; smiled at him across the red head of the potted geranium, as if when the heart bleeds the heart grows light.

"Here's *to* you, Max!"

He raised his glass and drank in through his rather heavy mustache, then flecked it this way and that with his napkin. "Ahh-h-h-h, that's the stuff!"

"S'more?"

"Yah-h-h-h-h-h!"

"Such a cotton mouth my bad boy brought home."

"Aha! Fee, fie, fum! Aha!"

"I broiled it under the single burner, Max, slow like you like. Here, you carve it, dearie. Just like always, eh?"

His fleshy, blue-shaved face took on the tenseness of concentrated effort, and he cut deep into the oozing beef, the red juice running out in quick streams.

"Ah-h-h-h-h!"

"No, no, you keep that, Max; it's your rare piece."

"Gravy?"

"Yes, dearie."

The small dog shook himself and rose from sleep and the depths of a pillow, nosing at her bare elbow.

"Was muvver's ittsie Snookie Ookie such a hungry bow-wow?"

He yapped shortly, pawing her.

"Ask big bossie sitting over there carving his din-din if him got chocolate tandy in him pocket like always for Snookie Ookie. No, no, bad red meat no good for ittsie bittsie bow-wow. Go ask big bossie what him got this time in him pocket for Snookie. Aw, look at him, Max; he remembers how you used to bring him—"

"Get down! Get down, I said! For God's sake get that little red-eyed, mangy cur out of here while we're eating, can't you? Good gad! can't a man eat a meal in this joint without having that dirty cur whining around? Get him down off your dress there, Mae. Get out, you little cur! G-e-t out!"

"Max!"

"Chocolate candy in my pocket. Chocolate arsenic, you mean! My damnfool days are over."

"What's got you, Max? Didn't you buy him for me yourself that day at the races five whole years ago? Wasn't the first things you asked for, when you woke in the hospital with your burns, me and—and Snookie? What's soured you, Max? What? What?"

"I'm soured on seeing a strapping, healthy woman sniveling over a little sick-eyed cur. Ain't that enough to sour any man? Why don't you get up and out and exercise yourself like the right kind of wimmin do? Play tennis or get something in you besides the rotten air of this flat, and mewling over that sick-eyed cur. Get out! Scc-c-c-c-c!"

The animal bellied to the door, tail down, and into the rear darkness of the hallway.

"Max, what's got you? What do I know about tennis or—things like that? You—you never used to want—things like that."

"Aw, what's the use of wasting breath?"

He flecked at his mustache, inserting the napkin between the two top buttons of his slight bay of waistcoat; carved a second helping of meat, masticating with care and strength so that his temples, where the hair thinned and grayed, contracted and expanded with the movements of his jaws.

"What's the use?"

"Max, I—"

"Thigh bother you?"

"A—a little."

"Didn't I tell you not to spare expense on trying new doctors if—"

"That ain't my real trouble, Max; it—"

"Been out to-day?"

"No, Max, I been sick as a dog, I tell you."

"No wonder you're sick, cooped up in this flat with nobody but a servant-girl for company. Gad! Ain't you ashamed to get so low that your own servant-girl is your running-mate? Ain't you?"

"Max, she—"

"I know. I know."

"I been so blue, Max. Loo can tell you how I been waiting and wondering. I—Lord, I been so blue, Max. She's good to me, Max, and—and I been so blue."

"Never knew one of you wimmin that wasn't that way half her time. You're a gang of sob sisters, every one of you—whining like you got your foot caught in a machine and can't get it out."

"How you mean, Max?"

"Aw, you're all either in the blues or nagging. Why ain't you sports enough to take the slice of life you get handed you? None of you ain't healthy enough, anyways, I tell you, indoors, eating and sleeping and mewling over poodle-dogs all the time. I'm damn sick of it all. Damn sick, if you want to know it."

"But, Max, what's put this new stuff into your head all of a sudden? You never used to care if—"

"And you got to quit writing me them long-winded letters, Mae, about what's come over me. Sometimes a fellow just comes to his senses, that's all."

"Max!"

"And you got to quit butting in my business hours on the telephone. I don't want to get ugly, but you got to cut it out. Cut it out, Mae, is what I said!"

He quaffed his wine.

"Max dear, if you'll only tell me what's hurting you I'll find a way to make good. I—I can learn lawn-tennis, if that's what you want. I can take off ten pounds in—"

"Aw, I don't want nothing. Nothing, I tell you!"

"If I only knew, Max, what's itching you. This way there's days when I just feel like I can't go on living if you don't tell me what's got you. I just feel like I can't go on living this way, Max."

Tears hot and ever ready flowed over her words and she fumbled for her handkerchief, sobs rumbling up through her.

"I just can't, I—I just can't!"

He pushed back from his half-completed meal, rising, but stooping to rap his fist sharply against the table.

"Now, lemme tell you this much right now, Mae, either you got to cut this sob stuff and get down to brass tacks and tell me what you want, or, by gad! I'll get out of here so quick it'll make your head swim. I ain't going to be let in for no tragedy-queen stuff, and the sooner you know it the better. Business! I'm a business man."

She swallowed her tears, even smiling, and with her hand pat against her bosom as if to suppress its heaving.

"I'm all right now, Max. I'm so full up with worry it—it just slipped out. I'm all right now, Max. Sit down. Sit down and finish, dearie."

But he fell to pacing the red carpet in angry staccato strides. His napkin dropped from his waistcoat to the floor and he kicked it out of his path.

"By gad! I didn't want to come, anyhow. I knew the sniveling I'd be let in for. Gimme a healthy woman with some outdoors in her. Gimme—"

"I ain't going to let out any more, Max; I swear to God I ain't. Sit down, dear, and finish your supper. Looka, your coffee's all cold. Lemme go out and heat it up for you. I—"

"I'm done. I'm done before I even begin. Now, Mae, if you can behave yourself and hold in long enough, just say what you got me up here for, and for God's sake let's have it over!"

He planted himself before her, feet well apart, and she rose, pushing back her chair, paling.

"I—I 'ain't got much of anything to say, Max, except I—I thought maybe you'd tell me what's eating you, dearie."

"I—"

"After all these years we been together, Max, so—so happy, all of a sudden, dear, these last two months dropping off from every other night to—to twice a week and then to—to once, and this last week—not at all. I—I—heavens above, Max, I 'ain't got nothing to say except what's got you. Tell me, dearie, is it anything I've done? Is it—"

"You talk like a loon, Mae, honest you do. You 'ain't done nothing. It's just that the—the time's come, that's all. You know it had to. It always has to. If you don't know it, a woman like—like you ought to. Gad! I used to think you was the kind would break clean as a whistle when the time came to break."

"Break, Max?"

"Yes, break. And don't gimme the baby-stare like that, neither. You know what I mean alrighty. You wasn't born yesterday, old girl!"

The blood ran from her face, blanching it. "You mean, Max—"

"Aw, you know what I mean alrighty, Mae, only you ain't sport enough to take things as they come. You knew all these years it had to come sooner or later. I 'ain't never quizzed into your old life, but if you didn't learn that, you—well you ought to. There never was a New Year came in, Mae, that I didn't tell you that, if you got the chance, for you to go out after better business. I never stood in your light or made no bones about nothing!"

"My God! Max, you—you're kidding!"

"All these years I been preaching to you, even before I joined Forest Park Club out there. 'Don't get soft, Mae. Keep down. Use the dumb-bells. Hustle around and do a little housework even if I do give you a servant. Walk in the park. Keep your looks, girl; you may need 'em,' I used to tell you."

"Oh you— You!—"

She clapped her hands over her mouth as if to stanch hysteria.

"Another let-out like that, Mae, and, by gad! I'll take my hat and—"

"No, no, Max, I—I didn't mean it. I'm all right. I— Only after all these years you wouldn't do it, Max. You wouldn't. You wouldn't throw me over and leave me cold, Max. What can I do after all these years? I—I 'ain't got a show in a chorus no more. You're kidding, Max. You're a white man, Max, and—you—you wouldn't do it, Max. You wouldn't. You—"

"Now, now, you can't say I 'ain't been white as silk, girl, and I'm going to be just as white as I've been, too. Don't worry, girl. For six years there 'ain't been a better-stocked flat than this in town, has there?"

"No, Max."

"The best none too good, eh?"

"No, Max."

"Just the same stuff comes here that I send up to my mother's flat, eh? All the drinks and all the clothes you want and a servant in the house as good as my mother's own, eh? No kick coming, eh, girl?"

"You—you wouldn't, Max—you wouldn't ditch me. What could I do? Nothing—nothing. I—I can't hire out as a scrubwoman, I—"

"Come, come now, girl, you're pretty slick, but you—you don't quite slide. What about that thirty-five hundred you got down in your jeans—eh? Them thirty-five hundred in the Farmers' Savings Bank—eh? Eh?"

"Max!"

"Hah! Knocked you off your pins that time, didn't I? I found your bankbook one morning, kiddo—found it on the floor right next to the dresser—"

"Max, I— Out of my checks I—I saved—I—"

"Sure! Gad! I ain't kicking about it, girl. Glad for you! Glad you got it, girl, only don't try to tell me you can't take care of yourself in this world alrighty, girl. Any old time you can't! Gad! thirty-five hundred she snitches out of her allowance in six years, lives on the fat of the land, too, and then tries to bamboozle me that she's flat. Thirty-five hundred in six years. Gad! I got to hand it to you there, kiddo; I got to hand it to you!"

"You can have it back, Max. I—I was going to surprise you when I had five thousand. I—"

"Gad! I don't want your money, girl. It's yours. You're fixed for life on it. I'm even going to hand you over a couple of thou extra to show you that I'm no cheap sport. I won't have a woman breathing can say I ain't white as silk with her."

"Max, you—you're killing me! Killing me! Killing me!"

"Now, now, Mae, if I was you I wouldn't show my hand so. I don't want to hurt you, girl. It ain't like I got any but the finest feelings for you. You're all right, you are. You are."

"Then, Max, for God's sake—"

"But what are you going to do about it? What the hell is anybody going to do about it? You ain't no baby. You know what life is. And you know that the seams has got to show on one of the two sides and it ain't your fault you got turned on the under side. But you should worry, girl! You're fixed. And I'm here to tell you I'm going to hand you on top of the two thou this here little flat just as it stands, Mae. Just as it stands, piano and all. I just guess you got a kick coming!"

Her hands flew to her bosom as if the steel of his words had slipped deep into the flesh. "You don't mean what you're saying, Max."

"Sure, I do! Piano and all, girl."

"No, no, you don't. You're just kidding me, Max, like you used to when you wanted to tease me and throw a scare in me that your mother was wise about the flat. Quit your kidding, Max, and take me in your arms and sing me 'Maizie you're a Daisie' like you used to after—after we had a little row. Lemme hear you call me 'Maizie,' dear, so I know you're only kidding. I'm a bum sport, dearie. I—I never could stand for guying. Cut the comedy, dear.'

She leaned to him with her lips twisted and dried in their frenzy to belie his words, but with little else to indicate that her heart lay ticking against her breast like a clock that makes its hour in half-time.

"Quit guying, Max, for God's sake! You—you got me feeling sick clear down inside of me. Cut it, dear. Too much is enough."

Her dress rustled with the faint swish of scything as she moved toward him, and he withdrew, taking hold of the back of his chair.

"Now, now, Mae; come, come! You're a sensible woman. I ain't stuck on this business any more than you are. You ought to have let me stay away and just let it die instead of raking up things like this. Come, buck up, old girl! Don't make it any harder than it's got to be. These things happen every day. This is business. There, there! Now! Now!"

The sudden bout of tenderness brought the tears stinging to her eyes and she was for ingratiating herself into his embrace, but he withdrew, edging toward the piano with an entire flattening of tone.

"Now, now, Mae, I tell you that you got to cut it. It would have been better if you had just let the old cat die. You oughtn't to tried that gag to get me here to-night. You'll get a lot more out of me if you do it dry, girl. A crying woman can drive me out of the house quicker 'n plague, and you ought to know it by now."

She sat down suddenly, feeling queasy.

"Now, now, old girl, buck up! Be a sport!"

"Gimme a drink, Max. I— Just a swallow. I—I'm all right." And she squeezed her eyes tight shut to blink out the tears.

He handed her a tumbler from the table, keeping his head averted, and after a bit she fell to sobbing and choking and trembling.

"It's her! It's your old woman. She's been chloroforming you with a lot of dope talk about hitting the altar rail with a bunch of white satin with a good fat wad sewed in the lining. It's your old—"

"Cut that!"

"It's your old woman. She—she don't know you like I do, Max. She—"

"Now, now, Mae! You knew this had to come sooner or later. I 'ain't never lied, have I? Right here in this room 'ain't you told me a dozen times you'd let me go quietly when the time came? 'Ain't you?"

"I never thought you meant it, Max. You don't mean it now. Don't let your old woman upset you, dear. What she don't know won't hurt her. Stick around her a little more if you think she's got a hunch about me and the flat. But she 'ain't, dearie; there ain't a chance in the world she's got a hunch about me. Don't let her make a mollycoddle out of you, Max. That old woman don't know enough about life and things to—"

"You cut that and cut it quick! I'm a decent fellow, I am. For six years I been tipping you off to leave my mother's name out—out of your mouth. There's a place for everything and, by gad! your mouth ain't no place for her name! By gad! I ain't no saint, but I won't stand for that! By gad! I—I won't!"

"Oh-h-h-h-h! Oh-h-h-h! Oh-h-h!"

She struck her breast twice with the flat of her hand, her voice so tight and high that it carried with it the quality of strangulation.

"Ain't fit to mention her name, ain't I? Ain't fit to mention her name? My kind ain't fit to mention her name, eh?"

"No, if you got to know it. Not—like that! My old mother's name. Not like that!"

"Not fit, eh? What are we fit for, then, us that only get the husks of you men and nothing else?"

"I—"

"What am I fit for? Fit to run to when your decent friends won't stand in for you? Fit to run to when you get mixed up in rotten customs deals? Fit to stand between you and hell when you got the law snapping at your heels for—for smuggling? Who was fit to run to then? Her whose name I ain't fit to mention? Her? Naw, you was afraid she'd turn on you. Naw, not her! Me! Me! I'm the one whose mouth is too dirty to mention your old lady's name—"

"By gad! You got to cut that or—"

"Just the same, who was it you hollered for when you woke up in the hospital with your back like raw meat? Who was it you hollered for then? Her whose name I ain't fit to mention? Naw, it wasn't! Me! Me! I was good enough then. I was good enough to smuggle you out of town overnight when you was dodging the law, and to sleep in my clothes for two weeks, ready to give the signal."

"That's right, dig up! Dig up! You might forget something."

"I been good enough to give you free all these years what you wasn't man enough to pay for. That's what we women are; we're the free lunch that you men get with a glass of beer, and what the hell do you care which garbage-pail what's left of us lands in after you're done with us!"

"Cut that barroom talk around here if—"

"Good enough for six years, wasn't I, to lay down like a door-mat for you to walk on, eh? Good enough. Good enough when it came to giving up chunks of my own flesh and blood when your burns was like hell's fire on your back and all your old woman could do to help was throw a swoon every time she looked at you. Good enough to—"

"Gad! I knew it! I knew it! Knew you'd show your yellow streak."

She fell to moaning in her hands. "No, no, Max, I—"

"Bah! you can't throw that up to me, though. I never wanted it! I could have bought it off any one of them poor devils that hang around hospitals, as many inches off any one of 'em as I wanted. I never wanted them to graft it on me off you. I told the doctor I didn't. I knew you'd be throwing it up to me some day. If I'd bought it off a stranger I—I wouldn't have that limp in front of me always to—to rub things in. I knew you'd throw it up to me. I— Gad! I knew it! I knew it!"

"No, no, Max, I didn't mean it. You—you just got me so crazy I don't know what I'm saying. Sure, I—I made you take it off me. I wanted 'em to cut it off me to graft on your burns because it—it was like finding a new way of saying how—how I love you, Max. Every drop of blood was like—like I could see for myself how—how I loved you, Max. I—"

"Oh, my God!" he said, folded his arms atop the piano, and let his head fall into them. "Oh, my God!"

"That's how I love you, Max. That's how you—you're all in the world I got, Max. That's why I—I can't, just can't let you go, dear. Don't throw me over, Max. Cut the comedy and come down to earth. You 'ain't had a holy spell for two years now since the old woman sniffed me and wanted to marry you off to that cloak-and-suit buyer with ten thou in the bank and a rush of teeth to the front. You remember how we laffed, dearie, that night we seen her at the show? Don't let your old lady—"

"Cut that, I tell you!"

"You'd be a swell gink hitting the altar trail with a bunch of white satin, wouldn't you? At your time of life, forty and set in your ways, you'd have a swell time landing a young frisky one and trying to learn one of them mother's darlings how to rub in your hair-tonic and how to rub your salad-plate with garlic? Gosh-golly! I burst right out laffing when I even think about it! Come down to earth, Max! You'd be a swell hit welded for life with a gold band, now, wouldn't you?"

She was suddenly seized with immoderate laughter not untinctured with hysteria, loud and full of emptiness, as if she were shouting for echoes in a cave.

"Like hell you would! *You* tied to a bunch of satin and tending the kids with the whooping-cough! Whoops la, la!" She fell to rocking herself backward and forward, her rollicking laughter staining her face dark red.

"Whoops la, la! Whoops la, la!"

Suddenly Max Zincas rose to his height, regarding her sprawling uncontrolled pose with writhing lips of distaste, straightened his waistcoat, cleared his throat twice, and, standing, drank the last of his wine. But a pallor crept up, riding down the flush.

"Funny, ain't it? Laff! Laff! But I'd wait till you hear something funnier I got to tell you. Funny, ain't it? Laff! Laff!"

She looked up with her lips still sagging from merriment, but the dark red in her face darker.

"Huh?"

His bravado suddenly oozed and the clock ticked roundly into the silence between them.

"Huh?" she repeated, cocking her head.

"You got to know it, Mae, and the sooner I get it out of me the better. But, remember, if you wanna drive me out before I'm finished, if you wanna get rid of me a damn sight quicker than any other way, throw me some sob stuff and watch. You— Well— I— The sooner I get it out of me the better, Mae."

"Huh?"

"She's a—a nice little thing, Mae. Her mother's a crony with my old lady. Lives in a brownstone out on Lenox Avenue. Met her first at—at a tennis-match she was winning at—at Forest Park Club."

"Huh?"

"Not a high-stepper or a looker like you in your day, Mae, none of—that chorus pep you used to have. Neat, though. Great little kid for outdoors. Nice little shape, too. Not in your class, but—but neat. Eyes like yours, Mae, only not—not in your class. A—a little cast in one of them, but all to the good, Mae. Nice clean little—girl, fifteen thou with her, and her old man half owner in the Weeko Woolen Mills. I—I need the money, Mae. The customs is digging up dirt again. It ain't like I 'ain't been on the level with you, girl. You knew it had to come sooner or later. Now, didn't you, Mae? Now, there's the girl. Didn't you?"

Reassured, he crossed to where she sat silent, and placed a large, heavy hand on her shoulder.

"There's nothing needs to worry you, old girl. Thirty-five hundred in your jeans and a couple of thou and the flat from me on top. Gad! it's a cinch for you, old girl. I've seen 'em ready for the dump at your age, and you—you're on the boom yet. Gad! you're the only one I ever knew kept her looks and took on weight at the same time. You're all right, Mae, and— and, gad! if I don't wish sometimes the world was different! Gad! if—if I don't!"

And, rather reassured, he tilted her chin and pinched her cold cheek and touched the corner of his eyes with the back of his wrist.

"Gad, if—if I don't!"

It was as if the flood of her emotion had risen to a wave and at his words frozen on its crest. She opened her lips to speak, but could only regard him with eyes as hard as ice-fields.

"Now, now, Mae, don't look thataway. You're a sensible woman and know the world's just built thataway. I always told you it don't cost us men nothing but loose change to show ourselves a good time. You girls gotta pay up in different coin. If I hadn't come along some other fellow would, so what's the use a fellow not showing himself a good time? You girls know where you get off. Come, be a sport, old girl! With thirty-five hundred in your jeans and me wanting to do the square thing—the piano and all, lemme say to you that you 'ain't got a kick coming. Just lemme say that to you—piano and all, Mae!"

Sobs trembled up, thawing the edge of ice that incased her. A thin blur of tears rose to her eyes like a premonitory ripple before the coming of the wind.

"You can't! You can't! You—you can't ditch me like that, I tell you. You—"

"By God! If you're going to begin to holler I'll get out of here so quick it'll make your head swim!"

"Oh no, you don't! Aw, no, you don't! You ain't going to quit so easy for a squint-eyed little hank that—that your old woman found for you. Max, you ain't! You wouldn't! Tell me you wouldn't, dear. Tell me! Tell me!"

"Get off your knees there and behave yourself, Mae! Looka your dress there, all torn. This ain't no barroom. Get up and behave yourself! Ain't you ashamed! Ain't you ashamed!"

She was trembling so that her knees sent little ripples down the tight white silk drop-skirt.

"You can't ditch me like this and get away with it. You and me can't—can't part peaceful. You can't throw me over after all these years for a little squint-eyed hank and get away with it! By Heaven! you can't!"

He drew tight fists to his sides, his lower jaw shot forward. "You start a row here and, by gad! if I don't—"

"I ain't! I ain't! But don't throw me over, Max, after all these years! Don't, Max! You need me. There ain't a woman on God's earth will do for you what I will. I—I 'ain't got nobody but you, Max, to do for. I tell you, Max, you— you need me. Think, dear, all them months when the customs was after you. Them hot days when you couldn't show your face, and I used to put you to bed and fan and fan you eight hours straight till you forgot to be scared and fell asleep like a baby."

"Now, now, Mae, I—"

"Them nights we used to mix a few drinks when we came home from a show or something and sit right here in this room and swill 'em off, laffing and laffing till we got a little lit up. That time when we sneaked down to Sheepshead and you lost your wad at the wheel and I won it back for you. All them times, Max! That—that Christmas Eve you sneaked away from your old woman! Remember? I tell you, Max, you can't throw me away after what we been through together, and get away with it. You can't, not by a damn sight! You can't!"

In spite of herself her voice would slip up, raucous sobs tore through her words, tears rained down her frankly distorted face, carrying their bitter taste of salt to her lips.

"You can't! You can't! I 'ain't got the strength! I 'ain't got a thing in life that ain't wrapped around you. I can't go back to hit or miss like—like I could ten years ago. I 'ain't got nothing saved out of it all but you. Don't try to ditch me, Max! Don't! I—I'll walk on my knees for you. I—"

"For God's sake, Mae, I—"

"If there's a way to raise two times fifteen thou for you, Max, I—I'll raise it. I'll find a way, Max. I tell you I will! I'm lucky at the wheel, Max. You watch and see. You just watch and see. I can work. Max, I—"

"Get up, Mae, get up. There's a good girl. Get up and—"

"I'll work my fingers down, Max, only don't try to ditch me, don't try to ditch me! I'll go out to the country where your old woman can't ever sniff me. I—I'll fix it, Max, so you—so you just can't lose. Don't ditch me, dear; take your Maizie back. Take me in your arms and call me Maizie. Take me!"

"Girl, 'ain't you—'ain't you got no shame!"

"Just try me back for a month, Max. For a month, Max, and see if—if I don't fix things so they come out right. Gimme a month, Max! Gimme, Max! Gimme! Gimme!"

And with her last remnant of restraint gone, she lay downright at his feet, abandoned to virulent grief, and in her naked agony a shapeless mass of frill and flounce, a horrible and not dramatic spectacle of abandonment; decencies gone down before desire, the heart ruptured and broken through its walls. In such a moment of soul dishabille and her own dishabille of bosom bulging over the tight lacing of her corset-line as she lay prone, her mouth sagging and wet with tears, her lips blowing outward in bubbles, a picture, in fact, to gloss over, Mae Munroe dragged herself closer, flinging her arms about the knees of Mr. Zincas, sobbing through her raw throat.

"Just a month, Max! Don't ditch me! Don't! Don't! Don't!"

He looked away from the sorry spectacle of her bubbling lips and great, swollen eyelids.

"Leggo! Leggo my knees!"

"Just a month, Max, just—"

"Leggo! Leggo my knees! Leggo, girl! Ain't you ashamed!"

"Just a month, Max, I—"

"Gad! 'ain't you got no shame, girl! Get up! Leggo! I can't stand this, I tell you. Be a sport and leggo me quiet, Mae. I—I'll send you everything, a—a check that'll surprise you, old girl! Lemme go quiet! Nothing can't change things. Quit your blubbering. It makes me sick, I tell you. Quit your blubbering, old girl, and leggo. Leggo! Leg-go! Leg-go, I say!"

Suddenly he stooped and with a backward turn of her wrist unloosed himself and, while the pain still staggered her, side-stepped the huddle of her body, grasped his hat from the divan and lunged to the door, tugging for a frantic moment with the lock.

On her knees beside the piano, in quite the attitude he had flung her, leaning forward on one palm and amid the lacy whirl of her train, Mae Munroe listened to his retreating steps; heard the slam of a lower door.

You who recede before the sight of raw emotions with every delicacy shamed, do not turn from the spectacle of Mae Munroe prone there on the floor, her bosom upheaved and her mouth too loose. When the heart is torn the heart bleeds, whether under cover of culture and a boiled shirt-front or without shame and the wound laid bare. And Mae Munroe, who lay there, simple soul, only knew or cared that her heart lay quivering like a hurt thing, and for the sobs that bubbled too frankly to her lips had no concern.

But after a while they ceased of exhaustion, and she rose to her feet, her train threatening to throw her; walked toward the cold, cloyed dinner, half-eaten and unappetizing on the table; and fell to scooping some of the cold gravy up from its dish, letting it dripple from the spoon back again. The powder had long since washed off her cheeks and her face was cold as dough. The tears had dried around her mouth.

Presently she pinned up the lacy train about her, opened a cabinet door and slid into a dark, full-length coat, pinned on a hat with a feather that dropped over one side as if limp with wet, dabbed at her face with a pink powder-chamois and, wheezing ever so slightly, went out, tweaking off two of the three electric lights after her—down two flights of stairs through a quiet foyer and out into the fluid warmth of late October. Stars were out, myriads of them.

An hour she walked—down the cross-town street and a bit along the wide, bright, lighted driveway, its traffic long since died down to an occasional night-prowling cab, a skimming motor-car; then down a flight of curving stone steps with her slightly perceptible limp, and into the ledge of parkway where shadows took her into their velvet silence; down a second flight, across a railroad track, and to the water's edge, where a great coal-station ran a jut of pier out into the river. She could walk its length, feeling it sway to the heavy tug of current.

Out at the very edge the water washed up against the piles with a thick, inarticulate lisp, as if what it had to say might only be understood from the under side.

A Boob Spelled Backward

First Published: *Cosmopolitan,* April 1918
Reprinted: *Humoresque and Other Stories*, Harper & Bros., 1919

How difficult it is to think of great lives in terms of the small mosaics that go to make up the pattern of every man's day-by-day—the too tepid shaving-water; the badly laundered shirt-front; the three-minute egg; the too-short fourth leg of the table; the draught on the neck; the bad pen; the neighboring rooster; the misplaced key; the slipping chest-protector.

Richelieu, who walked with kings, presided always at the stitching of his red robes. Boswell says somewhere that a badly starched stock could kill his Johnson's morning. It was the hanging of his own chintzes that first swayed William Morris from epic mood to household utensils. Seneca, first in Latin in the whole Silver Age, prepared his own vegetables. There is no outgrowing the small moments of life, and to those lesser ones of us how often they become the large ones!

To Samuel Lipkind, who, in a span of thirty years, had created and carried probably more than his share of this world's responsibilities, there was no more predominant moment in all his day, even to the signing of checks and the six-o'-clock making of cash, than that matinal instant, just fifteen minutes before the stroke of seven, when Mrs. Lipkind, in a fuzzy gray wrapper the color of her eyes and hair, kissed him awake, and, from across the hall, he could hear the harsh sing of his bath in the drawing.

There are moments like that which never grow old. For the fifteen years that Samuel Lipkind had reached the Two Dollar Hat Store before his two clerks, he had awakened to that same kiss on his slightly open mouth, the gray hair and the ever-graying eyes close enough to be stroked, the pungency of coffee seeming to wind like wreaths of mundane aroma above the bed, and always across the aisle of hallway that tepid cataract leaping in glory into porcelain.

Take the particular morning which ushers in our story, although it might have been any of twelve times three hundred others.

"Sammy!" This upon opening his door, then crossing to close the conservative five inches of open window and over to the bedside for the kissing him awake. "Sammy, get up!"

The snuggle away into the crotch of his elbow.

"Sammy! *Thu, thu!* I can't get him up! Sammy, a quarter to seven! You want to be late? I can't get him up!"

"M-m-m-m-m-m!"

"You want your own clerks to beat you to business so they can say they got a lazy boss?"

"I'm awake, ma." Reaching up to stroke her hair, thin and gray now, and drawn back into an early-morning knob.

"Don't splash in the bath-room so this morning, Sammy; it's a shame for the wall-paper."

"I won't"—drawing the cord of his robe about his waist, and as if they did not both of them know just how faithfully disregarded would be that daily admonition.

Then Mrs. Lipkind flung back the snowy sheets and bed-coverings, baring the striped ticking of the mattress.

"Hurry, Sammy! I'm up so long I'm ready for my second cup of coffee."

"Two minutes." And off across the hall, whistling, towel across arm.

It was that little early moment sublimated by nothing more than the fusty beginnings of a workaday, the mere recollecting of which was one day to bring a wash of tears behind his eyes and a twist of anguish into his heart.

Next breakfast, and to dine within reach of the coal-range which brews it is so homely a fashion that even Mr. Lipkind, upon whom such matters of bad form lay as a matter of course, was wont to remonstrate.

"What's the matter with the dining-room, ma? Since when have dining-rooms gone out of style?"

Pouring his coffee from the speckled granite pot, Mrs. Lipkind would smile up and over it.

"All I ask is my son should never have it worse than to eat all his lifetime in just such a kitchen like mine. Off my kitchen floor I would rather eat than off some people's fine polished mahogany."

The mahogany was almost not far-fetched. There was a blue-and-white spick-and-spanness about Mrs. Lipkind's kitchen which must lie within the soul of the housewife who achieves it—the lace-edged shelves, the scoured armament of dishpan, soup-pot, and what not; the white Swiss window-curtains, so starchy, and the two regimental geraniums on the sill; the roller-towel too snowy for mortal hand to smudge; the white sink, hand-polished; the bland row of blue-and-white china jars spicily inscribed to nutmeg, cinnamon, and cloves. That such a kitchen could be within the tall and brick confines of an upper-Manhattan apartment-house was only another of the thousand thousand paradoxes over which the city spreads her glittering skirts. The street within roaring distance, the highway of Lenox Avenue flowing dizzily constantly past her windows, the interior of Mrs. Lipkind's apartment, from the chromos of the dear dead upon its walls to the upholstery of another decade against those walls, was as little of the day as if the sweep of the city were a gale across a mid-Victorian plain and the flow past the windows a broad river ruffled by wind.

"You're right, ma; there's not a kitchen in New York I'd trade it for. But what's the idea of paying rent on a dining-room?"

"Sa-y, if not for when Clara comes and how in America all young people got extravagant ideas, we was just as well off without one in our three rooms in Simpson Street."

"A little more of that mackerel, please."

You to whom the chilled grapefruit and the eggshell cup of morning coffee are a gastronomic feat not always easy to hurdle, raise not your digestive eyebrows. At precisely fifteen minutes past seven six mornings in the week, seven-thirty, Sundays, Mrs. Lipkind and her son sat down to a breakfast that was steamingly fit for those only who dwell in the headacheless kingdom of long, sleepful nights and fur-coatless tongues.

"A few more fried potatoes with it, Sammy?"

"Whoa! You want to feed me up for the fat boys' regiment!"

Mrs. Lipkind glanced quickly away, her profile seeming to quiver. "Don't use that word, Sam—even in fun—it's a knife in me."

"What word?"

"'Regiment.'"

He reached across to pat the vein-corduroyed back of her hand.

"My little sweetheart mamma," he said.

She, in turn, put out her hand over his, her old sagging throat visibly constricting in a gulp, and her eyes as if they could never be finished with yearning over him. "You're a good boy, Sammy."

"Sure!"

"I always say no matter what it is bad my life has had for me with my twenty-five years a widow, my only daughter to marry out six hundred miles away from me, my business troubles when I had to lose the little store what your papa left me, nothing ain't nothing, Sammy, when a mother can raise for herself a boy like mine."

"You mean when a fellow can pick out for himself a little sweetheart mamma like mine."

"Sammy, stop it with your pinching-me nonsense like I was your best girl!"

"Well, ain't you?"

She paused, her cup of coffee half-way to her lips, the lines on her face seeming to want to lift into what would be a smile. "No, Sammy; your mother knows she ain't, and if she was anything but a selfish old woman, she would be glad that she ain't."

"'Sh! 'Sh!" said Mr. Lipkind, reaching this time half across the table for a still steaming muffin and opening it so that its hot fragrance came out. "'Sh! No April showers! Uh! Uh! Don't you dare!"

"I ain't," said Mrs. Lipkind, smiling through her tear and dashing at it with the back of her hand. "For why should I when I got only everything to be thankful for?"

"Now you're shouting!"

"How you think, Sammy, Clara likes a cheese pie for supper to-night? Last week I could see she didn't care much for the noodle pudding I baked her."

Mr. Lipkind, who was ever so slightly and prematurely bald and still more slightly and prematurely rotund, suffered a rush of color then, his ears suddenly and redly conspicuous.

"That's—that's what I started to tell you last night, ma. Clara telephoned over to the store in the afternoon she—she thought she wouldn't come to supper this Wednesday night, ma."

"Sammy—you—you and Clara 'ain't got nothing wrong together, the way you don't see each other so much these two months?"

"Of course not, ma; it's just happened a few times that way. The trade's in town; that's all."

"How is it all of a sudden a girl in the wholesale ribbon business should have the trade to entertain like she was in the cloak-and-suit chorus?"

"It's not that Clara's busy to-night, ma. She—she only thought she—for a change—there's a little side table for two—for three—where she boards—she thought maybe if—if you didn't mind, I'd go over to her place for Wednesday-night supper for a change. You know how a girl like Clara gets to feeling obligated."

"Obligated from eating once a week supper in her own future house!"

"She asked I should bring you, too, ma, but I know how bashful you are to go in places like that."

"In such a place where it's all style and no food—yes."

"That's it; so we—I thought, ma, that is, if you don't mind, instead of Clara here to-night for supper, I—I'd go over to her place. If you don't mind, ma."

There was a silence, so light, so slight that it would not have even held the dropping of a pin, but yet had a depth and a quality that set them both to breathing faster.

"Why, of course, Sammy, you should go!"

"I—we thought for a change."

"You should have told me yesterday, Sammy, before I marketed poultry."

"I know, ma; I—just didn't. Clara only 'phoned at four."

"A few more fried potatoes?"

"No more."

"Sit up straight, Sam, from out your round shoulders."

"You ain't—mad, ma?"

"For why, Sammy, should I be mad that you go to Clara for a change to supper. I'm glad if you get a change."

"It's not that, ma. It's just that she asked it. You know how a person feels, her taking her Wednesday-night suppers here for more than five years and never once have I—we—set foot in any of her boarding-houses. She imagines she's obligated. You know how Clara is, so independent."

"You should go. I hear, too, how Mrs. Schulem sets a good table."

"I'll be home by nine, ma—you sure you don't mind?"

"I wouldn't mind, Sammy, if it was twelve. Since when is it that a grown-up son has to apologize to his mother if he takes a step without her?"

"You can believe me, ma, but I've got it so it don't seem like theater or nothing seems like going out without my little sweetheart mamma on one arm and Clara on the other."

"It's not right, Sammy, you should spoil me so. Don't think that even if you don't let me talk about it, I don't know in my heart how I'm in yours and Clara's way."

"Ma, now just you start that talk and you know what I'll do—I'll get up and leave the table."

"Sammy, if only you would let me talk about it!"

"You heard what I said."

"To think my son should have to wait with his engagement for five years and never once let his mother ask him why it is he waits. It ain't because of to-night I want to talk about it, Sam, but if I thought it was me that had stood between you and Clara all these five years, if—if I thought it was because of me you don't see each other so much here lately, I—"

"Ma!"

"I couldn't stand it, son. If ever a boy deserved happiness, that boy is you. A boy that scraped his fingers to the bone to marry his sister off well. A boy that took the few dollars left from my notion-store and made such a success in retail men's hats and has given it to his mother like a queen. If I thought I was standing in such a boy's way, who ain't only a grand business man and a grand son and brother, but would make any girl the grandest husband that only his father before him could equal, I couldn't live, Sammy, I couldn't live."

"You should know how sick such talk makes me!"

"I haven't got hard feelings, Sammy, because Clara don't like it here."

"She does."

"For why should an up-to-date American girl like Clara like such an old-fashioned place as I keep? Nowadays, girls got different ideas. They don't think nothing of seventy-five dollar suits and twelve-dollar shoes. I can't help it that it goes against my grain no matter how fine a money-maker a girl is. In the old country my sister Carrie and me never even had shoes on our feet until we were twelve, much less—"

"But, ma—"

"Oh, I don't blame her, Sam. I don't blame her that she don't like it the way I dish up everything on the table so we can serve ourselves. She likes it passed the way they did that night at Mrs. Goldfinger's new daughter-in-law's, where everything is carried from one to the next one, and you got to help yourself quick over your shoulders."

"Clara's like me, ma; she wants you to keep a servant to do the waiting on you."

"It ain't in me, Sam, to be bossed to by a servant, just like I can't take down off the walls pictures of your papa *selig* and your grandma, because it ain't stylish they should be there. It's a feeling in me for my own flesh and blood that nothing can change."

"Clara don't want you to change that, ma."

"She's a fine, up-to-date girl, Sam. A girl that can work herself up to head floor-lady in wholesale ribbons and forty dollars a week has got in her the kind of smartness my boy should have in his wife. I'm an old woman standing in the way of my boy. If I wasn't, I could go out to Marietta, Ohio, by Ruby, and I wouldn't keep having inside of me such terrible fears for my boy and—and how things are now on the other side and—and—"

"Now, now, ma; no April showers!"

"An old woman that can't even be happy with a good daughter like Ruby, but hangs always on her son like a stone around his neck!"

"You mean like a diamond."

"A stone, holding him down."

"Ma!" Mr. Lipkind pushed back, napkin awry at his throat and his eyes snapping points of light. "Now if you want to spoil my breakfast, just say so and I—I'll quit. Why should you be living with Ruby out in Marietta if you're happier here with me where you belong? If you knew how sore these here fits of yours make me, you'd cut them out—that's what you would. I'm not going over to Clara's at all now for supper, if that's how you feel about it."

Mrs. Lipkind rose then, crossed, leaning over the back of his chair and inclosing his face in the quivering hold of her two hands. "Sammy, Sammy, I didn't mean it! I know I ain't in your way. How can I be when there ain't a day passes I don't invite you to get married and come here to live and fix the flat any way what Clara wants or even move downtown in a finer one where she likes it? I know I ain't in your way, son. I take it back."

"Well, that's more like it."

"You mustn't be mad at mamma when she gets old-fashioned ideas in her head."

He stroked her hand at his cheek, pressing it closer.

"Sit down and finish your breakfast, little sweetheart mamma."

"Is it all right now, Sammy?"

"Of course it is!" he said, his eyes squeezed tightly shut.

"Promise mamma you'll go over by Clara's to-night."

"But—"

"Promise me, Sammy; I can't stand it if you don't."

"Alright, I'll go, ma."

The Declaration of Economic Independence is not always a subtle one. There was that about Clara Bloom, even to the rather Hellenic swing of her very tailor-made back and the firm, neat clack of her not too high heels, which proclaimed that a new century had filed her fetter-free from the nineteen-centuries-long chain of women whose pin-money had too often been blood-money or the filched shekels from trousers pocket or what in the toga corresponded thereto.

And yet, when Miss Bloom smiled, which upon occasion she did spontaneously enough to show a gold molar, there were not only Hypatia and Portia in the straight line of her lips, but lurked in the little tip-tilt at the corners a quirk from Psyche, who loved and was so loved, and in the dimple in her chin a manhole, as it were, for Mr. Samuel Lipkind.

At six o'clock, when the wintry workaday flows into dusk and Fifth Avenue flows across Broadway, they met, these two, finding each other out in the gaseous shelter of a Subway kiosk. She from the tall, thin, skylight-less skyscraper dedicated to the wholesale supply of woman's insatiable demand for the ribbon gewgaw; he from a plate-glass shop with his name inscribed across its front and more humbly given over to the more satiable demand of the male for the two-dollar hat. There was a gold-and-black sign which ran across the not inconsiderable width of Mr. Lipkind's storefront and which invariably captioned his four inches of Sunday-newspaper advertisement:

SAMMY LIPKIND WANTS YOUR HEAD

As near as it is possible for the eye to simulate the heart, there was exactly that sentiment in his glance now as he found out Miss Bloom, she in a purple-felt hat and the black scallops of escaping hair, blacker because the red was out in her cheeks.

He broke into the kind of smile that lifted his every feature, screw-lines at his eyes coming out, head bared, and his greeting beginning to come even before she was within hearing distance of it.

There was in Mr. Lipkind precious little of Lothario, Launcelot, Galahad, or any of that blankety-blank-verse coterie. There remains yet unsung the lay of the five-foot-five, slightly bald, and ever so rotund lover. Falstaff and Romeo are the extremes of what Mr. Lipkind was the not unhappy medium. Offhand in public places, men would swap crop conditions and city politics with him. Twice, tired mothers in railway stations had volunteered him their babies to dandle. Young women, however, were not all impervious to him, and uncrossed their feet and became consciously unconscious of him across street-car aisles. In his very Two Dollar Hat Store, Sara Minniesinger, hooked of profile, but who had impeccably kept his debts and credits for twelve years back under the stock-balcony and a green eye-shade, was wont to cry of evenings over and for him into her dingy pillow. He was so unconscious of this that, on the twelfth anniversary of her incarceration beneath the stock-balcony, he commissioned his mother to shop her a crown of thorns in the form of a gold-handled umbrella with a bachelor-girl flash-light attachment.

There are men like that, to whom life is not only a theosophy of one God, but of one woman who is sufficient thereof. When Samuel Lipkind greeted Clara Bloom there was just that in his ardently appraising glance.

"Didn't mean to keep you waiting, Clara—a last-minute customer. *You* know."

"I've been counting red heads and wishing the Subway was pulled by white horses."

"Say, Clara, but you look a picture! Believe me, Bettina, that is some lid!"

Miss Bloom tucked up a rear strand of curl, turning her head to extreme profile for his more complete approval.

"Is it an elegant trifle, Sam? I ask you is it an elegant trifle?"

"Clara, it's—immense! The best yet! What did it set you back?"

"Don't ask me! I'm afraid just saying it would give your mother heart-failure by mental telepathy."

He linked her arm. "Whatever you paid, it's worth the money. It sets you off like a gipsy queen."

"None of that, Sam! Mush is fattening."

"Mush nothing! It's the truth."

"Hurry. Schulem's got a new rule—no reserving the guest-table."

They let themselves be swept into the great surge of the underground river with all of the rather thick-skinned unsensitiveness to shoulder-to-shoulder contact which the Subway engenders. Swaying from straps in a locked train, which tore like a shriek through a tube whose sides sweated dampness, they talked in voices trained to compete with the roar.

"What's the idea, Clara? When you telephoned yesterday I was afraid maybe it was—Eddie Leonard cutting in on my night again."

"Eddie nothing. Is it a law, Sam, that I have to eat off your mother every Wednesday night of my life?"

"No—only—you know how it is when you get used to things one way."

"I told you I had something to talk over, didn't I?"

They were rounding a curve now, so that they swayed face to face, nose to nose.

A few crinkles, frequent with him of late, came out in rays from his eyes.

"Is it anything you—you couldn't say in front of ma?"

"Yes."

He inserted two fingers into his collar, rearing back his head.

"Anything wrong, Clara?"

"You mean is anything right."

They rode in silence after that, both of them reading in three colors the border effulgencies of frenzied advertising.

But when they emerged to a quieter up-town night that was already pointed with a first star, he took her arm as they turned off into a side-street that was architecturally a barracks to the eye, brownstone front after brownstone front after brownstone front. Block after block of New York's side-streets are sunk thus in brown study.

"You mustn't be so ready to be put out over every little thing I say, Clara. Is it anything wrong to want you up at the house just as often as we can get you?"

"No, Sam; it ain't that."

"Well then, what is it?"

"Oh, what's the use beginning all that again? I want to begin to-night where we usually leave off."

"Is it—is it something we've talked about before, Clara?"

"Yes—and no. We've talked so much and so long without ever getting anywheres—what's the difference whether we've ever talked it before or not?"

"You just wait, Clara; everything is going to come out fine for us."

Her upper lip lifted slightly. "Yes," she said; "I've heard that before."

"We're going to be mighty happy some day, just the same, and don't you let yourself forget it. We've got good times ahead."

"Oh dear!" she sighed out.

"What?"

"Nothing."

He patted her arm. "You'll never know, Clara, the torture it's been for me even your going out those few times with Eddie Leonard has put me through. You're mine, Clara; a hundred Eddies couldn't change that."

"Who said anybody wanted to change it?"

He patted her arm again very closely. "You're a wonderful girl, Clara."

They turned up the stoop of Mrs. Schulem's boarding-house, strictly first-class. How they flourish in the city, these institutions of the Not Yet, the Never Was, the Never Will Be, and the Has Been! They are the half-way houses going up and the mausoleums coming down life's incline, and he who lingers is lost to the drab destiny of this or that third-floor-back hearth-stone, hot and cold running water, all the comforts of home. That is why, even as she moved up from the rooming- to the boarding-house and down from the third-floor back to the second-story front, there was always under Clara Bloom's single bed the steamer-trunk scarcely unpacked, and in her heart the fear that, after all, this might not be transiency, but home. That is why, too, she paid her board by the week and used printed visiting-cards.

And yet, if there exists such a paradox as an aristocracy among boarding-houses, Mrs. Schulem's was of it. None of the boiled odors lay on her hall-ways, which were not papered, but a cream-colored fresco of better days. There was only one pair of bisques, no folding-bed, and but the slightest touch of dried grasses in her unpartitioned front parlor. The slavey who opened the door was black-faced, white-coated, and his bedraggled skirts were trousers with a line of braid up each seam. Two more of him were also genii of the basement dining-hall, two low rooms made into one and entirely bisected by a long-stemmed T of dining-table, and between the lace-curtained windows a small table for two, with fairly snowy napkins flowering out of its water-tumblers, and in its center a small island of pressed-glass vinegar-cruet, bottle of darkly portentous condiment, glass of sugar, and another of teaspoons.

It was here that Miss Bloom and Mr. Lipkind finally settled themselves, snugly and sufficiently removed from the T-shaped battalion of eyes and ears to insure some privacy.

"Well," said Mr. Lipkind, unflowering his napkin, spreading it across his knees, and exhaling, "this is fine!"

There was an aura of authoritativeness seemed to settle over Miss Bloom.

This to one of the black-faced genii. "Take care of us right to-night, Johnson, and I'll fix it up with you. See if you can't manage it in the kitchen to bring us a double portion of those banana fritters I see they're eating at the big table. Say they're for Miss Bloom. I'll fix it up with you."

"Now, Clara, don't you go bothering with extras for me. This is certainly fine. Sorry you never asked me before."

"You know why I never asked you before."

"Why, you never saw the like how pleased ma was. She was the first one to fall in with the idea of my coming to-night."

She dipped into a shallow plate of amber soup. "I know," she said, "all about that."

"Ma's a good sport about being left at home alone."

"How do you know? You never tried it until to-night. I bet it's the first time since that night you first met me, five years ago, at Jerome Fertig's, and it wouldn't have been then if she hadn't had the neuralgia and it was your own clerk's wedding."

He laid down his spoon, settling back a bit from the table, pulling the napkin across his knees out into a string.

"I thought we'd gone all over that, Clara."

"Yes; but where did it get us? That's why we're here to-night, Sam—to get somewheres."

He crumbed his bread. "What do you mean, Clara?"

She forced his slow gaze to hers calmly, her hands outstretched on the table between them. "I've made up my mind, Sam. Things can't go on this way no longer between us."

"Just what do you mean by that?"

"I mean that we've either got to act or quit."

He was rolling the bread pills again, a flush rising. "You know where I stand, Clara, on things between us."

"Yes, Sam, and now you know where I stand." The din of the dining-room surged over the pause between them. Still in the purple hat, and her wrap thrown back over her chair, she held that pause coolly, level of eye. "I'm thirty-one now, Sam, three weeks and two days older than you. I don't see the rest of my days with the Arnstein Ribbon Company. I'm not getting any younger. Five years is a long time out of a girl's life. Five of the best ones, too. She likes to begin to see her future when she reaches my age. A future with a good providing man. You and me are just where we started five years ago."

"I know, Clara, and I'd give my right hand to change things."

"If I'd been able to save a cent, it might be different. But I haven't—I'm that way. I make big and spend big. But you can't blame a girl for wanting to see her future. That's me, and I'm not ashamed to say it."

"If only, Clara, I could get you to see things my way. If you'd be willing to try it with ma. Why, with a little diplomacy from you, ma'd move heaven and earth to please you."

"There's no use beginning that, Sam; it's a waste of time. Why—why, just the difference in the way me and—and your mother feel on money matters is enough. There's no use to argue that with me; it's a waste of time."

He lifted and let droop his shoulders with something of helplessness in the gesture. "What's the use, then? I'm sure I don't know what more to say to you, Clara. Oh, don't think my mother don't realize how things are between us—it's all I can do to keep denying and denying."

"Well, you can't say she knows from my telling."

"No; but there's not a day she don't say to me, particularly these last few times since you been breaking your dates with us pretty regular—I—well she sees how it worries me, and there's not a day she don't say to me, 'Sammy,' she said to me, only this morning, 'if I thought I was keeping you and Clara apart—'"

"A blind man could see it."

"There's not a day passes over her head she don't offer to go live with my sister in Ohio, when I know just how that one month of visiting her that time nearly killed her."

"Funny visiting an own daughter could nearly kill anybody."

"It's my brother-in-law, Clara. My mother couldn't no more live with Isadore Katz than she could fly. He's a fine fellow and all that, but she's not used to a man in the house that potters around the kitchen and the children's food and things like Isadore loves to. She's used to her own little home and her own little way."

"Exactly."

"If I want to kill my mother, Clara, all I got to do is put her away from me in her old age. Even my sister knows it. 'Sammy,' she wrote to me that time after ma's visit out there, 'I love our mother like you do, but I got a nervous husband who likes his own ways about the housekeeping and the children and the cooking, and nobody knows better than me that the place for ma to be happy is with you in her own home and her own ways of doing.'"

"I call that a nerve for a sister to let herself out like that."

"It's not nerve, Clara; it's the truth. Ruby's a good girl in her way."

"What about you—ain't your life to be thought of? Ain't it enough she was married off with enough money for her husband to buy a half-interest in a ladies' ready-to-wear store out there?"

"Why, if I was to bring my little wife to that flat of ours, Clara, or any other kind further down-town that she'd want to pick out for herself, I think my mother would just walk on her hands and knees to make things pleasant for her. Maybe you don't know it, but on your Wednesday nights up at the house, she is up at five o'clock in the morning fixing around and cooking the things she thinks you'll like."

"I'm not saying a word against your mother, Sam. I think she's a grand woman, and I admire a fellow that's good to his mother. I always say, 'Give me a fellow every time that is good to his mother and that fellow will be good to his wife.'"

"I'm not pretending to say ma mayn't be a little peculiar in her ways, but you never saw an old person that wasn't, did you? Neither am I saying it's exactly any girl's idea to start out married life with a third person in—"

"I've always swore to myself, Sam, and I'm not ashamed to admit it, that if I can't marry to improve myself, I'm going to stay single till I can. I'm not a six-dollar-a-week stenog that has to marry for enough to eat. I can afford to buy a seventy-five dollar suit every winter of my life and twelve-dollar shoes every time I need them. The hat on my head cost me eighteen-fifty wholesale, without having to be beholding to nobody, and—"

"Ma don't mean those things, Clara. It's just when she hears the price girls pay for things nowadays she can't help being surprised the way things have changed."

"I'm not a small potato, Sam. I never could live like a small potato."

"Why, you know there's nothing I like better than to see you dressed in the best that money can buy. You heard what I said about that hat just now, didn't you? Whatever it cost, it's worth it. I can afford to dress my little wife in the best that comes. There's nothing too good for her."

"Yes; but—"

"All ma needs, Clara, is a little humoring. She's had to stint so all her life, it's a little hard to get her used to a little prosperity. Take me. Why, if I bring her home a little shawl or a pockabook that cost, say, ten dollars, you think I tell her? No. I say, 'Here's a bargain I picked up for three ninety-eight,' and right away she's happy with something reduced."

"Your mother and me, Sam, and mind you, I'm not saying she isn't a grand old lady, wasn't no more made to live together than we was made to fly. I couldn't no more live her way than she could live mine. I've got a practical head on my shoulders—I don't deny it—and I want to improve ourselves in this world when we marry, and have an up-to-date home like every young couple that starts out nowadays."

"Sure, we—"

"That flat of yours up there or any other one under the conditions would be run like the ark. I'm an up-to-date girl, I am. There's not a girl living would be willing to marry a well-off fellow like you and go huck herself in a place she couldn't even have the running of herself or have her own say-so about the purse-strings. It may sound unbecoming, but when I marry I'm going to better myself, I am."

"I—why—"

"If she can't even stand for her own son-in-law walking into his own kitchen in his own house—Oh, you don't find me starting my married life that way at this late date. I haven't held off five years for that."

Mr. Lipkind pushed back his but slightly tasted food, lines of strain and a certain whiteness out in his face. "It—it just seems awful, Clara, this going around in a circle and not getting anywheres."

"I'm at the end of my rope, I am."

"I see your point in a way, Clara, but, my God! A man's mother is his mother! It's eating up my life just as it's eating yours, but what you going to do about it? It just seems the best years of our life are going, waiting for God knows what."

Hands clasped until her finger-nails whitened, Miss Bloom leaned across the table, her voice careful and concentrated. "Now you said something! That's why you and me are here alone together to-night. There's not going to be a sixth year of this kind of waiting between us. Things have got to come to a head. I've got a chance, Sam, to marry. Eddie Leonard has asked me."

"I—thought so."

"Eddie Leonard ain't a Sam Lipkind, but after the war his five-thousand-dollar job is down at Arnstein's waiting for him, and he's got a good stiff bank-account saved as good as yours and—and no strings to it. I believe in a girl facing those facts the same as any other facts. Why, I—this war and all—why if anything was to happen to you to-morrow—us unmarried this way—I'd be left high and dry without so much as a penny to show for the best five years of my life. We've got to do one thing or another, Sam. I believe in a girl being practical as well as romantic."

"I—see your point, Clara."

"I'm done with going around in this circle of ours."

"You mean—"

"You know what I mean."

The lower half of Mr. Lipkind's face seemed to lock, as it were, into a kind of rigidity which shot out his lower jaw. "I'll see Eddie Leonard burning like brimstone before I let him have you!"

"Well?"

"God! I don't know what to say—I don't know what to say!"

"That's your trouble, Sam; you're so chickenhearted you—"

"My father died when I was five, Clara, and no matter what my feelings are to you, there's no power on earth can make me quit having to be him as well as a son to my mother. Maybe it sounds softy to you—but if I got to pay with her happiness for—ours—then I never want happiness to the day I die."

"In other words, it's the mother first."

"Don't put it that way—it's her—age—first. It ain't what she wants and don't want; it's what she's got to have. My mother couldn't live away from me."

"She could if you were called to war."

There was something electric in the silence that followed, something that seemed to tighten the gaze of each for the other.

"But I haven't been—yet."

"The next draft will get you."

"Maybe."

"Well, what'll you do then?"

"That's something me and ma haven't ever discussed. The war hasn't been mentioned in our house for two years—except that the letters don't come from Germany, and that's a grief to her. There's enough time for her to cross that bridge when we come to it. She worries about it enough."

"If I was a man I'd enlist, I would!"

"I'd give my right hand to. Every other night I dream I'm a lieutenant."

"Why, there's not a fellow I know that hasn't beaten the draft to it and enlisted for the kind of service he wants. I know a half a dozen who have got in the home guard and things and have saved themselves by volunteering from being sent to France."

"I wouldn't dodge the front thataway. I'd like to enlist as a private and then work myself up to lieutenant and then on up to captain and get right into the fray on the front. I—"

"You bet, if I was a fellow, I'd enlist for the kind of home service I wanted—that's what Eddie and all the fellows are doing."

"So would I, Clara, if I was what you call a—free man. There's nobody given it more thought than me."

"Well, then, why don't you? Talk's cheap."

"You know why, Clara, to get back to going around in a circle again."

"But you've got to go, sooner or later. You've got a comfortable married sister and independent circumstances of your own to keep your mother; you haven't got a chance for exemption."

"I don't want exemption."

"Well, then, beat the draft to it."

"I— Most girls ain't so anxious to—to get rid of their best fellows, Clara."

"Silly! Can't you see the point? If—if you'd enlist and go off to camp, I—I could go and live near you there like Birdie Harberger does her husband. See?"

"You mean—"

"Then—God forbid anything should happen to you!—I'm your wife. You see, Sam?"

"Why, Clara—"

"You see what I mean. But nothing can happen this way, because if you try to enlist in some mechanical department where they need you in the country—you see, Sam? See?"

"I—see."

"Your mother would have to get used to things then, Sam—it would be the easiest for her. An old lady like her couldn't go trailing around the outskirts of a camp like your wife could. Think of the comfort it'll be to her to have me with you if she can't be. She'll get so used to—living—alone—"

"I— You mustn't talk that way to me, Clara. When I'm called to serve my country, I'm the first one that will want to go. I've given more money already than I can afford to help the boys who are at the front. So far as I'm concerned, enlisting like this with—with you—around, would be the happiest thing ever happened to me, but—well, you see for yourself."

"You mean, then, you won't?"

"I mean, Clara, I can't."

She was immediately level of tone again and pushed back, placing her folded napkin beside her place, patting it down.

"Well, then, Sam, I'm done."

"'Done,' Clara?"

"Yep. That lets me out. I've given you every chance to make this thing possible. Your mother is no better and no different than thousands and thousands of other mothers who are giving their sons, only, she is better off than most, because she's provided for. It's all right for a fellow's mother to come first, maybe, but if his wife isn't even to come second or third or tenth, then it's about time to call quits. I haven't made up my mind to this in a day. I'm done."

"Clara—"

"Ed has asked me. I don't pretend he's my ideal, but he's more concerned about my future than he is about anybody else's. If I'm ready to leave with him on that twelve-o'clock train for Boston to-morrow, where he's going to be put in the clerical corps at Camp Usonis, we'll be married there to-morrow night, and I'll settle down somewhere near camp as long as I can. He's got a good nest-egg if—God forbid!—anything should happen. That's the whole thing in a nutshell."

"My God! Clara, this is awful! Eddie Leonard he's not your kind; he—"

"I've given you first chance, Sam. That proves how you stand with me. A one! Ace high! First! Nobody can ever take your place with me. Don't be a boob coming and going, Sam; you're one now not to see things and you'll be another one spelled backward if you don't help yourself to your chance when it comes. You've got your life in front of you, and your mother's got hers in back of her. Now choose."

"My God! Clara, this is—terrible! Why—I'd rather be a thousand boobs than take my mother's heart and tear it to pieces."

"You won't?"

"I can't."

"Don't say that, Sam. Go home and—sleep on it. Think it over. Please! Come to your senses, honey. Telephone me at eleven to keep me from catching that twelve-o'clock train. Don't let me take it with Eddie. Think it over, Sam. Honey—our—future—don't throw it away! Don't let me take that twelve-o'clock train!"

There were tears streaming from her eyes, and her lips, so carefully firm, were beginning to tremble. "You can't blame a girl, Sam, for wanting to provide for her future. Can you, Sam? Think it over. Please! I'll be praying when eleven o'clock comes to-morrow morning for you to telephone me. Please, Sam—think!"

He dropped his face low, lower toward the table, trembling under the red wave that surged over him and up into the roots of his hair. "I'll think it over, Clara—my girl—my own girl!"

As if the moments themselves had been woven by her flying amber needles into a whole cloth of meditation, Mrs. Lipkind, beside a kitchen lamp that flowed in gracious light, knitted the long, quiet hours of her evening into fabric, her face screwed and out of repose and occasionally the lips moving. Age is prone to that. Memories love to be mumbled and chewed over—the unconscious kind of articulation which comes with the years and for which youth has a wink and a quirk.

A tiger cat with overfed sides and a stare that seemed to doze purred on the window-ledge, gold and unswerving of eye. The silence was like the singing inside of a shell, and into it rocked Mrs. Lipkind.

By nine o'clock she was already glancing up at the clock, cocking her head to each and every of night's creaks.

By half after nine there were small and frequent periods of peering through cupped hands down into a street so remote that its traffic had neither shape nor identity. Once she went down a long slit of hallway to the front door, opening it and gazing out upon a fog-filled corridor that was papered in embossed leatherette, one speckled incandescent bulb lighting it sadly. There was something impregnable, even terrible to her in the featureless stare of the doors of three adjoining apartments. She tiptoed, almost ran, poor dear! with the consciousness of some one at her heels, back to the kitchen, where at least was the warm print of the cat's presence; fell to knitting again, clacking her needles for the solace of explainable sound.

Identically with the round moment of ten Mr. Lipkind entered, almost running down the hallway.

"Hello, ma! Think I got lost? Just got to talking and didn't realize. Haven't been worried, ma? Afraid?"

She lifted her head from his kiss. "'Afraid!' What you take me for? For why should I be worried at only ten o'clock? Say, I'm glad if you stay out for recreation."

He kissed her again, shaking out of his coat and unwinding his muffler. "I could just see you walking the floor and looking out of the window."

"Sa-y, I been so busy all evening I didn't have time to think. I'm not such a worrier no more like I used to be. Like the saying is—life is too short."

He drew up beside her, lifting her needles off her work. "Little sweetheart mamma, why don't you sit on the big sofa in the front room where it's more comfortable?"

"You can't make, Sammy, out of a pig's ear a silk stocking."

He would detain her hands, his eyes puckered and, so intent upon her. "You had a good time, Sammy?"

"You'd be surprised, ma, what a nice place Clara boards at."

"What did they have to eat? Good cooking?"

"Not for a fellow that's used to my boarding-house."

"What?"

"I couldn't tell if it was soup or finger-bowls they served for the first course."

"I know—stylish broth. Let me warm you up a little of my thick barley soup that's left over from—"

He pressed her down. "Please, ma! I'm full up. I couldn't. They had pink ice cream, too, with pink cake and—"

"Such mess-food what is bad for you. I'm surprised how Clara keeps her good complexion. Let me fix you some fried—"

"Ma, I tell you I couldn't. It's ten o'clock. You mustn't try to fatten me up so. In war-time a man has got to be lean."

She sat back suddenly and whitely quiet. "That's—twice already to-day, Sam, you talk like that."

He took up her lax hand, moving each separate finger up and down, eyes lowered. "Why not? Doesn't it ever strike you, mamma, that you and me are—are kidding ourselves along this war business, pretending to each other there ain't no war?"

She laid a quick hand to her breast. "What you mean, Sammy?"

"Why, you know what I mean, ma. I notice you read the war news pretty closely, all right."

"Sammy, you mean something!"

"Now, ma, there's no need to get excited right away. Think of the mothers who haven't even got bank-accounts whose sons have got to go."

"Sammy—you 'ain't been—"

"No, no; I haven't."

"You have! I can see it in your face! You've come home with some news to break. You've been drafted!"

He held her arms to her sides, still pressing her down to her chair. "I tell you I haven't! Can't you take my word for it?"

"Swear to me, Sammy!"

"All right; I swear."

"Swear to me on your dead father who is an angel in heaven!"

"I swear—thataway."

She was still pressing against her breathing. "You're keeping something back. Sammy, is it that we got mail from Germany? From Aunt Carrie? Bad news— O my God!"

"No! No! Who could I get mail from there any more than you've been getting it for the last two years? Mamma, if you're going to be this excitable and get yourself sick, I won't talk over anything with you. I'll quit."

"You got something, Sammy, to break to me. I can read you like a book."

"I'm done. If I can't talk facts over with you without your going to pieces this way, I'm done. I quit."

She clasped her hands, her face pleading up to him. "Sammy, what is it? If you don't tell me, I can't stand it. Sammy?"

"Will you sit quiet and not get excited?"

"Please, Sammy, I will."

"It's this: you see, ma, the way the draft goes. When a fellow's called to war, drafted, he's got to go, no questions asked. But when a fellow enlists for war, volunteers, you see, before the government calls him, then thataway he can pick out for himself the thing he wants to be in the army. Y'see? And then maybe the thing he picks out for himself can keep him right here at home. Y'see, ma—so he don't have to go away. See the point?"

"You mean when a boy enlists he offers himself instead of gets offered."

"Exactly."

"You got something behind all this. You mean you—you want to enlist."

"Now, ma—you see, if I was to enlist—and stay right here in this country—with you near the camp or, as long as it's too rough life for you, with—with Clara there—a woman to look in on—"

"Sammy—you mean it's enlistment!"

Her voice rose in velocity; he could feel her pulse run beneath his fingers.

"It's the best way, ma. The draft is sure to get me. Let me beat it and keep myself home—near you. We might as well face the music, ma. They'll get me one way or another. Let me enlist now, ma. Like a man. Right away. For my country!"

Do you know the eyes of Bellini's "Agony in a Garden"? Can you hear for yourself the note that must have been Cassandra's when she shouted out her forebodings? There were these now in the glance and voice of Mrs. Lipkind as she drew back from him, her face actually seeming to shrivel.

"No, Sammy! No! No! No!"

"Ma—please—"

"You wouldn't! You couldn't! No, Sammy—my son!"

"Ma, for God's sake don't go on so!"

"Then tell me you wouldn't! Against your own flesh and blood! Tell me you wouldn't!"

"No, no, ma! For God's sake, don't take a fit—a stroke—no, no; I wouldn't—I wouldn't!"

"Your own blood, Sammy! Your own baby cousins what I tucked you in bed with—mine own sister's children! Her babies what slept with you. Mine own sister who raised me and worked down her hands to the bone to make it so with my young husband and baby we could come to America—no—no!"

"Mamma, for God's sakes—"

"Three years like a snake here inside of it's eating me—all night—all day—I'm a good American, Sammy; I got so much I should be thankful for to America. Twenty-five years it's my home, the home where I had prosperity and good treatment, the home where I had happiness with your papa and where he lies buried, but I can't give you to fight against my own, Sammy—to be murdered by your own—my sister what never in her life harmed a bird—my child and her children—cousins—against each other. My beautiful country what I remember with cows and green fields and clover—always the smell of clover. It ain't human to murder against your own flesh and blood for God knows what reason!"

"Mamma, there is a reason it—"

"I tell you I'm a good American, Sammy. For America I give my last cent, but not to stick knives in my own—it ain't human— Why didn't I die before we got war? What good am I here? In my boy's way for his country—his marriage—his happiness—why don't I die?"

"Ma, I tell you you mustn't! You're making yourself sick. Let me fan you. Here, ma, I didn't mean it. See—I'm holding you tight. I won't never let go. You're my little sweetheart mamma. You mustn't tremble like that. I'm holding you tight—tight—little mamma."

"My boy! My little boy! My son! My all! All in their bed together. Three.

Her two. Mine. The smell of clover—my boy—Sammy—Sam—" She fainted back into his arms suddenly, very white and very quiet and very shriveled.

He watched beside her bed the next five hours of the night, his face so close above hers that, when she opened her eyes, his were merged into one for her, and the clasp of his hand never left hers.

"You all right, ma? Sure? Sure you don't need the doctor?"

She looked up at him with a tired, a burned-out, an ashamed smile. "The first time in my life, Sammy, such a thing ever happened to me."

He pressed a chain of close kisses to the back of her hand, his voice far from firm. "It was me, ma. I'll never forgive myself. My little mamma, my little mamma sweetheart!"

"I feel fine, son; only, with you sitting here all night, you don't let me sleep for worry that you ain't in bed."

"I love it. I love to sit here by you and watch you sleep. You're sure you've no fever? Sure?"

"I'm well, Sammy. It was nothing but what you call a fainting-fit. For some women it's nothing that they should faint every time they get a little bit excited. It's nothing. Feel my hands—how cool! That's always a sign—coolness."

He pressed them both to his lips, blowing his warm breath against them. "There now—go to sleep."

The night-light burning weakly, the great black-walnut bedstead ponderous in the gloom, she lay there mostly smiling and always shamefaced.

"Such a thing should happen to me at my age!"

"Try to sleep, ma."

"Go in your room to bed, and then I get sleep. Do you want your own clerks should beat you to business to-morrow?"

"A little whisky?"

"Go away; you got me dosed up enough with such *Schnapps*."

"The light lower?"

"No. If you don't go in your room, I lay here all night with my eyes open, so help me!"

He rose, stiff and sore-kneed, hair awry, and his eyes with the red rims of fatigue. "You'll sure ring the little bell if you want anything, ma?"

"Sure."

"You promise you won't get up to fix breakfast."

"If I don't feel good, I let you fix mine."

"Good night, little sweetheart mamma."

"You ain't—mad at me, Sam?"

"Mad! Why, ma, you mustn't ask me a—a thing like that; it just kills me to hear you. Me that's not even fit to black your shoes! Mad at you? Why, I—

I— Good night—good—night—ma."

At just fifteen minutes before seven, to the pungency of coffee and the harsh sing of water across the hall, Mrs. Lipkind in a fuzzy wrapper the color of her eyes and hair, kissed her son awake.

"Sam! Sammy! Get up! *Thu, thu!* I can't get him up in the morning!"

The snuggle away and into the crotch of his elbow.

"Sam-my—quarter to seven!"

He sprang up then, haggard, but in a flood of recollection and remorse. "Ma, I must 'a' dropped off at the last minute. You all right? What are you doing up? Go right back! Didn't I tell you not to get up?"

"I been up an hour already; that's how fine I feel. Get up, Sammy; it's late."

He flung on his robe, trying to withdraw her from the business of looping back the bed-clothing over the foot-board and pounding into the pillows.

"I tell you I won't have it! You got to lay in bed this morning."

"I'm all right, Sammy. Wouldn't I say so if I wasn't?" But she sat down rather weakly on the edge of the bed, holding the right side of her, breathing too hard.

"I—I shouldn't have beat that pillow is all. Let me get my breathing. I'm all right." Nevertheless, she let him relax her to his pillow, draw the covers down from the footboard, and cover her.

"This settles it," he said, quietly. "I'm going to get a doctor."

She caught his hand. "If—if you want to get me excited for sure, just you call a doctor—now—before I talk with you a minute—I want to talk—I'm all right, Sammy, if you let me talk to you. One step to that telephone, and I get excited—"

"Please, ma—"

"Sammy?"

"Yes."

"Will you listen to me and do like I want it?"

"Yes."

"I—been a bad old woman."

"That's right—break my heart."

"I got a brave boy for a son, and I want to make him a coward."

"Ma—please!"

"I laid saying to myself all night, a mother should have such a son like mine and make things hard for him yet!"

"Please, get it all out of your head—"

"From America what has given to me everything I should hold back my son from fighting for. In war, it ain't your own flesh and blood what counts; it's the flesh and blood of your country—not, Sam? I been thinking only it's my family affair. If God lets be such a terrible thing like war, there is some-where a good reason for it. I want you to enlist, Sammy, for your country. Not for in an office, but for where they need you. I want you to enlist to get some day to be such a lieutenant and a captain like you used to play it with tin soldiers. I want—"

"Mamma, mamma, you know you don't mean it!"

"I want it, I tell you. All night I worked on it how dumb I've been, not right away to see it—last night. With Clara near you in the camp—"

"Ma, I didn't mean it that way; I—"

"Clara near you for a woman to look in on, I been so dumb not to right away see it. I'm glad you let it out, Sam. I wouldn't take five thousand dollars it didn't happen— I feel fine—I want it—I—"

"I didn't mean it, ma—I swear! Don't rub it in this way—please—please—"

"Why, I never wanted anything in my life like I want this, Sammy—that you should enlist—a woman to look in on—I been a bad woman, Sammy, I—I—oh—"

It was then that Mr. Lipkind tore to the telephone, his hands so frenzied that they would not properly hold the receiver.

At eight o'clock, and without even a further word, Mrs. Lipkind breathed out quietly, a little tiredly, and yet so eloquent of eye. To her son, pleading there beside her for the life she had not left to give, it was as if the swollen bosom of some stream were carrying her rapidly but gently down its surface, her gaze back at him and begging him to stay the current.

"Mamma! Darling! Doctor—please—for God's sakes—please—she wants something—she can't say it—give it to her! Try to make her tell me what she wants—she wants something—this is terrible—don't let her want some-thing—mamma—just one word to me—try—try—O my God—Doctor—"

A black arm then reached down to withdraw him from the glazed stare which had begun to set in from the pillow.

By ten o'clock a light snow had set in, blowing almost horizontally across the window-pane. He sat his second hour there in a rather forward huddle beside the drawn shade of that window, the *sotto-voce* comings and goings, all the black-coated *parvenus* that follow the wake of death, moving about him. A clock shaped like a pilot's wheel, a boyhood property which had marked the time of twenty years, finally chimed the thin, tin stroke of eleven and after a swimming, nebulous interval, twelve. He glanced up each time with his swollen eyes, and then automatically out to the wall telephone in the hall opposite the open door. But he did not move. In fact, for two more hours sat there impervious to proffered warmth of word or deed. Meanwhile, the snow behind the drawn shade had turned to rain that beat and washed against the pane.

Just so the iciness that had locked Samuel Lipkind seemed suddenly to melt in a tornado of sobs that swept him, felled him into a prostration of the terrible tears that men weep.

At a training-camp—somewhere—from his side of a tent that had flapped like a captive wing all through a wind-swept night, Lieutenant Lipkind stirred rather painfully for a final snuggle into the crotch of an elbow that was stiff with chill and night damp.

Out over the peaked city that had been pitched rather than built, and on beyond over the frozen stubble of fields, sounded the bugle-cry of the reveille, which shrills so potently:

> I can't get 'em up; I can't get 'em up;
> I can't get 'em up in the morn—ing!

She Also Serves

First Published: *Cosmopolitan*, October 1918

When Eddie Snuggs was drafted, a titter rippled over the Main Floor.

Not but what The Parisian had already once, twice, even thrice been rudely jerked to the exigencies, the rather hurried expediencies of war; but there were limits to the quirks of fate and the rapid shunting of destinies into a world in maelstrom.

Denny MacGinn, erstwhile of the Silks and now an "ace" in France, was a stretch which tested the ductility of the imagination; Joe Viviano, so inalienable from the Sheet-Music Department, was not easy to visualize among the hero-survivors flung by a bone-cracking sea against the wildest coast of Scotland; or Morris Aaronson, shipping-clerk, of annual-outing tango fame, driving an ambulance into the intermittent blackness and white fury of a shell-shot road. Yet compared with the inconceivability of Eddie Snuggs in khaki—

"I could just as soon think of the 'Floradora' sextet doin' the gas-mask gavotte in No Man's Land as Cissie Snuggs in patch-pockets and panier pants." This from Miss Elise Hite, of the Jewelry.

Miss Mabel Dobschutz (*of the rhinestone hair-ornaments*): I wonder if he could use a pair of pink-silk sleeve-garters.

Miss Essie White (*blond to the roots*): You two stack up about as funny as a casualty list.

Miss Dobschutz lifted her gaze, then crinkled it to slits.

"'What have we here? What have we here?'"—cried out in the key of off-C of a popular refrain. "Since when is the fatal blond beauty on twitterin' terms with Cissie Snuggs again?"

"I ain't; but that's no reason that I'm goin' to join in the haw-haw that this store ain't got the sense to keep bottled up. I don't feel no feather tickler on my funny-bone these war days."

Miss Hite smoothed down her hipless hip-line. Her silhouette was like the quick stroke of a hard pencil.

"If I felt that way about my poor, ittsie-bittsie floor-walker that's been drafted by great big, bad government, I'd make it up with ittsie-bittsie perfect lady of a floor-walker, I would."

"You let Eddie Snuggs alone! The fellows in this store can't all be class-beauties like Archie Tupp. The kind of hero-stuff you girls got on the brain only comes in five reels to soft music."

"'What have we here? What have we here?' Say, dearie, if I felt that way and had had a row with my pittsie-ittsie floor-walker, just because he slapped me on the wristwatch for gettin' fresh with a customer, I'd smile myself in with him again. I'd give him a flash of my ruby teeth and my pearly lips."

"You just bet your life I'll make it up to him! I had no right to sass that dame over the earrings, and you know it. You bet your life I'll make it up to him! No boy I know is goin' into that mess over there with a mad from me hangin' on."

"Here he comes, dearie; let's see you get religion."

"You better watch out, darling"—moving down the counter—"it might be catchin'."

Late afternoon lay rather drowsily over The Parisian. A thin trickle percolated through the aisles, pausing to finger, to price, and, semi-occasionally, to purchase. There was a somnolence over the jewelry counter, a sort of afternoon apathy for the paste pearl and the gilt-back diamond. Miss White, her own ears depending long, slim stalactites of jet, leaned across the glass-topped counter. She was not unlike the Psyche of Apuleius in the lift of desire to her mouth-corners, the nose tip-tilting, eager, curious, the three-tier coiffure cascading curls that were so the color of sunlight.

"Eh-ud!"

Mr. Snuggs, turning the counter corner, paused as if, through the din of the workaday, he had heard a bird-note.

"Oh, Eh-ud!"

He shot his cuffs and reared his neck. A slow red began to creep out of his tight, high collar and up into a too smoothly pomaded pompadour that was high and thick of nap.

"Eh?"

Miss White leaned further. Her own face had pinkened, the color flowing down into the very V of her very sheer blouse.

"The colors are calling, tra-la, tra-la!" she paraphrased, hands on hips, head tilted to an angle of insouciance.

Mr. Snuggs drew up. He was hit at the knees by the kind of frock coat that convention reserves for her floor-walkers, undertakers, bankers, and park statues of patriots. A rose cravat stabbed with a freshwater pearl enhanced the rosiness of his state of unmistakable and growing agitation. He drew from his cuff a kerchief, touching it ever so slightly to each of the rather finely etched nostrils.

"Yeh," he said; "Uncle Sam knocked at my door last night and invited me to training-camp." His voice was like the butler's-pantry epiphoneum of thin glass in the shattering, high, brittle, and, it must be owned, soprano.

"The—the customer's always right, Ed. I oughtn't to have given her sass about them green earrings."

"It was my fault, Essie. You gave her what was coming to her, trying to get credit for them when you sat right next to her at the movies with them in her ears."

"I sold 'em to her Ed—so help me!—Saturday morning; I'd have known her red hair anywhere, and that very same night didn't I find myself sittin' right next to her, wearin' them big as life and—"

"It was my fault, Essie; I apolo—"

"You mean it was mine, Ed. They're watchin' you anyways for showin' me partiality. You could 'a' been fired for not jerkin' me up when the customer is always right, and—"

"What's the difference whose fault it was, Essie—now?"

"That's just it, Ed. I—I didn't want you to go—off—with things this a-way—mixed—between us."

"I—that's fine of you, Ess—gee; that's mighty fine of you!"

"How you feelin' about things, Ed?"

"Me—oh, I—fine!"

"Don't let the goings-on in this cheap joint of a store get under your skin, Ed."

"Let 'em laugh. I guess, if the truth is known, I don't look so very long on the soldier-boy stuff; but I feel fine. Fine!"

"Every fellow that's drafted don't have to be a Archie Tupp or a roughneck to make good."

"I'm going to give 'em the best I got in me. A fellow can't do more than that, can he?"

"You bet your life he can't!"

"The way I look at it, I'm darn lucky to even measure up to Uncle Sam's idea of a soldier. Lord, you could have knocked me down with a feather the way I passed muster."

"I'd like to stand up here on this counter and give this here store a piece of my mind, I would! I don't see no medals on nobody around here for hero-stuff. There's been some exemption goin' on in this shebang I wouldn't want a brother of mine to have on his head and not a dozen counters away from here, neither. Some girls, too, that helped the whole dirty business through."

"Now, I wouldn't let myself get worked up that way, Ess. I can see where I'd be a joke to some of 'em. I guess, if the truth was known, the Lord didn't exactly cut me out for a tin soldier. Not that I'm afraid. Lord, you only got one life to lose, and that's little enough for a fellow to hand over to his country if she happens to need it."

"Honest, Ed, when I hear you talk like that, I—I get sore. Why don't you say things like that out—to all of 'em when they kid you? Lots of times, when just a word from you would set things right with the—knockers—all you do is stand and not say a word."

"That's me every time, Ess. Lots of times, when just a word from me might square me, I—I can't—it just sticks—I can't say it."

"I never seen a fellow that wouldn't turn a finger to set himself right with people. 'Sissy!' I'd like to see a gang of knockers call me a sissy if I was a fellow with as much—"

"It's my voice, Ess. All my life I been up against it with these second-story vocal cords of mine. A fellow can't expect to make much of a hit anywheres, Ess, much less in the war-business, if he ain't what you call a 'man's man.' I'm not, and I know it. Put me with a bunch of fellows, and I'm a committee of one, off by myself. High C ain't a popular tone of voice among fellows."

"If you'd only listened to me, Ed! No girl on earth could have took more trouble to get you to train down your voice than I have."

"Didn't I buy some of them graphophone lessons to please you?"

"It's them little things, Ed. The yellow gloves and the pink ties and the wrist handkerchief. You—like I've told you a thousand times—you just can't expect regular fellows like Viviano and Archie Tupp and MacGinn to fall for that kind of stuff. You—you'll last with the boys in the army about fifteen minutes, Ed, if you go in that a-way. I know you for what you are, really and truly, Ed, but the fellows in the army—they'll take you at your face value and—and make it hot for you if—"

"A fellow's got to be himself, Ess. You know there never was a leopard that was cured of his spots. I can't help what I am no more than Archie Tupp over there can help his white forelock or old Mason his humpback."

"Say; if it suits you, it's got to suit me."

"It don't suit me, Ess. God knows I'd never win a popularity contest with myself!"

"I hate to see a fellow stand in his own light."

"I wonder, Ess, if—if you'll hate to see me go—just a little bit."

"You bet your life I will, Ed! We've had our scraps and all, but I ain't worked on the floor with you fourteen months for—for nothin.'"

"You'll never guess, Ess, the first thing I packed up to take to camp with me. That little snap-shot of you next to the smoke-stack of that Coney Island boat last August. Remember?"

"That old thing!"

"It's the sweetest little pose, Ess, like you was ready to tinkle right off the cardboard, curls and cuteness and all."

"That old thing!"

"There's just one other remembrance I'm going to carry over there, Ess. Guess?"

"What?"

"Gowann; guess."

"Can't."

"Try."

"Can't, I tell you."

"That little old snap-shot is one, and the smell of that there sweet cologne you always got so strong on you is the other. It's a grand smell, Ess. Saturday afternoon, me feeling rotten after our little row, I sat next to a girl in the subway with it on, and it just seemed like it was your little ghost sitting there. Honest, I can close my eyes any minute of the day or night and smell that perfume and see that yellow head of yours and them blue eyes as plain as day. Funny how a smell can get a fellow, ain't it?"

"It's my favorite perfume, Azelia is."

"And you're my favorite perfume."

"Sh-h-h-h!"

"We—we fuss a lot, Ess, like kids, but that's just what you are to me, like Azelia is to you. My favorite kind of perfume."

"Honest, Ed, you—you're the funniest fellow, kind of three-in-one sort of guy! Every once in a while I get to seein' a real man stickin' out all over you, and the very next you're a cissy talkin' Azelia perfume."

"That's one of my leopard's spots, I guess, Ess—it's just in me to like sweet smells and you."

"Honest, if a fellow like you can go dippy over cologne one minute and then lift his head and go to war without a whimper the next, I'm goin' to get in on this war-job, too, and get some education. If you and MacGinn and Viviano have got such stuff bottled up in you, I'm goin' to show this old war where I come in."

"Say, Ess; wouldn't it be immense with you over there a Red Cross girlie? Why don't you try it again, honey, to get in—wouldn't you just make one immense Red Cross girlie?"

"I've had my little turn-down for foreign service, once. Shakespeare never repeats. They don't need my kind; what they need is brains. I've got about as much education and language and hoity-toity stuff for nursin' over there as a house-fly has."

"Why, Ess, it would be worth getting all kinds of a hole in the head to have you nurse it!"

"Well, about all they're goin' to let me do for any of you fellows with holes in your heads is make the bandages. You ought to see me Saturday afternoon, Ed, sittin' in a plate-glass window on Fifth Avenue, rolling gauze. Some class! If not for the green earrings and the row with you, I'd have made the speed-record that afternoon—my first try at it, too. I'm goin' to give all my Saturday afternoons and—"

"Is—is that why you sassed the dame, Ess—because she was making you late for—for there?"

"What did you think I was afraid of being late for—Lady Aubrey's garden-party?"

"Why, you—you wonderful little Essie, you! You wonderful little—you—you—a little kitten like you giving your Saturday afternoons on top of that twenty dollars you just gave to the Red Cross. A little kitten like you, sweating them twenty dollars out of her nine a week, and now, on top of it—her Saturday afternoons—you—little—"

"What's twenty bucks? What's anything to show how us stay-at-homes are back of the fellows over there that are dyin' in the mud for us while we sleep. If I had a thousand times twenty dollars in my pocket this minute, I'd want each one of them dollars to say for me, 'Boys, I'm with you!'"

"Why—why there's just no fellow in the draft is going away with more than I'm going. I don't care who he is. A little Azelia back here bucking him up with every kind of sacrifice a girl can make for him. I—I *am* going with you in back of me, Ess, ain't I? You back here, caring if—if I come back? Ess? Essie?"

"You bet your life you goin' thataway, Eddie Snuggs—Charles Edward Snuggs," said Miss White, placing her hand over his, her eyes widening, filling.

In a hastily improvised hospital-ward—somewhere in France—a nurse, not quite so white as she might have been, bent over a cot, the mud-drenched edges of her sleeves rolled back. Stenches rose there—stenches so over-whelming that the senses sickened, then reeled at the shrieks of the ether-imprisoned, the not-to-be-endured agonies beneath the knife, the sobbings of men too delirious to bite back the groans, the tear of blood-soaked linen that had stuck fast to living flesh.

"I doubt if he will come out of it," said the nurse not so white as she might have been to her newly appointed aide. "It's not the hip that bothers us, it's the hole in his head. We've been hoping it didn't touch the brain. They'd better decorate the poor brave boy before he—"

Cried the aide:

"Let's try a fresh dressing! There may be a surface-clot. I saw a corporal yesterday come out of worse than this."

"Hurry, then. There's that poor fellow three cots down, the one with the white forelock that this poor child here dragged in from No Man's Land—he's coming out of ether."

"Quick!"

There was a shifting, a swabbing, a sobbing through blue lips, and then a fresh swathing of bandage that was merciful to the dented brow.

A scent rose up, even through that stench insidious and insinuating.

THE NURSE: This is the third bandage I've used to-night that has smelled of cheap perfume. We'd better not use the rest of that carton.

The whiff of Azelia rose higher and with each winding of the gauze more and more insistent.

The rather finely etched nostrils on the pillow quivered, then lifted ever so lightly.

The eyes opened, the glaze seeming to fade before a smile.

"I told you I've seen them come out of worse!" cried the newly apprenticed aide, trembling a little, crying a little, smiling a little.

Humoresque

First Published: *Cosmopolitan*, March 1919
Reprinted: *Humoresque and Other Stories*, Harper & Bros., 1919
Filmed: *Humoresque*, dir. Frank Borzage, 1920
Humoresque, dir. Jean Negulesco, 1946

On either side of the Bowery, which cuts through like a drain to catch its sewage, Every Man's Land, a reeking march of humanity and humidity, steams with the excrement of seventeen languages, flung in *patois* from tenement windows, fire-escapes, curbs, stoops, and cellars whose walls are terrible and spongy with fungi.

By that impregnable chemistry of race whereby the red blood of the Mongolian and the red blood of the Caucasian become as oil and water in the mingling, Mulberry Street, bounded by sixteen languages, runs its intact Latin length of push-carts, clothes-lines, naked babies, drying vermicelli; black-eyed women in rhinestone combs and perennially big with child; whole families of buttonhole-makers, who first saw the blue-and-gold light of Sorrento, bent at home work round a single gas flare; pomaded barbers of a thousand Neapolitan amours. And then, just as suddenly, almost without osmosis and by the mere stepping down from the curb, Mulberry becomes Mott Street, hung in grill-work balconies, the moldy smell of poverty touched up with incense. Orientals whose feet shuffle and whose faces are carved out of satinwood. Forbidden women, their white, drugged faces behind upper windows. Yellow children, incongruous enough in Western clothing. A draughty areaway with an oblique of gaslight and a black well of descending staircase. Show-windows of jade and tea and Chinese porcelains.

More streets emanating out from Mott like a handful of crooked rheumatic fingers, then suddenly the Bowery again, cowering beneath Elevated trains, where men burned down to the butt end of soiled lives pass in and out and out and in of the knee-high swinging doors, a veiny-nosed, acid-eaten race in themselves.

Allen Street, too, still more easterly, and half as wide, is straddled its entire width by the steely, long-legged skeleton of Elevated traffic, so that its third-floor windows no sooner shudder into silence from the rushing shock of one train than they are shaken into chatter by the passage of another. Indeed, third-floor dwellers of Allen Street, reaching out, can almost touch the serrated edges of the Elevated structure, and in summer the smell of its hot rails becomes an actual taste in the mouth. Passengers, in turn, look in upon this horizontal of life as they whiz by. Once, in fact, the blurry figure of what might have been a woman leaned out, as she passed, to toss into one Abrahm Kantor's apartment a short-stemmed pink carnation. It hit softly on little Leon Kantor's crib, brushing him fragrantly across the mouth and causing him to pucker up.

Beneath, where even in August noonday, the sun cannot find its way by a chink, and babies lie stark naked in the cavernous shade, Allen Street presents a sort of submarine and greenish gloom, as if its humanity were actually moving through a sea of aqueous shadows, faces rather bleached and shrunk from sunlessness as water can bleach and shrink. And then, like a shimmering background of orange-finned and copper-flanked marine life, the brass-shops of Allen Street, whole rows of them, burn flamelessly and without benefit of fuel.

To enter Abrahm Kantor's—Brasses, was three steps down, so that his casement show-window, at best filmed over with the constant rain of dust ground down from the rails above, was obscure enough, but crammed with copied loot of khedive and of czar. The seven-branch candlestick so biblical and supplicating of arms. An urn, shaped like Rebecca's, of brass, all beaten over with little pocks. Things—cups, trays, knockers, ikons, gargoyles, bowls, and teapots. A symphony of bells in graduated sizes. Jardinières with fat sides. A pot-bellied samovar. A swinging-lamp for the dead, star-shaped. Against the door, an octave of tubular chimes, prisms of voiceless harmony and of heatless light.

Opening this door, they rang gently, like melody heard through water and behind glass. Another bell rang, too, in tilted singsong from a pulley operating somewhere in the catacomb rear of this lambent vale of things and things and things. In turn, this pulley set in toll still another bell, two flights up in Abrahm Kantor's tenement, which overlooked the front of whizzing rails and a rear wilderness of gibbet-looking clothes-lines, dangling perpetual specters of flapping union suits in a mid-air flaky with soot.

Often at lunch, or even the evening meal, this bell would ring in on Abrahm Kantor's digestive well-being, and while he hurried down, napkin often bib-fashion still around his neck, and into the smouldering lanes of copper, would leave an eloquent void at the head of his well-surrounded table.

This bell was ringing now, jingling in upon the slumber of a still newer Kantor, snuggling peacefully enough within the ammoniac depths of a cradle recently evacuated by Leon, heretofore impinged upon you.

On her knees before an oven that billowed forth hotly into her face, Mrs. Kantor, fairly fat and not yet forty, and at the immemorial task of plumbing a delicately swelling layer-cake with broom-straw, raised her face, reddened and faintly moist.

"Isadore, run down and say your papa is out until six. If it's a customer, remember the first asking-price is the two middle figures on the tag, and the last asking-price is the two outside figures. See once, with your papa out to buy your little brother his birthday present, and your mother in a cake, if you can't make a sale for first price."

Isadore Kantor, aged eleven and hunched with a younger Kantor over an oilcloth-covered table, hunched himself still deeper in a barter for a large crystal marble with a candy stripe down its center.

"Izzie, did you hear me?"

"Yes'm."

"Go down this minute—do you hear? Rudolph, stop always letting your big brother get the best of you in marbles. Iz-zie!"

"In-a-minute."

"Don't let me have to ask you again, Isadore Kantor!"

"Aw, ma, I got some 'rithmetic to do. Let Esther go!"

"Always Esther! Your sister stays right in the front room with her spelling."

"Aw, ma, I got spelling, too."

"Every time I ask that boy he should do me one thing, right away he gets lessons! With me, that lessons-talk don't go no more. Every time you get put down in school, I'm surprised there's a place left lower where they can put you. Working-papers for such a boy like you!"

"I'll woik—"

"How I worried myself! Violin lessons yet—thirty cents a lesson out of your papa's pants while he slept! That's how I wanted to have in the family a profession—maybe a musician on the violin! Lessons for you out of money I had to lie to your papa about! Honest, when I think of it—my own husband—it's a wonder I don't potch you just for remembering it. Rudolph, will you stop licking that cake-pan? It's saved for your little brother Leon. Ain't you ashamed even on your little brother's birthday to steal from him?"

"Ma, gimme the spoon?"

"I'll give you the spoon, Isadore Kantor, where you don't want it. If you don't hurry down, the way that bell is ringing, not one bite do you get out of your little brother's birthday-cake to-night!"

"I'm goin', ain't I?"

"Always on my children's birthdays a meanness sets into this house! Rudolph, will you put down that bowl! Iz-zie—for the last time I ask you—for the last time—"

Erect now, Mrs. Kantor lifted an expressive hand, letting it hover.

"I'm goin', ma; for golly sakes, I'm goin'!" said her recalcitrant one, shuffling off toward the staircase, shuffling, shuffling.

Then Mrs. Kantor resumed her plumbing, and through the little apartment, its middle and only bedroom of three beds and a crib lighted vicariously by the front room and kitchen, began to wind the warm, the golden-brown fragrance of cake in the rising.

By six o'clock the shades were drawn against the dirty dusk of Allen Street and the oilcloth-covered table dragged out center and spread by Esther Kantor, nine in years, in the sturdy little legs bulging over shoe-tops, in the pink cheeks that sagged slightly of plumpness, and in the utter roundness of face and gaze, but mysteriously older in the little-mother lore of crib and knee-dandling ditties and in the ropy length and thickness of the two brown plaits down her back.

There was an eloquence to that waiting, laid-out table, the print of the family already gathered about it; the dynastic high chair, throne of each succeeding Kantor; an armchair drawn up before the paternal mustache-cup; the ordinary kitchen chair of Mannie Kantor, who spilled things, an oilcloth sort of bib dangling from its back; the little chair of Leon Kantor cushioned in an old family album that raised his chin above the table. Even in cutlery the Kantor family was not lacking in variety. Surrounding a centerpiece of thick Russian lace were Russian spoons washed in washed-off gilt; forks of one, two, and three tines; steel knives with black handles; a hartshorn carving-knife. Thick-lipped china in stacks before the armchair. A round four-pound loaf of black bread waiting to be torn, and to-night, on the festive mat of cotton lace, a cake of pinkly gleaming icing, encircled with five pink little candles.

At slightly after six Abrahm Kantor returned, leading by a resisting wrist Leon Kantor, his stemlike little legs, hit midship, as it were, by not sufficiently cut-down trousers and so narrow and birdlike of face that his eyes quite obliterated the remaining map of his features, like those of a still wet nestling. All except his ears. They poised at the sides of Leon's shaved head of black bristles, as if butterflies had just lighted there, whispering, with very spread wings, their message, and presently would fly off again. By some sort of muscular contraction he could wiggle these ears at will, and would do so for a penny or a whistle, and upon one occasion for his brother Rudolph's dead rat, so devised as to dangle from string and window before the unhappy passer-by. They were quivering now, these ears, but because the entire little face was twitching back tears and gulp of sobs.

"Abrahm—Leon—what is it?" Her hands and her forearms instantly out from the business of kneading something meaty and floury, Mrs. Kantor rushed forward, her glance quick from one to the other of them. "Abrahm, what's wrong?"

"I'll feedle him! I'll feedle him!"

The little pulling wrist still in clutch, Mr. Kantor regarded his wife, the lower half of his face, well covered with reddish bristles, undershot, his free hand and even his eyes violently lifted. To those who see in a man a perpetual kinship to that animal kingdom of which he is supreme, there was something undeniably anthropoidal about Abrahm Kantor, a certain simian width between the eyes and long, rather agile hands with hairy backs.

"Hush it!" cried Mr. Kantor, his free hand raised in threat of descent, and cowering his small son to still more undersized proportions. "Hush it or, by golly! I'll—"

"Abrahm—Abrahm—what is it?"

Then Mr. Kantor gave vent in acridity of word and feature.

"*Schlemmil!*" he cried. "*Momser! Ganef! Nebich!*" by which, in smiting mother tongue, he branded his offspring with attributes of apostate and ne'er-do-well, of idiot and thief.

"Abrahm!"

"*Schlemmil!*" repeated Mr. Kantor, swinging Leon so that he described a large semicircle that landed him into the meaty and waiting embrace of his mother. "Take him! You should be proud of such a little *momser* for a son! Take him, and here you got back his birthday dollar. A feedle! Honest—when I think on it—a feedle!"

Such a rush of outrage seemed fairly to strangle Mr. Kantor that he stood, hand still upraised, choking and inarticulate above the now frankly howling huddle of his son.

"Abrahm, you should just once touch this child! How he trembles! Leon—mamma's baby—what is it? Is this how you come back when papa takes you out to buy your birthday present? Ain't you ashamed?"

Mouth distended to a large and blackly hollow O, Leon, between terrifying spells of breath-holding, continued to howl.

"All the way to Naftel's toy-store I drag him. A birthday present for a dollar his mother wants he should have, all right, a birthday present! I give you my word till I'm ashamed for Naftel, every toy in his shelves is pulled down. Such a cow—that shakes with his head—"

"No—no—no!" This from young Leon, beating at his mother's skirts.

Again the upraised but never quite descending hand of his father.

"By golly! I'll 'no—no' you!"

"Abrahm—go 'way! Baby, what did papa do?"

Then Mr. Kantor broke into an actual tarantella of rage, his hands palms up and dancing.

"'What did papa do?' she asks. She's got easy asking. 'What did papa do?' The whole shop, I tell you. A sheep with a baa inside when you squeeze on him—games—a horn so he can holler my head off—such a knife like Izzie's with a scissors in it. 'Leon,' I said, ashamed for Naftel, 'that's a fine knife like Izzie's so you can cut up with. All right, then'—when I see how he hollers—'such a box full of soldiers to have war with.' 'Dollar seventy-five,' says Naftel. 'All right, then,' I says when I seen how he keeps hollering. 'Give you a dollar fifteen for 'em.' I should make myself small for fifteen cents more. 'Dollar fifteen,' I says—anything so he could shut up with his hollering for what he seen in the window."

"He seen something in the window he wanted, Abrahm?"

"Didn't I tell you? A feedle! A four-dollar feedle! A moosicer, so we should have another feedler in the family for some thirty-cents lessons."

"Abrahm—you mean—he—our Leon—wanted a violin?"

"'Wanted,' she says. I could potch him again this minute for how he wanted it! *Du*—you little bum you—*chammer*—*momser*—I'll feedle you!"

Across Mrs. Kantor's face, as she knelt there in the shapeless cotton-stuff uniform of poverty, through the very tenement of her body, a light had flashed up into her eyes. She drew her son closer, crushing his puny cheek up against hers, cupping his bristly little head in her by no means immaculate palms.

"He wanted a violin! It's come, Abrahm! The dream of all my life—my prayers—it's come! I knew it must be one of my children if I waited long enough—and prayed enough. A musician! He wants a violin! He cried for a violin! My baby! Why, darlink, mamma'll sell her clothes off her back to get you a violin. He's a musician, Abrahm! I should have known it the way he's fooling always around the chimes and the bells in the store!"

Then Mr. Kantor took to rocking his head between his palms.

"Oi—oi! The mother is crazier as her son. A moosician! A *fresser,* you mean. Such an eater, it's a wonder he ain't twice too big instead of twice too little for his age."

"That's a sign, Abrahm; geniuses, they all eat big. For all we know, he's a genius. I swear to you, Abrahm, all the months before he was born I prayed for it. Each one before they came, I prayed it should be the one. I thought that time the way our Isadore ran after the organ-grinder he would be the one. How could I know it was the monkey he wanted? When Isadore wouldn't take to it I prayed my next one, and then my next one, should have the talent. I've prayed for it, Abrahm. If he wants a violin, please, he should have it."

"Not with my money."

"With mine! I've got enough saved, Abrahm. Them three extra dollars right here inside my own waist. Just that much for that cape down on Grand Street. I wouldn't have it now, the way they say the wind blows up them—"

"I tell you the woman's crazy—"

"I feel it! I know he's got talent! I know my children so well. A—a father don't understand. I'm so next to them. It's like I can tell always everything that will happen to them—it's like a pain—somewheres here—like in back of my heart."

"A pain in the heart she gets."

"For my own children I'm always a prophet, I tell you! You think I didn't know that—that terrible night after the pogrom after we got out of Kief to across the border! You remember, Abrahm, how I predicted it to you and then—how our Mannie would be born too soon and—and not right from my suffering! Did it happen on the ship to America just the way I said it would? Did it happen just exactly how I predicted our Izzie would break his leg that time playing on the fire-escape? I tell you, Abrahm, I get a real pain here under my heart that tells me what comes to my children. Didn't I tell you how Esther would be the first in her confirmation-class and our baby Boris would be red-headed? At only five years, our Leon all by himself cries for a fiddle—get it for him, Abrahm—get it for him!"

"I tell you, Sarah, I got a crazy woman for a wife! It ain't enough we celebrate eight birthdays a year with one-dollar presents each time and copper goods every day higher. It ain't enough that right to-morrow I got a fifty-dollar note over me from Sol Ginsberg; a four-dollar present she wants for a child that don't even know the name of a feedle."

"Leon, baby, stop hollering. Papa will go back and get the fiddle for you now before supper. See, mamma's got money here in her waist—"

"Papa will go back for the feedle *not*—three dollars she's saved for herself he can holler out of her for a feedle!"

"Abrahm, he's screaming so he—he'll have a fit."

"He should have two fits."

"Darlink—"

"I tell you the way you spoil your children it will some day come back on us."

"It's his birthday night, Abrahm—five years since his little head first lay on the pillow next to me."

"All right—all right—drive me crazy because he's got a birthday."

"Leon baby—if you don't stop hollering you'll make yourself sick. Abrahm, I never saw him like this—he's green—"

"I'll green him. Where is that old feedle from Isadore—that seventy-five-cents one?"

"I never thought of that! You broke it that time you got mad at Isadore's lessons. I'll run down. Maybe it's with the junk behind the store. I never thought of that fiddle. Leon darlink—wait! Mamma'll run down and look. Wait, Leon, till mamma finds you a fiddle."

The raucous screams stopped then, suddenly, and on their very lustiest crest, leaving an echoing gash across silence. On willing feet of haste Mrs. Kantor wound down backward the high, ladder-like staircase that led to the brass-shop.

Meanwhile to a gnawing consciousness of dinner-hour had assembled the house of Kantor. Attuned to the intimate atmosphere of the tenement which is so constantly rent with cry of child, child-bearing, delirium, delirium tremens, Leon Kantor had howled no impression into the motley din of things. There were Isadore, already astride his chair, leaning well into center table, for first vociferous tear at the four-pound loaf; Esther, old at chores, settling an infant into the high chair, careful of tiny fingers in lowering the wooden bib.

"Papa, Izzie's eating first again."

"Put down that loaf and wait until your mother dishes up, or you'll get a potch you won't soon forget."

"Say, pop—"

"Don't 'say, pop' me! I don't want no street-bum freshness from you!"

"I mean, papa, there was an up-town swell in, and she bought one of them seventy-five-cent candlesticks for the first price."

"*Schlemmil! Chammer!*" said Mr. Kantor, rinsing his hands at the sink. "Didn't I always tell you it's the first price, times two, when you see up-town business come in? Haven't I learned it to you often enough a slummer must pay for her nosiness?"

There entered then, on poor, shuffling feet, Mannie Kantor, so marred in the mysterious and ceramic process of life that the brain and the soul had stayed back sooner than inhabit him. Seventeen in years, in the down upon his face and in growth unretarded by any great nervosity of system, his vacuity of face was not that of childhood, but rather as if his light eyes were peering out from some hinterland and wanting so terribly and so dumbly to communicate what they beheld to brain-cells closed against himself.

At sight of Mannie, Leon Kantor, the tears still wetly and dirtily down his cheeks, left off his black, fierce-eyed stare of waiting long enough to smile, darkly, it is true, but sweetly.

"Giddy-app!" he cried. "Giddy-app!"

And then Mannie, true to habit, would scamper and scamper.

Up out of the traplike stair-opening came the head of Mrs. Kantor, disheveled and a smudge of soot across her face, but beneath her arm, triumphant, a violin of one string and a broken back.

"See, Leon—what mamma got! A violin! A fiddle! Look! The bow, too, I found. It ain't much, baby, but it's a fiddle."

"Aw, ma—that's my old violin. Gimme. I want it. Where'd you find—"

"Hush up, Izzie! This ain't yours no more. See, Leon, what mamma brought you. A violin!"

"Now, you little *chammer,* you got a feedle, and if you ever let me hear you holler again for a feedle, by golly! if I don't—"

From his corner, Leon Kantor reached out, taking the instrument and fitting it beneath his chin, the bow immediately feeling, surely and lightly, for string.

"Look, Abrahm, he knows how to hold it! What did I tell you? A child that never in his life seen a fiddle, except a beggar's on the street!"

Little Esther suddenly cantered down-floor, clapping her chubby hands. "Lookie—lookie—Leon!"

The baby ceased clattering his spoon against the wooden bib. A silence seemed to shape itself.

So black and so bristly of head, his little clawlike hands hovering over the bow, Leon Kantor withdrew a note, strangely round and given up almost sobbingly from the single string. A note of warm twining quality, like a baby's finger.

"Leon—darlink!"

Fumbling for string and for notes the instrument could not yield up to him, the birdlike mouth began once more to open widely and terribly into the orificial O.

It was then Abraham Kantor came down with a large hollow resonance of palm against that aperture, lifting his small son and depositing him plop upon the family album.

"Take that! By golly! one more whimper out of you and if I don't make you black-and-blue, birthday or no birthday! Dish up, Sarah, quick, or I'll give him something to cry about."

The five pink candles had been lighted, burning pointedly and with slender little smoke wisps. Regarding them owlishly, the tears dried on Leon's face, his little tongue licking up at them.

"Look how solemn he is, like he was thinking of something a million miles away except how lucky he is he should have a pink birthday-cake. Uh—uh—uh! Don't you begin to holler again. Here, I'm putting the feedle next to you. Uh—uh—uh!"

To a meal plentifully ladled out directly from stove to table, the Kantor family drew up, dripping first into the rich black soup of the occasion. All except Mrs. Kantor.

"Esther, you dish up. I'm going somewhere. I'll be back in a minute."

"Where you going, Sarah? Won't it keep until—"

But even in the face of query, Sarah Kantor was two flights down and well through the lambent aisles of the copper-shop. Outside, she broke into run, along two blocks of the indescribable bazaar atmosphere of Grand Street, then one block to the right.

Before Naftel's show-window, a jet of bright gas burned in a jibberwock land of toys. There was that in Sarah Kantor's face that was actually lyrical as, fumbling at the bosom of her dress, she entered.

To Leon Kantor, by who knows what symphonic scheme of things, life was a chromatic scale, yielding up to him, through throbbing, living nerves of sheep-gut, the sheerest semitones of man's emotions.

When he tucked his Stradivarius beneath his chin the book of life seemed suddenly translated to him in melody. Even Sarah Kantor, who still brewed for him, on a small portable stove carried from city to city and surreptitiously unpacked in hotel suites, the blackest of soups, and, despite his protestation, would incase his ears of nights in an old home-made device against their flightiness, would oftentimes bleed inwardly at this sense of isolation.

There was a realm into which he went alone, leaving her as detached as the merest ticket purchaser at the box-office.

At seventeen Leon Kantor had played before the crowned heads of Europe, the aching heads of American capital, and even the shaved head of a South Sea prince. There was a layout of anecdotal gifts, from the molar tooth of the South Sea prince set in a South Sea pearl to a blue-enameled snuff-box incrusted with the rearing-lion coat-of-arms of a very royal house.

At eighteen came the purchase of a king's Stradivarius for a king's ransom, and acclaimed by Sunday supplements to repose of nights in an ivory cradle.

At nineteen, under careful auspices of press agent, the ten singing digits of the son of Abrahm Kantor were insured at ten thousand dollars the finger.

At twenty he had emerged surely and safely from the perilous quicksands which have sucked down whole Lilliputian worlds of infant prodigies.

At twenty-one, when Leon Kantor played a Sunday-night concert, there was a human queue curling entirely around the square block of the opera-house, waiting its one, two, even three and four hours for the privilege of standing room only.

Usually these were Leon Kantor's own people pouring up from the lowly lands of the East Side to the white lands of Broadway, parched for music, these burning brethren of his—old men in that line, frequently carrying their own little folding camp-chairs, not against weariness of the spirit, but of the flesh; youth with Slavic eyes and cheek-bones. These were the six-deep human phalanx which would presently slant down at him from tiers of steepest balconies and stand frankly emotional and jammed in the unreserved space behind the railing which shut them off from the three-dollar seats of the reserved.

At a very special one of these concerts, dedicated to the meager purses of just these, and held in New York's super opera-house, the Amphitheater, a great bowl of humanity, the metaphor made perfect by tiers of seats placed upon the stage, rose from orchestra to dome. A gigantic cup of a Colosseum lined in stacks and stacks of faces. From the door of his dressing-room, leaning out, Leon Kantor could see a great segment of it, buzzing down into adjustment, orchestra twitting and tuning into it.

In the bare little room, illuminated by a sheaf of roses, just arrived, Mrs. Kantor drew him back by the elbow.

"Leon, you're in a draught."

The amazing years had dealt kindly with Mrs. Kantor. Stouter, softer, apparently even taller, she was full of small new authorities that could shut out cranks, newspaper reporters, and autograph fiends. A fitted-over-corsets black taffeta and a high comb in the graying hair had done their best with her. Pride, too, had left its flush upon her cheeks, like two round spots of fever.

"Leon, it's thirty minutes till your first number. Close that door. Do you want to let your papa and his excitement in on you?"

The son of Sarah Kantor obeyed, leaning his short, rather narrow form in silhouette against the closed door. In spite of slimly dark evening clothes worked out by an astute manager to the last detail in boyish effects, there was that about him which defied long-haired precedent. Slimly and straightly he had shot up into an unmannered, a short, even a bristly-haired young manhood, disqualifying by a close shave for the older school of hirsute virtuosity.

But his nerves did not spare him. On concert nights they seemed to emerge almost to the surface of him and shriek their exposure.

"Just feel my hands, ma. Like ice."

She dived down into her large silk what-not of a reticule.

"I've got your fleece-lined gloves here, son."

"No—no! For God's sake—not those things! No!"

He was back at the door again, opening it to a slit, peering through.

"They're bringing more seats on the stage. If they crowd me in I won't go on. I can't play if I hear them breathe. Hi—out there—no more chairs! Pa! Hancock—"

"Leon, Leon, ain't you ashamed to get so worked up? Close that door. Have you got a manager who is paid just to see to your comfort? When papa comes, I'll have him go out and tell Hancock you don't want chairs so close to you. Leon, will you mind mamma and sit down?"

"It's a bigger house than the royal concert in Madrid, ma. Why, I never saw anything like it! It's a stampede. God! this is real—this is what gets me, playing for my own! I should have given a concert like this three years ago. I'll do it every year now. I'd rather play before them than all the crowned heads on earth. It's the biggest night of my life. They're rioting out there, ma—rioting to get in."

"Leon, Leon, won't you sit down, if mamma begs you to?"

He sat then, strumming with all ten fingers upon his knees.

"Try to get quiet, son. Count—like you always do. One—two—three—"

"Please, ma—for God's sake—please—please!"

"Look—such beautiful roses! From Sol Ginsberg, an old friend of papa's he used to buy brasses from eighteen years ago. Six years he's been away with his daughter in Munich. Such a beautiful mezzo they say, engaged already for Metropolitan next season."

"I hate it, ma, if they breathe on my neck."

"Leon darlink, did mamma promise to fix it? Have I ever let you play a concert where you wouldn't be comfortable?"

His long, slim hands suddenly prehensile and cutting a streak of upward gesture, Leon Kantor rose to his feet, face whitening.

"Do it now! Now, I tell you. I won't have them breathe on me. Do you hear me? Now! Now! Now!"

Risen also, her face soft and tremulous for him, Mrs. Kantor put out a gentle, a sedative hand upon his sleeve.

"Son," she said, with an edge of authority even behind her smile, "don't holler at me!"

He grasped her hand with his two and, immediately quiet, lay a close string of kisses along it.

"Mamma," he said, kissing again and again into the palm, "mamma—mamma."

"I know, son; it's nerves!"

"They eat me, ma. Feel—I'm like ice! I didn't mean it; you know I didn't mean it!"

"My baby," she said, "my wonderful boy, it's like I can never get used to the wonder of having you. The greatest one of them all should be mine—a plain woman's like mine!"

He teased her, eager to conciliate and to ride down his own state of quivering.

"Now, ma—now—now—don't forget Rimsky!"

"Rimsky! A man three times your age who was playing concerts before you were born! Is that a comparison? From your clippings-books I can show Rimsky who the world considers the greatest violinist. Rimsky he rubs into me!"

"All right, then, the press-clippings, but did Elsass, the greatest manager of them all, bring me a contract for thirty concerts at two thousand a concert? Now I've got you! Now!"

She would not meet his laughter. "Elsass! Believe me, he'll come to you yet! My boy should worry if he makes fifty thousand a year more or less. Rimsky should have that honor—for so long as he can hold it. But he won't hold it long. Believe me, I don't rest easy in my bed till Elsass comes after you. Not for so big a contract like Rimsky's, but for bigger—not for thirty concerts, but for fifty!"

"*Brava! Brava!* There's a woman for you. More money than she knows what to do with, and then not satisfied!"

She was still too tremulous for banter. "'Not satisfied'? Why, Leon, I never stop praying my thanks for you!"

"All right, then," he cried, laying his icy fingers on her cheek; "to-morrow we'll call a *mignon*—a regular old-fashioned Allen Street prayer-party."

"Leon, you mustn't make fun."

"Make fun of the sweetest girl in this room!"

"'Girl'! Ah, if I could only hold you by me this way, Leon. Always a boy —with me—your poor old mother—your only girl. That's a fear I suffer with, Leon—to lose you to a—girl. That's how selfish the mother of such a wonder-child like mine can get to be."

"All right! Trying to get me married off again. Nice! Fine!"

"Is it any wonder I suffer, son? Twenty-one years to have kept you by me a child. A boy that never in his life was out after midnight except to catch trains. A boy that never has so much as looked at a girl and could have looked at princesses. To have kept you all these years—mine—is it any wonder, son, I never stop praying my thanks for you? You don't believe Hancock, son, the way he keeps always teasing you that you should have a— what he calls—affair—a love-affair? Such talk is not nice, Leon—an affair!"

"Love-affair poppycock!" said Leon Kantor, lifting his mother's face and kissing her on eyes about ready to tear. "Why, I've got something, ma, right here in my heart for you that—"

"Leon, be careful your shirt-front!"

"That's so—so what you call 'tender,' for my best sweetheart that I— Oh, love-affair—poppycock!"

She would not let her tears come.

"My boy—my wonder-boy!"

"There goes the overture, ma."

"Here, darlink—your glass of water."

"I can't stand it in here; I'm suffocating!"

"Got your mute in your pocket, son?"

"Yes, ma; for God's sake, yes! Yes! Don't keep asking things!"

"Ain't you ashamed, Leon, to be in such an excitement! For every concert you get worse."

"The chairs—they'll breathe on my neck."

"Leon, did mamma promise you those chairs would be moved?"

"Where's Hancock?"

"Say—I'm grateful if he stays out. It took me enough work to get this room cleared. You know your papa how he likes to drag in the whole world to show you off—always just before you play. The minute he walks in the room right away he gets everybody to trembling just from his own excitement. I dare him this time he should bring people. No dignity has that man got, the way he brings every one."

Even upon her words came a rattling of door, of door-knob, and a voice through the clamor.

"Open—quick—Sarah! Leon!"

A stiffening raced over Mrs. Kantor, so that she sat rigid on her chair-edge, lips compressed, eye darkly upon the shivering door.

"Open—Sarah!"

With a narrowing glance, Mrs. Kantor laid to her lips a forefinger of silence.

"Sarah, it's me! Quick, I say!"

Then Leon sprang up, the old prehensile gesture of curving fingers shooting up.

"For God's sake, ma, let him in! I can't stand that infernal battering."

"Abrahm, go away! Leon's got to have quiet before his concert."

"Just a minute, Sarah. Open quick!"

With a spring his son was at the door, unlocking and flinging it back.

"Come in, pa."

The years had weighed heavily upon Abrahm Kantor in avoirdupois only. He was himself plus eighteen years, fifty pounds, and a new sleek pomposity that was absolutely oleaginous. It shone roundly in his face, doubling of chin, in the bulge of waistcoat, heavily gold-chained, and in eyes that behind the gold-rimmed glasses gave sparklingly forth his estate of well-being.

"Abrahm, didn't I tell you not to dare to—"

On excited balls of feet that fairly bounced him, Abrahm Kantor burst in.

"Leon—mamma—I got out here an old friend—Sol Ginsberg. You remember, mamma, from brasses—"

"Abrahm—not now—"

"Go 'way with your 'not now'! I want Leon should meet him. Sol, this is him—a little grown up from such a *nebich* like you remember him—*nu?*"

"Abrahm, you must ask Mr. Ginsberg please to excuse Leon until after his concert—"

"Shake hands with him, Ginsberg. He's had his hand shook enough in his life, and by kings, too—shake it once more with an old bouncer like you!"

Mr. Ginsberg, not unlike his colleague in rotundities, held out a short, a dimpled hand.

"It's a proud day," he said, "for me to shake the hands from mine old friend's son and the finest violinist livink to-day. My little daughter—"

"Yes, yes, Gina. Here, shake hands with him. Leon, they say a voice like a fountain. Gina Berg—eh, Ginsberg—is how you stage-named her? You hear, mamma, how fancy—Gina Berg? We go hear her, eh?"

There was about Miss Gina Berg, whose voice could soar to the tirra-lirra of a lark and then deepen to mezzo, something of the actual slimness of the poor, maligned Elsa so long buried beneath the buxomness of divas. She was like a little flower that in its crannied nook keeps dewy longest.

"How do you do, Leon Kantor?"

There was a whir through her English of three acquired languages.

"How do *you* do?"

"We—father and I—traveled once all the way from Brussels to Dresden to hear you play. It was worth it. I shall never forget how you played the 'Humoresque.' It made me laugh and cry."

"You like Brussels?"

She laid her little hand to her heart, half closing her eyes.

"I will never be so happy again as with the sweet little people of Brussels."

"I, too, love Brussels. I studied there four years with Ahrenfest."

"I know you did. My teacher, Lyndahl, in Berlin, was his brother-in-law."

"You have studied with Lyndahl?"

"He is my master."

"I—will I sometime hear you sing?"

"I am not yet great. When I am foremost like you, yes."

"Gina—Gina Berg; that is a beautiful name to make famous."

"You see how it is done? Gins—berg. Gina Berg."

"Clev-er!"

They stood then smiling across a chasm of the diffidence of youth, she fumbling at the great fur pelt out of which her face flowered so dewily.

"I—well—we—we are in the fourth box— I guess we had better be going—fourth box left." He wanted to find words, but for consciousness of self could not. "It's a wonderful house out there waiting for you, Leon Kantor, and you—you're wonderful too!"

"The—flowers—thanks!"

"My father, he sent them. Come, father—quick!"

Suddenly there was a tight tensity that seemed to crowd up the little room.

"Abrahm—quick—get Hancock. That first rows of chairs—has got to be moved—there he is, in the wings—see the piano ain't dragged down too far! Leon, got your mute in your pocket? Please Mr. Ginsberg—you must excuse— Here, Leon, is your glass of water. Drink it, I say. Shut that door out there, boy, so there ain't a draught in the wings. Here, Leon, your violin. Got your neckerchief? Listen how they're shouting! It's for you, Leon—dar-link— Go!"

The center of that vast human bowl which had shouted itself out, slim, boylike, and in his supreme isolation, Leon Kantor drew bow and a first thin, pellucid, and perfect note into a silence breathless to receive it.

Throughout the arduous flexuosities of the Mendelssohn E minor concerto, singing, winding from tonal to tonal climax, and out of the slow movement which is like a tourniquet twisting the heart into the spirited *allegro molto vivace*, it was as if beneath Leon Kantor's fingers the strings were living vein-cords, youth, vitality, and the very foam of exuberance racing through them.

That was the power of him. The vichy and the sparkle of youth, so that, playing, the melody poured round him like wine and went down seething and singing into the hearts of his hearers.

Later, and because these were his people and because they were dark and Slavic with his Slavic darkness, he played, as if his very blood were weeping, the "Kol Nidre," which is the prayer of his race for atonement.

And then the super-amphitheater, filled with those whose emotions lie next to the surface and whose pores have not been closed over with a water-tight veneer, burst into its cheers and its tears.

There were fifteen recalls from the wings, Abrahm Kantor standing counting them off on his fingers and trembling to receive the Stradivarius. Then, finally, and against the frantic negative pantomime of his manager, a scherzo, played so lacily that it swept the house in lightest laughter.

When Leon Kantor finally completed his program they were loath to let him go, crowding down the aisles upon him, applauding up, down, around him until the great disheveled house was like the roaring of a sea, and he would laugh and throw out his arm in widespread helplessness, and always his manager in the background gesticulating against too much of his precious product for the money, ushers already slamming up chairs, his father's arms out for the Stradivarius, and, deepest in the gloom of the wings, Sarah Kantor, in a rocker especially dragged out for her, and from the depths of the black-silk reticule, darning his socks.

"Bravo—bravo! Give us the 'Humoresque'—Chopin Nocturne—Polonaise—'Humoresque.' Bravo—bravo!"

And even as they stood, hatted and coated, importuning and pressing in upon him, and with a wisp of a smile to the fourth left box, Leon Kantor played them the "Humoresque" of Dvořák, skedaddling, plucking, quirking—that laugh on life with a tear behind it. Then suddenly, because he could escape no other way, rushed straight back for his dressing-room, bursting in upon a flood of family already there: Isadore Kantor, blue-shaved, aquiline, and already graying at the temples; his five-year-old son, Leon; a soft little pouter-pigeon of a wife, too, enormous of bust, in glittering ear-drops and a wrist watch of diamonds half buried in chubby wrist; Miss Esther Kantor, pink and pretty; Rudolph; Boris, not yet done with growing-pains.

At the door Miss Kantor met her brother, her eyes as sweetly moist as her kiss.

"Leon darling, you surpassed even yourself!"

"Quit crowding, children. Let him sit down. Here, Leon, let mamma give you a fresh collar. Look how the child's perspired. Pull down that window, Boris. Rudolph, don't let no one in. I give you my word if to-night wasn't as near as I ever came to seeing a house go crazy. Not even that time in Milan, darlink, when they broke down the doors, was it like to-night—"

"Ought to seen, ma, the row of police outside—"

"Hush up, Roody! Don't you see your brother is trying to get his breath?"

From Mrs. Isadore Kantor: "You should have seen the balconies, mother. Isadore and I went up just to see the jam."

"Six thousand dollars in the house to-night, if there was a cent," said Isadore Kantor.

"Hand me my violin, please, Esther. I must have scratched it, the way they pushed."

"No, son, you didn't. I've already rubbed it up. Sit quiet, darlink!"

He was limply white, as if the vitality had flowed out of him.

"God! Wasn't it—tremendous?"

"Six thousand, if there was a cent," repeated Isadore Kantor. "More than Rimsky ever played to in his life!"

"Oh, Izzie, you make me sick, always counting—counting!"

"Your sister's right, Isadore. You got nothing to complain of if there was only six hundred in the house. A boy whose fiddle has made already enough to set you up in such a fine business, his brother Boris in such a fine college, automobiles—style—and now because Vladimir Rimsky, three times his age, gets signed up with Elsass for a few thousand more a year, right away the family gets a long face—"

"Ma, please! Isadore didn't mean it that way!"

"Pa's knocking, ma! Shall I let him in?"

"Let him in, Roody. I'd like to know what good it will do to try to keep him out."

In an actual rain of perspiration, his tie slid well under one ear, Abrahm Kantor burst in, mouthing the words before his acute state of strangulation would let them out.

"Elsass—it's Elsass outside! He—wants—to sign—Leon—fifty concerts—coast to coast—two thousand—next season! He's got the papers—already drawn up—the pen outside waiting—"

"Abrahm!"

"Pa!"

In the silence that followed, Isadore Kantor, a poppiness of stare and a violent redness set in, suddenly turned to his five-year-old son, sticky with lollipop, and came down soundly and with smack against the infantile, the slightly outstanding and unsuspecting ear.

"*Momser!*" he cried. "*Chammer! Lump! Ganef!* You hear that? Two thousand! Two thousand! Didn't I tell you—didn't I tell you to practise?"

Even as Leon Kantor put pen to this princely document, Franz Ferdinand of Serbia, the assassin's bullet cold, lay dead in state, and let slip were the dogs of war.

In the next years, men, forty deep, were to die in piles; hayricks of fields to become human hayricks of battle-fields; Belgium disemboweled, her very entrails dragging, to find all the civilized world her champion, and between the poppies of Flanders, crosses, thousand upon thousand of them, to mark the places where the youth of her allies fell, avenging outrage. Seas, even when calmest, were to become terrible, and men's heart-beats, a bit sluggish with the fatty degeneration of a sluggard peace, to quicken and then to throb with the rat-a-tat-tat, the rat-a-tat-tat of the most peremptory, the most reverberating call to arms in the history of the world.

In June, 1917, Leon Kantor, answering that rat-a-tat-tat, enlisted.

In November, honed by the interim of training to even a new leanness, and sailing-orders heavy and light in his heart, Lieutenant Kantor, on two days' home-leave, took leave of home, which can be cruelest when it is tenderest.

Standing there in the expensive, the formal, the enormous French parlor of his up-town apartment de luxe, from not one of whose chairs would his mother's feet touch floor, a wall of living flesh, mortared in blood, was throbbing and hedging him in.

He would pace up and down the long room, heavy with the faces of those who mourn, with a laugh too ready, too facetious, in his fear for them.

"Well, well, what is this, anyway, a wake? Where's the coffin? Who's dead?"

His sister-in-law shot out her plump, watch-encrusted wrist. "Don't, Leon!" she cried. "Such talk is a sin! It might come true."

"Rosie-posy-butter-ball," he said, pausing beside her chair to pinch her deeply soft cheek. "Cry-baby-roly-poly, you can't shove me off in a wooden kimono that way."

From his place before the white-and-gold mantel, staring steadfastly at the floor tiling, Isadore Kantor turned suddenly, a bit whiter and older at the temples.

"I don't get your comedy, Leon."

"'Wooden kimono'—Leon?"

"That's the way the fellows at camp joke about coffins, ma. I didn't mean anything but fun! Great Scott! Can't any one take a joke!"

"O God! O God!" His mother fell to swaying softly, hugging herself against shivering.

"Did you sign over power of attorney to pa, Leon?"

"All fixed, Izzie."

"I'm so afraid, son, you don't take with you enough money in your pockets. You know how you lose it. If only you would let mamma sew that little bag inside your uniform with a little place for bills and a little place for the asafœtida!"

"Now, please, ma—please! If I needed more, wouldn't I take it? Wouldn't I be a pretty joke among the fellows, tied up in that smelling stuff! Orders are orders, ma. I know what to take and what not to take."

"Please, Leon, don't get mad at me, but if you will let me put in your suit-case just one little box of that salve, for your finger-tips, so they don't crack—"

Pausing as he paced to lay cheek to her hair, he patted her. "Three boxes, if you want. Now, how's that?"

"And you won't take it out so soon as my back is turned?"

"Cross my heart."

His touch seemed to set her trembling again, all her illy concealed emotions rushing up. "I can't stand it! Can't! Can't! Take my life—take my blood, but don't take my boy—don't take my boy—"

"Mamma, mamma, is that the way you're going to begin all over again, after your promise?"

She clung to him, heaving against the rising storm of sobs. "I can't help it—can't! Cut out my heart from me, but let me keep my boy—my wonder-boy—"

"Oughtn't she be ashamed of herself? Just listen to her, Esther! What will we do with her? Talks like she had a guarantee I wasn't coming back. Why, I wouldn't be surprised if by spring I wasn't tuning up again for a coast-to-coast tour—"

"Spring! That talk don't fool me. Without my boy, the springs in my life are over—"

"Why, ma, you talk like every soldier who goes to war was killed! There's only the smallest percentage of them die in battle—"

"'Spring,' he says; 'spring'! Crossing the seas from me! To live through months with that sea between us—my boy maybe shot—my—"

"Mamma, please!"

"I can't help it, Leon; I'm not one of those fine mothers that can be so brave. Cut out my heart, but leave my boy! My wonder-boy—my child I prayed for!"

"There's other mothers, ma, with sons!"

"Yes, but not wonder-sons! A genius like you could so easy get excused, Leon. Give it up. Genius it should be the last to be sent to—the slaughter-pen. Leon darlink—don't go!"

"Ma, ma—you don't mean what you're saying. You wouldn't want me to reason that way! You wouldn't want me to hide behind my—violin."

"I would! Would! You should wait for the draft. With my Roody and even my baby Boris enlisted, ain't it enough for one mother? Since they got to be in camp, all right, I say, let them be there, if my heart breaks for it, but not my wonder-child! You can get exemption, Leon, right away for the asking. Stay with me, Leon! Don't go away! The people at home got to be kept happy with music. That's being a soldier, too, playing their troubles away. Stay with me, Leon! Don't go leave me—don't—don't—"

He suffered her to lie, tear-drenched, back into his arms, holding her close in his compassion for her, his own face twisting.

"God! ma, this—this is awful! Please—you make us ashamed—all of us! I don't know what to say. Esther, come quiet her—for God's sake quiet her!"

From her place in that sobbing circle Esther Kantor crossed to kneel beside her mother.

"Mother darling, you're killing yourself. What if every family went on this way? You want papa to come in and find us all crying? Is this the way you want Leon to spend his last hour with us—"

"Oh, God—God!"

"I mean his last hour until he comes back, darling. Didn't you just hear him say, darling, it may be by spring?"

"'Spring'—'spring'—never no more springs for me—"

"Just think, darling, how proud we should be! Our Leon, who could so easily have been excused, not even to wait for the draft."

"It's not too late yet—please—Leon—"

"Our Roody and Boris both in camp, too, training to serve their country. Why, mamma, we ought to be crying for happiness. As Leon says, surely the Kantor family, who fled out of Russia to escape massacre, should know how terrible slavery can be. That's why we must help our boys, mamma, in their fight to make the world free! Right, Leon?" trying to smile with her red-rimmed eyes.

"We've got no fight with no one! Not a child of mine was ever raised to so much as lift a finger against no one. We've got no fight with no one!"

"We have got a fight with some one! With autocracy! Only this time it happens to be Hunnish autocracy. You should know it, mamma—oh, you should know it deeper down in you than any of us, the fight our family right here has got with autocracy! We should be the first to want to avenge Belgium!"

"Leon's right, mamma darling, the way you and papa were beaten out of your country—"

"There's not a day in your life you don't curse it without knowing it! Every time we three boys look at your son and our brother Mannie, born an—an imbecile—because of autocracy, we know what we're fighting for. We know. You know, too. Look at him over there, even before he was born, ruined by autocracy! Know what I'm fighting for? Why, this whole family knows! What's music, what's art, what's life itself in a world without freedom? Every time, ma, you get to thinking we've got a fight with no one, all you have to do is look at our poor Mannie. He's the answer. He's the answer."

In a foaming sort of silence, Mannie Kantor smiled softly from his chair beneath the pink-and-gold shade of the piano-lamp. The heterogeneous sounds of women weeping had ceased. Straight in her chair, her great shelf of bust heaving, sat Rosa Kantor, suddenly dry of eye; Isadore Kantor head up. Erect now, and out from the embrace of her daughter, Sarah looked up at her son.

"What time do you leave, Leon?" she asked, actually firm of lip.

"Any minute, ma. Getting late."

This time she pulled her lips to a smile, waggling her forefinger.

"Don't let them little devils of French girls fall in love with my dude in his uniform."

Her pretense at pleasantry was almost more than he could bear.

"Hear! Hear! Our mother thinks I'm a regular lady-killer! Hear that, Esther?" pinching her cheek.

"You are, Leon—only—only, you don't know it!"

"Don't you bring down too many beaux while I'm gone either, Miss Kantor!"

"I—won't, Leon."

Sotto voce to her: "Remember, Esther, while I'm gone, the royalties from the discaphone records are yours. I want you to have them for pin-money and—maybe a dowry?"

She turned from him. "Don't, Leon—don't—"

"I like him! Nice fellow, but too slow! Why, if I were in his shoes I'd have popped long ago."

She smiled with her lashes dewy.

There entered then, in a violet-scented little whirl, Miss Gina Berg, rosy with the sting of a winter's night, and, as usual, swathed in the high-napped furs.

"Gina!"

She was for greeting every one, a wafted kiss to Mrs. Kantor, and then, arms wide, a great bunch of violets in one outstretched hand, her glance straight, sure, and sparkling for Leon Kantor.

"Surprise—everybody—surprise!"

"Why, Gina—we read—we thought you were singing in Philadelphia to-night!"

"So did I, Esther darling, until a little bird whispered to me that Lieutenant Kantor was home on farewell leave."

He advanced to her down the great length of room, lowering his head over his hand, his puttee-clad legs clicking together. "You mean, Miss Gina—Gina—you didn't sing?"

"Of course I didn't! Hasn't every prima donna a larynx to hide behind?" She lifted off her fur cap, spilling curls.

"Well, I—I'll be hanged!" said Lieutenant Kantor, his eyes lakes of her reflected loveliness.

She let her hand linger in his. "Leon—you—really going? How—terrible! How—how—wonderful!"

"How wonderful—your coming!"

"I— You think it was not nice of me—to come?"

"I think it was the nicest thing that ever happened in the world."

"All the way here to the train I kept saying, 'Crazy—crazy—running to tell Leon—Lieutenant—Kantor good-by—when you haven't seen him three times in three years—'"

"But each—each of those three times we—we've remembered, Gina."

"But that's how I feel toward all the boys, Leon—our fighting boys—just like flying to them to kiss them each one good-by."

"Come over, Gina. You'll be a treat to our mother. I—Well, I'm hanged! All the way from Philadelphia!"

There was even a sparkle to talk, then, and a let-up of pressure. After a while Sarah Kantor looked up at her son, tremulous, but smiling.

"Well, son, you going to play—for your old mother before—you go? It'll be many a month—spring—maybe longer, before I hear my boy again except on the discaphone."

He shot a quick glance to his sister. "Why, I—I don't know. I—I'd love it, ma, if—if you think, Esther, I'd better."

"You don't need to be afraid of me, darlink. There's nothing can give me the strength to bear—what's before me like—like my boy's music. That's my life, his music."

"Why, yes; if mamma is sure she feels that way, play for us, Leon."

He was already at the instrument, where it lay, swathed, atop the grand piano. "What'll it be, folks?"

"Something to make ma laugh, Leon—something light, something funny."

"'Humoresque,'" he said, with a quick glance for Miss Berg.

"'Humoresque,'" she said, smiling back at him.

He capered through, cutting and playful of bow, the melody of Dvořák's, which is as ironic as a grinning mask.

Finished, he smiled at his parent, her face still untearful.

"How's that?"

She nodded. "It's like life, son, that piece. Crying to hide its laughing and laughing to hide its crying."

"Play that new piece, Leon—the one you set to music. You know. The words by that young boy in the war who wrote such grand poetry before he was killed. The one that always makes poor Mannie laugh. Play it for him, Leon."

Her plump little unlined face innocent of fault, Mrs. Isadore Kantor ventured her request, her smile tired with tears.

"No, no—Rosa—not now! Ma wouldn't want that!"

"I do, son; I do! Even Mannie should have his share of good-by."

To Gina Berg: "They want me to play that little arrangement of mine from Allan Seegar's poem. 'I Have a Rendezvous . . . .'"

"It—it's beautiful, Leon. I was to have sung it on my program to-night—only, I'm afraid you had better not—here—now—"

"Please, Leon! Nothing you play can ever make me as sad as it makes me glad. Mannie should have, too, his good-by."

"All right, then, ma, if—if you're sure you want it. Will you sing it, Gina?"

She had risen. "Why, yes, Leon."

She sang it then, quite purely, her hands clasped simply together and her glance mistily off, the beautiful, the heroic, the lyrical prophecy of a soldier-poet and a poet-soldier:

> "But I've a rendezvous with Death
> On some scarred slope of battered hill,
> When spring comes round again this year
> And the first meadow-flowers appear."

In the silence that followed, a sob burst out, stifled, from Esther Kantor, this time her mother holding her in arms that were strong.

"This, Leon, is the most beautiful of all your compositions. What does it mean, son, that word, 'rondy-voo'?"

"Why, I—I don't exactly know. A rendezvous—it's a sort of meeting, an engagement, isn't it, Miss Gina? Gina? You're up on languages. As if I had an appointment to meet you some place—at the opera-house, for instance."

"That's it, Leon—an engagement."

"Have I an engagement with you, Gina?"

She let her lids droop. "Oh, how—how I hope you have, Leon."

"When?"

"In the spring?"

"That's it—in the spring."

Then they smiled, these two, who had never felt more than the merest butterfly wings of love brushing them, light as lashes. No word between them, only an unfinished sweetness, waiting to be linked up.

Suddenly there burst in Abrahm Kantor, in a carefully rehearsed gale of bluster.

"Quick, Leon! I got the car down-stairs. Just fifteen minutes to make the ferry. Quick! The sooner we get him over there the sooner we get him back! I'm right, mamma? Now, now! No water-works! Get your brother's suit-case, Isadore. Now, now! No nonsense! Quick—quick—"

With a deftly manœuvered round of good-bys, a grip-laden dash for the door, a throbbing moment of turning back when it seemed as though Sarah Kantor's arms could not unlock their deadlock of him, Leon Kantor was out and gone, the group of faces point-etched into the silence behind him.

The poor, mute face of Mannie, laughing softly. Rosa Kantor crying into her hands. Esther, grief-crumpled, but rich in the enormous hope of youth. The sweet Gina, to whom the waiting months had already begun their reality.

Not so Sarah Kantor. In a bedroom adjoining, its high-ceilinged vastness as cold as a cathedral to her lowness of stature, sobs dry and terrible were rumbling up from her, only to dash against lips tightly restraining them.

On her knees beside a chest of drawers, and unwrapping it from swaddling-clothes, she withdrew what at best had been a sorry sort of fiddle.

Cracked of back and solitary of string, it was as if her trembling arms, raising it above her head, would make of themselves and her swaying body the tripod of an altar.

The old twisting and prophetic pain was behind her heart. Like the painted billows of music that the old Italian masters loved to do, there wound and wreathed about her clouds of song:

> But I've a rendezvous with Death
> On some scarred slope of battered hill,
> When spring comes round again this year
> And the first meadow-flowers appear.

She Walks in Beauty

First Published: *Cosmopolitan*, August 1921
Reprinted: *The Vertical City*, Harper & Bros., 1922
The Best Short Stories of 1921, ed. Edward J. O'Brien, Small, Maynard & Co., 1922
*Creating the Short Story: A Symposium Anthology with an Introduction
by Henry Goodman*, Harcourt, Brace & Co., 1929
The World's One Hundred Best Short Stories, Vol. 7 [Women],
ed. Grant M. Overton, Funk, 1927

By that same architectural gesture of grief which caused Jehan at Agra to erect the Taj Mahal in memory of a dead wife and a cold hearthstone, so the Bon Ton hotel, even to the pillars with red-freckled monoliths and peacock-backed lobby chairs, making the analogy rather absurdly complete, reared its fourteen stories of "elegantly furnished suites, all the comforts and none of the discomforts of home."

A mausoleum to the hearth. And as true to form as any that ever mourned the dynastic bones of an Augustus or a Hadrian.

An Indiana-limestone and Vermont-marble tomb to Hestia.

All ye who enter here, at sixty dollars a week and up, leave behind the lingo of the fireside chair, parsley bed, servant problem, cretonne shoe bags, hose nozzle, striped awnings, attic trunks, bird houses, ice-cream salt, spare-room matting, fruit jars, spring painting, summer covers, fall cleaning, winter apples.

The mosaic tablet of the family hotel is nailed to the room side of each door and its commandments read something like this:

One ring: Bell Boy.
Two rings: Chambermaid.
Three rings: Valet.
Under no conditions are guests permitted to use electric irons in rooms.
Cooking in rooms not permitted.
No dogs allowed.
Management not responsible for loss or theft of jewels.
Same can be deposited for safe-keeping in the safe at office.

Note:

Our famous two-dollar Table d'Hôte dinner is served in the
Red Dining Room from six-thirty to eight. Music.

It is doubtful if in all its hothouse garden of women the Hotel Bon Ton
boasted a broken finger nail or that little brash place along the forefinger that
tattles so of potato peeling or asparagus scraping.

The fourteenth-story manicure, steam bath, and beauty parlors saw to all
that. In spite of long bridge table, lobby divan, and table-d'hôte séances, "tea"
where the coffee was served with whipped cream and the tarts built in four
tiers and mortared in mocha filling, the Bon Ton hotel was scarcely more
than an average of fourteen pounds overweight.

Forty's silhouette, except for that cruel and irrefutable place where the
throat will wattle, was almost interchangeable with eighteen's. Indeed, Bon
Ton grandmothers with backs and French heels that were twenty years
younger than their throats and bunions, vied with twenty's profile.

Whistler's kind of mother, full of sweet years that were richer because she
had dwelt in them, but whose eyelids were a little weary, had no place there.

Mrs. Gronauer, who occupied an outside, southern-exposure suite of five
rooms and three baths, jazzed on the same cabaret floor with her grand-
daughters.

Many of the Bon Ton afternoon devoted entirely to the possible lack of
length of the new season's skirts or the intricacies of the new filet-lace pat-
terns.

Fads for the latest personal accoutrements gripped the Bon Ton in sea-
sonal epidemics.

The permanent wave swept it like a tidal one.

In one winter of afternoons enough colored-silk sweaters were knitted in
the lobby alone to supply an orphan asylum, but didn't.

The beaded bag, cunningly contrived, needleful by needleful, from little
strands of colored-glass caviar, glittered its hour.

Filet lace came then, sheerly, whole yokes of it for crêpe-de-Chine nightgowns and dainty scalloped edges for camisoles.

Mrs. Samstag made six of the nightgowns that winter—three for herself
and three for her daughter. Peach-blowy pink ones with lace yokes that were
scarcely more to the skin than the print of a wave edge running up sand, and
then little frills of pink-satin ribbon, caught up here and there with the most
delightful and unconvincing little blue-satin rosebuds.

It was bad for her neuralgic eye, the meanderings of the filet pattern, but she liked the delicate threadiness of the handiwork, and Mr. Latz liked watching her.

There you have it! Straight through the lacy mesh of the filet to the heart interest.

Mr. Louis Latz, who was too short, slightly too stout, and too shy of likely length of swimming arm ever to have figured in any woman's inevitable visualization of her ultimate Leander, liked, fascinatedly, to watch Mrs. Samstag's nicely manicured fingers at work. He liked them passive, too. Best of all, he would have preferred to feel them between his own, but that had never been.

Nevertheless, that desire was capable of catching him unawares. That very morning as he had stood, in his sumptuous bachelor's apartment, strumming on one of the windows that overlooked an expansive tree-and-lake vista of Central Park, he had wanted very suddenly and very badly to feel those fingers in his and to kiss down on them.

Even in his busy broker's office, this desire could cut him like a swift lance.

He liked their taper and their rosy pointedness, those fingers, and the dry, neat way they had of stepping in between the threads.

Mr. Latz's nails were manicured, too, not quite so pointedly, but just as correctly as Mrs. Samstag's. But his fingers were stubby and short. Sometimes he pulled at them until they cracked.

Secretly he yearned for length of limb, of torso, even of finger.

On this, one of a hundred such typical evenings in the Bon Ton lobby, Mr. Latz, sighing out a satisfaction of his inner man, sat himself down on a red-velvet chair opposite Mrs. Samstag. His knees, widespread, taxed his knife-pressed gray trousers to their very last capacity, but he sat back in none the less evident comfort, building his fingers up into a little chapel.

"Well, how's Mr. Latz this evening?" asked Mrs. Samstag, her smile encompassing the question.

"If I was any better I couldn't stand it," relishing her smile and his reply.

The Bon Ton had just dined, too well, from fruit flip *à la* Bon Ton, mulligatawny soup, filet of sole *sauté,* choice of or both *poulette eminé* and spring lamb *grignon,* and on through to fresh strawberry ice cream in fluted paper boxes, *petits fours,* and *demi-tasse.* Groups of carefully corseted women stood now beside the invitational plush divans and peacock chairs, paying twenty minutes' after-dinner standing penance. Men with Wall Street eyes and blood pressure slid surreptitious celluloid toothpicks and gathered around the cigar stand. Orchestra music flickered. Young girls, the traditions of demure sixteen hanging by one-inch shoulder straps, and who could not walk across a hardwood floor without sliding the last three steps, teetered in bare arm-in-arm groups, swapping persiflage with pimply, patent-leather-haired young men who were full of nervous excitement and eager to excel in return badinage.

Bell hops scurried with folding tables. Bridge games formed.

The theater group got off, so to speak. Showy women and show-off men. Mrs. Gronauer, in a full-length mink coat that enveloped her like a squaw, a titillation of diamond aigrettes in her Titianed hair, and an aftermath of scent as tangible as the trail of a wounded shark, emerged from the elevator with her son and daughter-in-law.

"Foi!" said Mr. Latz, by way of somewhat unduly, perhaps, expressing his own kind of cognizance of the scented trail.

"*Fleur de printemps,*" said Mrs. Samstag, in quick olfactory analysis. "Eight-ninety-eight an ounce." Her nose crawling up to what he thought the cunning perfection of a sniff.

"Used to it from home—not? She is not. Believe me, I knew Max Gronauer when he first started in the produce business in Jersey City and the only perfume he had was at seventeen cents a pound and not always fresh killed at that. *Cold storage de printemps!*"

"Max Gronauer died just two months after my husband," said Mrs. Samstag, tucking away into her beaded handbag her filet-lace handkerchief, itself guilty of a not inexpensive attar.

"Thu-thu!" clucked Mr. Latz for want of a fitting retort.

"Heigh-ho! I always say we have so little in common, me and Mrs. Gronauer, she revokes so in bridge, and I think it's terrible for a grandmother to blondine so red, but we've both been widows for almost eight years. Eight years," repeated Mrs. Samstag on a small, scented sigh.

He was inordinately sensitive to these allusions, reddening and wanting to seem appropriate.

"Poor little woman, you've had your share of trouble."

"Share," she repeated, swallowing a gulp and pressing the line of her eyebrows as if her thoughts were sobbing. "I— It's as I tell Alma, Mr. Latz, sometimes I think I've had three times my share. My one consolation is that I make the best of it. That's my motto in life, 'Keep a bold front.'"

For the life of him, all he could find to convey to her the bleeding quality of his sympathy was, "Poor, poor little woman!"

"Heigh-ho!" she said, and again, "Heigh-ho!"

There was quite a nape to her neck. He could see it where the carefully trimmed brown hair left it for a rise to skillful coiffure, and what threatened to be a slight depth of flesh across the shoulders had been carefully massaged of this tendency, fifteen minutes each night and morning, by her daughter.

In fact, through the black transparency of her waist Mr. Latz thought her plumply adorable.

It was about the eyes that Mrs. Samstag showed most plainly whatever inroads into her clay the years might have gained. There were little dark areas beneath them like smeared charcoal, and two unrelenting sacs that threatened to become pouchy.

Their effect was not so much one of years, but they gave Mrs. Samstag, in spite of the only slightly plump and really passable figure, the look of one out of health. Women of her kind of sallowness can be found daily in fashionable physicians' outer offices, awaiting X-ray appointments.

What ailed Mrs. Samstag was hardly organic. She was the victim of periodic and raging neuralgic fires that could sweep the right side of her head and down into her shoulder blade with a great crackling and blazing of nerves. It was not unusual for her daughter Alma to sit up the one or two nights that it could endure, unfailing through the wee hours in her chain of hot applications.

For a week, sometimes, these attacks heralded their comings with little jabs, like the pricks of an exploring needle. Then the under-eyes began to look their muddiest. They were darkening now and she put up two fingers with a little pressing movement to her temple.

"You're a great little woman," reiterated Mr. Latz, rather riveting even Mrs. Samstag's suspicion that here was no great stickler for variety of expression.

"I try to be," she said, his tone inviting out in her a mood of sweet forbearance.

"And a great sufferer, too," he said, noting the pressing fingers.

She colored under this delightful impeachment.

"I wouldn't wish one of my neuralgia spells to my worst enemy, Mr. Latz."

"If you were mine—I mean—if—the—say—was mine—I wouldn't stop until I had you to every specialist in Europe. I know a thing or two about those fellows over there. Some of them are wonders."

Mrs. Samstag looked off, her profile inclined to lift and fall as if by little pulleys of emotion.

"That's easier said than done, Mr. Latz, by a—a widow who wants to do right by her grown daughter and living so—high since the war."

"I—I— " said Mr. Latz, leaping impulsively forward on the chair that was as tightly upholstered in effect as he in his modish suit, then clutching himself there as if he had caught the impulse on the fly, "I just wish I could help."

"Oh!" she said, and threw up a swift brown look from the lace making and then at it again.

He laughed, but from nervousness.

"My little mother was an ailer, too."

"That's me, Mr. Latz. Not sick—just ailing. I always say that it's ridiculous that a woman in such perfect health as I am should be such a sufferer."

"Same with her and her old joints."

"Why, except for this old neuralgia, I can outdo Alma when it comes to dancing down in the grill with the young people of an evening, or shopping."

"More like sisters than any mother and daughter I ever saw."

"Mother and daughter, but which is which from the back, some of my friends put it," said Mrs. Samstag, not without a curve to her voice; then, hastily: "But the best child, Mr. Latz. The best that ever lived. A regular little mother to me in my spells."

"Nice girl, Alma."

"It snowed so the day of—my husband's funeral. Why, do you know that up to then I never had an attack of neuralgia in my life. Didn't even know what a headache was. That long drive. That windy hilltop with two men to keep me from jumping into the grave after him. Ask Alma. That's how I care when I care. But, of course, as the saying is, 'time heals.' But that's how I got my first attack. 'Intenseness' is what the doctors called it. I'm terribly intense."

"I—guess when a woman like you—cares like—you—cared, it's not much use hoping you would ever—care again. That's about the way of it, isn't it?"

If he had known it, there was something about his intensity of expression to inspire mirth. His eyebrows lifted to little Gothic arches of anxiety, a rash of tiny perspiration broke out over his blue shaved face, and as he sat on the edge of his chair it seemed that inevitably the tight sausagelike knees must push their way through mere fabric.

Ordinarily he presented the slightly bay-windowed, bay-rummed, spatted, and somewhat jowled well-being of the Wall Street bachelor who is a musical-comedy first-nighter, can dig the meat out of the lobster claw whole, takes his beefsteak rare and with two or three condiments, and wears his elk's tooth dangling from his waistcoat pocket and mounted on a band of platinum and tiny diamonds.

Mothers of débutantes were by no means unamiably disposed toward him, but the débutantes themselves slithered away like slim-flanked minnows.

It was rumored that one summer at the Royal Palisades Hotel in Atlantic City he had become engaged to a slim-flanked one from Akron, Ohio. But on the evening of the first day she had seen him in a bathing suit the rebellious young girl and a bitterly disappointed and remonstrating mother had departed on the Buck Eye for "points west."

There was almost something of the nudity of arm and leg he must have presented to eighteen's tender sensibilities in Mr. Latz's expression now as he sat well forward on the overstuffed chair, his overstuffed knees strained apart, his face nude of all pretense and creased with anxiety.

"That's about the way of it, isn't it?" he said again into the growing silence.

Suddenly Mrs. Samstag's fingers were rigid at their task of lace making, the scraping of the orchestral violin tearing the roaring noises in her ears into ribbons of alternate sound and vacuum, as if she were closing her ears and opening them, so roaringly the blood pounded.

"I— When a woman cares for—a man like—I did—Mr. Latz, she'll never be happy until—she cares again—like that. I always say, once an affectionate nature, always an affectionate nature."

"You mean," he said, leaning forward the imperceptible half inch that was left of chair—"you mean—me—?"

The smell of bay rum came out greenly then as the moisture sprang out on his scalp.

"I—I'm a home woman, Mr. Latz. You can put a fish in water, but you cannot make him swim. That's me and hotel life."

At this somewhat cryptic apothegm Mr. Latz's knee touched Mrs. Samstag's, so that he sprang back full of nerves at what he had not intended.

"Marry me, Carrie," he said, more abruptly than he might have, without the act of that knee to immediately justify.

She spread the lace out on her lap.

Ostensibly to the hotel lobby they were as casual as, "My mulligatawny soup was cold to-night," or, "Have you heard the new one that Al Jolson pulls at the Winter Garden?" But actually the roar was higher than ever in Mrs. Samstag's ears and he could feel the plethoric red rushing in flashes over his body.

"Marry me, Carrie," he said, as if to prove that his stiff lips could repeat their incredible feat.

With a woman's talent for them, her tears sprang.

"Mr. Latz—"

"Louis," he interpolated, widely eloquent of eyebrow and posture.

"You're proposing, Louis!" She explained rather than asked, and placed her hand to her heart so prettily that he wanted to crush it there with his kisses.

"God bless you for knowing it so easy, Carrie. A young girl would make it so hard. It's just what has kept me from asking you weeks ago, this getting it said. Carrie, will you?"

"I'm a widow, Mr. Latz—Louis—"

"Loo—"

"L—loo. With a grown daughter. Not one of those merry-widows you read about."

"That's me! A bachelor on top, but a home man underneath. Why, up to five years ago, Carrie, while the best little mother a man ever had was alive, I never had eyes for a woman or—"

"It's common talk what a grand son you were to her, Mr. La—Louis—"

"Loo."

"Loo."

"I don't want to seem to brag, Carrie, but you saw the coat that just walked out on Mrs. Gronauer? My little mother she was a humpback, Carrie, not a real one, but all stooped from the heavy years when she was helping my father to get his start. Well, anyway, that little stooped back was one of the reasons why I was so anxious to make it up to her. Y'understand?"

"Yes—Loo."

"But you saw that mink coat. Well, my little mother, three years before she died, was wearing one like that in sable. Real Russian. Set me back eighteen thousand, wholesale, and she never knew different than that it cost eighteen hundred. Proudest moment of my life when I helped my little old mother into her own automobile in that sable coat.

"I had some friends lived in the Grenoble Apartment when you did—the Adelbergs. They used to tell me how it hung right down to her heels and she never got into the auto that she didn't pick it up so as not to sit on it.

"That there coat is packed away in cold storage now, Carrie, waiting, without me exactly knowing why, I guess, for—the one little woman in the world besides her I would let so much as touch its hem."

Mrs. Samstag's lips parted, her teeth showing through like light.

"Oh," she said, "sable! That's my fur, Loo. I've never owned any, but ask Alma if I don't stop to look at it in every shop window. Sable!"

"Carrie—would you—could you— I'm not what you would call a youngster in years, I guess, but forty-four isn't—"

"I'm—forty-one, Louis. A man like you could have younger."

"No. That's what I don't want. In my lonesomeness, after my mother's death, I thought once that maybe a young girl from the West, nice girl with her mother from Ohio—but I—funny thing, now I come to think about it— I never once mentioned my little mother's sable coat to her. I couldn't have satisfied a young girl like that, or her me, Carrie, any more than I could satisfy Alma. It was one of those mamma-made matches that we got into because we couldn't help it and out of it before it was too late. No, no, Carrie, what I want is a woman as near as possible to my own age."

"Loo, I—I couldn't start in with you even with the one little lie that gives every woman a right to be a liar. I'm forty-three, Louis—nearer to forty-four. You're not mad, Loo?"

"God love it! If that ain't a little woman for you! Mad? Why, just your doing that little thing with me raises your stock fifty per cent."

"I'm—that way."

"We're a lot alike, Carrie. For five years I've been living in this hotel because it's the best I can do under the circumstances. But at heart I'm a home man, Carrie, and unless I'm pretty much off my guess, you are, too—I mean a home woman. Right?"

"Me all over, Loo. Ask Alma if—"

"I've got the means, too, Carrie, to give a woman a home to be proud of."

"Just for fun, ask Alma, Loo, if one year since her father's death I haven't said, 'Alma, I wish I had the heart to go back housekeeping.'"

"I knew it!"

"But I ask you, Louis, what's been the incentive? Without a man in the house I wouldn't have the same interest. That first winter after my husband died I didn't even have the heart to take the summer covers off the furniture. Alma was a child then, too, so I kept asking myself, 'For what should I take an interest?' You can believe me or not, but half the time with just me to eat it, I wouldn't bother with more than a cold snack for supper, and everyone knew what a table we used to set. But with no one to come home evenings expecting a hot meal—"

"You poor little woman! I know how it is. Why, if I so much as used to telephone that I couldn't get home for supper, right away I knew the little mother would turn out the gas under what was cooking and not eat enough herself to keep a bird alive."

"Housekeeping is no life for a woman alone. On the other hand, Mr. Latz—Louis—Loo, on my income, and with a daughter growing up, and naturally anxious to give her the best, it hasn't been so easy. People think I'm a rich widow, and with her father's memory to consider and a young lady daughter, naturally I let them think it, but on my seventy-four hundred a year it has been hard to keep up appearances in a hotel like this. Not that I think you think I'm a rich widow, but just the same, that's me every time. Right out with the truth from the start."

"It shows you're a clever little manager to be able to do it."

"We lived big and spent big while my husband lived. He was as shrewd a jobber in knit underwear as the business ever saw, but—well, you know how it is. Pneumonia. I always say he wore himself out with conscientiousness."

"Maybe you don't believe it, Carrie, but it makes me happy what you just said about money. It means I can give you things you couldn't afford for yourself. I don't say this for publication, Carrie, but in Wall Street alone, outside of my brokerage business, I cleared eighty-six thousand last year. I can give you the best. You deserve it, Carrie. Will you say yes?"

"My daughter, Loo. She's only eighteen, but she's my shadow—I lean on her so."

"A sweet, dutiful girl like Alma would be the last to stand in her mother's light."

"But, remember, Louis, you're marrying a little family."

"That don't scare me."

"She's my only. We're different natured. Alma's a Samstag through and through. Quiet, reserved. But she's my all, Louis. I love my baby too much to—to marry where she wouldn't be as welcome as the day itself. She's precious to me, Louis."

"Why, of course! You wouldn't be you if she wasn't. You think I would want you to feel different?"

"I mean—Louis—no matter where I go, more than with most children, she's part of me, Loo. I—Why, that child won't so much as go to spend the night with a girl friend away from me. Her quiet ways don't show it, but Alma has character! You wouldn't believe it, Louis, how she takes care of me."

"Why, Carrie, the first thing we pick out in our new home will be a room for her."

"Loo!"

"Not that she will want it long, the way I see that young rascal Friedlander sits up to her. A better young fellow and a better business head you couldn't pick for her. Didn't that youngster go out to Dayton the other day and land a contract for the surgical fittings for a big new clinic out there before the local firms even rubbed the sleep out of their eyes? I have it from good authority Friedlander Clinical Supply Company doubled their excess-profit tax last year."

A white flash of something that was almost fear seemed to strike Mrs. Samstag into a rigid pallor.

"No! No! I'm not like most mothers, Louis, for marrying their daughters off. I want her with me. If marrying her off is your idea, it's best you know it now in the beginning. I want my little girl with me—I have to have my little girl with me!"

He was so deeply moved that his eyes were embarrassingly moist.

"Why, Carrie, every time you open your mouth you only prove to me further what a grand little woman you are!"

"You'll like Alma, when you get to know her, Louis."

"Why, I do now! Always have said she's a sweet little thing."

"She is quiet and hard to get acquainted with at first, but that is reserve. She's not forward like most young girls nowadays. She's the kind of child that would rather go upstairs evenings with a book or her sewing than sit down here in the lobby. That's where she is now."

"Give me that kind every time in preference to all these gay young chickens that know more they oughtn't to know about life before they start than my little mother did when she finished."

"But do you think that girl will go to bed before I come up? Not a bit of it. She's been my comforter and my salvation in my troubles. More like the mother, I sometimes tell her, and me the child. If you want me, Louis, it's got to be with her, too. I couldn't give up my baby—not my baby."

"Why, Carrie, have your baby to your heart's content! She's got to be a fine girl to have you for a mother, and now it will be my duty to please her as a father. Carrie, will you have me?"

"Oh, Louis—Loo!"

"Carrie, my dear!"

And so it was that Carrie Samstag and Louis Latz came into their betrothal.

None the less, it was with some misgivings and red lights burning high on her cheek bones that Mrs. Samstag at just after ten that evening turned the knob of the door that entered into her little sitting room.

The usual horrific hotel room of tight green-plush upholstery, ornamental portières on brass rings that grated, and the equidistant French engravings of lavish scrollwork and scroll frames.

But in this case a room redeemed by an upright piano with a green-silk-and-gold-lace-shaded floor lamp glowing by. Two gilt-framed photographs and a cluster of ivory knickknacks on the white mantel. A heap of handmade cushions. Art editions of the gift poets and some circulating-library novels. A fireside chair, privately owned and drawn up, ironically enough, beside the gilded radiator, its headrest worn from kindly service to Mrs. Samstag's neuralgic brow.

From the nest of cushions in the circle of lamp glow Alma sprang up at her mother's entrance. Sure enough, she had been reading, and her cheek was a little flushed and crumpled from where it had been resting in the palm of her hand.

"Mamma," she said, coming out of the circle of light and switching on the ceiling bulbs, "you stayed out so late."

There was a slow prettiness to Alma. It came upon you like a little dawn, palely at first and then pinkening to a pleasant consciousness that her small face was heart-shaped and clear as an almond, that the pupils of her gray eyes were deep and dark, like cisterns, and to young Leo Friedlander (rather apt the comparison, too) her mouth was exactly the shape of a small bow that had shot its quiverful of arrows into his heart.

And instead of her eighteen she looked sixteen, there was that kind of timid adolescence about her, and yet when she said, "Mamma, you stayed down so late," the bang of a little pistol shot was back somewhere in her voice.

"Why—Mr. Latz—and—I—sat and talked."

An almost imperceptible nerve was dancing against Mrs. Samstag's right temple. Alma could sense, rather than see, the ridge of pain.

"You're all right, mamma?"

"Yes," said Mrs. Samstag, and sat down on a divan, its naked greenness relieved by a thrown scarf of black velvet stenciled in gold.

"You shouldn't have remained down so long if your head is hurting," said her daughter, and quite casually took up her mother's beaded hand bag where it had fallen in her lap, but her fingers feeling lightly and furtively as if for the shape of its contents.

"Stop that," said Mrs. Samstag, jerking it back, a dull anger in her voice.

"Come to bed, mamma. If you're in for neuralgia, I'll fix the electric pad."

Suddenly Mrs. Samstag shot out her arm, rather slim-looking in the invariable long sleeve she affected, drawing Alma back toward her by the ribbon sash of her pretty chiffon frock.

"Alma, be good to mamma to-night! Sweetheart—be good to her."

The quick suspecting fear that had motivated Miss Samstag's groping along the beaded hand bag shot out again in her manner.

"Mama—you haven't—?"

"No, no! Don't nag me. It's something else, Alma. Something mamma is very happy about."

"Mamma, you've broken your promise again."

"No! No! No! Alma, I've been a good mother to you, haven't I?"

"Yes, mamma, yes, but what—"

"Whatever else I've been hasn't been my fault—you've always blamed Heyman."

"Mamma, I don't understand."

"I've caused you worry, Alma—terrible worry. I know that. But everything is changed now. Mamma's going to turn over such a new leaf that everything is going to be happiness in this family."

"Dearest, if you knew how happy it makes me to hear you say that."

"Alma, look at me."

"Mamma, you—you frighten me."

"You like Louis Latz, don't you, Alma?"

"Why, yes, mamma. Very much."

"We can't all be young and handsome like Leo, can we?"

"You mean—?"

"I mean that finer and better men than Louis Latz aren't lying around loose. A man who treated his mother like a queen and who worked himself up from selling newspapers on the street to a millionaire."

"Mamma?"

"Yes, baby. He asked me to-night. Come to me, Alma; stay with me close.

He asked me to-night."

"What?"

"You know. Haven't you seen it coming for weeks? I have."

"Seen what?"

"Don't make mamma come out and say it. For eight years I've been as grieving a widow to a man as a woman could be. But I'm human, Alma, and he—asked me to-night."

There was a curious pallor came over Miss Samstag's face, as if smeared there by a hand.

"Asked you what?"

"Alma, it don't mean I'm not true to your father as I was the day I buried him in that blizzard back there, but could you ask for a finer, steadier man than Louis Latz? It looks out of his face."

"Mamma, you— What—are you saying?"

"Alma?"

There lay a silence between them that took on the roar of a simoon and Miss Samstag jumped then from her mother's embrace, her little face stiff with the clench of her mouth.

"Mamma, you— No—no! Oh, mamma—oh—!"

A quick spout of hysteria seemed to half strangle Mrs. Samstag so that she slanted backward, holding her throat.

"I knew it. My own child against me. O God! Why was I born? My own child against me!"

"Mamma—you can't marry him. You can't marry—anybody."

"Why can't I marry anybody? Must I be afraid to tell my own child when a good man wants to marry me and give us both a good home? That's my thanks for making my child my first consideration—before I accepted him."

"Mamma, you didn't accept him. Darling, you wouldn't do a—thing like that!"

Miss Samstag's voice thickened up then quite frantically into a little scream that knotted in her throat, and she was suddenly so small and stricken that, with a gasp for fear she might crumple up where she stood, Mrs. Samstag leaned forward, catching her again by the sash.

"Alma!"

It was only for an instant, however. Suddenly Miss Samstag was her coolly firm little self, the bang of authority back in her voice.

"You can't marry Louis Latz."

"Can't I? Watch me."

"You can't do that to a nice, deserving fellow like him!"

"Do what?"

"That!"

Then Mrs. Samstag threw up both her hands to her face, rocking in an agony of self-abandon that was rather horrid to behold.

"O God! why don't you put me out of it all? My misery! I'm a leper to my own child!"

"Oh—mamma—!"

"Yes, a leper. Hold my misfortune against me. Let my neuralgia and Doctor Heyman's prescription to cure it ruin my life. Rob me of what happiness with a good man there is left in it for me. I don't want happiness. Don't expect it. I'm here just to suffer. My daughter will see to that. Oh, I know what is on your mind. You want to make me out something—terrible—because Doctor Heyman once taught me how to help myself a little when I'm nearly wild with neuralgia. Those were doctor's orders. I'll kill myself before I let you make me out something terrible. I never even knew what it was before the doctor gave his prescription. I'll kill—you hear?—kill myself."

She was hoarse. She was tear splotched so that her lips were slippery with them, and while the ague of her passion shook her, Alma, her own face swept white and her voice guttered with restraint, took her mother into the cradle of her arms and rocked and hushed her there.

"Mamma, mamma, what are you saying? I'm not blaming you, sweetheart. I blame him—Doctor Heyman—for prescribing it in the beginning. I know your fight. How brave it is. Even when I'm crossest with you, I realize. Alma's fighting with you dearest every inch of the way until—you're cured! And then—maybe—some day—anything you want! But not now. Mamma, you wouldn't marry Louis Latz now!"

"I would. He's my cure. A good home with a good man and money enough to travel and forget myself. Alma, mamma knows she's not an angel. Sometimes when she thinks what she's put her little girl through this last year she just wants to go out on the hilltop where she caught the neuralgia and lie down beside that grave out there and—"

"Mamma, don't talk like that!"

"But now's my chance, Alma, to get well. I've too much worry in this big hotel trying to keep up big expenses on little money and—"

"I know it, mamma. That's why I'm so in favor of finding ourselves a sweet, tiny little apartment with kitch—"

"No! Your father died with the world thinking him a rich man and they will never find out from me that he wasn't. I won't be the one to humiliate his memory—a man who enjoyed keeping up appearances as he did. Oh, Alma, Alma, I'm going to get well now! I promise. So help me God if I ever give in to—it again."

"Mamma, please! For God's sake, you've said the same thing so often, only to break your promise."

"I've been weak, Alma; I don't deny it. But nobody who hasn't been tortured as I have can realize what it means to get relief just by—"

"Mamma, you're not playing fair this minute. That's the frightening part. It isn't only the neuralgia any more. It's just desire. That's what's so terrible to me, mamma. The way you have been taking it these last months. Just from—desire."

Mrs. Samstag buried her face, shuddering, down into her hands.

"O God! My own child against me!"

"No, mamma. Why, sweetheart, nobody knows better than I do how sweet and good you are when you are away from—it. We'll fight it together and win! I'm not afraid. It's been worse this last month because you've been nervous, dear. I understand now. You see, I—didn't dream of you and—Louis Latz. We'll forget—we'll take a little two-room apartment of our own, darling, and get your mind on housekeeping, and I'll take up stenography or social ser—"

"What good am I, anyway? No good. In my own way. In my child's way. A young man like Leo Friedlander crazy to propose and my child can't let him come to the point because she is afraid to leave her mother. Oh, I know—I know more than you think I do. Ruining your life! That's what I am, and mine, too!"

Tears now ran in hot cascades down Alma's cheeks.

"Why, mamma, as if I cared about anything—just so you—get well."

"I know. I know the way you tremble when he telephones, and color up when he—"

"Mamma, how can you?"

"I know what I've done. Ruined my baby's life, and now—"

"No!"

"Then help me, Alma. Louis wants me for his happiness. I want him for mine. Nothing will cure me like having a good man to live up to. The minute I find myself getting the craving for—it—don't you see, baby, fear that a good husband like Louis could find out such a thing about me would hold me back? See, Alma?"

"That's a wrong basis to start married life on—"

"I'm a woman who needs a man to baby her, Alma. That's the cure for me. Not to let me would be the same as to kill me. I've been a bad, weak woman, Alma, to be so afraid that maybe Leo Friedlander would steal you away from me. We'll make it a double wedding, baby!"

"Mamma! Mamma! I'll never leave you."

"All right, then, so you won't think your new father and me want to get rid of you, the first thing we'll pick out in our new home, he said it himself to-night, 'is Alma's room.'"

"I tell you it's wrong. It's wrong!"

"The rest with Leo can come later, after I've proved to you for a little while that I'm cured. Alma, don't cry! It's my cure. Just think, a good man! A beautiful home to take my mind off—worry. He said to-night he wants to spend a fortune, if necessary, to cure—my neuralgia."

"Oh, mamma! Mamma! If it were only—that!"

"Alma, if I promise on my—my life! I never felt the craving so little as I do—now."

"You've said that before—and before."

"But never with such a wonderful reason. It's the beginning of a new life. I know it. I'm cured!"

"Mamma, if I thought you meant it."

"I do. Alma, look at me. This very minute I've a real jumping case of neuralgia. But I wouldn't have anything for it except the electric pad. I feel fine. Strong. Alma, the bad times with me are over."

"Oh, mamma! Mamma, how I pray you're right."

"You'll thank God for the day that Louis Latz proposed to me. Why, I'd rather cut off my right hand than marry a man who could ever live to learn such a—thing about me."

"But it's not fair. We'll have to explain to him, dear, that we hope you're cured now, but—"

"If you do—if you do—I'll kill myself! I won't live to bear that! You don't want me cured. You want to get rid of me, to degrade me until I kill myself! If I was ever anything else than what I am now—to Louis Latz—anything but his ideal—Alma, you won't tell! Kill me, but don't tell—don't tell!"

"Why, you know I wouldn't, sweetheart, if it is so terrible to you. Never."

"Say it again."

"Never."

"As if it hasn't been terrible enough that you should have to know. But it's over, Alma. Your bad times with me are finished. I'm cured."

There were no words that Miss Samstag could force through the choke of her tears, so she sat cheek to her mother's cheek, the trembling she could no longer control racing through her like a chill.

"Oh—how—I hope so!"

"I know so."

"But wait a little while, mamma—just a year."

"No! No!"

"A few months."

"No, he wants it soon. The sooner the better at our age. Alma, mamma's cured! What happiness! Kiss me, darling. So help me God to keep my promises to you! Cured, Alma, cured."

And so in the end, with a smile on her lips that belied almost to herself the little run of fear through her heart, Alma's last kiss to her mother that night was the long one of felicitation.

And because love, even the talk of it, is so gamy on the lips of woman to woman, they lay in bed, heartbeat to heartbeat, the electric pad under her pillow warm to the hurt of Mrs. Samstag's brow, and talked, these two, deep into the stillness of the hotel night.

"I'm going to be the best wife to him, Alma. You see, the woman that marries Louis has to measure up to the grand ideas of her he got from his mother."

"You were a good wife once, mamma. You'll be it again."

"That's another reason, Alma; it means my—cure. Living up to the ideas of a good man."

"Mamma! Mamma! You can't backslide now—ever."

"My little baby, who's helped me through such bad times, it's your turn now, Alma, to be carefree like other girls."

"I'll never leave you, mamma, even if—he—Latz—shouldn't want me."

"He will, darling, and does! Those were his words. 'A room for Alma.'"

"I'll never leave you!"

"You will! Much as Louis and I want you with us every minute, we won't stand in your way! That's another reason I'm so happy, Alma. I'm not alone any more now. Leo's so crazy over you, just waiting for the chance to—pop—"

"Shh-sh-h-h!"

"Don't tremble so, darling. Mamma knows. He told Mrs. Gronauer last night when she was joking him to buy a ten-dollar carnation for the Convalescent Home Bazaar, that he would only take one if it was white, because little white flowers reminded him of Alma Samstag."

"Oh, mamma!"

"Say, it is as plain as the nose on your face. He can't keep his eyes off you. He sells goods to Doctor Gronauer's clinic and he says the same thing about him. It makes me so happy, Alma, to think you won't have to hold him off any more."

"I'll never leave you. Never!"

Nevertheless, she was the first to drop off to sleep, pink there in the dark with the secret of her blushes.

Then for Mrs. Samstag the travail set in. Lying there with her raging head tossing this way and that on the heated pillow, she heard with cruel awareness the minutæ, all the faint but clarified noises that can make a night seem so long. The distant click of the elevator depositing a nighthawk. A plong of the bedspring. Somebody's cough. A train's shriek. The jerk of plumbing. A window being raised. That creak which lies hidden in every darkness, like a mysterious knee joint. By three o'clock she was a quivering victim to these petty concepts, and her pillow so explored that not a spot but was rumpled to the aching lay of her cheek.

Once Alma, as a rule supersensitive to her mother's slightest unrest, floated up for the moment out of her young sleep, but she was very drowsy and very tired, and dream tides were almost carrying her back as she said:

"Mamma, you all right?"

Simulating sleep, Mrs. Samstag lay tense until her daughter's breathing resumed its light cadence.

Then at four o'clock the kind of nervousness that Mrs. Samstag had learned to fear began to roll over her in waves, locking her throat and curling her toes and fingers and her tongue up dry against the roof of her mouth.

She must concentrate now—must steer her mind away from the craving!

Now then: West End Avenue. Louis liked the apartments there. Luxurious. Quiet. Residential. Circassian walnut or mahogany dining room? Alma should decide. A baby-grand piano. Later to be Alma's engagement gift from "mamma and—papa." No, "mamma and Louis." Better so.

How her neck and her shoulder blade and now her elbow were flaming with the pain. She cried a little, quite silently, and tried a poor, futile scheme for easing her head in the crotch of her elbow.

Now then: She must knit Louis some neckties. The silk-sweater stitch would do. Married in a traveling suit. One of those smart dark-blue twills like Mrs. Gronauer, junior's. Topcoat—sable. Louis' hair thinning. Tonic. O God! Let me sleep! Please, God! The wheeze rising in her closed throat. That little threatening desire that must not shape itself! It darted with the hither and thither of a bee bumbling against a garden wall. No! No! Ugh! The vast chills of nervousness. The flaming, the craving chills of desire!

Just this last giving-in. This one. To be rested and fresh for him to-morrow. Then never again. The little beaded hand bag. O God! Help me! That burning ache to rest and to uncurl of nervousness. All the thousand thousand little pores of her body, screaming each one to be placated. They hurt the entire surface of her. That great storm at sea in her head; the crackle of lightning down that arm—

"Let me see—Circassian walnut—baby grand—" The pores demanding, crying—shrieking—

It was then that Carrie Samstag, even in her lovely pink nightdress a crone with pain, and the cables out dreadfully in her neck, began by infinitesimal processes to swing herself gently to the side of the bed, unrelaxed inch by unrelaxed inch, softly and with the cunning born of a travail.

It was actually a matter of fifteen minutes, that breathless swing toward the floor, the mattress rising after her with scarcely a whisper and her two bare feet landing patly into the pale-blue room slippers, there beside the bed.

Then her bag, the beaded one on the end of the divan. The slow, taut feeling for it and the floor that creaked twice, starting the sweat out over her.

It was finally after more tortuous saving of floor creaks and the interminable opening and closing of a door that Carrie Samstag, the beaded bag in her hand, found herself face to face with herself in the mirror of the bathroom medicine chest.

She was shuddering with one of the hot chills. The needle and little glass piston out of the hand bag and with a dry little insuck of breath, pinching up little areas of flesh from her arm, bent on a good firm perch, as it were.

There were undeniable pockmarks on Mrs. Samstag's right forearm. Invariably it sickened her to see them. Little graves. Oh! oh! little graves! For Alma. Herself. And now Louis. Just once. Just one more little grave—

And Alma, answering her somewhere down in her heartbeats: "No, mamma. No, mamma! No! No! No!"

But all the little pores gaping. Mouths! The pinching up of the skin. Here, this little clean and white area.

"No, mamma! No, mamma! No! no! no!"

"Just once, darling?" Oh—oh—little graves for Alma and Louis. No! No! No!

Somehow, some way, with all the little mouths still parched and gaping and the clean and quite white area unblemished, Mrs. Samstag found her way back to bed. She was in a drench of sweat when she got there and the conflagration of neuralgia, curiously enough, was now roaring in her ears so that it seemed to her she could hear her pain.

Her daughter lay asleep, with her face to the wall, her flowing hair spread in a fan against the pillow and her body curled up cozily. The remaining hours of the night, in a kind of waking faint she could never find the words to describe, Mrs. Samstag, with that dreadful dew of her sweat constantly out over her, lay with her twisted lips to the faint perfume of that fan of Alma's flowing hair, her toes curling in and out. Out and in. Toward morning she slept. Actually, sweetly, and deeply, as if she could never have done with deep draughts of it.

She awoke to the brief patch of sunlight that smiled into their apartment for about eight minutes of each afternoon.

Alma was at the pretty chore of lifting the trays from a hamper of roses. She placed a shower of them on her mother's coverlet with a kiss, a deeper and dearer one, somehow, this morning.

There was a card, and Mrs. Samstag read it and laughed:

> Good morning, Carrie.
> Louis.

They seemed to her, poor dear, these roses, to be pink with the glory of the coming of the dawn.

On the spur of the moment and because the same precipitate decision that determined Louis Latz's successes in Wall Street determined him here, they were married the following Thursday in Lakewood, New Jersey, without even allowing Carrie time for the blue-twill traveling suit. She wore her brown-velvet, instead, looking quite modish, a sable wrap, gift of the groom, lending genuine magnificence.

Alma was there, of course, in a beautiful fox scarf, also gift of the groom, and locked in a pale kind of tensity that made her seem more than ever like a little white flower to Leo Friedlander, the sole other attendant, and who during the ceremony yearned at her with his gaze. But her eyes were squeezed tight against his, as if to forbid herself the consciousness that life seemed suddenly so richly sweet to her—oh, so richly sweet!

There was a time during the first months of the married life of Louis and Carrie Latz when it seemed to Alma, who in the sanctity of her lovely little ivory bedroom all appointed in rose enamel toilet trifles, could be prayerful with the peace of it, that the old Carrie, who could come pale and terrible out of her drugged nights, belonged to some grimacing and chimeric past. A dead past that had buried its dead and its hatchet.

There had been a month at a Hot Springs in the wintergreen heart of Virginia, and whatever Louis may have felt in his heart of his right to the privacy of these honeymoon days was carefully belied on his lips, and at Alma's depriving him now and then of his wife's company, packing her off to rest when he wanted a climb with her up a mountain slope or a drive over piny roads, he could still smile and pinch her cheek.

"You're stingy to me with my wife, Alma," he said to her upon one of these provocations. "I don't believe she's got a daughter at all, but a little policeman instead."

And Alma smiled back, out of the agony of her constant consciousness that she was insinuating her presence upon him, and resolutely, so that her fear for him should always subordinate her fear of him, she bit down her sensitiveness in proportion to the rising tide of his growing, but still politely held in check, bewilderment.

Once, these first weeks of their marriage, because she saw the dreaded sign of the muddy pools under her mother's eyes and the little quivering nerve beneath the temple, she shut him out of her presence for a day and a night, and when he came fuming up every few minutes from the hotel veranda, miserable and fretting, met him at the closed door of her mother's darkened room and was adamant.

"It won't hurt if I tiptoe in and sit with her," he pleaded.

"No, Louis. No one knows how to get her through these spells like I do. The least excitement will only prolong her pain."

He trotted off, then, down the hotel corridor, with a strut to his resentment that was bantam and just a little fighty.

That night as Alma lay beside her mother, holding off sleep and watching, Carrie rolled her eyes sideways with the plea of a stricken dog in them.

"Alma," she whispered, "for God's sake! Just this once. To tide me over. One shot—darling. Alma, if you love me?"

Later there was a struggle between them that hardly bears relating. A lamp was overturned. But toward morning, when Carrie lay exhausted, but at rest in her daughter's arms, she kept muttering her sleep:

"Thank you, baby. You saved me. Never leave me, Alma. Never—never—never. You saved me, Alma."

And then the miracle of those next few months. The return to New York. The happily busy weeks of furnishing and the unlimited gratifications of the well-filled purse. The selection of the limousine with the special body that was fearfully and wonderfully made in mulberry upholstery with mother-of-pearl caparisons. The fourteen-room apartment on West End Avenue with four baths, drawing-room of pink-brocaded walls, and Carrie's Roman bath-room that was precisely as large as her old hotel sitting room, with two full-length wall mirrors, a dressing room canopied in white lace over white satin, and the marble bath itself, two steps down and with rubber curtains that swished after.

There were evenings when Carrie, who loved the tyranny of things with what must have been a survival within her of the bazaar instinct, would fall asleep almost directly after dinner, her head back against her husband's shoulder, roundly tired out after a day all cluttered up with matching the blue upholstery of their bedroom with taffeta bed hangings. Shopping for a strip of pantry linoleum that was just the desired slate color. Calculating with electricians over the plugs for floor lamps. Herself edging pantry shelves in cotton lace.

Latz liked her so, with her fragrantly coiffured head, scarcely gray, back against his shoulder, and with his newspapers, Wall Street journals and the comic weeklies which he liked to read, would sit an entire evening thus, moving only when his joints rebelled, his pipe smoke carefully directed away from her face.

Weeks and weeks of this, and already Louis Latz's trousers were a little out of crease, and Mrs. Latz, after eight o'clock and under cover of a very fluffy and very expensive negligée, would unhook her stays.

Sometimes friends came in for a game of small-stake poker, but after the second month they countermanded the standing order for Saturday night musical-comedy seats. So often they discovered it was pleasanter to remain at home. Indeed, during these days of household adjustment, as many as four evenings a week Mrs. Latz dozed there against her husband's shoulder, until about ten, when he kissed her awake to forage with him in the great white porcelain refrigerator and then to bed.

And Alma. Almost she tiptoed through these months. Not that her scorching awareness of what must have lain low in Louis' mind ever diminished. Sometimes, although still never by word, she could see the displeasure mount in his face.

If she entered in on a tête-à-tête, as she did once, when by chance she had sniffed the curative smell of spirits of camphor on the air of a room through which her mother had passed, and came to drag her off that night to share her own lace-covered-and-ivory bed.

Again, upon the occasion of an impulsively planned motor trip and week-end to Long Beach, her intrusion had been so obvious.

"Want to join us, Alma?"

"Oh—yes—thank you, Louis."

"But I thought you and Leo were—"

"No, no. I'd rather go with you and mamma, Louis."

Even her mother had smiled rather strainedly. Louis' invitation, politely uttered, had said so plainly, "Are we two never to be alone, your mother and I?"

Oh, there was no doubt that Louis Latz was in love and with all the delayed fervor of first youth.

There was something rather throat-catching about his treatment of her mother that made Alma want to cry.

He would never tire of marveling, not alone at the wonder of her, but at the wonder that she was his.

"No man has ever been as lucky in women as I have, Carrie," he told her once in Alma's hearing. "It seemed to me that after—my little mother there couldn't ever be another—and now you!"

At the business of sewing some beads on a lamp shade Carrie looked up, her eyes dewy.

"And I felt that way about one good husband," she said, "and now I see there could be two."

Alma tiptoed out.

The third month of this she was allowing Leo Friedlander his two evenings a week. Once to the theater in a modish little sedan car which Leo drove himself. One evening at home in the rose-and-mauve drawing-room. It delighted Louis and Carrie slyly to have in their friends for poker over the dining-room table these evenings, leaving the young people somewhat indirectly chaperoned until as late as midnight. Louis' attitude with Leo was one of winks, quirks, slaps on the back, and the curving voice of innuendo.

"Come on in, Leo; the water's fine!"

"Louis!" This from Alma, stung to crimson and not arch enough to feign that she did not understand.

"Loo, don't tease," said Carrie, smiling, but then closing her eyes as if to invoke help to want this thing to come to pass.

But Leo was frankly the lover, kept not without difficulty on the edge of his ardor. A city youth with gymnasium-bred shoulders, fine, pole-vaulter's length of limb, and a clean tan skin that bespoke cold drubbings with Turkish towels.

And despite herself, Alma, who was not without a young girl's feelings for nice detail, could thrill to this sartorial svelteness and to the patent-leather lay of his black hair which caught the light like a polished floor.

In the lingo of Louis Latz, he was "a rattling good business man, too." He shared with his father partnership in a manufacturing business— "Friedlander Clinical Supply Company"—which, since his advent from high school into the already enormously rich firm, had almost doubled its volume of business.

The kind of sweetness he found in Alma he could never articulate even to himself. In some ways she seemed hardly to have the pressure of vitality to match his, but, on the other hand, just that slower beat to her may have heightened his sense of prowess. His greatest delight seemed to lie in her pallid loveliness. "White honeysuckle," he called her, and the names of all the beautiful white flowers he knew. And then one night, to the rattle of poker chips from the remote dining room, he jerked her to him without preamble, kissing her mouth down tightly against her teeth.

"My sweetheart! My little white carnation sweetheart! I won't be held off any longer. I'm going to carry you away for my little moonflower wife."

She sprang back prettier than he had ever seen her in the dishevelment from where his embrace had dragged at her hair.

"You mustn't," she cried, but there was enough of the conquering male in him to read easily into this a mere plating over her desire.

"You can't hold me at arm's length any longer. You've maddened me for months. I love you. You love me. You do. You do," and crushed her to him, but this time his pain and his surprise genuine as she sprang back, quivering.

"No, I tell you. No! No! No!" and sat down trembling.

"Why, Alma!" And he sat down, too, rather palely, at the remote end of the divan.

"You— I—mustn't!" she said, frantic to keep her lips from twisting, her little lacy fribble of a handkerchief a mere string from winding.

"Mustn't what?"

"Mustn't," was all she could repeat and not weep her words.

"Won't—I—do?"

"It's—mamma."

"What?"

"Her."

"Her what, my little white buttonhole carnation?"

"You see—I— She's all alone."

"You adorable, she's got a brand-new husky husband."

"No—you don't—understand."

Then, on a thunderclap of inspiration, hitting his knee:

"I have it. Mamma-baby! That's it. My girlie is a cry-baby, mamma-baby!" And made to slide along the divan toward her, but up flew her two small hands, like fans.

"No," she said, with the little bang back in her voice which steadied him again. "I mustn't! You see, we're so close. Sometimes it's more as if I were the mother and she my little girl."

"Alma, that's beautiful, but it's silly, too. But tell me first of all, mamma-baby, that you do care. Tell me that first, dearest, and then we can talk."

The kerchief was all screwed up now, so tightly that it could stiffly unwind of itself.

"She's not well, Leo. That terrible neuralgia—that's why she needs me so."

"Nonsense! She hasn't had a spell for weeks. That's Louis' great brag, that he's curing her. Oh, Alma, Alma, that's not a reason; that's an excuse!"

"Leo—you don't understand."

"I'm afraid I—don't," he said, looking at her with a sudden intensity that startled her with a quick suspicion of his suspicions, but then he smiled.

"Alma!" he said, "Alma!"

Misery made her dumb.

"Why, don't you know, dear, that your mother is better able to take care of herself than you are? She's bigger and stronger. You—you're a little white flower, that I want to wear on my heart."

"Leo—give me time. Let me think."

"A thousand thinks, Alma, but I love you. I love you and want so terribly for you to love me back."

"I—do."

"Then tell me with kisses."

Again she pressed him to arm's length.

"Please, Leo! Not yet. Let me think. Just one day. To-morrow."

"No, no! Now!"

"To-morrow."

"When?"

"Evening."

"No, morning."

"All right, Leo—to-morrow morning—"

"I'll sit up all night and count every second in every minute and every minute in every hour."

She put up her soft little fingers to his lips.

"Dear boy," she said.

And then they kissed, and after a little swoon to his nearness she struggled like a caught bird and a guilty one.

"Please go, Leo," she said. "Leave me alone—"

"Little mamma-baby sweetheart," he said. "I'll build you a nest right next to hers. Good night, little white flower. I'll be waiting, and remember, counting every second of every minute and every minute of every hour."

For a long time she remained where he had left her, forward on the pink divan, her head with a listening look to it, as if waiting an answer for the prayers that she sent up.

At two o'clock that morning, by what intuition she would never know, and with such leverage that she landed out of bed plump on her two feet, Alma, with all her faculties into trace like fire horses, sprang out of sleep.

It was a matter of twenty steps across the hall. In the white-tiled Roman bathroom, the muddy circles suddenly out and angry beneath her eyes, her mother was standing before one of the full-length mirrors—snickering.

There was a fresh little grave on the inside of her right forearm.

Sometimes in the weeks that followed a sense of the miracle of what was happening would clutch at Alma's throat like a fear.

Louis did not know.

That the old neuralgic recurrences were more frequent again, yes. Already plans for a summer trip abroad, on a curative mission bent, were taking shape. There was a famous nerve specialist, the one who had worked such wonders on his mother's cruelly rheumatic limbs, reassuringly foremost in his mind.

But except that there were not infrequent and sometimes twenty-four-hour sieges when he was denied the sight of his wife, he had learned, with a male's acquiescence to the frailties of the other sex, to submit, and, with no great understanding of pain, to condone.

And as if to atone for these more or less frequent lapses, there was something pathetic, even a little heartbreaking, in Carrie's zeal for his well-being. No duty too small. One night she wanted to unlace his shoes and even shine them—would have, in fact, except for his fierce catching of her into his arms and for some reason his tonsils aching as he kissed her.

Once after a "spell" she took out every garment from his wardrobe and, kissing them piece by piece, put them back again, and he found her so, and they cried together, he of happiness.

In his utter beatitude, even his resentment of Alma continued to grow but slowly. Once, when after forty-eight hours she forbade him rather fiercely an entrance into his wife's room, he shoved her aside almost rudely, but, at Carrie's little shriek of remonstrance from the darkened room, backed out shamefacedly, and apologized next day in the conciliatory language of a tiny wrist watch.

But a break came, as she knew and feared it must.

One evening during one of these attacks, when for two days Carrie had not appeared at the dinner table, Alma, entering when the meal was almost over, seated herself rather exhaustedly at her mother's place opposite her stepfather.

He had reached the stage when that little unconscious usurpation in itself could annoy him.

"How's your mother?" he asked, dourly for him.

"She's asleep."

"Funny. This is the third attack this month, and each time it lasts longer. Confound that neuralgia!"

"She's easier now."

He pushed back his plate.

"Then I'll go in and sit with her while she sleeps."

She, who was so fastidiously dainty of manner, half rose, spilling her soup.

"No," she said, "you mustn't! Not now!" And sat down again hurriedly, wanting not to appear perturbed.

A curious thing happened then to Louis. His lower lip came pursing out like a little shelf and a hitherto unsuspected look of pigginess fattened over his rather plump face.

"You quit butting into me and my wife's affairs, you, or get the hell out of here," he said, without raising his voice or his manner.

She placed her hand to the almost unbearable flutter of her heart.

"Louis! You mustn't talk like that to—me!"

"Don't make me say something I'll regret. You! Only take this tip, you! There's one of two things you better do. Quit trying to come between me and her or—get out."

"I— She's sick."

"Naw, she ain't. Not as sick as you make out. You're trying, God knows why, to keep us apart. I've watched you. I know your sneaking kind. Still water runs deep. You've never missed a chance since we're married to keep us apart. Shame!"

"I— She—"

"Now mark my word, if it wasn't to spare her I'd have invited you out long ago. Haven't you got any pride?"

"I have. I have," she almost moaned, and could have crumpled up there and swooned her humiliation.

"You're not a regular girl. You're a she-devil. That's what you are! Trying to come between your mother and me. Ain't you ashamed? What is it you want?"

"Louis—I don't—"

"First you turn down a fine fellow like Leo Friedlander, so he don't come to the house any more, and then you take out on us whatever is eating you, by trying to come between me and the finest woman that ever lived. Shame! Shame!"

"Louis!" she said, "Louis!" wringing her hands in a dry wash of agony, "can't you understand? She'd rather have me. It makes her nervous trying to pretend to you that she's not suffering when she is. That's all, Louis. You see, she's not ashamed to suffer before me. Why, Louis—that's all! Why should I want to come between you and her? Isn't she dearer to me than anything in the world, and haven't you been the best friend to me a girl could have? That's all—Louis."

He was placated and a little sorry and did not insist further upon going into the room.

"Funny," he said. "Funny," and, adjusting his spectacles, snapped open his newspaper for a lonely evening.

The one thing that perturbed Alma almost more than anything else, as the dreaded cravings grew, with each siege her mother becoming more brutish and more given to profanity, was where she obtained the soluble tablets.

The well-thumbed old doctor's prescription she had purloined even back in the hotel days, and embargo and legislation were daily making more and more furtive and prohibitive the traffic in drugs.

Once Alma, mistakenly, too, she thought later, had suspected a chauffeur of collusion with her mother and abruptly dismissed him, to Louis' rage.

"What's the idea?" he said, out of Carrie's hearing, of course. "Who's running this shebang, anyway?"

Again, after Alma had guarded her well for days, scarcely leaving her side, Carrie laughed sardonically up into her daughter's face, her eyes as glassy and without swimming fluid as a doll's.

"I get it! But wouldn't you like to know where? Yah!" And to Alma's horror slapped her quite soundly across the cheek so that for an hour the sting, the shape of the red print of fingers, lay on her face.

One night in what had become the horrible sanctity of that bed-chamber— But let this sum it up. When Alma was nineteen years old a little colony of gray hairs was creeping in on each temple.

And then one day, after a long period of quiet, when Carrie had lavished her really great wealth of contrite love upon her daughter and husband, spending on Alma and loading her with gifts of jewelry and finery, somehow to express her grateful adoration of her, paying her husband the secret penance of twofold fidelity to his well-being and every whim, Alma, returning from a trip taken reluctantly and at her mother's bidding down to the basement trunk room, found her gone, a modish black-lace hat and the sable coat missing from the closet.

It was early afternoon, sunlit and pleasantly cold.

The first rush of panic and the impulse to dash after stayed, she forced herself down into a chair, striving with the utmost difficulty for coherence of procedure.

Where in the half hour of her absence had her mother gone? Matinée? Impossible! Walking? Hardly possible. Upon inquiry in the kitchen, neither of the maids had seen nor heard her depart. Motoring? With a hand that trembled in spite of itself Alma telephoned the garage. Car and chauffeur were there. Incredible as it seemed, Alma, upon more than one occasion, had lately been obliged to remind her mother that she was becoming careless of the old pointedly rosy hands. Manicurist? She telephoned the Bon Ton Beauty Parlors. No. Where? O God! Where? Which way to begin? That was what troubled her most. To start right so as not to lose a precious second.

Suddenly, and for no particular reason, Alma began a hurried search through her mother's dresser drawers of lovely personal appointments. Turning over whole mounds of fresh white gloves, delving into nests of sheer handkerchiefs and stacks of webby lingerie. Then for a while she stood quite helplessly, looking into the mirror, her hands closed about her throat.

"Please, God, where?"

A one-inch square of newspaper clipping, apparently gouged from the sheet with a hairpin, caught her eye from the top of one of the gold-backed hairbrushes. Dawningly, Alma read.

It described in brief detail the innovation of a newly equipped narcotic clinic on the Bowery below Canal Street, provided to medically administer to the pathological cravings of addicts.

Fifteen minutes later Alma emerged from the Subway at Canal Street, and, with three blocks toward her destination ahead, started to run.

At the end of the first block she saw her mother, in the sable coat and the black-lace hat, coming toward her.

Her first impulse was to run faster and yoo-hoo, but she thought better of it and, by biting her lips and digging he finger nails, was able to slow down to a casual walk.

Carrie's fur coat was flaring open and, because of the quality of her attire down there where the bilge waters of the city tide flow and eddy, stares followed her.

Once, to the stoppage of Alma's heart, she saw Carrie halt and say a brief word to a truckman as he crossed the sidewalk with a bill of lading. He hesitated, laughed, and went on.

Then she quickened her pace and went on, but as if with a sense of being followed, because constantly as she walked she jerked a step, to look back, and then again, over her shoulder.

A second time she stopped, this time to address a little nub of a woman without a hat and lugging one-sidedly a stack of men's basted waistcoats, evidently for home work in some tenement. She looked and muttered her ununderstanding at whatever Carrie had to say, and shambled on.

Then Mrs. Latz spied her daughter, greeting her without surprise or any particular recognition.

"Thought you could fool me! Heh, Louis? I mean Alma."

"Mamma, it's Alma. It's all right. Don't you remember, we had this appointment? Come, dear."

"No, you don't! That's a man following. Shh-h-h-h, Louis! I was fooling. I went up to him in the clinic" (snicker) "and I said to him, 'Give you five dollars for a doctor's certificate.' That's all I said to him, or any of them. He's in a white carnation, Louis. You can find him by the—it on his coat lapel. He's coming! Quick—"

"Mamma, there's no one following. Wait, I'll call a taxi!"

"No, you don't! He tried to put me in a taxi, too. No, you don't!"

"Then the Subway, dearest. You'll sit quietly beside Alma in the Subway, won't you, Carrie? Alma's so tired."

Suddenly Carrie began to whimper.

"My baby! Don't let her see me. My baby! What am I good for? I've ruined her life. My precious sweetheart's life. I hit her once—Louis—in the mouth. It bled. God won't forgive me for that."

"Yes, He will, dear, if you come."

"It bled. Alma, tell him in the white carnation that mamma lost her doc-tor's certificate. That's all I said to him. Saw him in the clinic—new clinic—'give you five dollars for a doctor's certificate.' He had a white carnation—right lapel. Stingy. Quick!—following!"

"Sweetheart, please, there's no one coming."

"Don't tell! Oh, Alma darling—mamma's ruined your life! Her sweetheart baby's life."

"No, darling, you haven't. She loves you if you'll come home with her, dear, to bed, before Louis gets home and—"

"No. No. He mustn't see. Never this bad—was I, darling? Oh! Oh!"

"No, mamma—never—this bad. That's why we must hurry."

"Best man that ever lived. Best baby. Ruin. Ruin."

"Mamma, you—you're making Alma tremble so that she can scarcely walk if you drag her so. There's no one following, dear. I won't let anyone harm you. Please, sweetheart—a taxicab."

"No. I tell you he's following. He tried to put me into a taxicab. Followed me. Said he knew me."

"Then, mamma, listen. Do you hear? Alma wants you to listen. If you don't—she'll faint. People are looking. Now I want you to turn square around and look. No, look again. You see now, there's no one following. Now I want you to cross the street over there to the Subway. Just with Alma who loves you. There's nobody following. Just with Alma who loves you."

And then Carrie, whose lace hat was quite on the back of her head, relaxed enough so that through the enormous maze of the traffic of trucks and the heavier drags of the lower city, her daughter could wind their way.

"My baby! My poor Louis!" she kept saying. "The worst I've ever been. Oh—Alma—Louis—waiting—before we get there—Louis!"

It was in the tightest jangle of the crossing and apparently on this conjur-ing of her husband that Carrie jerked suddenly free of Alma's frailer hold.

"No—no—not home—now. Him. Alma!" And darted back against the breast of the down side of the traffic.

There was scarcely more than the quick rotation of her arm around with the spoke of a truck wheel, so quickly she went down.

It was almost a miracle, her kind of death, because out of all that jam of tonnage she carried only one bruise, a faint one, near the brow.

And the wonder was that Louis Latz, in his grief, was so proud.

"To think," he kept saying over and over again and unabashed at the way his face twisted—"to think they should have happened to me. Two such women in one lifetime as my little mother—and her. Fat little old Louis to have had these two. Why, just the memory of my Carrie—is almost enough.

To think old me should have a memory like that—it is almost enough—isn't it, Alma?"

She kissed his hand.

That very same, that dreadful night, almost without her knowing it, her throat-tearing sobs broke loose, her face to the waistcoat of Leo Friedlander.

He held her close—very, very close.

"Why, sweetheart," he said, "I could cut out my heart to help you! Why, sweetheart! Shh-h-h! Remember what Louis says. Just the beautiful memory—of—her—is—wonderful—"

"Just—the b-beautiful—memory—you'll always have it, too—of her—my mamma—won't you, Leo? Won't you?"

"Always," he said when the tight grip in his throat had eased enough.

"Say—it again—Leo."

"Always."

She could not know how dear she became to him then, because not ten minutes before, from the very lapel against which her cheek lay pressed, he had unpinned a white carnation.

Forty-Five

First Published: *Cosmopolitan*, December 1922
Reprinted: *Song of Life*, A.A. Knopf, 1927

There is the Paris o' your heart and my heart, the Paris of Little Billee, Hugo and Maupassant, and the Paris to which George Moore confessed.

There is the Paris that butters its radishes and eats its crabs with the whiskers on.

There is the Left Bank, that on *Quat'z Arts* nights paints its slim body Tuscan bronze and walls up its eyes in gold-leaf, but of any morning, except the morning after, carries home its breakfast bread by the yard, and cuts its cheese with a palette scraper. There is Montmartre with a courtplaster lizard on her shoulder, red heels, no stockings, petticoat ruffles not always fresh, but all the passions smoking to slow flame in her come-hither eyes, and the soot reservoirs in half shells beneath them.

There is the terrible Paris of Zola, the harlequin Paris of Merrick, and the Baedekered Paris of Cook's.

The Paris that smells of chypre and of closed plumbing; of cognac and sawdust; of love and of too few baths.

The Paris of Comédie Française and the Folies Bergères. The Paris of undraped dancing girls, their beautiful bodies revealing and disclosing in just the proportion to make that beauty horrid. Paris with her thumb to her nose.

Paris at sunrise with the wagon-loads of carrots coming into market, little pink tongues sticking out. . . .

Then there is the Paris of Edith Whatley and her daughter, May. Of them and the thousands like them, who book annual passage on the steamships that ply between the smart tea and shopping districts of the slightly east fifties and the smart tea and shopping districts of Rue Castiglione and Place Vendôme.

The Paris of Rumplemeyer's and Eugénie's Electrical Eyebrow Plucking Parlours (English spoken); of Worth, Jenny, Lanvin and Captain Molyneux (English spoken). The Paris of six fittings, a massage and a look-in at Cartier's in the forenoon. Snails and Amer Picon at Prunier's for luncheon. Longchamps. Wood strawberries at tea-time on the Bois. Dinner at the Ritz. Russian ballet. Irene Castle at Pré Catalan. Dancing at Café Madrid and Maxim's.

The Paris of lavender manicures (English spoken), Polaire pedicures, and of those thousand-franc Indian turbans at Renée's studded in chrysoprase and red jasper. The Paris of "facial liftings" where the years are cut out of the face as surely as the heart can be carved from a bull.

That is the Paris of the Whatleys and the thousands like them who sail annually and who keep the plate-glass fronts of the Rue de la Paix sown with chalcedony perfume tripods, topaz cigarette-cases, diamond collarettes forked with the lightning of rubies, pearls as mysterious as flesh and dark ones the identical color and quality of a bruise on a woman's arm.

May Whatley of this Paris had the scorn of sophistication for the Paris of Baedeker. The Paris carried about in a small red volume by middle-aged English ladies with fallen arches and by American school-teachers with Irish lace collars on their dust-coloured travelling suits, who clutter up the mail department of the American Express every morning and carry mono-grammed wash-cloths in rubber bags and "My Trip Abroad" diaries.

Theirs the Paris of the Louvre and the Panthéon, Eiffel Tower and Versailles on Fountain Sunday. Arc de Triomphe, Musée de Cluny, Duval's, Galerie Lafayette, Notre Dame.

Nineteen years previously Edith Whatley had made her first trip to Paris with just such a group of time-and-money-limited teachers and librarians from Munsie. Four of them in a deck D stateroom. The cotton crêpe night-ies that could be washed without ironing. The Anderson "seconds" and post-card reproductions of masterpieces to be bought in the foyer of the Louvre!

Ah me, she had met Gordon Whatley on shipboard that first trip! Her thrill at beholding "The Angelus" and Whistler's "Mother" in the flesh of the original paint. Notre Dame as she had seen it for the first time with a Cook's courier and a shy young thing of a Paris moon between the towers.

It could still do something to her that was lovely, Notre Dame. A flutter that would get caught in her breathing.

And yet she knew—May had thrown it out one day as they sped past in Lowell Jackson's racer—that architecturally Notre Dame had its tongue in its cheek.

Curiously clever girl, May. Somehow, between manicures and fittings, she had a squirrel-like way of storing up nuts of supercilious and superficial information.

She knew the difference between a Manet and a Monet. The Old Masters were all right if one still had time for "literalism" (quotes). She rebelled against the "Corinthian column invasion" (quotes). Attended exhibitions of the abstract schools of coloured cubes. Paid annual dues to a Secessionist Society which gravely called a purple rhomboid a spade; considered Shelley a "rank rhymist" but a "greater humanitarian than Lycurgus, Nietzsche or

Godwin" (quotes); referred cryptically to "The Spoon River Anthology" as the "dawn of American consciousness" (quotes); knew who Dorothy Richardson, Gertrude Stein, Leo Ornstein and Theodore Dreiser were.

A pat phrase from the Literary Digest stuck to her. An arty word overheard in a café. Dadaism, Batik; names like Max Reinhardt, D. H. Lawrence, Amy Lowell.

These glibnesses, caught on the fly, amused her mother, puzzled and even impressed her. May was a student neither of life, nor of art, nor of self, but she presented to the cant phrase, the erudite comment, the smiting word, a surface of fly-paper.

She had been to the Louvre only once, when a child at that, but she challenged the authenticity of the Rubens collections and referred to his as the "pounds-of-flesh school."

May hated fat. Which brings us to May herself. She was nineteen, about as slim as a lath, and when she stepped out of her bath—a strictly American one as to hot and cold water, price and nickel-plated fittings, in the Hotel Griffon, Rue de Rivoli—the ribs not only rippled through her peach-pink young skin, but she had the flexity and breastlessness of Greek youth, the same flash of skeleton through her, and the tiny cave-in at the stomach.

It was toward this Hellenic end that May exercised her mother for fifteen minutes night and morning on the bath-mat spread out before the open window.

One, two, three, stoop. Fifty times. Up on toes, breathe deeply. Squat on toes, breathe deeply. Fifty times. Touch floor with finger-tips without bending knees, fifty times. And so on, until the rounds of colour were high in her cheeks.

The result was remarkable. The shadow of concavity about Edith's waistline was scarcely fainter than her daughter's. Except for a slight and lyre-shaped swing to the hips, the onus of motherhood lay not upon her. She was straight, she was breastless, she was boyish. Even her bobbed hair, where it sprang out, had left a little rough area on the back of her neck, like a young boy's after his first visits the barber.

On her bath-mat before the open window she might have posed, with her narrow loins, cultivated flatness of chest, un-rich bosom and bony line from hip to knee, for the perfect type of the motherhood of a short-haired civilization.

May's admiration for this Frankenstein mother of her own creation was her one deepest and sincerest enthusiasm.

She drank cocktails, grenadines and the surreptitious white absinthes with greedy-looking lips, but a wry sensation at the pit of her stomach; perfumed her pink nostrils before going to bed to get the odour of her swankily inhaled cigarettes out of them; could swear down, drink down, jazz down, any respectable girl among the smarter (English spoken) cabarets of Paris.

These enthusiasms were so long simulated that simulation could be May Whatley at her best; but for her mother, enthusiasm came easily, richly, like a gusher.

On a June morning, after the bath-mat exercises and still in their pastel-coloured pajamas and their shaggy heads not yet dry from the bath, they sat over a Continental breakfast of coffee, rolls and honey, served in their suite.

"Old darling," said May suddenly, mashing out her third cigarette of the day, kissing her second and third finger-tips and leaning over to transfer them to her mother's lips, "you look fit as a top this morning."

May belonged to the genus offspring who call their parents by Christian name; and because it has never yet been uttered except in the key of being modern, she jerked up a bit each time she said it as if waiting for the applause to die down.

Edith answered her daughter by caressing the toe of her pastel-coloured mule against the muled toe of her daughter.

"May, stop egging me on in my old-age nonsense," she said and flushed with pleasure, but her right hand sprang rather guiltily to a seamed and scarcely visible welt just under the flare of hair off her brow.

Yes, there is something else that may as well be told now and over with.

Edith's face had been "lifted." Fifteen years in crow's-feet, a little tan mole on her right cheek which her father had teased her about up to the very night he died, two rather well-defined mouth-braces the piquant shape of Edith's laugh, and all the little smile wrinkles up around her eyes, had, presto-change-o, vanished under ten thousand francs' worth of the skill of the most famous beauty doctor in Paris (English spoken).

Even to May, the new Edith who emerged from those five bandaged weeks in Beauty's nursing home had been somewhat of a shock. Something dear about the old Edith had scurried away on the crow's-feet, leaving an astonishingly girly Edith, it is true, but a new suave Edith too, with the propped-up smile of one of those masks above the proscenium arch.

You knew, almost creepily, that back somewhere was the old Edith, but there was the new one who would not allow the old so much as the indenture of a mouth-brace, and then those erased-looking eyes. They were not the windows of Edith's soul at all, but alfrescoed imitations of them.

And yet when May, transferring her kissed finger-tips to her mother's lips, said, "Darling, you look fit as a top," she meant it. Indisputably, Edith Whatley looked twenty-four.

"These all-night dancing parties of yours, May, are hard on even my 'facial.'"

"Nonsense—I don't let you do anything that isn't good for you. Lowell said you had more toddle left in you at two this morning than all the rest of us put together."

"Lowell is overdoing the all-night parties, though, May. Last night must have cost him five thousand francs."

"Bosh! If he doesn't spend his millions on us, he will on someone else. The surest way to disgust a boy like Lowell is to show consideration for his pocket nerve. I let him buy wine until I have to pour it into the flower-boxes."

"I think that's disgusting."

"No, you don't. It's wise. Which reminds me, there's some Malays dancing over at Le Faun that everybody is talking about. I thought I'd ring up Speed and see if he would take us to-night after the Coq d'Or."

"Malays?"

"Yes. Muscle dancers. Adele Stetlow says it's awful. They don't move off one spot. All flesh shuddering."

"Ugh! Really, May, for a girl as fastidious as you are . . ."

"But it's the rage of Paris," said May. "Everybody's going." And in her little mauve pajamas, and kicking off her mules, she walked over to the pier-mirror between windows, and began to indulge in a little series of muscular non-senses.

"Uh, dum de dum, dum, eh, uh, uh . . ."

"The rage of *American* Paris, you mean, May. A Frenchman and his fam-ily would be a real curiosity at the places we frequent."

"Darling, how naïve! As if the Paris of the Frenchman mattered. They're only running the show. They sit behind the scenes, scrape in American dol-lars and eat tripe."

"Just the same, it will be good to get back home and order a real French dish off an American menu. I'm so tired of American dishes off French menus."

"Darling, you shall have *escargots bordelaises, babas au rhum* and cham-pagne cocktail in demi-tasses at Petit Rat Mort the very first night we land in New York. Meanwhile, Mrs. Whatley, get a little hurry on. We have two fit-tings at Lanvin at eleven, Renée has our turbans at eleven-thirty. Cartier will have the pearl tassels to show us at twelve and there are your eyebrows to be done before we drop in at Café de Paris for lunch. Henri's holding our table for one o'clock."

"Not the eyebrows, May! I couldn't stand it right after going through the facial. They're not so heavy, dear."

Miss Whatley kissed her mother on each ear lobe. "You're the only smart woman in Paris, Edith Whatley, with unplucked eyebrows. The first sixty-eight yanks are the hardest."

Mrs. Whatley regarded her daughter out of a face that would not and could not trouble up. "May, leave me my eyebrows, I prithee. They make my face seem less nude."

"Aha! The Munsie instinct, always latent in my parent, is now lifting its head to meow!"

"But May, I—the pain—"

"What's the matter, old dear? Feeling logy? Mix you an eye-opener?"

"No, I hate the stuff—and so do you," said Edith Whatley, wanting to grimace out of a face that insisted upon remaining as bland as summer sky.

So there were the fittings that morning, the pearl tassels, the Italian turbans and the eyebrow-pluckings to the accompaniment of such spurts of pain that the agony rolled in cold tears down Edith's cheeks and when she emerged into the sunlight of Rue St. Honoré there was only a superciliously shaped hair-line flaming beneath her turban to indicate where had been brows.

"You're wonderful, Edith. You look like Irene Castle and you make me feel sixteen. I'm damn proud of you."

"I—think I feel faint—"

"Nonsense! Let's jump into a taxi and go over to the Café de Paris, and I'll get Henri to mix you a brandy-and-soda—"

"A cup of tea, dear—if you don't mind."

It was upon stepping from the taxicab on Rue de l'Opéra, the flame in her brow somewhat subsided and a little of the flesh glow back in her cheeks, that Edith Whatley walked straight into the path of Julie Bell Anderson Sears, Munsie Central High School, class of 1899.

One of those stunned movements of open-mouthed and silent ejaculation.

"Why—Julie Bell Anderson!"

Julie Bell, in an excellent quality blue-and-white foulard that followed her curves, and an excellent quality blue Milan short-back sailor with cornflowers, stopped short, her round-as-an-apple face wrinkling into honest perplexity.

"I—I'm sorry, but you have the advantage," she said in the Lancashire of Indiana and threw a humorously helpless appeal to her companion, a young girl, also pretty, but cruelly bisected, at just the line Lanvin disapproves most, by a shirtwaist and skirt.

"Julie Bell, don't you say you don't know me! Munsie Central High. Rock Church Choral Sextette. I never could remember your married name, but you're Julia Bell Anderson! Sears—that's it. You married Edward Sears from Fort Worth."

"If this isn't like me," said Julie Bell and blew upward at a distracted-looking strand of brown-grey hair that had started to dangle; "stupid at remembering names."

"Why, mama, you're usually splendid at recalling old friends from Munsie. Try to think, dear."

"For heaven's sake then, old dear," said May, who loathed sidewalk reunions, "unburden your dark identity to your friends."

"Remember the night at Christian Endeavour strawberry festival out at Linden Wood, Julie, when you cut your hand scooping up ice-cream and I bound it with my petticoat ruffle and you were so worried over the waste of embroidery? Remember the night you slept at our house on Dover Street and helped me write the class prophecy—"

Julia Bell Anderson Sears's face then did a curious thing. It froze. Froze into an amazement that thawed into actual silliness. "You—can't be—Edith Mastason? No—no—it couldn't be—"

"Of course I'm Edith, you old darling, you. Now, give me a great big hug right here in the middle of Rue de l'Opéra."

"Edith, I'll skip along in and whisper the brandy-and-soda to Henri—"

"No, no, May, I want you to stay here and meet this dear old friend of mine—my daughter, Julie, and of course this is your daughter, and—and—oh, just tell me everything about everybody and let me get my fill of looking at dear old Julie Bell Anderson, whom I haven't seen for—for nineteen years!"

For the life of her Julie Bell could not get past the spluttering stage. "Why I—you—Edith—twenty-three—different—funny eyes—slimmer—mole?—wouldn't recognize—bobbed hair—why, Edith, you're a regular flapper!"

"Of course I am, you old outspoken darling you, and so are you going to be after we get hold of you and get some of that dear good-natured fat off of you. And to think this dear girl is your daughter . . ."

"I say, dear, we're blocking the traffic. Make an engagement for some other time. Henri won't hold our table—"

"Julie Bell, you and—your daughter—"

"Cornelia."

"Cornelia—come in and lunch with May and me!"

"No sirree, you and May are coming right around the corner to a little place we are just devoted to on the Rue des Pyramides. Cornelia, you and May walk on ahead and break your own ice. Edith—why, honey, I just don't know where to begin!"

Something cold and slit-like had happened to May's eyes. Slim as a sardine, every undulation of her through the artful simplicity of her modish black dress emphasizing her emancipation from everything nether except glove silk and precious little of that, she placed a frigid and squeezing restraint upon her mother's arm. "But Edith—we're lunching *here*."

"But darling, Julie Bell and I haven't seen one another in nineteen—"

"Where is this place on the Rue des Pyramides?"

"May, you'll love it. It's a little restaurant near the Louvre. Not even table-cloths, and the dearest little old French proprietor who tosses up a perfect salad before your very eyes."

"I know. Where they rub the dessert plates with garlic and red wine tastes like tooth-paste. I like your party, Edith, but you'll have to choose between it and me this time. I hate quaintness. It smells."

"So does chypre," spoke up Cornelia in a voice rather surprisingly loud. No light and shade. An American desert of a voice. "Only garlic is an honester smell than chypre."

"But at least the way of the transgressor is fragrant," said Edith, and lifted her lips daintily off her teeth in a tantalizing little smile she had.

Edith held out persuasive hands.

"Please, darlings," she said through the biting admonition of May's pointed finger-nails into her forearm, "we've reserved our table here and Henri strikes you off his bowing list if you disappoint. . . . Let's not squabble over places. Now which of these two girls of ours will give in first?"

"Why, I will, of course," said Cornelia, out of the little pause that followed, and jerking up her skirt band where it seemed to glory in sagging away to reveal the grin of gathers.

Across fourteen canary-bird bathtubs of *hors d'œuvres* and then *ham-an'-eggs* and *pommes frites*—which is the French way of catering to the American appetite for ham and eggs and fried potatoes—the patter ran something like this:

"Julie Bell, whatever became of the Ponscarme family that used to live on the corner of Spruce and Third?"

"Why honey, the old man died the year I married and moved to Fort Worth, and they say that Shirley took her share in the estate and bought herself a Polish nobleman."

"And Mary Nipher?"

"Same old Mary. Her second daughter visited us in Fort Worth last summer. Mary's grey as a bat, though. Edith, honey, I just can't keep my eyes off of you. It's not human for a woman to look fifteen years younger than the day she graduated with her hair on her head in a Psyche and a long train dress."

"My daughter just won't let me grow old, Julie. Says I owe it to her to keep her young by keeping that way myself."

"You see, Connie, it's May's doing. Just think, Edith and I were girls together and look at us now."

"Mama, you can't stand dieting and you know it. It makes you nervous and gives you circles under your eyes."

"Circles at least can be *intéressant*. Fat's fat."

"Why, I wish you could have seen, May, one day when my shampoo woman put a little henna in the water just to touch up the grey. Between Connie and her father you would have thought me a fallen woman. Mere henna, mind you!"

"Mama dear, it wasn't that and you know it. But it did something horrid and gilt to her. Oh, I don't know, made her look like the sort of woman who would wear tarnished silver evening slippers down to breakfast!"

"You see what tyrants my family are with me?"

"Never you mind, Julie Bell, May and I will take hold of you. I know just how Connie feels—you've such a pretty face and the grey makes it even softer; but as May says, women simply don't let themselves go grey any more."

"Mama hasn't let herself go, and as for her face and hair, I wouldn't let anyone tamper with them for anything."

"You see."

"Why I only meant, dear—"

"Let herself go! Why, she's the leading spirit in Fort Worth. She took political history and international law with me my whole last two years at the State University. She's stumped the State for the Governor of Texas and for Child Welfare. She's president of the Fort Worth Wednesday Club and can talk the technicalities of pretty nearly every corporation law case that my father handles. If you call that letting herself go!"

"Oh, but that's splendid, Julie! It does my heart good to hear Connie brag about you."

"I'm not bragging, merely trying to—show you that—"

"You always did have a perfectly splendid head on your shoulders, Julie. That's not the issue. But since you've brought up the other subject, you don't mind my saying something, do you, dear?"

"You come right out with it, Edith. Probably won't do me one bit of good when my two tyrants begin to interfere, but any woman who can look like you can speak with authority."

"Well, Julie, first of all, you—and Connie too; I'm going not to let that young lady off—don't study yourselves."

"Honey, you just have your finger in as many community pies as I have, and see—"

"And look at Connie there. Just as pretty as a picture, making herself all tubby in a shirtwaist and skirt."

"Edith, you don't half appreciate Connie. That child took Phi Beta Kappa last year and—"

"Mama, please—no mutual admiration society—"

"Don't interrupt. And Julie, dotted foulard! I didn't think they were perpetrated any more."

"Why, a little dressmaker I just give work to, sort of to keep her going, made this—I know it isn't much."

"With all your money! Julie, it's not fair to yourselves. Oh yes, I've heard about that show place of yours down in Fort Worth that you throw open to school children once a month! Haven't you been to any of the French dressmakers, dear?"

"Well, Edith, you'll laugh at us, but we—Ed and all of us in fact—we believe in patronizing home talent. Fort Worth gives us our living and we try to give her hers back."

"Altruistic, but rather hard on the altruist."

"Not that a French dress now and then could matter a great deal, I guess. Do you know, Connie, it might be a good idea to take back home one or two and give Miss Effie the advantage of copying them for her fall trade."

"Oh Julie Bell, Julie Bell, I just couldn't have you any different, foulard and all!"

"You do see now what I mean! Mama's just mama!"

"And Connie is her mother's daughter."

"The fact of the matter is, Edith, when Connie and I get to Paris we don't get our noses up out of our Baedekers long enough to much more than buy the folks back home a trinket or two."

"Oh la, la!"

"I know it, May. Regular old cut-and-dried Cook's tourists. But for the life of me I can't help it. I feel guilty being in the same town with the Barbizon collection and Sorbonne lectures and wasting my time on the Rue de la Paix."

"You're not all wrong, Julie. Now hear this, May. We can stand a little scolding too."

"You should see my dining-room, Edith. Really, it is a Gothic gem and every piece copied by a Fort Worth cabinet-maker from pictures I brought back five summers ago from the Musée de Cluny. Those of us who live in the small American towns and cities and who can afford to travel owe it to the community to carry home some of this culture to them, Edith."

"Of course," said May, poising a forkful of Mousse Niagara before her slightly too emphasized lips and her voice curving out into an elaborate fan of satire, "and of course there is the Fort Worth Culture Club."

"Of course, yes," said Cornelia, as suddenly as a pounce, and fastening her rather noonday eyes upon May's slitted ones, "and mama's president of it, and we have Owen Meredith afternoons, and last year our vice-president prepared just the sweetest paper on 'Shakespeare's Heroines.'"

"That's right, Connie, don't let my young daughter tease you."

"Oh, Connie can hold her own! May has probably lived in New York too long to realize what the intellectual isolation of our country can mean."

"Yes, but we travel more than any nation in the world."

"Granted, but even so, what about the proportion of Americans who have never been abroad or even seen their own country, for that matter?"

"That's true, Julie. Right in my own family I'm the only one who has ever been to Europe."

"We all know the Culture Club joke, even down our way. But just let me tell you it is those little groups of women with busy-business-men husbands who are carrying the first banners of the real intellectual awakening in our country."

"Hear, hear!"

"May!"

"Let her alone, Edith. My riot act will peter out in a minute."

"*Garçon, donnez-moi une lumière,*" said May, tilting her cigarette up at the waiter, who lighted it with fervent servility.

"Certainly, miss," he said.

"Oh! I'm not ashamed to say, just to emphasize my point to you, that my very first club paper next winter is going to be on Rodin and the pieces in the Rodin Museum here."

"You know where that is, May. Over on the Left Bank, near the Rotonde and all those places we went the night Lowell took us slumming."

"M-m-m."

"Most of Rodin's things somehow remind me of home, Edith. Intellectually or culturally, as the Germans would say, we are only half out of the marble. The features of an awakening beauty are there, lovely as life, but they haven't emerged. Our little culture clubs and art circles that afford you sophisticates so much amusement are in a way the Rodins of American culture. Tearing an intellectual curiosity out of the cold marble."

Suddenly May leaned forward.

"Edith, there is that Pennystetter girl from Philadelphia coming in with Tom Sutter. She's wearing that Grueze model of Lanier's. See her sleeves! They're quite large. Eugenie told me before she sailed that she had it on very inside information that Lanier's sleeves would be larger."

"Edith, the name Pennystetter reminds me! You'll never guess whom I ran into at the American Express the other morning. Bob Pennyrich!"

"No!"

"I knew he was over, but thought he was in London. Same old Bob. We heard him laughing clear upstairs in the mail department, and I said to Connie, 'That laugh belongs to no one in the world but Bob Pennyrich.'"

"Why, Julie—Bob in Paris! I haven't seen him for—let me see—going on twenty years."

"Bob liked you mighty well in the old days, Edith, when you used to sit in the grandstand and root for him and the Central High football team."

"I hear he has done so wonderfully well, Julie."

"Well? Why, honey, Bob just owns about half of Munsie, is director in three banks there, officer in two or three corporations, owns the largest block of stock in the Suwanee Rubber Company, drives the fastest cars, does the most charity, owns the finest private art gallery and laughs the loudest of any man in Munsie. I wouldn't be surprised to see Bob Pennyrich on the gubernatorial ticket one of these days."

"You've heard me speak of this Bob Pennyrich, May. He's the one who sent me that little tear-shaped diamond I always keep in safety deposit, for a wedding present."

"A very appropriate gift. The fact that Bob liked you pretty well and has never married has always sort of tied up in my mind, Edith."

"Julie, what utter nonsense!"

"Bob Pennyrich is almost about the realest man I know," spoke up Cornelia.

"Please not the 'almost.' Bobby Fowler, Bob's nephew, is Connie's candidate for realest."

"Mama, dear—"

"Connie, why not? Edith is one of my very oldest friends. You may as well know, dear, that's why Connie's father packed us over to Europe this summer. 'Treat your mother to her last son-in-lawless summer, Connie,' was the way he put it."

Sisters under their skin suddenly tightened in a circle about that table.

"Connie engaged!" cried Edith in a church-whisper voice that rose and fell in a little Gothic arch of reverence.

Connie held out a left third finger with a small blue diamond gleaming up from it.

"October," she said, and blushed furiously.

"He's a nice clean boy, Edith, twenty-four—"

"Twenty-five, mama."

"Oh dear yes, excuse the error!" said her mother.

"Well, bless their hearts!"

"His mother, Aila Pennyrich, was about five years ahead of us in High, Edith. Good clean Hoosier stock. Bobby is in one of his uncle's banks and has a nice future, if he earns it. I can't see what more two young people with their health and enthusiasm and a pretty little bungalow from the blushing bride's parents and a good thriving town like Munsie to start in, could ask for, do you?"

"Why, no," said May with her lips apart. "Why, no. No." And down now came May's voice, and gone were the provokingly tilted eyebrows, and two little hands pounced on Connie's own. "Listen, dear, I'm a whippersnapper at knowing the right places. I know the sweetest place for peach-coloured trousseau lingerie, and have you seen those adorable little platinum anklets at Cartier's? So amusing! Cunning little satires, you know, on the ball-and-chain idea—"

There suddenly rang out above the crystal and silver clatter of Café de Paris an enormous laugh, as if one of those telescoping traveller's cups as big as a barrel had clattered apart on a stone floor, each segment with a resonance all its own, and on it, Edith, Connie and Julie Bell turned simultaneously.

"Edith, that laugh belongs to only one human being!"

"Bob Pennyrich!"

"There he is, mama, over there in the doorway talking to some people!"

"Run and tell him, Connie, to come right over here, but don't let on whom we are with. Law, I wouldn't miss this!"

It was a noisy, well-met reunion, with May a little splinter of disapproval on the edge. She hated the hubbub, she hated the grin of gathers above Connie's sagging skirt-band, she hated the Indiana burr that had suddenly raised itself on her mother's voice; and how Bob Pennyrich could laugh!

The Ritter twins, Baltimore, a few tables removed, were giggling behind their Poiré moire vanity cases.

"You're fooling! Well, I'm hanged! Heaven above, girl, what have you been doing? Running the clock backward? 'Pon my soul, I took you for a chicken."

"Bob!"

"Fact! I'm not sure yet that this wet little town with the goatee under its chin isn't playing a trick on me. I'm seeing things! Where's that little cheek mole, honey, that I used to dot all my *i*'s with? Where's all those little sun's-rays crinkles that used to squeeze back your eyes when you laughed? Push back that hat a little—bobbed hair—b-bobbed—" It was then that he threw back his head and laughed, and the Ritter twins wielded their vanity cases. "Great Caesar's ghost, our little class beauty of 'ninety-nine in her high head-dress, long train, turned flapper twenty years after!"

Quick, excited, exclamatory talk. Pennyrich's laughter dominating all the clatter, and May more than ever the little splinter on the edge, with the circumflex high in her eyebrows again and smoking coldly at her cigarette.

He wanted to order luncheon all over again. He paid the check. He bought up the flower-girl's stock of violets and jonquils and was constantly diving into his left breast pocket for snapshots of his new Alsatian wolfhound, a cablegram from Bobby Fowler and banknotes to pay the waiter.

"Lemonade—or lemon squash or whatever it is they call it over here in this land of no ice. Come, girls, have a lemonade."

"No, thank you," said May and smiled down at her grenadine.

"Well, Edith, I don't mind telling you this is the greatest treat I've had in Europe. Take off that there Hindu toga and let me get a real good look at you, honey." And suiting the action to the word he reached over, lifting the solemn fez off Edith's small clipped head.

"Don't, Bob!" she cried, and her hands flew up to the still quivering line of her plucked eyebrows.

"Well, I'm darned!" he said, a rather comical perplexity out on his American Indian cast of face, and his mouth a little humorous, a little vexed, a little sad.

"I don't see the point, Bob. Nobody seems to be sitting around with their eyes hanging out over *you,* and you look so fit it's breath-taking."

"But you look fit, Edy, in a way that sets us back a generation. Am I right, Julie? But by Jove, I can't help kind of missing that little brown mole—"

"Oh, cheer up! Why ooze sentimentality over a mole? There must be plenty of them flourishing on native cheek-bones back in Munsie." Of course this was from the cool lips of May, and her eyes were like slits of cold fire at him when she said it.

He looked at her, at her little slim, cross-kneed angle of insouciance, and back went his head for a blast of the easy laughter.

"You sassy little milk-and-honey-fed-chicken, you! Tell your mama to take you home and wash some of that nature-faking purple off those lips of yours."

"Now, Bob, don't you and May start in like that—"

"Look here, girls, where do you all live? I'll drive you home now, and then what say to a ride in the Bois about six and dinner later at one of those Chumps Elysses places? What say, Edy? Julie?"

"Oh, Bob, we'd love it!"

"But Edith, we're—"

"No buts from you, Miss Slimpsy. For once you have to put up with your mama's country friends, or I'll carry you kicking and screaming every inch of the way."

"May's right, Bob. I forgot. May means that she—we have a partial engagement for this evening—"

"May doesn't mean anything of the sort. She's probably got her heart set on one of those Paris nights especially staged for the sucker Americans who—"

"No, Edith, Mr.—Pennyrich is quite right. I didn't mean anything at all. Of course we will join him. This is one of the times when it is so much easier to give in than to be let in for what is sure to be an argument. One dreads the noise."

"Great!" cries the not-a-gentleman from Indiana, seizing his vulgar opportunity. "Where are you stopping, girls? I'll pick you all up at five."

"Connie and I are at the Hotel de Staël."

"The where?"

"A little hotel on the Rue Cambon. A dear little courtyard and French food—so really French. Connie and I always stop there, but our rooms aren't so good this year—"

"Julie, with all your money! A little dump like that!"

"I don't blame her, Edith. I'm at the Esplanade. Hundred francs a day for the kind of room and bath that wouldn't cost me a penny above six bucks a day in New York; the lobby about as foreign-looking as an Elks' convention; American only spoken, and about the only thing French that I can see about the place is a palm out every which way I turn."

"We're at the Griffon, just across from the Tuileries Gardens, and just as comfy as can be. Why don't you move over to our hotel, Julie? We'll all be here some weeks. You too, won't you, Bob?"

"The girl is inspired! Connie, stop pouting or I'll cable a certain nephew of mine that his fiancée is given to fits of irascible temper—"

"Connie means—"

"Not a word out of you, Julie Bell, or I'll include a report on the mother-in-law."

"But reservations at our hotel are not easy to—"

"And don't worry about our not getting all the rooms at your hotel we want, Miss Slimpsy. Just make a noise like an American dollar any place in Europe this summer and you can buy anything from the Kaiser's spurs to a spurious Rembrandt."

"Oh, how utterly—utter!"

"I know. Pretty awful, isn't it? But now grit your little teeth some more and prepare to bear up under the invasion of the Indianese. We're going to stage a rousing Old Home Week that will put some of those good old sense-of-humour crinkles back in your mama's face."

"It is very possible," said May, lifting back her lips in the cool, neat way she had, "that Edith will have need of those sense-of-humour crinkles in view of the impending invasion you mention."

"*Zouee!*" he cried, making a mock feint.

Her head was back now, and the slits in her eyes said "War!"

And it was. But war of the roaring cannonade of Pennyrich's laughter and the little barbed spearings of May Whatley's tongue. She had a way of watching him while he talked, almost as if behind the arched bow of her teeth, the arrow of her tongue was tautening ready to fly.

Her mother would observe all this with anxiety, ready always with the intercepting or deflecting word, because often and more often, as the gay Paris weeks fled on, May drew blood, and Pennyrich's laughter would die down into quick pools of silence.

"May, for the few weeks that we are all to be here in the hotel together, you might make yourself a little more agreeable to my friends. You are sweet, dear, to Julie and Connie these days, but—Bob—"

"Oh, Edith, don't you worry about Bob! He's too pleased with his man-from-home rôle to be on to himself."

"There are limits to fun."

"Who said fun? He's one of those noisy, assertive Americans who think that the only way to impress a woman is to throw violent cave-man contortions and treat her as if she still rode side-saddle and held her little finger out from the teacup."

"I wouldn't exactly say that Bob is trying to impress you, May."

"His is the grand old spirit of 'ninety-six. He likes women who still call a leg a limb and say 'when baby came.' Don't want to seem to wound your native enthusiasm, dear, but the pride of dear old Munsie High is impossible."

Edith's reply came from her a little too fast for her to control.

"But I notice that you haven't missed one of our impossible friend's parties. If I felt as you say you do, I'd go off with Lowell and the old crowd, dear."

Miss Whatley, who was at breakfast, nibbled at the heel of her morning roll.

"Not at all; I enjoy it. Besides, I'm what he needs."

"You, what he needs!" Something that was slow and humorous came out in Edith's voice, and the mask of her face gave a little twitch as if a mute was trying to speak. "Why, May Whatley, one Bob Pennyrich in this world is worth ten of you."

"Possibly."

"And of me, for that matter."

"No, Edith, not you." May was fierce at that, pressing down her mother's hands to the tray and kissing them in a little hot string clear up to the wrists. "He's not worth ten of you! Nobody is."

"Oh May—May—"

"Yum—yum—yum—bad hands, stop twitching in that silly nervous way"—and kissed them all over again.

The little unusual tremolo in her daughter's voice and the string of soft kisses sent surprising and easy tears spurting to Edith's eyes.

"Oh, May, that's just it. Nerves. I—us—oh—I'm silly! But May, sometimes when I get to thinking of us—our kind of—lives—and what a silly, inconsequential mother I must be to—well, I mean how much I am to blame for—for things and I—oh, silly nerves, I know!"

Miss Whatley regarded her parent with the dispassionate eyes of supreme youth. They were like bright shallow pans with gilt bottoms.

"You *are* developing nerves, Edith. I've noticed it lately. Bad. Mustn't."

"I can't seem to help it, May. Sometimes I—the queerest sensation. I want to laugh, May, and no sooner do I want to laugh than I want to cry, and then I just sort of want to do both at the same time. Sort of hysteria, I guess."

"And no wonder. It's the Uplift family across the hall. I could forgive even Connie her shirtwaists and her mother her pince-nez on the gold hook, if only they weren't so damn noble. When they begin to drag you to morning lectures in the mummy room at the Louvre and buy Anderson prints of Le Brun and daughter to take home to the Fort Worth assistant librarian, I don't want to laugh and cry, at the same time; I want to grunkle like a gorilla, or whatever it is gorillas do."

Edith Whatley pressed her fingers into her eyelids until the darkness spun starpoints. "Oh May, May, May, where am I letting you lead us! Connie isn't exactly a blaze of personality, and Julie's bromidic in spots, but just the same I sometimes think she has kept young in a different way than I have. A finer way."

"Fat," said May, the word spinning from her lips like a disk.

"She's not fat in spirit! I've cut the wrinkles out of my face, but Julie Bell's kept them out of her heart."

"Whatever that means."

"No, May, under our skins Julie and I are the same age—forty-five—and it's being forty-five underneath this bobbed hair of mine and my plucked eyebrows that makes me want to laugh when I want to cry and cry when I want to laugh."

"Laugh, darling, laugh, if it makes you feel any better."

"That's why I love to have Julie these days, May. I need her. Don't scoff! It's these little nervousnesses that come with forty-five that make me ache to take down my hair, climb into a kimono and talk it all out with someone my own—"

"If you're feeling nervous, we'll both stop in later for a facial. There's a little line next to your nose, dear, that I want out and quick too, because if Bob spies it he'll want it to wear in his watch. That must be he now on the telephone. Even central always rings noisiest when it's Bob."

"I'll answer it, May."

"Oh no, never mind! I'll soothe his savage breast with my dulcet tones. Hello . . . Well, it all depends upon which lady you mean. The young and pretty one or the young and pretty one. . . . Well, that will be about enough Hoosier horridness out of you. Won't I do?"

"I'll take the receiver, dear."

"Shh-h. . . . What? . . . She's not feeling any too fit this morning."

"Please, May, don't let on to Bob! Here, give me the receiver; I want to thank him for my flowers—"

"Oh, we loved the 'posies and secretive buds'! Of course, the marigolds were for me, *n'est-ce pas?* . . . Why? Why, because they're for remembrance or something of the sort, aren't they? . . . Oh rosemary, of course, if you must quibble over terms!"

"May, let me—"

"Shh-h. . . . Where? . . . To-day? Why on earth does one take a boat up the Seine with mussy little French families and their *enfants terribles* when one has the smartest car in Paris at his beck and call?"

"Oh May, it's a perfect day for our picnic up the Seine!"

"Wait, Bob, I can't understand a word. Edith—please—it's maddening to have you talk in on me like this. Hello—"

"But Connie and Julie Bell are counting on it. You keep your engagement with the Stetlows, dear, and we'll get the hotel to fix us up a picnic basket—"

"The sweet girl graduate is all agog, so I suppose I must. I cannot trust my young parent out alone on these wild Indianese debauches. I suppose there'll be hard-boiled eggs and *jambon froid,* warm wine out of fluted paper cups and crumbly cake with the icing stuck to the tissue paper. . . . All right, then, eleven o'clock if I must. Good-bye."

"But May," said Edith, risen and regarding her daughter with very dark and very bright eyes, "if you don't want to go—"

"But I do want to go, Edith," said May. Her voice was dead level now and the moment of silence that floated in between them was crowded with heartbeat.

They sat on deck and watched the French countryside, florid with June, slide past, Pennyrich at great ease in knickerbockers, one knee flung high over the other and his restless fingers playing an incessant tune upon it.

"That's a perfect Claude Lorraine sky, mama," said Connie.

"Oh, I would not say that!" said May, who could not quite remember ever having seen a Claude Lorraine.

"Well, girls, what do you think I bought myself to-day that about set me back the price of a couple diamond tiara-ra-ras, a motor boat and a grand piano or two?"

"Whew, Bob, setting some Munsie pin-money in motion?"

"No, Julie, I'm pretty much like you when it comes to rolling the American dollar along the Rue de la Paix, but I blew myself to something that doesn't exactly come under the heading of home industry. Yes, saw something I liked; couldn't get the thing off my mind. Wanted it. Got an expert fellow to do the parley-vooing, got the price down from the eighty per cent. advance quoted to Americans and now I'm the proud possessor of—guess!"

"Oh Bob, not a hydroplane or something dangerous?"

"Zero for Edith."

"A château!"

"Zero for the milk-fed chicken. Come on, Julie and Connie—next!"

"A—a—oh, what could have cost more than all those things put together! I have it! A Gobelin."

"No."

"A—a—"

"A Meissonier, girls."

"There, I was going to guess an automobile in the beginning. What is it, Bob, one of those wonderful French racers?"

There was a moment of pause, with Edith darting out a quick gesture as if to push back May's words, and Connie, it must be owned, rippling up into a giggle. But Julie Bell leaned forward, her mouth ardent.

"Bob, how wonderful to be able to gratify a gorgeous whim like that!"

"I got it from the same fellow who sold me my small Jan Steen two years ago. I don't know the technical points that make me like it, but it's considered a very fine little canvas, and by Jove, it's full of the prance of horses and hurt eyes kind of dying gloriously and red smoke and—well, it got me."

"I hope you'll let us hang it in our club rooms during Federated Art Circle week, the way you did your Zorn etchings, Bob."

"Certainly I will, but before I let you hang it I want to drive my new Meissonier down Elm Street and see what the folks back home think of my French racer—"

A kind of suppressed laugh went up in a little explosion, and May, whose face still stung red and whose lips were none too steady, lifted them then, bravely.

"I must brush up on my Baedeker."

"Baedeker won't help you, sister. What you need is a spanking. A good old Indiana back-of-the-hairbrush brand, and by Jove, Edith, I'd like to be the one to administer it to your young daughter."

"Bob, don't you and May begin, now!"

"Never have been able to make much of an impression upon the mother, but I'd like to try my hand at making a literal one on the daughter."

"Subtle wit, I suppose."

"A spanking, sister, that's all you need to set you straight. Some of that kalsomine washed off that pretty face of yours, your point of view aired, and I'll show you a close runner-up to the Edith Mastason who sang 'Alice, Where Art Thou?' on the graduating platform of the Munsie High."

But instead of her usual curved scimitar of a retort, small jade-white areas had sprung out and were quivering about May's nostrils, and she jumped up so precipitately that her deck-chair toppled over.

"You're horrid," she said, her lips pulled this way and that in her desperate effort to steady them, "perfectly, perfectly horrid," and then before the avalanche of her tears turned and ran.

"Why, May dear—come back—come back—Bob was only teasing!"

"Good heavens," he said, "I've hurt the child!" and began to rise up in what seemed interminable sections of his length.

"I'll go to her," said Edith, who had paled. "Bob, you were cruel."

"No. Let me. I must have come down like an elephant," he said, and stalked after her with the wind lifting his strong black hair.

He found her in a crumple off in a deserted corner of the bow, her arms crossed on top of a coil of canvas fire-hose and her face down in them.

"Why, now, May!" he said, in the voice with which he told children Jack the Giant-Killer. "Is this the girl I thought was such a good sparring-partner? Shame!"

"Go away!" she said furiously into her arms. "Go away!"

He stood looking down at her crush of small figure, her smart outing hat with its patent leather rose awry, and her back all curved up with crying.

"May—"

"Go away!"

"I'm sorry if I've hurt you."

"You sorry!" she cried, flashing her tear-lashed face up at him. "You sorry if you've hurt me! Why, you thrive on it!"

"I do not."

"You do. You revel in it. There's never a remark you direct to me or at me that hasn't been carefully barbed beforehand." And down went her head into her arms again.

He cleared a little of the fire-hose and sat down beside her.

"You don't mean that, May."

"I do. I do. I do. I can't stand it any more. Your sarcasm. Your blistering, horrid way of trying to belittle me."

"Doesn't it occur to you, May, if I seem to belittle you, it might be that unconsciously I am trying to barricade myself against being belittled by you?"

"Oh, no! You flung down the gauntlet to me the first instant you clapped eyes on me. You've too much disdain for anything I might say to let it belittle you."

"You're wrong. No, May—listen, stop crying and we will talk this thing out."

"I'm so hurt. So wounded by what your attitude toward me has been from the very start. So hurt that I've rammed my pillow into my mouth, if you want to know it, so Edith wouldn't hear me crying in the night. That's how you've hurt me. And to-day it wasn't any worse than—than usual, but I guess I—I just snapped."

"It's just as well you did, May," he said, reaching out for her arm with the gesture of a doctor feeling for a pulse. "It's the first glimpse I've ever had of you with your eyebrows down."

"There you go again. For a man of the world such as you profess to be—"

"I've never professed any such thing. You've just sized me up right, honey, that's all."

"Indeed I have. Your ideas about life are carpet-slippered and your ideas about women mid-Victorian."

"Both much maligned institutions."

"You think a girl who reads Freud or Havelock Ellis is a brazen hussy—"

"You're wrong again. I object to the girl who doesn't read Freud or Havelock Ellis but juggles their cant phrases up into a cocktail of dangerous misconceptions."

"You belong to the school that dotes on the 'good old days' when we slept with closed windows and closed minds. Why, I—I actually believe your grudge against me is because I've kept my mother young and good-looking and free from her native school of Owen Meredith and hips. And I—as for my eyebrows—well, they're my affair, aren't they?"

"Bless your heart, indeed they are. Pluck them all out, honey, if you like them better that way. What does an old Hoosier like me know about such things? I think you look darn cute if you ask me. I could write a sonnet to them. How's that? Modern enough, isn't it? Sonnet to a Lady's Plucked Eyebrows."

"No, that isn't modern—it's merely you—being smart."

"May, you're wrong. I hold no brief against you flappers. I'd like to have a half dozen of you with your bobbed hair and your rolled stockings and your naughty little jazzy shoulders, each one of you waving a different-coloured feather fan above my coach, the way the Egyptians did. Those fellows had the right idea."

She laughed through her tears and the wet of her lashes with the glow of her eyes behind them was like shower-in-sun, and he took both her hands in his and now his voice was the Jack-the-Giant-Killer voice again, just about the time the children are getting drowsy.

"Why, May, you girls have about fifty-one per cent. the right idea. Throwing off restraints that haven't any more meaning left to them than Chinese feet. That's not my tirade. The swing of the pendulum is too far, that's all. I'm for the new values every time, but it is the false ones that have crept in with them."

"That's the hue and cry over every young generation," said May in the recitative voice of one who has said it all before. "The Brontë sisters were considered shocking because they travelled about a bit and taught school, the 'Gibson Girl' because she wore rainy-day skirts, and now—"

"The flapper generation because she jazzes, boozes, regards the crowning glory of womanhood her bobbed hair and is directly responsible for the male genus lounge-lizard."

"Yes, and then settles down and makes just as good a wife and mother as any of them in the maligned generations before her."

"Exactly. That's just why you youngsters sometimes get on my nerves. What's it all about? Setting aside old ideals for new ideas. No reality. No sincerity. Syncopated thinking. Piffle."

"Good old moss-grown spirit of 'ninety-six."

"Drinking down cocktails when they make you sick to your tummy. Sorry, honey, if I have to talk facts. Sneering down the old merely because it isn't new. Wiping the Meissoniers off the slate because someone came along later and squirted on the pigment straight from the tube. God knows I don't take you all seriously . . ."

"We must be brave and bear up under it—"

"I'd just as soon buy the whole generation of you an all-day sucker, tell you to go home and wash your eyebrows, they look sore, and go to bed."

"Ah, my cave man! There is nothing left for me to do but fall in love with you at the end of the fifth instalment."

"I know the good old wife-and-mother stuff is there. But meanwhile you youngsters are taking yourselves too seriously. Honestly, now, you mustn't. Ellen Key and Jane Addams and Madam Curie are the real modern woman of to-day. Why don't you flappers emulate them?"

"We can't all be Ellen Keys and Jane Addamses, you know."

"No, but you can hitch your sixty-horse-power runabouts to the kind of modernity for women that they represent, instead of this new generation piffle that you are all impudent with."

"I won't be talked to like this!"

"Yes, you will. It's good for you. It isn't so very important that you hap-pened to confuse my Meissonier with a motor car—but it's the point of view behind the error. I refuse to accept Dadaism, futurism, free verse and the Russian ballet as the only movements in the history of the world that matter. I think Cézanne is a mighty artist, but so was Meissonier. Debussy hasn't yet overshadowed Bach for me nor James Joyce one Mr. William Makepeace Thackeray. Wow, but that last will give the 'esoteric few' the ascetic shud-ders!"

"You flatter yourself."

"Ah, but joking aside, we are all making a mountain out of a mole-hill, about you youngsters and your goings-on. As you say, you are young and will settle down some day. But what have you done to Edith, May? What you can get away with charmingly can—can even be rather horrible on an older woman. What have you done with the old Edith whose hair grew up off her neck in the shyest, sweetest way and whose eyes used to squeeze right in behind laugh-crinkles?"

"And don't forget the mole on the cheek."

"You're getting Edith's laugh-crinkles, May. No—don't fight them back. Sometimes when I look at you I get a fleeting glimpse of the old Edith—the sweetest girl in Munsie. What have you done with her? She's gone. I can't find her behind that polite-faced mask. She keeps trying to look out at me, but no use; and then, just when I am about giving up, along you come with some unconscious twist or turn. A replica of the old Edith I am looking for and cannot find."

Scalding, angrily hot tears were out in May's eyes.

"Don't drag Edith into this! Ridicule me all you want, but not her. I can't stand that."

"We are not mincing words to-day, May. I hold you to account. Edith is not really the—the caricature on youth which you have made out of her. She's as real behind her mask as Munsie or Julie or—you!"

"What Edith is, she is—for me. Because I've moulded her sweet nature against—stodginess. She went through ten years of unmitigated married hell with my father and I've rejuvenated her from forty-five to twenty-five and I'm proud of it."

"You've perpetrated—"

"A woman doesn't have to look fair, fat and forty to proclaim the mater-nity you prate about. Behind what you are pleased to term her mask there never was a dearer—a—a—dearer—"

"Why, May," he said, and by now the children in his Jack-the-Giant-Killer voice were sound asleep, "I love you when you're like this!" And touched her cheek, and they both sprang apart from the contact. Surprised. Startled. Young.

"I—why—" she said.

"Why—I—" he said.

"Let's go back," she cried and stood up rumpled and red.

"There—there's the rippingest little crinkle, May, like Edith used to have, curled up under your eye. No—don't touch it."

"Let's go," she repeated, and jerked her hand away from the sting of his.

They turned up-deck, wind in their faces.

It was wonderful to lie very straight and very still upon the bed after the long day on the water, and May, in orchid-coloured pajamas that made a sort of boy doll of her, was stretched on top of the violet-coloured taffeta coverlet, her arms stiff along her sides, her lips prim, and eyelids that, because of the little flashing through her body, were not quite steady.

It was only an interim. At seven Pennyrich's car would gather them up again, all five, for outdoor dinner in the Bois and, because May wanted it, dancing later at Les Acacias.

Edith, who could not sleep, sat beside the window. She was still in her white outing frock and there was a red welt across her brow where the hat had pressed. She kept rubbing it. Opposite, the Tuileries Gardens swam in the haze of late sun.

The welt hurt, and because she could not sleep she tiptoed finally across the hall to the Anderson suite.

Julie Bell had a headache. Her hair was down and there were frank patches of dark shadow out here and there in her face. She wore a dark challie wrapper with a shirred waist-line and an outlining of narrow red satin ribbon. A practical wrapper for slithering through Pullman cars.

"Why, Julie Bell, I haven't seen one of those 'solid Comforts' since I left Munsie. Are the girls still swapping them at Christmas?"

"Connie made me mine. Wouldn't be without one. Come right in, honey. Shove over those things and curl up here on the foot of the bed. I'm done up. Splitting headache. Bob will have to count me out of the second instalment of his party."

"Oh Julie, I am sorry!"

"Getting old, Edy. You look twenty-five and I feel it most of the time, but the fact remains that these two hundred and thirty-seven bones of ours, or however many it is, have been cavorting for forty-five years, and these nerves of ours—"

"Oh, Julie, you too—nerves?"

"Me too? Why Edy, you can't know—"

"Don't I! The unreasonable depressions. That dreadful, hot, stifled feeling of wanting to laugh and cry—that horrid, irresistible inclination sometimes to laugh—"

"How well I know it! Connie has invented a little treatment all her own for it, and it works; a little massage—the back of my neck—up under my hair, and my face in her lap—and an old nonsense song about 'old corn pone' that she sings to me. That's when a daughter more than anyone else in the world can understand, can help you over the bad half-hours, isn't it? But I can't get over you, Edy. Young you!"

"Young me. Under our skins, Julie, we're both forty-five."

"I guess that's about the size of it."

"Do you mind my being here, dear?"

"I love it. Reminds me of old days."

"It was heavenly, wasn't it, on the river to-day?"

"Isn't Bob a wonder, Edy? Ed always says of him that he treats life as if it were a tandem of spirited horses. He drives with a laugh and his hand is light, but he is master of the reins every second."

"Bob has everything," said Edith, her eyes seeming to ignore the wall and see into some beyond that was her very own.

"No, not everything," said Julie Bell in a curving tone that stabbed into Edith so pleasantly that she reddened, started and then slapped a pillow very hard to make the start seem part of that gesture.

"If you will be literal—of course no one has—everything."

"Bob hasn't you."

"Why—Julie—"

"Oh come now, Edy! Everyone knows how much he liked you and what a blow it was to him when you married Gordon Whatley."

"That was twenty years ago and I've been a widow ten, so if Bob liked me so much—"

"Now, now, that all sounds logical enough, but men aren't logical in such matters. Bob's been making his way all these years and your paths simply didn't happen to cross. That's the man of it—and life—outside of romances. But now—"

"Why, Julie Bell!" said Edith, afraid that her voice must be much too high, but she could not seem to get it down. "I simply won't have you talking like this."

"Why?"

"Why—because."

"Well, well, what an excellent reason! Why, you old darling, I wish you wouldn't be all inhibited when you're talking to me. Good heavens, Edy, if we can't settle down to a good old heart-to-heart, who can?"

"There are some things, Julie—not even us—oh, I know what you mean, dear! But if Bob is so dominant—he is dominant—a man who is a captain in industry—in life—should be captain in lo—dominate that part too—I mean. I—see the way he handled May to-day. The way he brought her back—happy—dominated."

"The way he handles May in general is rich, Edith. He knows that down under all her nonsense is just another adorable Edith Mastason. All that flapper nonsense just tickles him except when he gets right annoyed and gives her a verbal spanking. He knows his May."

"It's true, Julie. Down under all the things that her father's money and my weakness have done for May, she's as Munsie as you or I ever were, Julie. She loves to putter about the kitchen, adores youngsters and will spoil to death the man she marries."

"She looks like you used to, Edy, more and more every day. Something about the eyes. The little cunning crinkling-in expression like you used to have before you had your face fiddled with. Bob and I were saying the other evening, sometimes it is uncanny to see you sitting there with your face so calm and untouched and all your little funninesses cropping out in May, as if your expression had merely been transferred to her."

"It must seem—uncanny. But you see, I'm behind myself and can't notice it."

"Edy, while we're on the subject will you be angry if I say something?"

"You old darling, I couldn't be at anything you might say."

"Edy, let your hair grow long again. Oh, I know it's my generation and Munsie speaking, but—let it grow! It is sweet and young and boyish on May, and as the saying is, she is young enough to get away with it. So are you, dear, for that matter, except—not quite."

"I'm as silly in it, then, as I feel, Julie?"

"Oh no, not that, except—it takes something away from you! I miss it. Bob—misses it. It's one of the reasons he can't seem to find you. What is adorable on May, and she is too cunning, isn't quite right with you because—well, it's the contour of these forty-five-year-old bones of ours showing through. Bones can't be lifted like wrinkles. Not that I'm holding myself up as an example. Heaven forbid!"

"I know, Julie Bell, you're dead right," said Edith. "So right that—that it hurts to talk about it."

"Edith, I have offended you!"

"You haven't. You've helped. I hate to talk about anything that hurts—always have. But Julie—you wait and watch. Sometimes a talk like this—coming at just the psychological moment can—can—Bob—Julie, do you think—"

"I don't think, I know," said Julie, and they kissed and held one another cheek to cheek, and that way Edith could somehow talk easier.

"You see, with me, Julie—all those dreadful ten years with Whatley broke my spirit, I guess. And then May began to grow up, and I let her fashionable school and social ideas picked up from the new generation and her sweet kind of dominating youth, get on top of me. We Americans do revere our young so. And then, without caring very much one way or another—it just happened this way."

"As Ed always says when we drag him off to a dinner-party after a hard day in court, 'thank God for the flappers, they are so easy to sleep to.'"

"Julie, I've tired you. Your eyelids are all blue."

"I've loved having you."

"You're sure you can't go along this evening, dear? Bob's in his glory giving us what he calls a real party. And Connie?"

"There's no use. She's napping in the other room, but she won't budge. That's the pity of it. Says she wants to stay at home and write to Bobbie, but I know the truth of it is that she is on ache-and-pain duty with me. Why don't you pack May off with Lowell and some of her group, Edith, and you go off by yourself on a real old-fashioned talk-fest with Bob?"

"Oh Julie—shame on you!" cried Edith, but she kissed her and ran back across the hall with the rather silly consciousness that she was giggling.

May, already in the apricot frock, was just turning from the telephone, and her lips, *au naturel,* were bunched as if they had been kissed.

"It's Bob," she said and giggled too, but at nineteen it was a freshet of delight.

"What?"

"Just some nonsense he telephoned down to me. Tease."

"You're dressed early, dear."

"Oh no, the car is at the door, Bob is ready any time! We—thought we would sit down in the car and wait."

"There's a little dark shadow under your eye, dear. Powder it out."

"No. No. Please."

"Why—May—"

"Why—nothing—"

"Julie and Connie aren't going. Julie's a little done up."

"Not going?"

"No, dear, and I thought if Lowell—"

"Why, Edith dear, if you're too tired! It's been a long glaring day, and dear—you've a headache! I can see it. You mustn't think of going either."

It was the welt from the hat that Edith stood rubbing, the rims to her eyes widening a bit as bewilderment set in.

"Why no—dear—I'm not—"

"You are. You're worn out and I'm a pig. I've had my forty winks and you haven't, and I don't mind a bit putting up with your Big Bear Bob alone for one evening."

"But May—"

"No buts—Edith, please! You're a darling little wreck—you need sleep and you shall have it," and she was gone, on a kiss that smelled of chypre, a waft of tulle and a flash of white summer fur.

Quite automatically, after a moment of standing there stunned, Edith walked after, but only across the hall to Julie Bell's door. It was closed and she knocked softly, without any definite notion of what she wanted, but rather with the idea of avoiding the chypre-scented silence that May had so precipitately left behind her.

There was no answer, and finally she opened the door, quietly, to save the squeak. Julie was still on the bed, but her face was buried in Connie's lap, and Connie, manipulating clever and boneless fingers up under her mother's hair and along the back of her neck, was chanting some nonsense about "good corn pone and an ole ham bone."

It was not easy to close the door noiselessly again, and the horrid quiet was waiting for her when she regained her room, and she went over as if with destination and began to screw the top on a jar of cold cream that May had left uncovered.

That dreadful impulse had her by the throat. She wanted to laugh. This time she let it come. Dry. Brittle. Like glass, breaking.

The Brinkerhoff Brothers

First Published: *Cosmopolitan*, April 1923
Reprinted: *Song of Life*, A.A. Knopf, 1927

The beat to the day-by-day of the brothers Brinkerhoff was rather like the tick-tock of one of those family clocks with a nosegay painted on the glass door. The kind that stands on the mantelpiece between the blue glass vases with the warts blown into them.

The odour of the room that contained that clock hung over the brothers Brinkerhoff. Odour of horse-hair. Of the carpet hassock that always felt damp. Of the hard-coal stove when the soot was cold.

But it was nineteen years since the brothers had known that identical room in the house on Papin Street in South St. Louis. A father with a spade-shaped beard had died there one night in a high black-walnut bedstead, his face as four-cornered in death as it had been in life.

A mother who had tended him and the two sons through the long lethal silences into which these men could sink at meals, had died two months later while reddening the strip of brick walk that led up to the white scoured steps of the house on Papin Street.

The brothers had boarded the nineteen years since with a "private family" on Maffit Avenue on the North Side. It was nearer the St. Louis Coal and Ice Company.

There were about eighteen months between them, but most people thought them twins. You never felt quite right about their names. Somehow, Oscar's should have been Ichabod. And Henry's, well—Ichabod too.

You remember the nymph of Crete who named all her little nymphs Ariel because they simply would not resemble any other name?

Poor little Mrs. Brinkerhoff, who bore her sons in the big black-walnut bedstead the very first thing after she arrived from a cisalpine village, and who in all her years of mothering her three silent men had not learned how not to call them Uscar, Hennery and Puppa—poor little Mrs. Brinkerhoff, she should have called them just Ichabods all.

Oscar was the younger. His head had slightly the look of being set on a pole. The pole of his body. And his arms were very long, so long that—but

"Ichabod" says it all again. Before the swift descriptive potency of "Ichabod," further to describe the brothers Brinkerhoff, their little doilies of thinning hair or the dry crackle of Henry's finger-joints, were redundancy.

And now back to the tick and tock of their daily lives. It was just that. Tick for Monday. Tock for Tuesday. Tick. Tock. And the little spangs of silence in between were the nights, when the brothers slept side by side in the second-storey back of the private family named Burby on Maffit Avenue.

It was a square room with one window which overlooked the Burbys' long, narrow back-yard with a brick ash-pit at the far end, and little Bettina Burby's rag doll and kiddie-car usually kicked into the dry stubble of city grass. It contained a double light-oak bed, chiffonier with two equidistant burnt-wood collar-and-cuff boxes (the brothers wore detachable cuffs), and on the mantelpiece, regarding each other from little fretwork balconies, velvet-framed photographs of the father whose jaw was grim with the bite of false teeth and the mother who always said Uscar and Hennery and Puppa, her face full of the ravages of the years of reddening the bricks of Papin Street and her decent crocheted collar closed at the throat with a brooch photograph of her sons, aged four and a half and six, Oscar's left ear mashed softly against Henry's right.

Mrs. Burby kept a red velvet rocker from the parlour up in the brothers' room, because the springs rose up so when guests sat down on it, and up over the doorway, looking down into the calm tick and tock of Brinkerhoff comings and goings, was a large crayon portrait of a deceased Burby who looked like Brigham Young.

That picture exercised a slow and rather pleasant hypnosis over Henry. He liked, for instance, to start fastening his suspenders in one corner of the room and watch the eyes slide right after him over to the chiffonier for his sleeve-garters. The brothers wore both suspenders and sleeve-garters. They would. Well, standing, say, between the red velvet chair and the bed, these eyes above the transom could seem to press against Henry's own light blue ones like hot pennies, or sitting down on the bed-edge to clump off his shoes, or shaving in the square of mirror over the washstand, he could feel their warm ball-like quality and even imagine they would give slightly if he pressed against them.

"By George, it's right human the way those photographers get those eyes to move. Just like they're human."

This was quite a speech for Henry, who as a rule merely grunted while he did things such as dive into his shirt (yes, the brothers still wore them that way) or lift up a triangle of cheek to the razor.

More frequently the silence of their dressing was broken only by Bettina Burby shrilling in the back yard, the opening and shutting of a drawer, or

Mrs. Burby sizzling their breakfast beefsteak in the kitchen, which was directly beneath their room; or mostly just by Henry's grunts, which were nothing more than the leak of the vocal into his breathing.

There was something rather wonderful about the silences between these men. By the time they were around forty it had gathered in between them like a deep sunless pool beside which they could sit and smoke their pipes in an endless *pu, pu,* of utter passivism.

The Burbys, after years of these stilly men, came to regard them as "two of the family," and talk flew about them at the dinner-table in a merry hailstorm that seemed literally to bounce off the slightly bald heads of the brothers.

Burby had a wall-paper store on Easton Avenue, a street of small businesses that skirted the North Side. He was enormously stout and wheezed so that when he was at home it was exactly as if a small motor were at work in the house. Mrs. Burby, who was pretty in the jelled sort of way that the overweight can be pretty, wore her apron in a perpetual muff about her short dimpled arms. She had an eighteen-year-old son in the navy and a three-year-old daughter, Bettina. The neighbourhood regarded the interval as not quite nice.

The brothers she called Mr. O. and Mr. H. to their faces, but to the neighbours with whom she held endless back-yard and telephone conferences, she could wax facetious.

"Don't faint, but the Brinkeys won't be home to supper to-night. Nineteenth meal they've missed in nineteen years. St. Louis Coal and Ice Company's annual bonus picnic"; or "I don't own a clock that runs. But I should worry about a clock when my Brinkeys' comings and goings are as much to the minute as the sun is."

And so it was. To the dot, at twenty minutes past seven, in their alpaca suits in summer and mixture sack suits in winter, the rather stern black string ties and the square-toed shoes, well blacked, the brothers Brinkerhoff breakfasted.

First, four drops in a glass of water out of a bottle of raspberry-coloured liquid that stood in the centre of the table beside the vinegar cruet (the brothers were subject to acid stomach), then a piece of well-pounded, well-done beefsteak, hashed browned potatoes, coffee from a granite pot that stood on a raffia mat, and two slices of thick untoasted bread.

Since the advent of little Bettina, Oscar, always a little the spokesman for the two, invariably left two cone-shaped chocolate bon-bons on the wooden bib of her empty high-chair. They were fond of the goldy little girl, after a Brinkerhoff fashion. Oscar said "Boo" to her, and Henry made noises in between his teeth and cheek that sounded like his tin-tired buggy turning a short curb.

The St. Louis Coal and Ice Company still used horses. Round-bellied, three-ton teams with splendid shaggy forelegs and veins that under the drag could bulge thick as a wrist as they moved with the dignity of leisure, through the motor maze of the city's traffic.

The Company, for the brothers' lighter purposes of city collecting, supplied the Brinkerhoffs each with a chestnut filly and a two-seated storm buggy with a black apron which buttoned over the front against rain. Henry covered a portion of North St. Louis and Oscar what was known as the more or less fashionable West End. The St. Louis Coal and Ice Company did not mail its city and county bills.

The brothers Brinkerhoff were city collectors. Long satisfactory uninterrupted records. True, that one Aloysius Jones, who had once shared a portion of the North St. Louis route with Oscar, was now a vice-president of the firm, and whenever a death or resignation moved certain employees a notch along in advancement, the eyes of the corporation seemed resolutely turned away from the brothers Brinkerhoff.

But in the twenty-one years there had been five advances in salary. It was forty dollars a week now, and often a bonus at Christmas.

They were content. Little fishes, little bones, as the saying goes. The brothers apparently wanted but little here below.

Summer evenings, with the Burbys buzzing on the square of front porch and the brick wall of the house next door for their vistas, they tilted their straight chairs against the side of the house, puffing their pipes; and the pool formed between them, the pool of silence, their bodies like tall cypresses bordering it.

"That Briggs account over on De Tony Street don't look any too strong."

"So?"

"Seventeen ton bituminous."

"So?"

Pu. Pu. Pu.

Long, cool, purple intervals, tip-tilted there against the side of the house until ten o'clock and to bed. Empty pods of evenings with the brothers' silent thoughts rattling about in them like dried peas.

Bricks that breathed out like a feverish little child sleeping in the dark with its mouth open.

Often a radio in the house next door caught up a woman's singing voice from the air and flung it like a scarf across the darkness. A lovely fluctuating scarf that had colour to it. It was not difficult to squeeze sibilant colours out of the darkness. Squinting the eyes did it. Orange, for instance, had a soaring note to it that could mount and mount until it became just a gleaming point of melody, like a star. Trills were sort of the blue of running water. Coloratura, that adorable watermelon pink of a woman's mouth when she yawns—these particular fancies could play the very devil with Oscar. No sooner conceived than they could confuse him violently. Colour has melody. No—melody has colour. Oh, nonsense—joost nonsense.

"Sofia's got a stone bruise on her left hind leg, Henry, bothering her right much."

"So?"

"Yes."

"Freckert's Liniment."

"M-m-m."

There! That little note from the radio! A wounded mouse-coloured note with a woman crying down in it. A Mrs. Snyder on Newstead Avenue, who opened the door for him the first of every month, had a throat that must hold a note like that. It throbbed a little when she talked, like the bleating breast of a dove. He must turn in that claim. Otto B. Snyder. Three thousand pounds of ice— Her lips. No, no. Not her lips. Any lovely lips. He could conjure a curved and scented pair into the darkness that poised like butterfly wings against the brick wall opposite. Lips. Even Mrs. Burby's, which dragged a bit and could be greasy from gnawing along a chop bone—even her lips— fluty—bah—

"Freckert's Liniment is too weak."

"Try iodine."

Oscar had never touched a woman's lips, except his mother's. He had kissed them when they lay dead, they were so pitiful to him. But not—that way. The way of the lips in the darkness.

These imagings, modernly called suppressed desires and picked at random, might have been either Oscar's or Henry's. Except that, of the two, Henry was perhaps the more ascetic. Extraordinary that these two men could have slid through life so narrowly. Like slab-sided cats oozing between porcelains. Deep down in the secret places of Henry's pool, his own submerged water-lilies of fancy could open too, under the silence. They were so naïvely free of desire, his fancies. Almost ludicrous because they belonged to Henry. He really had a lovely favourite lily-pad. It was the colour of Bettina. All goldy it could rise and flaunt in an enormous rosette right before his eyes. Somewhere imprisoned in his spangled fancy was the innocent Bettina herself. And so his darkness, all inchoate, could vignette off into just a gold-dust kind of haze with little-girl laughter in it. Henry, whose adolescence had been even more languid than Oscar's, dozed in this haze. The haze of the golden laughter of the little girl Bettina.

At ten o'clock, then, by the thick disk of Oscar's watch, bed. The thud of four shoes. The decent black string ties laid straight beneath the mattress.

Pipes cleaned and airing on the window sill. The brothers kept two pipes each going. For sweetness. Monday's pipe airing on Tuesday, and Tuesday's pipe airing on Wednesday.

These were the Brinkerhoff brothers when Mrs. Burby took to her bed of sciatic rheumatism and Miss Trina Blankenmeister, a sister of Mrs. Burby's step-mother, came from Herculaneum, Missouri, to run the house.

It all happened so suddenly. Henry first detected it in a laugh. An upward rush of it from Oscar one morning when Trina handed him the coffee-pot, as if a lot of unsuspected emotions over which he had absolutely no control had suddenly clattered out over everything like a dropped tray of tin things. It was horrible. Henry felt his pores begin to swell outward and then seem to pick open as if he were a nutmeg-grater, and Trina jumped back with the pot so that she splashed coffee up her bare arm.

Oscar alone seemed innocent of his plight. The plight of baring his long horsy teeth to laugh out loud and then reaching over, with a killing expression, to fleck off with his napkin the stain on Trina's arm.

Henry felt actually sick for him, and as if not another bite of beefsteak nor his Adam's apple would ever swallow down again.

For the first time in nineteen years, and for highly different reasons, two portions of unfinished beefsteak went back to the kitchen that morning. When Mrs. Burby, from her bed of pain, heard about it she said, "Great heavens, it's the millennium."

But then that sharply faceted thing, her woman's intuition, pounced and just lifted Trina up, so that she saw several different lights on her at once.

"Don't throw it away," she said, meaning the beefsteak, of course; "you can grind it up for Burby's lunch."

But her eyes from their angle on the pillow followed Trina out of the room. The little swing to the uncorseted hips. The cling of the gingham skirt to their roundiness.

Trina was blonde and nervous and twenty-eight. She wore such high-power glasses, the rimless kind with gold ear frames, that her eyes seemed to swim right up against the lenses like an enormous and terribly intent gaze that could remain open in water and stare through it.

When she removed the spectacles, they left a red welt across her nose and a sort of doused Trina, as if someone had put out a light. She was so nervous she would jump if you spoke without first clearing your throat or indicating that you had intentions, as she did when Oscar's laugh spilled over the breakfast; and for the life of her she could not keep one particular strand of hair, which she crimped with an iron, from dangling.

The one gesture which describes her most clearly was the arc of her narrow arm going up to wind that strand behind her ear. Her indulgence of it was mammoth. It made you hot inside each time she wound it, as if a nerve of your very private own were suddenly going to throw up its hands and yell. It made Henry feel that way. Trina, passing him the hashed browned potatoes with one hand and winding with the other.

But Oscar. Suddenly and for the first unsuppressed time, that upward curve of a woman's arm, with the little white nest at the elbow, shot through him with the lancinating jab of a hypodermic.

All those darting elusive gadflies across the pool of the silence. The shimmer of submerged sensation. The golden flank of half an ecstasy that never rose to the surface. That shiny, slimy pool beside the cypress of himself, full of the forbidden thoughts of women's lips and sound that was like a coloured scarf across his senses. All suddenly concrete in Trina. Trina, risen luminous out of this pool of scuttling desires. Trina, who must have floated down-stream looking at him with her blue eyes magnified by water, here at his side passing him the kohlrabi and the stewed rhubarb, and scalding her preciously real arm because he had startled her with the long-toothed laugh of his ecstasy at her nearness.

She had come to him so suddenly, turning the long dull years of his feeble adolescence into a garden that led to her. Oscar was in love to the beating of shawms and cymbals in his brain.

To Henry, the three events that led to his marriage were every bit as decisive as the battles of Marathon and Arbelu and Tours. The Tuesday evening that Oscar stopped Trina in the pantry and asked her to walk out with him after the dishes were washed. The Labour Day excursion ride down the Mississippi to Cahokia. The Sunday afternoon that Henry surrendered his place and Oscar took Trina instead, for a drive in the storm buggy to Chain of Rocks. This last, of course, was the precipitant event. Oscar and Trina came home engaged.

That evening, no sooner were the brothers in their room than Oscar suddenly faced Henry, two round spots of colour on top of his cheeks as if they had been placed there with a rubber stamp. It is doubtful whose heart beat loudest, Oscar's or Henry's, whose Adam's apple would not swallow down again.

"Henry," said Oscar, "that little gold band from Mutter. You don't mind if I got use for it now? Trina—"

It was the first reference between them to Trina. Henry, who wanted to answer, only stood there sort of waving his eyelids, and so finally, when his throat would not unlock, he walked over to the chiffonier and drew out of a drawer the little pasteboard box of their joint relics. There were a pair of gold-and-black ear-rings shaped like urns. A gold-and-black bracelet to match. The ceramic of the two little boys with their ears touching and the band ring set with a chip diamond, the gold cut out in little rays around it.

Handing it to Oscar, something that he would have burst his throat to avoid happened to Henry. He broke out crying. A long bruise of a sob, as if some fugitive, terribly wounded, were hiding in a marsh. The marsh of Henry's heart.

And on that moan from the innermost of Henry, Oscar, who felt as if he were drowning in his brother's tears, went down before the first sobs these men had ever known.

It was too awful. Henry who kept his lips lashed against his teeth and his mouth working up and down like some poor old man with empty gums, and Oscar who flung one hand on his brother's shoulder and let his head sink down on his outstretched arm.

"Don't, Brother; I can't stand it."

Not since their mother's funeral had they addressed one another as Brother.

"I'm glad for you, Brother."

"She's a goot girl, Henry."

"So?"

"A goot worker. A companion."

"We've been goot companions too, Oscar."

"Yes, Henry. But—a woman. That's life."

"We've been well off by ourselves, Oscar. Quiet. No heartaches. A quiet life is goot."

The brothers under stress did that to their d's.

"I need a little heart-ache in my life, Henry. A happy heart-ache—like I got from Trina."

Lower sank Henry's head.

"A woman is a woman. They make troubles."

"Without troubles, Henry, I have thought it out for myself, a man has no contrast to know when he has happiness."

"Women, Oscar—I've seen it a hundred times. The best of them the same. Shenanigans. Sickness. Doctor bills. Bearing-down pains like Mrs. Burby, and pink pills."

"Not Trina. She's goot. And strong, Henry. Strong as Sofia. Her nerves are on top, but strong."

"We've been so well off alone, Oscar. Quiet."

"A woman, Henry. God made man to want her."

"Not every man. There have always been men like us in the world. It's been so goot together, so long—without."

"Not any more for me—since Trina."

Suddenly Henry knew it was no use. So he took Oscar's hand and pressed it, digging the gold trinkets up into it until they cut.

"Brother," he said.

"It will never be different with us, Henry. Trina is a grand girl. You will always have it goot with us—in our home."

Over the phrase "in our home" Oscar seemed to swell up in a way that was actually froggy. Little puffs came out over his eyebrows and on the spots where his ears lapped on to his cheeks.

"Thank you, Brother," said Henry, but in his heart the tears were still running. He knew. This was his last of Oscar.

Trina and Oscar were married four weeks later in the Garrison Avenue Church. Bettina Burby carried the bride's veil and spread it about her so that when she knelt down she was in the bower of her tulle. There were no other attendants, but Henry and the Burbys and the bride's sister from Herculaneum occupied half of the first front row. Mr. Burby wheezed, the organ played "Melody in F," and the rector's voice, intoning the service, seemed to mount to the double archings of the church and the gargoyles to chew it into echoes and mouth it out again.

In the yellow light from a stained window there was something terrible in the sternness of Oscar. His face was so square with his will to respond in mighty "I do"'s. His long black coat so solemn. Hired, and giving him the odour of a park statue of a statesman.

And Trina. She dropped her bouquet of white narcissus, and twice during the ceremony, in the agony of her nervousness, wound at the strand of hair. But her eyes were soft. Like bluebells under water. And they did not seem to protrude so against the lenses, and when she kissed her sister from Herculaneum they dissolved into big fluffy tears. And there was great ado of removing the spectacles, which had become entangled in the veiling, and Oscar, who stood by, kept reaching out his hand and drawing it back.

She was his now. More than anything else he wanted to untangle Trina's spectacles from her wedding veil and fit them back on the dear little red welt on the bridge of her nose. That little red welt was his now. His hand kept moving backward and forward like a shuttle.

And already Henry, standing by, was hurting with the sense of his thirdness.

The Oscars went to housekeeping in a four-room flat on Kennerly Avenue. There had been talk of a room for Henry. Trina, in fact, had marched up to his door one evening while Oscar stood at the foot of the stairs waiting, and knocked. Henry, with his entire going to bed at loose ends since Oscar was remaining out on the porch so late, a-wooing, had already removed one shoe and was staring at the wall. The knock startled him, and he limped to the door, opening it an inch.

"It's me, Henry. Trina."

He was horribly embarrassed and linked his foot in the white balbriggan sock, up behind his knee.

"Oh," he said. "Trina! Joost a minute. I'm in bed almost," and closed the door its half inch.

"Never mind, Henry. I can say it from here." And then Trina began to recite, Oscar's eyes down at the foot of the stairs burning up against her back.

"Henry, we want you to come and live with us. We've got to know, because we're going hunting to-morrow for a flat with the extra room."

It was a peculiar thing about Trina's voice. Just say "Herculaneum" as if your vocal chords were strung along your frontal bone and you have it. The rise to the antepenultimate syllable of Trina's home town contained the full range of her vocal inflection.

Poor Henry. Listening to her voice now, every shade of it started him trembling. It was like tearing something as close as his right side off of him, leaving him bleeding, that Oscar should go. He wanted that room in his home. Wanted it with a sob in his throat.

"Why, Trina," he said, "that's goot. I appreciate it. But young married couples, it's an old saying, they got it best by themselves."

"Now, Henry, there's a room waiting if you say the word."

If he said the word! He wanted to, but it stuck in his throat, and the little grunts in his breathing tumbled over themselves. He wanted, more than anything he had ever wanted in his life, that room in the home of his sharer of eloquent silences. But the plating on Trina's voice was so pitifully thin, and well Henry knew, deep down in his heart where he kept the little adder of a thought resolutely tucked away, that Oscar and Trina should have found the flat with his room in it first, and then swept, rather than interrogated him.

And so he stood rubbing his white-stockinged foot against the back of his leg, wanting to say yes. Wanting to, and instead only repeating what he hoped she would not accept from him.

"If I thought I wasn't in the way—"

"We've got to know, Henry. There's a four-room flat over on Kennerly just suits fine. But it's no trouble to look for a five."

"Oh Trina, Trina," sighed poor Henry's heart.

"No trouble at all, Henry."

"I know that young married couples they like it best sometimes alone. I wouldn't be in the way, I could promise you that, only, I'm afraid it's not right—"

And then for the first time Trina's voice lost its pie-pan shallowness and came out with heartiness.

"Well, Henry, I don't want to insist, you're so used to it here, but remember, that extra plate and knife and fork are always waiting for you on our table in our home. 'Always welcome' is our motto."

And Oscar at the bottom of the stairs, drunk on the phrases "our table," "our home," "our motto," had his little adder of discomfort too, which he would not so much as let lift its head.

After all, both Trina and he had done their best. Henry's ways were set. But well the little adder down in Oscar knew—it knew.

Gaunt, lank, unlaughing Oscar. Life had been the colour of horse-hair and the smell of damp hassocks for him. He wanted his Trina in their flat where he could have her nearness for his very own.

And so the next day, the four-room flat in the two-family house on Kennerly Avenue was rented and announced at the supper table to many: "Now aren't you sorry you turned us down!" and "See now, Mr. Hoitiy Toity, what you're missing!" flung merrily to Henry, who grunted and grunted as if he really believed the indictment.

And how Trina, who for almost the twenty-eight years of her life had lived with the married sister in Herculaneum, worn her cast-off clothing and cooked for a family of five and three farmhands, did blossom. It was a pleasure to see her thin nervous face pinken up, and because she had never in all her experience known the intoxication of handling money, she spent lavishly on the furnishings of the flat. A little too lavishly. There was a hundred-and-thirty-five-dollar Victrola with a balcony-front mahogany case for the parlour, and a dining-room set, mission-finished oak with coloured glass in the buffet doors, cost two hundred and seventy-five. And Trina could not resist a life-size plaster Negro boy, in such true-to-life ragged trousers, you could almost want to mend the rents, and holding half a watermelon in the form of a card-receiver, to stand between the folding doors.

But there was the five-hundred-dollar wedding present, half of his savings, from Henry; and Oscar's own nest-egg, which from the years of natural penury was nicely around a thousand, could easily stand the strain.

And so they were married and Henry moved up to the third floor, in what Mrs. Burby called her "single-gent room"; and except that there was one collar-and-cuff box on the chiffonier now and the velvet-framed photographs of the dead-and-buried Brinkerhoffs reposed on the Kennerly Avenue mantel-piece, there was not much change in the daily scheme of things for Henry Brinkerhoff.

Even the deceased Burby who looked like Brigham Young had followed him upstairs, and the red velvet rocker that bulged of old springs.

It was as natural that every act of Henry's should fall into routine as it was that his Monday, Wednesday, and Friday pipe should alternate with the remaining days of the week. It happened that his first dinner at the home of the Oscars was on a Friday evening, and thereafter, tick-tock, Friday evenings it continued to be.

With this exception of the one evening a week, the old after-dinner intervals were his, pretty much as they had always been, tilted up against the house on his straight-back chair in summer, and in winter reading his Home Edition beside the gas lamp in the Burby reception hall.

He was quiet, and more than ever Henry had come to love the swoon-like depths of his silence.

Almost from the beginning things did not go so well with the Oscars.

In the first place, Oscar sprained a ligament in his leg the first month, reaching from a ladder to hang an oval picture with a convex glass to it, of Queen Louise, on the stairs. Trina had bought it from a man at the door.

For the first time in twenty-one years Oscar missed a day on his route, but after that he hobbled with a cane and managed pretty well.

Then didn't the new hat-rack in the hall do the top-heavy act of toppling over on a boy who was delivering some curtain-rods from a neighbourhood hardware store, breaking his collarbone and banging him up pretty badly. There was some talk of a lawsuit, but Oscar settled finally for fifty dollars and almost an equal amount in doctor bills.

Well, that blew over, and when Henry came on his Fridays it was to find a state of beatitude that gave him the same hottish feeling he had experienced when Oscar had laughed that first morning and shown his long, seldom exposed teeth. Positively, it was embarrassing to see Oscar's hand linger too long on Trina's if she so much as passed him the syrup jug. Once he walked in on them playing clip-clap-clop with the palms of their hands, and another time at the supper-table, when the electric current gave out and came on so suddenly that it revealed Oscar and Trina breaking apart from having taken advantage of the darkness to embrace, he was so embarrassed that he could scarcely look up again during the meal. Not so much for himself as for Oscar. Dark, narrow Oscar in this ridiculous plight. It was kinder somehow not to look.

And he didn't. As the months wore on, for every time that Oscar's hand lingered too long over the syrup jug, Henry would be assiduously looking out of the window; and when Trina stumbled once over a rug and landed plump in Oscar's lap, and to his supreme embarrassment, knowing Henry, could not get up for laughing, Henry rose hastily from his chair to pretend to search for something among the uncut pages of Lives of Famous Men which Trina had bought at the door on "monthlies."

It was after the first year that things turned not so good in earnest. Trina, true to Henry's unwitting prophecy, developed "bearing-down pains." It was pitiful to see her newly acquired pinkiness recede and the circles and a little crop of water-bubbles come out under her eyes. At first she tried the sample remedies thrown around at front doors by old men carrying canvas bags like sowers. It was no unusual thing for Oscar to come home and find her with the potatoes peeled but not frying, sitting on the edge of the kitchen table poring over booklet testimonials from beneficiaries of this or that pill.

Pills. Trina was a great believer in their efficacy. But when these minor remedies failed, and Trina would pause in the midst of her sweeping to clutch at the small of her back, for all the world like the before-taking pictures on the pamphlet, Oscar took to bringing home drug-store remedies. Once Mrs. Sydney on Newstead Avenue, who had had an operation, recommended a home brew of herbs and some sort of bitters, giving Oscar the first herbs from her own store of them, and for a while it seemed that the mixture would do the work; but one morning Trina just could not get up until, as she put it, until she had laid some of the back-ache out of her, so Oscar prepared his breakfast and hers and carried it in to her and came off his route at eleven to see how she felt.

After that Trina no longer got up for breakfast, and Oscar became quite adept at puttering over the stove, even taking a hand at the evening meal while Trina was so poorly. Once, while frying himself a piece of his invariable breakfast beefsteak, the gas stove exploded up into his face with quite a report, but there was no damage and the stove was repaired. He learned the trick of corn bread too, tying one of Trina's aprons around his waist and kneading for dear life.

Poor Trina. That first year or two she tried. Valiantly. Nailing up lace shelf-paper with her face screwed of her complaint. Surprising Oscar with the oil-cloth on the stairs laid when he came home one evening. Gilding the imitation gas-logs in the imitation gas-grate and running up to greet him that night all smelling, as Oscar put it when he kissed her between the smears of gilt, "just like a little banana."

And Trina loved being a little banana, and she loved her home and her sovereignty of it. With a stack of unwashed dishes in the sink and the bedroom pretty untidy, she liked to putter in the parlour, secure against the whanging voice of her sister, or the dirty little yanking fingers of her nieces and nephews.

And how that parlour seemed to become smaller and smaller as Trina jammed it fuller and fuller. It came to have somewhat the look of a small boy fairly crammed with bon-bons and about to be very uncomfortable. Trina could no more withstand the front-door canvasser than she could too many of the cone-shaped chocolates which Oscar brought her now, as he used to bring them to Bettina. At her front door, by the easy signing of a slip and fifty cents down, she negotiated for a dozen cabinet-size photographs of herself with coloured enlargement. "Little Pet" carpet-sweeper came that way, and of course the Queen Louise and the Lives of Great Men. Also a brown pottery jardinière which contained her rubber-tree, a glossy-leaved beauty which she tended like a baby, washing the leaves in milk to make them shine.

Then the sick headaches set in. "Sikkedicks," as Henry came horridly to know them from Trina's pronunciation. The surest barometer of Trina's state of head came to be the fold of flesh between Oscar's eyes. When the brothers met, as they did each morning at the livery stable for their horses and runabouts, Henry could tell at a glance by that worried furrow if the cloud of one of Trina's all too frequents sikkedicks hung over the land.

"Not so goot with Trina to-day," was about Oscar's summing-up of it, or, if it happened to be Friday: "You should stop by at Finney's for the bread to-night, Henry. I'll bring some smelts from the community market. Trina's got sikkedick."

And off they drove in opposite directions, the long narrow buggies somber as deacons and in a way distinctly resembling the brothers themselves. Oscar with the worried dent between his eyes. Henry settling down low in his seat, lulled with the sedative order of his life. More and more as the sense of his brother's eruptive little home, with the sink of unwashed dishes and Trina often with her hair in a pug and her shoes slattern, began to grow on him, Henry clung to the simple geometry of his scheme of things. The long identical evenings. Seven-thirty breakfasts with never an ado. The little room with the burnt-wood collar-box and the alternate pipe airing on the window-sill. Nobody's headache.

Henry, whose loyalty to his brother was like a candle flame, long and unwavering and white, came to castigate himself soundly for his many invading states of mind toward Trina.

For instance, he wanted honestly and whole-heartedly to sympathize with her "sikkedicks." Although he had never experienced one and could not remember that his little mother had ever sallowed under the complaint, it was evidently a malady that could wrack its victim, and cast it aside like a rag doll. But for the life of him Henry could not help a major sensation of disgust when he arrived at the flat to find Trina with her eyes looking spilled and the lids just far enough over the pupils to rob them of any expression whatsoever. Sort of like a baby's who sleeps with his eyes not quite closed.

How that "sikkedick" predominated over the house. Henry could feel it when he set foot on the lowermost step. The smell of camphor or witch-hazel or whatever it was that Trina daubed up her brow with. Oscar, tiptoeing clumsily over boards that creaked under rugs, and looking outlandish in the gingham apron about his middle as he puttered away at supper. Trina in the unaesthetic headcloth, pinned over with a safety-pin in back and for ever holding on to the small of her back as if she were broken and in danger of falling in two parts.

Deep-dyed disgust of her filled Henry. There was something not nice about her "heddicks." Something almost not—clean. People with decent reticences didn't have them, or at least, if they did, never dragged them about in public that way. There was something that offended Henry horribly about her sick eyes and the way she would grab up Oscar's hand suddenly and press it to her brow. Oscar sitting meanwhile stiff and embarrassed and going on with his other hand at whatever he was doing, as if nothing had happened. Only, up against her brow, Trina could feel the little tremor of sympathy from him which he so shamefacedly concealed from his brother, who upon such occasions and many similar ones immediately sought retreat among the uncut pages of The Lives of Great Men.

And then she could be testy with Oscar. That almost killed Henry. One evening, when he tried to make her lie down, instead of standing sick and staggering over the pungency of frying smelts, she cried out to him, "Oh, go to the devil. I can't call my hired girl in to fix supper, can I? Somebody has to do it." And another time, ministering to the crick in her back, he spilled liniment down it and she cried out in pain: "Great big boob, you!" And then a few minutes later when Oscar came into the parlour, that looped-up smile on his face smeared over the hurt, as it were, it was all Henry could do to keep the tears from splashing down on Volume Four, The Lives of Great Men.

On the other hand, Trina on her good days was the loving and honouring and obeying wife whom Oscar had so solemnly taken at the altar, babying him, smoothing his widening bald spot and serving him in a hundred nervous little solicitous ways. Neither was she without a very definite kind of affection for her brother-in-law, calling him Grunty, and on her well Fridays she invariably had "kale" boiled with ham-end, a dish of which he was inordinately fond.

Sitting alone in his side yard evening after evening, tilted against the brick wall, pipe in its slow journeys from his knee to his lips, Henry was tireless at his cogitations about Oscar, pondering for hours upon these new and secret places in his brother's life. Places no longer of the pool. Places that Oscar never by word or act revealed to him. To what extent was Oscar realizing the nervous unaesthetic woman who was his? Trina bit her finger-nails. Trina let her corsets and tired-looking bits of clothing droop over chairs from day's end to day's end. She was fast losing what looks she had, too. Her arms were bony now from their incessant darting to and fro, no doubt, and the water-bubbles beneath her eyes pulled at her expression.

More than once when Oscar walked to the corner with Henry, as he did on Friday nights, Oscar's eyes, as they parted with just "Goot-night," had ridden through the darkness with Henry into the waiting quiet of Mrs. Burby's room as if they too had wanted to come.

Was Oscar envying Henry?

One October morning, when the brothers met at the livery stable, Oscar's face, which if one thought about it at all was usually the colour of strong burlap, presented the peculiar ashen of rope instead. Dry. Fibrous. Without the suggestion of blood running through it.

"Oscar?" cried Henry, putting startled interrogation into the word.

"Trina had the doctor last night. Next Saturday morning. St. Anthony's Hospital. Operation."

That was all. The brothers rode their ways that morning with the whips in their sockets unflecked. It was misting, and above the storm-curtains their faces looked out squarely. For all the world like gaunt Abraham Lincolns.

Trina came through splendidly. In fact, her first two months out of the hospital she gained flesh so rapidly that Oscar spanked her one evening as she passed him to water the rubber-plant and called her "Fatty." All her skirt-bands had to be let out and gussets set into her waists. The "sikkedicks" persisted, but not so frequently, and except that it remained impossible for Trina to feel well enough to get up to prepare Oscar's breakfast, conditions in the little flat improved.

Indeed Trina, who came to love afternoon "movies," could return home quite flushed and pretty-looking, often barely in time to throw together the evening meal and, as she put it, "redd up the place a bit."

Oscar indulged her love of entertainment, often providing the ticket for Mrs. Burby too, but there was a little pinch in the household. Trina's operation and doctor bills had mounted to over six hundred dollars, and then on top of it, with the mechanical gesture of a firm which has turned into a corporation, Henry's salary was raised to fifty dollars.

Not Oscar's. He had been falling off, you see. Irregularities. Trina's operation had taken him off the route daily for weeks. Oscar's collections were not up to mark.

And the first thing Henry knew, Oscar, white with the ignominy of it, was at him for a loan. Four hundred dollars, which he gave over, cheerfully.

The first hundred was paid back within the sixmonth, but Trina, still lavish with the *élan* of one unaccustomed to handling money, had her heart set on one of those new-fangled washing-machines which had appeared at the door, and Oscar, with Henry's wide indulgence, let the payment of the second hundred lapse a month.

But before that month had rounded out an event stalked in that fairly knocked Oscar over the head with a slapstick.

Trina was with child. For three months, with a reticence not at all typical of her, she had carried this secret from Oscar, finally sobbing it out to him one evening because she could not eat her dinner.

He sat stunned, with his hand on her humped little shoulders as she told him, and he kissed her, and Trina cried and cried and wanted it and didn't want it, and cried and cried some more.

But it was almost two more months before Oscar could bring himself to tell Henry, and then only because Trina was developing a querulousness that needed justification and because Oscar could not see the second payment on that four hundred clearly ahead.

Oscar told him on the corner one Friday evening as they parted.

"That's goot," was all Henry could find to say over and over again as they wrung hands and parted. "That's very fine. That's goot."

But all the way home, in a wild kind of pain for his brother, Henry kept asking himself over and over again, was it so goot? Was it?

It wasn't, because Trina's baby was born in such agony of travail that Oscar, standing waiting through the black aisle of the night, finally laid his head down on the parlour table and sobbed in long audible sounds like corn-husks rasping off the ear. Sobs that cut him in two—and Henry.

At high noon of the next day, in the midst of Trina's cries and entreaties and callings upon God, her son was born. It was Sunday, and straight through the chime-lit morning the brothers had waited side by side on two stiff-backed chairs in the parlour. When the nurse placed his son in Oscar's arms, he began to laugh, sillily again and in the manner that had so fright-fully embarrassed Henry that time at breakfast. So sillily and so full of hys-teria that Henry, without so much as glancing at the little living bundle of his nephew, hurried over to the shelf that bore The Lives of Great Men.

It was two months before Trina set foot out of bed. Three before the nurse could be dismissed. And then for another month Mrs. Burby did all the cook-ing, sending it over by Henry or Bettina in buckets covered with paper napkins.

There was not much left of the spick-and-span newness of the little flat of three years before. The furniture had dulled, and the carpets. The rubber-plant had one lone leaf, and Trina's erstwhile pride, the black plaster boy, had a crack in his face that bisected it on the diagonal.

They were bitter days, those first few months of the life of Oscar's son. Trina, poor girl, shattered in health and nerves. Oscar at his wit's end and deeper in debt to Henry than ever. And the baby. Well, Oscar's son was the kind of child over whom people bend pitying heads and say "Poor little fellow, he may outgrow it. They often do, you know." His head was too large. So large that it drooped tiredly like an enormous mushroom on a slender stalk, the little chin resting against the chest. A sweet unfretful baby with a harassed face that said "Why?"

And how fiercely, and with a famished love that blazed colour into her thin cheeks, Trina tended and nursed and suffered from the cruel steel braces they put under his chin.

And Henry and Oscar de-daddling that child! It was to laugh, the solemn two of them, grimacing, trying to awaken that mysterious star of light that meant recognition in the poor little eyes that were set on top, almost like a frog's. Doing "This-little-piggy-went-to-market, that-little-piggy-stayed-at-home," the only nursery rhyme they knew, to each and every finger and each and every toe.

But Oscar's son regarded them blindly, almost as the mushroom a little too heavy on its stem might have.

"He knows me," cried Oscar, knowing it not to be true.

"The little fellow smiled at me," cried Henry, knowing that he hadn't smiled at all.

"He's muvver's darling darlingest," cried Trina, her eyes beautiful with the star-dust of being a mother.

And so the months wore on, and Trina's strength came back slowly, if at all, and the boy Buster's big head lolled on its puny stalk, and expenses kept just a little bit ahead of Oscar. And there the flat stood, dirty and cluttered from one week's end to the next, except when Mrs. Burby came over and lent a hand, or Oscar and Henry tidied a bit on Friday evenings, or Trina, with her old bearing-down pains again, dragged herself around in her nightgown and slip-slopping slippers, dusting and trying, when she could, to have a decent snack of supper for Oscar when he came home tired.

But at least little Buster seldom cried, and through the long days would lie almost meditatively in the tender cove of his mother's arm; and with every visit of the doctor a trail of good cheer, like a slant of sunshine, was left over the house.

"Don't you worry over that youngster. I've seen them a whole lot more backward than he is develop into bust-roarers."

And Trina's eyes would fill of gratitude and Oscar clear his throat and offer a cigar.

"And you too, Mrs. Brinkerhoff. You're going to gradually get back your strength and be three times the woman you were before the birth of this young rascal."

"Oh doctor—dear doctor."

And yet the weeks dragged on so, and one day, because Oscar could endure no more (she had acquired the habit of whining at him from the bed to do this and not for God's sake to do that), a flash of anger smote him in his eyes and he slammed blindly out of the house. At least slammed for him. Running down the front steps and closing the lower door on a burst of ejaculation that sounded to Trina, as she lay there appalled, terrifyingly like "God damn."

That afternoon at about five-thirty it happened.

Trina, jerked strangely enough into awareness, not anger, by this outburst, had pulled herself together and, with little Buster under one arm, was frying a mess of flounder for supper. Oscar liked flounder. She had cleaned the front room, too. Tied a ribbon bow around the crack in the jardinière that contained the rubber-plant. And for the first time, at least since Buster was born, her blond hair was crimped and held in place with her rhinestone combs, and she wore a dimity dress with a sash made of the same material.

Oscar had frightened Trina. Tears of self-pity spurted more than once as she probed into the fish with her fork, but she squeezed them back. All her intuition told her somehow that this was not the time for self-pity. Therefore the rhinestone combs and the dimity dress. Trina was not all fool. So she tasted back her tears and poked at the flounder and leaned to raise the gas flame . . .

It happened in a smear and a bang, a roar and a spurt of flame, and the very gas burner that had once popped into Oscar's face flew out with a great stain of flame over Trina as she stood there clutching her baby under one arm, her dimity sash standing out like a butterfly, doused into nothing by the very first flame.

"Baby—Oscar—oh God—oh—"

When Oscar came home the house was filled with neighbours and the stairs smelled cold and charred.

They were in the act of dressing Trina's arm, which was held in the air like a dreadful signal when Oscar entered the bedroom; and so Henry, coming in to Friday night supper some five minutes later, found his brother in a dead faint on the floor, a neighbour trying to force water down him, which ran off instead into a long mandarin moustache down his collar.

By ten o'clock Trina had not regained sufficient consciousness to feel her pain, and the baby too lay in a torpor that was merciful to it.

But once more the doctor was optimistic.

"There's a good fighting chance for both of them. No flame swallowed and eyes safe." Inferentially, when the bang came, Trina had displayed sufficient presence of mind to toss the baby well out of the flare, and in some way her own dodge had saved her eyes and throat. So far so good. At this early hour there was no foretelling future developments, but there were too many people about. The doctor and the nurse shooed them out like flies, Henry included.

He walked home through a September evening that was whitish with starlight. The Burbys were on their square of front porch. Gabble-gabble as usual. He cut across to the lawn for his chair, which was tilted and waiting against the side wall of the house.

He felt as a man must after he has lost a great deal of blood.

Rather as if life had a circular motion to it. The cushions of his fingers were shirred as if they had been long in water.

There stood his silence, waiting for him. Deep and cool as a well. It was almost as if he could lave it refreshingly to his face the way he did with water in his morning wash. And upstairs, his room, with the burnt-wood collar-box exactly as it had stood since Oscar's marriage, and his Tuesday, Thursday, Saturday and Sunday's pipe airing on the window-sill.

He lit his Monday, Wednesday, and Friday's.

Pu—pu—pu—pu—

Poor Oscar's pipe scheme was all awry. Sometimes he borrowed a few puffs off of Henry's, for the sweetness.

Oscar, who had fallen out of the order and the quiet as a child might plunge headlong out of a window. A great wave of bitterness made Henry's face wry, as if he were tasting something horrid. Oscar, who might so easily be sitting there now beside him. Oscar, who loved the tick and tock. Oscar, whose neat, square-toed shoes were broken and grinning now. It stabbed Henry to see him in these. His brother's shoes had always been as firm-toed and punctiliously blacked as his own. And now—

Suddenly a thought smote Henry. A gadfly of a thought that swam across the darkness and hung brilliantly and twenty times its natural size right before Henry's eyes.

What if Trina should die?

Trina, who was a drain, and poor little Buster, whose head would probably always be too large for his body. A brilliant persistent gadfly of a thought that was almost a hope, which, try as he would, Henry could not banish. Even when it receded and became smaller, it glittered so in the darkness. What if Trina should die? Oscar back once more in the well-ordered quiet. The second-storey room again with the twin collar-boxes—the deceased Burby's eyes—almost human— What if Trina should—

To throw off this thought which lit and glittered, Henry began to walk again toward Kennerly Avenue. It was after eleven and the streets quiet, so that his footsteps sort of followed him down the sidewalks.

There was still a light in the bedroom of the Oscar flat. He could see it from the side of the house as he approached. Was Trina better? Henry tried to buoy himself with his hope and ran up the porch steps insisting to himself, "I hope Trina's better. I hope Trina's better."

The screen door was unlatched and the parlour dark. But in the bedroom, the centre gas was burning full-size and up into the stifling etheric atmosphere. Oscar was on the bed-edge bending over, and Trina, with her arms, bandages and all, locked about his neck so that her head, bandaged too, was lifted from the pillow, was talking in her highest and most nervous voice. The strand of hair, discoloured with iodine, hung loose of the binding gauze.

Henry, who feared that she might be delirious, stood off in the darkened parlour to tremble and to wait.

"Am I going to die, Oscar? Is my baby going to die? I won't go alone."

"Why, Trina, of course you are not going to die. You are a little burnt, that's all. You and baby. Joost a little burnt."

"I ought to die, Oscar. Me and baby. And relieve you. You've had so little out of it, Oscar, but worry—and drain—oh—oh—poor Oscar—poor Trina—I ought to die—but not without baby—I can't go alone—I know I ought to die—for you—"

"Don't say that, Trina. Don't say that," cried the Oscar whom Henry, standing out there trembling in the darkness, had never seen before. "Don't say that. Don't die. Live, Trina. You and baby, live for me! I couldn't go back to things without you. Live, Trina, you and baby. Live. Live."

And to Henry's horror, as he stood there with the gooseflesh shuddering over him, Oscar pitched forward against Trina so that she had to hold him even with the bandaged part of her arm from crushing over on the sleeping little Buster, his words tumbling, crashing, slithering over each other like coals down a steel chute.

"Live, Trina. Live! For me—couldn't—go back—to things without you. Live, Trina—you and baby—live." And her voice, a banner of it, waving.

"We'll live, Oscar. We'll live. We'll live."

Somehow Henry got down the stairs again, stealthily, and out into the whitish darkness. There were no pedestrians, and by the time he reached home again, church chimes were tilting out a solemn midnight.

Up in his room, seated there on the side of the bed, the eyes of the deceased Burby, that were almost human, focused upon him, clump went one of Henry's shoes. And then, very much later, clump, the other. And still he sat round-backed and looking at the silence.

Henry, envying Oscar.

The Spangle That Could Be a Tear

First Published: *The Bookman*, December 1923

⚘

There were three heads in the one bed above the pulled coverlets.

Sheets that had been washed in one water without bluing. Two brown heads. Ellie's and Little Bill's. And then Teddy's. The baby. His was exactly the white of taffy. Curious languor of the pigment. It was the color of a very gentle old man's hair. And yet on baby Teddy it was so young and so tender. The thistle down of it lay along his lashes. That little rill of light along Teddy's closed bluish lids. Night after night, looking down at her three asleep there, it was, unconscionably enough, the tenderness along Teddy's lashes that could seem to hurt Millie most. Hurt at her heart and hurt and hurt there.

Every night, Millie hurting there beside her three and Big Bill over in his big bed on the other side of the room grunting to her through the shag of his enormous mustache.

"Come on to bed, Mil."

"Comin', Bill."

It was so hard for Bill to keep awake after eight. If you drove a two ton truck and unloaded it to the maniacal clatter of coal down a chute and the grime got into your pores and made your teeth and your eyeballs look as white as a Negro's and you sweated even in December, it was not easy to remain awake after a supper of Millie's strong stew and potatoes that steamed as you broke them open.

Frequently, even before she undressed the children, Millie had to draw off Big Bill's shoes. Clump. Clump. It was dreadful to see him, sprawled asleep in them beside the supper table, with his chin in his chest and his nose in his mustache. Those enormous clod shoes that weighted him down so to the soot ridden days. Like a drowned man standing erect on the floor of a sea. Weighted down. Weighted down. That was it. Millie and Big Bill and the children, weighted down.

Standing there at her children's bed, night after night after night with that sense of the weights at her heart.

Especially around Christmas time when the Five, Ten, and Twenty-five Cent Store that occupied the ground floor of the tenement began to light up with red tissue paper bells and Christmas tree canaries, all the little closed eyes of her children seemed to open at Millie, gazing at her right through the transparency of lids.

You. You. We are weighted down. Mother. Drowning at the very bottom of the days. Why?

And once Big Bill, the enormous hulk of him, had seemed to answer back from the other side of the room. "Come on to bed, Mil." Poor Millie, sometimes she put her hand to her mouth to hold back the sobs.

Little Bill who was almost fourteen and looked eight. Presently his birthday would ring out like a knell. Fourteen. Working papers. Little Bill who wanted to be an engineer.

And Ellie who was eleven but looked fourteen. Little Ellie who had violet in her irises and the roundest loveliest little bulge to her legs. Like lyres. McClosky, who ran the Five, Ten, and Twenty-Five, had pinched her there one dusk in the courtyard and made horrid clucking sounds between his teeth. Big Bill had almost killed him. Millie had torn him off and led him upstairs and washed the hair—McClosky's—out of his mouth. That courtyard where the dirty snow lingered until late spring and little girls heard horrid lurking things. The horrid lurking things that Ellie knew.

Sometimes, standing there beside her sleeping three, Millie put up both her hands to hold back the sobs.

And yet somehow, the hurt that lay deepest, until she could feel her heart move outward and press against her dirty old corsets, was Teddy. His bluish lids with the rill of light along them. The thin little lids through which the baby eyes could time and time again seem to look up at her.

You. You. We are weighted down, Mother. Drowning at the very bottom of the days. Why?

Teddy who had a spot on his lung and needed sun and wide days that tasted of pine, weighted down close to the foul old smells that came up from the courtyard.

Oh God, forgive me. I didn't want him. I prayed. I begged. Keep it God, I kept saying. Don't let me have another. I can't do for it. I haven't the right to another. I knew before he came. Big Bill knew! I begged him. No more, Bill. He promised. But Bill—he's just a man. You're God. You shouldn't have let him. God. I prayed so. And now I've got him and I can't give him up. It's a sin to keep having them God, when you can't do for them. We can't give ours a chance. But don't take him back now, God. My Teddy. You shouldn't have let me have him. Oh God, now that he's here, I won't give him back. Make it so that we can do for him. Make that spot on his lung well—God—God—

Bill's only a man. You're God—keep him from being bestial.

It was hardest of all near Christmas. Somehow when those six little eyes in the bed looked up through the closed lids. . . .

You. You. We are weighted down, Mother. . . . You couldn't look back. You couldn't meet those eyes. Six of them. Ellie who wanted a fur tippet and whose plump neck was all chapped. Little Bill who began to sniffle horridly as early as October. For two years Little Billy had been saving his pennies from running errands for Jo's garage for a radio set. Big Bill could grow pale under his shag every time he borrowed those never completed and never refunded savings from his son.

When December came around and the Five and Ten and Twenty-Five began to light up with tinsel, Millie's heart, from being heavy, hung in her body like the motionless clapper to a bell. To be furtive with one's own baby. To kiss the rill of light along his eyelids; kiss rather than dare to look down into the blue. To box Little Billy roundly across the ear when he sniffled for his savings that had gone to help out the emergency of a creosote lamp for Teddy's breathing. It was easier to box for reply than to look down into the troubled, thwarted eyes.

Of all the months in the year Millie hated December, with its twenty-fifth day mounted on it like a spangle. The spangle that could be a tear.

Ellie's tippet. You schemed and wore newspaper next to your skin when your ribbed undershirt would no longer hold the darns and you were glad when Big Bill, who had granulated eyelids from fatigue, had to work Sundays during the coal shortage. But still you could not manage Ellie's fur tippet. They cost four dollars. Rather dreadful, lumpy, dyed rat ones on the push-carts. But you boxed Ellie's ears when she cried for it. Boxed her soundly because you could not look her in the eye or along the ridge of flesh where her neck was chapped. Teddy should have had a coat at Christmas. A sweet warm one that fastened up in front with brass buttons with anchors on. You wanted those buttons with the anchors on for Teddy and a blue sailor's cap with the name of a battleship across the front.

You wanted it with your heart. The heart that hung in your body like a still clapper and the more you wanted it the more you slapped with your sudsy hands. Not hard. Just boxed, stinging, little ears.

There was a twitch to Ellie in her sleep. You noticed it as you stood there beside the bed. The tender curve of her body. Ellie who was about to be a woman. Lovely little mystery of that. Ellie exposed to the horrid scuttling things of the courtyard. . . . Little Bill who wanted to be an engineer. Oh God, not to be able to look them in the face. Afraid of those irises that could stare right up through the lids. Oh God—no more—please—to bring into this—

The twitching. Ellie twitching there.

"Ellie. Baby?"

"Mother!"

"Yes."

"Mother, you there?"

"Yes. Sh-h, go back to sleep."

"Mother?"

"Hush up. I was just covering you up before I go to bed. You kick so."

"Mother—"

"Ellie, you sick?"

"No—but Mother—stay by me—"

"Why Ellie—"

"I'm so—hot—"

"Fever?"

"No. Just—scary hot—give me, Mother—your hand."

"Sh-h-h, don't wake the baby."

"Mother—"

"Ellie, why are you twitching that way?"

"I—feel afraid, Mother."

"You've been dreaming."

"Moomie!"

"Ellie—Ellie—you haven't called me that since you were a baby!"

"Moomie—hold me—"

"Sh-h-h, don't wake the baby. Your father either. Sh-h, he's worn out."

"Moomie, you know Jo?"

"Jo who?"

"Jo."

"Ellie—Jo who?"

"The Jo in the garage next door? The Greek."

"Why, yes. But what Ellie—what—Ellie—what—what?"

"I didn't Moomie. I didn't. I didn't—"

"Didn't what, Ellie? Tell Moomie. Tell Moomie. Didn't what?"

"I didn't go, Moomie. He wanted. He tried to pull me—up. Where he lives. Over the garage. To show me—he said—his motorcycle to take me riding on. Upstairs. I didn't go, Moomie. He pinched. Look."

Oh God. Oh God.

"He pinched me, Moomie. See. But I didn't go."

"Ellie—Ellie—my baby—look at me Ellie. My all. My life. Tell me again and again that you didn't go."

"I swear. I didn't."

"Swear it!"

"You hurt!"

"Swear it!"

"I didn't, Moomie, but he hurt—where he pinched—"

"Ellie—my Ellie—Ellie—"

"Don't jerk so, Moomie."

"My baby. Go back to sleep. My baby. My life. Blood of my blood. My baby."

"It was right, wasn't it Moomie, not to go? It was right, wasn't it?"

"Yes, yes Ellie. Oh God, Ellie, never go. Never go. Carry that around in you. Mother's prayer. Never go, Ellie."

"Moomie, Moomie, what makes you jerk so when you breathe?"

"Sh-h-h, Ellie, don't wake your father. Go back to sleep. My baby. My precious. Ellie—promise Mother. Don't tell your father. Ever. He'll kill. It's so dark for you already, Ellie. Don't tell your father—"

"But it's all right Moomie, I didn't go."

"It's all right, Ellie. Now go back to sleep—"

Ellie's lids fluttering down. Precious curve of her. The room that was hot and a little sour with breath. The hot, sour gale of it in Millie's ears. The red, the rising gale—

God—God—Ellie—my Ellie—take her back, God—before they dirty her—take her back, God—now—

Millie in the red, the rising gale stumbling across the room and gathering herself until she hung in a hook of fury over the big bed and the shamble of Bill lying there dozing with his dry mouth open.

Damn you. Damn you. Damn you.

"Huh? What say? Millie, that you? What the hell—come to bed—"

Big good natured Bill who cried onto the back of his hand when he took Little Bill's savings for the creosote lamp.

"Millie—what say?"

"Yi—yi—yi—" shuddering lips too sick to speak.

"What say? Come to bed, Millie—m'girl—come—"

"Yi—yi—"

"Come—to—bed, m'girl—"

"Yi—"

"Y'hear!"

"Comin'—Bill—"

The Gold in Fish

First Published: *Cosmopolitan*, August 1925
Reprinted: *Song of Life*, A.A. Knopf, 1927;
More Aces: A Collection of Short Stories Compiled by the Community Workers of the N.Y. Guild for the Jewish Blind, G.P. Putnam's Sons, 1925
Filmed: *The Younger Generation*, dir. Frank Capra, 1929

There always had been, even when as a youngster he had used to shout it through years of a childhood spent in the din of Delancey Street, something about Morris's voice.

Something that approached a slow rich gargle. Centuries of Oriental unctuousness lay like salve on that voice. The unctuousness of the bazaar merchant. The unctuousness that accompanies the gesture of the rubbing of the hands. Rhythmic unctuousness of a dealer in things. Lover of things. Connoisseur of things. Silks. Scents. Cloth of gold. Sandalwood. Ivories. Apes. Peacocks.

All in the voice of Morris. There was a nap on it. The fuzz of centuries of suavities of salesmanship.

When Morris spoke, his long black eyes lay in two somnolent slits over the somnolent voice.

Mrs. Goldfish considered him her fairest child.

"It's a pity," she used to comment to almost every conclave of the shawled women that took place on the long, lean tenement stoop on Delancey Street, "it's a pity my Morris should have the beautiful curls for the family and my Reenie have only a little waviness, and my Birdie's, they're straight like a poker."

In a way it was a pity. Because one day Morris's curls were to lie in a little ruin on a bath towel over which his mother's tears were to flow. They were almost the only bitter tears she was ever to shed over him.

The slightly somnolent voice of Morris. It clung to your consciousness long after it had drifted into silence.

Sooner or later, Morris got his way.

A gentle, insidious way. A way that had transformed his father from a petty, puttering dealer in used furniture in Delancey Street—a lean, argumentative little old man with a protruding chin and a curl of goatee that was pretty constantly waggling from haggling—into the dim old man whose beard was mostly quiet now and faint with Havana where it had once reeked with meerschaum.

The old man's haggling days were over. He sat now most of the time in the bow of the brace of sunny living-room windows that overlooked waves of upper West Side roofs and a distant slash of Hudson River.

Once the old man summed it up rather grimly for himself, sitting there the long leisurely hours through, his head dozy on his chest. Not only were his haggling days over, the old man concluded. But his *days* were over.

The old man's days were over.

That was an ungrateful thought, to be smashed back like a jack-in-the-box.

By the time Morris Goldfish was nineteen, he was earning more per week than his father had ever in his life earned per month.

And as auctioneer!

Well, with that voice, his mother had once dared to dream of a rabbi. But from the first, when at fourteen he had voluntarily hired himself out to a Japanese who kept a trinket-goods shop in Mott Street (auction Saturdays) Morris found his way to that ancient trade.

It was his voice. With its strange insidiousness, furry, never raucous, plaintive, never aggressive; dulcet and pained at the undiscerning bidder, never bully-ragging; Morris was to establish a new precedent in an old, old craft. It just pierced, that voice, down into you like a hypodermic needle. Subtly. That was the voice that ended the haggling days of old man Goldfish and landed him in the sunny bow of window that overlooked the slash of the distant river. That was the voice that lowered the stridency of Mother Goldfish, that married Reenie Goldfish to Irving Silk, of Silk and Striker, that married itself to Irma, only daughter of Wolfheim Striker—Striker and Striker, Incorporated.

That was the voice. The insidious voice that had long since promoted the raucous job of auctioneering into a gentle art.

Some of the genuinely fine collections of his time, from the Dadarian Rock Crystal Collection and the Rienzi Palace tapestries to the Rinehardt group of ivory elephants and the Danzelli cryptics, had gone down before the lapis lazuli signet that Morris used as hammer. One of the Danzelli cryptics, signed with a seventeenth century Florentine signature, hung over the imported Gothic fireplace in Morris Goldfish's living-room in his house in West Seventy-third Street.

A stone-lace Renaissance house, fifty feet removed from Riverside Drive and facing the rococo splendor of the home of a steel magnate about which sight-seeing bus guards megaphoned.

The voice of Morris Goldfish. He was using it now in the bow-windowed living-room of the ten room and three baths apartment he furnished and maintained for his parents in West 110th Street.

Using it against an atmosphere of feeble rebellion. But it had stilled many more active rebellions, that voice. The rebellion against giving up the used-furniture store in Delancey Street. The rebellion against hats, where generations of shawls had swathed softly. The rebellion against loneliness of unneighborly neighbors and the upper West Side cost of rump for pot-roast. The rebellion against twin beds and loaf sugar and boiled collars. The rebellion against the installation of a second maid who changed the lower as well as the upper sheets every week.

There was one member of the Goldfish family into whose blood stream that voice had never slid, insidiously, like the hypodermic needle.

That was Birdie. But more, much more of Birdie later.

There was about this rebellion, hanging like haze over the living-room—Heppelwhite, that Morris had knocked down to himself from the G. P. Granadine sale—something special. Something ominous. Something that made Morris's upper lip, topped with a little black mustache that looked as if it had been kissed there, not quite so sure of itself.

"We been, Morris, up against lots of outrageousness since you got yourself so prosperous, but never nothing like this."

"Mother," said Morris and directed his somnolent eyes a little sadly toward the droop of her there in the Heppelwhite chair, "you're making a mountain out of a mole-hill."

"A mole-hill," said Mrs. Goldfish and wound her hands in a dry-wash. "A mole-hill! I should cut off my name in two like it was so much silk by the yard, and a mole-hill he calls it."

"Mother, you don't understand—"

"I don't understand! I understand that my son comes home and announces to me and his papa, like it was so much weather, that we ain't named Goldfish any more. We're named Fish!"

"No, no. Not like it was so much weather, mother. I've explained it to you so carefully at least six times since I entered this room ten minutes ago, that I have changed our name legally because it was a liability and not an asset. No man named Morris Goldfish can hope to achieve the position in life that I have mapped out for myself. For us."

"Forty years now, son, I been a Goldfish and—"

"Morris Goldfish and Maurice Fish are two different human beings, mother. Certain walks of life are closed to Morris Goldfish that I, as Maurice

Fish, propose to enter."

"You hear that, papa. The name that was good enough for you to get born into, and for me to marry into, is somethink to be ashamed of. Irma, ain't you got no pride in family? Ain't the name that was good enough for you to marry when you married my son, good enough now so you don't got to make laughing-stock of you and your children by changing it?"

Mrs. Maurice Fish, nee Irma Striker, had gray eyes and a nose that had been straightened. Bloodlessly. "It would have to be bloodlessly," had been Birdie's trite comment. "The stuff don't flow in her." Irma's finger nails were flaming ruby cabochons which hung from her hands in glowing convex surfaces. Irma's hair, bobbed, was marcelled so that only the boyish shave peak in the back revealed it.

Irma called her nurse-maid a *bonne*.

Irma weighed one hundred and fourteen pounds and attended Lyman Wastrel's Stretching Classes for weight reduction.

When Irma sat in a chair, she unloosed like a character doll. There simply were no bones to her. She sprawled like so much sawdust crammed into painted cloth.

"She don't sit," said old man Goldfish. "She splatters."

"Mother, you don't understand," said Irma and took a long puff at her cigaret and left a red rim on it.

You-don't-understand—you-don't-understand.

Said Birdie once: "Put those three words together every time she has said them to you, ma, and they will reach from here to Pocatello, Idaho, wherever and whatever that is."

"I don't understand?" repeated Mrs. Goldfish in three large shrugs. "Oh, I understand, all right! I understand I'm ashamed I should face anybody for being laughing-stock. My friends down-town should know it on me. I should call up over the telephone to Kramer my butcher—he should send me and charge me a miltz to Mrs. Julius *Fish*. I ask you, papa, sitting there like you was froze there, is that the way you want I should got to call up for my miltz?"

There was about Julius Goldfish, sitting there in Heppelwhite, with the Havana fragrant droop to the quiescent goatee of him, something of the curious kind of suspended animation of a figure sitting under water. Drowned there, but in the casual attitude of life.

When Julius Goldfish spoke, his goatee had the merest flip to it, none of the exuberant waggle of the old days of haggle.

"Fish," he repeated in the remote and watery tones. "Fish? For why, Morris, is it better we should be just Fish and not Goldfish? Ain't it commoner, son, to be just any old fish like a carp or a pike or a minnie? For why is it finer? Just Fish? With Goldfish you know right away it's a fancy fish sometimes with two tails what swims around all day in a glass bowl in the window. I know goldfish what sell so high as twenty dollars."

"Fish! My Reenie don't need to care—she's married herself out of her name. But Birdie—I want once to know what your sister Birdie has to say when she hears how she's had her tail cut off from her name—or is it her head? I—"

"It ain't good, son, you should move us out of our name all of a sudden like—like you moved us up out of our business and out of our old home. I know everything you do is for the better. But our name, son—when you cut it, is like cutting something so close like—like an arm or a something that's part of us."

There was the enormous nervelessness to old man Goldfish's voice of one caught in the lassitude of realizing his defeat in advance.

"You don't understand, dad," said Irma, and flipped cigaret ashes backward over the chair, because her knee as she slanted in Heppelwhite was higher than her head. "Goldfish, as it has been translated from whatever your forebears chose to call themselves, is a comedy name. Nobody bearing it can help being just a little ridiculous all of the time. It isn't the name that an important art connoisseur, or I should think the parents or sisters of an important art connoisseur, should bear. Maurice and I refuse to continue to be ridiculous because of a name, and certainly it is a subject upon which the family cannot afford to be divided."

"You must understand, father, that I would not be asking this of you and mother and—and the girls—if I didn't realize its important psychology. It is a matter of business with me, father."

"I know, son—I know—if it's for your good—"

"All right, papa, if it's for his good—but what about *ours?* You can do the calling up of—Kramer, with such a name like Fish. Not me!"

"Mama—mama," said old man Fish, dusting himself down the front, a recent and vacant mannerism of his, "you don't mean that. Always what has been good for Morris has been good for us. Look at what he has done for us all—"

"I know it. I know it. But, papa—like Birdie said once, a Goldfish out of water is one of the saddest sights in the world. Maybe Delancey Street was our water—"

"You don't mean that—mama—"

"Morris knows I ain't ungrateful, papa—every mother should have such a son. Say, I guess if it's best for him and Irma and the children we should be Fish and not Goldfish, for the few years I got left to be Fish, I should make a scandal about it."

"It *is* best, mother. Best from every angle. Best I can assure you for my business and social interests. See, mother, I've brought your new engraved cards for us all. Mrs. Julius Fish, Mr. Maurice Fish. Miss Birdie Fish."

"Such an extravagance, son. For what we need cards? To throw them around at doors in the apartment house so maybe we can get a little neighborliness out of some in the building? Callink cards. We're used to them from home. Not, papa?" The warmth of humor flowed back into Mrs. Goldfish's little cheeks. She could be like that. Surrender with grace and good spirit. "Only don't be so sure, son, with your cards here already made for Birdie, you got it so easy to turn your sister around your little finger like us."

"It's up to you, mother, and father, to help make Birdie understand from the start. I'm not going to have Birdie gumming up the machinery. She's gummed it up enough. More than I propose to tell right here. If Birdie is clever, she won't oppose—"

"That must be Birdie now in the keyhole with her key. Now, Morris, don't you start nothing with your sister. You neither, Irma. I hate always it should be such fussings and teasings between you."

There entered then into the Heppelwhite, into the pleasant lavender of a dusk which flowed into the bow window, Miss Birdie Goldfish. Better say ripped. Ripped into the Heppelwhite. Ripped into the lavender. Ripped into the dusk. Tearing the mood, the environment asunder as if it had all been so much paper stretched across a hoop.

Birdie entered a room precisely like that. As if she had splashed through a hoop.

"Hello, everybody," she said and pulled off by the brim one of those small, untrimmed soft felt hats in which nine out of ten women feel cunning whether they look it or not.

Birdie did not look cunning in it. To be fair, it is doubtful if she felt it. Birdie was one of those lower-middle-register people who come large and hoarse. There could have been nothing cunning about Birdie. When Birdie opened her mouth, she boomed. Literally that.

"Smells like a conference or a row, or both," said Miss Goldfish and spun her hat from her with a twist of wrist.

"Birdie!"

"What's the in-the-gloaming idea?" said Miss Goldfish and switched on some side bracket crystal chandeliers (Sinclair estate), ran her hand through her black bobbed hair, plucked her rather too close-fitting black satin dress away from its habit of clinging to her, walked over, threw open one of the windows and cocked herself on the sill.

"Birdie, you'll fall out."

"Spring is come and the birds are singing," said Miss Goldfish and leaned over to peck her father with a kiss on as much of the tip of his ear as she could reach, and proceeded, with the aid of the mirror in the lid of a small round vanity box, to tinker with the clipped edges of her hair.

"Well, your Holiness," said Miss Goldfish to her brother, but directing her gaze to her reflection in the bit of mirror, "what you got under your little round hat?"

"Birdie—shh-h, that ain't nice. Suppose some *goy* neighbors should hear you. You should have respect for everybody's religion even if it ain't your own."

"Oh ma, ring a bell every time you want to nag, honey. It's easier," said Miss Goldfish, smearing a plentiful area of red along her lips and with the tip of her little finger making it bow enormously under her nose.

"Ain't that fine! My daughter tells me I should ring a bell when—"

"Charming," said Mrs. Maurice Fish, and blew a smoke ring to the ceiling.

Miss Goldfish inclined a glance at her sister-in-law over a powder-puff about to make an onslaught. "Huh?"

"Charming, was all I said."

And then Miss Goldfish's voice took unto itself the tilt of a fog horn trying to be a pitch pipe. "My word! So glad you think so!"

"Birdie, you shouldn't talk so to Irma."

"Never mind, mother, she is no more disgusting than usual."

"Same to you, dear," said Miss Goldfish complacently to her reflection, and swinging her head on the pillar of short neck for a peer at her own profile.

In a family that by a principle of its own private biology insisted upon the infallibility of family resemblance, Birdie was said to be like unto her mother. Well, if Birdie resembled her mother, she had flowed a little over at that resemblance.

Where little Mrs. Goldfish's features had quite a little jut to them out of the bony structure of face, Birdie's were softly imbedded in heavy check, and her chin, instead of tapering down into wattles, threatened, ever so slightly, to double. There was a little ridge right on the back of Birdie's neck that the bobbed hair enhanced. That knob was not infrequently red. It was a careful habit of Birdie's to massage it during quiet periods at the Cutie Shop, where Birdie sold cutenesses to cuties.

And Birdie's opulence she managed somehow to pour into frocks slightly too small for it. There always was a straining across the bust line. That look of armholes about to burst.

It must have been because Birdie insisted upon wearing frocks ready-made out of the Cutie Shop. A little fourteen by eighteen feet mauve and wisteria concoction oozed in between a sheet-music shop and a theatrical ticket agency in the Broadway forties, and catering to a trade known along the Rialto as Squabs, Ponies, Flappers and Pets.

Somewhere imbedded in Birdie's face was a certain squab-young prettiness. A one-hundred-and-seventy-six pound prettiness.

When Birdie walked on the stilts of heels that threw her forward and her too modish dress clung and climbed about her calves, loiterers on Broadway's corners said "Whoops, la la!" and sometimes Birdie, who was neither timid nor flirtatious, turned on them with a shrug of her plump shoulders and a leer: "See anything green?"

When upon occasion her brother eyed her through his half slitted eyes, the somnolent ones that lay in a gaze that matched his voice, Birdie would put that same question.

She was putting it now: "See anything green, lovingest brother?" she said and involuntarily yanked at her skirt where it rode up to reveal the edge of purple and vermilion bloomer.

"Birdie, stop startink somethink right away with your brother. It's not nice. It's just as well, Morris, she should right away know it, what's happened to her. Look, Birdie, your brother has got a surprise for you. Here are your new callink cards. We had a liability and now we got an asset."

Birdie, still ensconced in window frame, reached to take the small cardboard box from her mother, but her eyes and her nose and her mouth crinkling toward her brother.

"What's rotten in Denmark this evening?" she said and automatically ran her finger across to feel of the engraving. "Miss Birdie Fish. Miss Bi—Say—hey—waiter—bring me the rest of my order. I didn't say half-portion. Where's the other half, waiter?"

"We ain't Goldfish no more, Birdie. For business and society reasons. It's a vulgarity, Birdie, a family like ours should call itself Goldfish. Morris has got the good sense we should get it changed by court. Birdie Fish. That sounds like something. Ain't it, papa?"

Miss Goldfish swung slowly out of the window frame, knees bent, head back, and palms on her hips beginning a paddywhack against her thighs.

"Oh! Oh! Oh!" she cried and gasped for breath and cried again. "Oh! Oh! Oh! This is the best yet. It's too good—too—rich! It cannot be; it could only happen in the funny-strips or a padded cell. My brother decides to change the family name. The family comes home and finds itself amputated—"

"You might have known, mother, she would act like an idiot and a vulgar one at that."

"Wild woman," said Irma and mashed out her cigaret on a chalcedony tray from the Ronald sale.

"You poor fish," cried Birdie and kept rocking. "Goldfish is a liability, is it? Well, how's gefüldte fish? Morris Gefüldte Fish. At least when you were amputating why didn't you cut off the tail, you poor Fish, and leave the Gold?"

"Because Gold is a common and obviously modified name. Everybody has done it that way. Look in the telephone and you'll see fifty Golds to one Fish. There is distinction to the name Fish. If it is good enough for Stuyvesant Fish and Hamilton Fish, it is good enough for Maurice Fish, and should be good enough for Birdie Fish. You have as much reason to be grateful, Birdie, as the rest of us. It cannot be much of an asset to a girl, even in the business you insist upon choosing for yourself, to have to sign herself Birdie Goldfish."

"Well," cried Birdie, her face suddenly congealing into angles, "let me tell you something, Morris Goldfish—and Morris Goldfish you'll be to me to the end of the chapter—just you put this in your jade and ivory cigaret holder and smoke it: I was born Birdie Goldfish, I was confirmed Birdie Goldfish, I was mar—I am Birdie Goldfish, and so help me, it will take more than a pack of Tiffany visiting cards to make me die anything but Birdie Goldfish. *Goldfish*, you hear me?"

"Mother, can't you—"

"No, she can't! You've worn them down until they aren't much more than a couple of transfer pictures that you've flattened out on a sheet of paper. I remember the time when ma would have turned and given you *makots* for even suggesting what you've gone and done. Pa too. Look at them now—trying to like it. It's enough to make you cry your eyes out."

"You—"

"Oh, you're the big mogul of the family, all right. I grant you that. You've pulled us up. But only so we don't pull you down. Well, I don't want to pull you down. I'm willing to put up with all this for ma and pa's sake. You've got them buffaloed, all right. But let me tell you there are limits and those limits are Fish!"

"No, those limits aren't Fish, Birdie. Those—those limits, my fine sister, are you! Your coarseness. Your vulgarity. Don't—don't rile me too much, Birdie—today of all days. If—it weren't for mother and father and Irma—I could tell you now what those limits are."

"You could, could you!"

"Children!"

"Well, let me tell you right here, my dear brother Mawruss Goldfish, there's nothing about me that you need to be afraid to discuss before ma and pa and anything you got to say to me will be baby-talk before Irma compared to what she hears wafted to her on the south wind patter of her Mah-Jong parties. So whatever you've got to say to me, Brother Mawruss, you can shoot to me right now."

There was a sucked-in look to Maurice Fish's lips as if anger had lashed them to his teeth.

"Don't rile me, Birdie, into saying things we both may regret."

"Then don't take it upon yourself to come home telling me you've changed my name on me as if it was a kitchen apron. You can put that over on ma and pa and maybe your sister Reenie. But I'm a Goldfish, get that. Make me ashamed of it if you can!"

"Morris don't mean, Birdie—"

"Don't he! Don't he? Then what does he mean, ma? He's ashamed of his name! A good name that you and pa have kept clean and decent for us kids."

"I mean that you're a disgrace to our family no matter what name you call us. No girl with an iota of respect for her surroundings and with every comfort hers for the asking will spend her time clerking in a little fourth-rate, hand-me-down, chorus-girl emporium, when she has the opportunity to stay at home and study and improve herself and—"

"Yes, opportunity! I'd be a smart one to get myself sucked down the way you've sucked down ma and pa. I admit I'm not stuck on my job, but it's the best a low-brow like me can hope for. I'm low-brow maybe, but I'm not browbeaten."

"Birdie, stop fussing with—"

"Why, ma and pa used to be two individuals before you set about killing them with kindness. Before you took the Goldfish family out of water. That's what they are. Two Goldfish out of water. I know them! I know every time ma puts a hat on her head it gives her a headache. I know how she goes on the sly and buys herself a miltz and sneaks in the kitchen on the cook's day out to fix it for her and pa. I know how pa'd rather haggle selling a second-hand, golden-oak, roller-top, Grand Rapids desk to Jacob Mintz than sit sunning himself all day in a Heppelwhite chair, that he cannot pronounce. Talk about a fish out of water! If ever there were fishes out of water, it's the Goldfishes."

"Birdie—you mustn't holler at your—"

"But not me! I know why I work in the Cutie Shop. Not because I'm any crazier about it than you are! But I pay my way and I go my way. I got a kosher nature and I'm not ashamed of it. Ma and pa have too, only they're bluffed. Well, I'm not. I pay as I go. Maybe I don't go very far, but just the same I'm my own mistress. Get that? My own mistress!"

There flashed across the face of Maurice Fish something over which he seemed to have no control. A grimace of anger that made words like hot coals hop off reluctant lips.

"Your own mistress maybe—but for all I know—more than that! Worse than that."

"What?"

"Oh, you know what I mean. I've been telling you all along. Those cheap traveling salesmen you've been running with. Those Broadway penny-sports you're about with, until a man is afraid to take his own wife to the theater for fear of running into you with one of them."

"What'll I do, sit at home and wait for you to send me some college professors?"

"And now—and now—worse—defaulters—gangsters—crooks—thieves. Talk about being your own mistress—if that was the worst—You've driven me to this—I will say it! Ma! Pa! She's running around town with men whose names aren't fit to be uttered by self-respecting people—she's going to drag us down three steps for every one step we've mounted. Either you cut out that gang, Birdie—those crooks—or I—if mother and father haven't any authority over you—I'll take it to court! Once more before them, I ask you. Are you or are you not going to stop running around town with that crook—that defaulter—that gangster that even today's papers mention in that bond stealing case? Isadore Slupsky."

"Birdie—you ain't been going out again with that Slupsky boy that Morris says ain't nice!"

"Well, well, answer her."

There actually seemed but little left of Morris except his pallor and the lashed lips against his teeth.

"Birdie—don't tell me you been out again with such a man like him."

"Yes, ma. Yes, pa. Yes. Yes. Yes. I had supper with him last night. I had lunch with him today. I can't bring him home so I meet him on street corners. If Isadore's a crook, then so am I. That's how sure I am that boy's being framed. One dirty frame-up after another."

"Oh, she has the lingo all right. Listen!"

"That's what's happened to that boy because he's only a kid. And a kid that's sweet and trusting and who has been raised with gangsters and nobody but a drunk old aunt who died in the d.t.'s to raise him, hasn't got much chance of fighting his way out. Alone. Yes, I been seen with him."

"And—go on—and—what—else?"

"And what else?" said Birdie and looked at her brother with her head forward and the lump on her neck out as if she would charge forward. "And what?"

"It's town talk you've been seen with him. And if they get him, and they'll get him sure if they round up the others on this bond theft, I guess our name, whether it's Fish or Goldfish, will be mixed up with it."

"Birdie!"

"You've been seen with him. Dinner. Lunch. But what else? Now that you've got me riled. Go on. I guess sooner or later mother and father will have to listen to the kind of tales a dealer walked into my office with this morning. Well, well? Where else have you been seen with him? Where did Birdie spend last night, ma?"

"Why—why, with—with Sadie, one of the girls, Morris, what works in her store. Morris—Birdie—I—papa—what?"

"Well, she was seen with—I'll say it if I choke—she was seen coming out of the Grand Lester Hotel this morning with Slupsky! Is it any wonder the name Goldfish is one to be rid of? That's where she was seen with him. Now what have you to say?"

"What have I to say?" said Birdie and smiled the slow kind of smile that a woman reserves for the smile she turns to her lover. "What have I to say? Why, you poor Fish. You poor decapitated Goldfish. I married Ike Slupsky yesterday at noon."

It was near that midnight when Isadore Slupsky, with Birdie breathing into his collar from the five flights of climb, unlocked the door to his flat in South Simpson Street, Bronx.

A sort of cave damp came out in a billow. Stale bad air. A single electric bulb on the narrow landing kept threatening to blink out.

"Hold your horses, Mr. Edison," said Birdie to it. "We need you to lead us into our rose-grown cottage."

"If I had only known we were coming here tonight, Bird, I'd have come up ahead and opened up the place. Whew!"

"Never mind, Boy. The way I spilled the beans all over the Heppelwhite tonight, we're lucky to have your flat to come to. Lucky too I managed to locate you at Tod's place. The family confab was still fabbing when I made a bee-line for the telephone, my overnightie bag and the front door."

"There," said Slupsky and clicked on a pale smear of hall light. It was hard to wedge in because of a pachyderm procession of trunks down the narrow aisle. "Wait here a minute, Birdie, and I'll go ahead and light up."

"Not on your life," said Birdie, lugging down the slit of hallway after him. "If I stand here long enough to get wedged, you'll have to shoe-horn me out."

The front room of Mr. Slupsky's apartment clicked on to the same blear of yellow light. It was a front room of no rug. Two deal chairs piled on a sofa that bulged springs. A detached cooking range. A wash-basket of dishes, waffle iron, huge ball of clothes-line and a lamp with a broken base. In a room that led off, a bed-spring tipped against the door barred entrance. Beneath the opened window, even at ebb-tide hour of midnight, Simpson Street flowed in distant babble.

"Well!" said Birdie and dropped her patent leather suitcase from nerveless fingers.

"I told you, Bird, we should have gone to the Grand Lester."

"At seven dollars per?"

"This is no place to bring you. It's been the darnedest place to sublet. Eleven months of lease signed by me on my hands after the old woman died. Long as I had to keep on coming across every month with the twenty-eight bucks for these rooms, I just been keeping this truck stored up here. My aunt wasn't much on style, but it never looked like this when she kept it. This is no place for you, Bird. It's not too late yet to go to a hotel."

There was something about the pale, the eager, the nervous face of Slupsky that reminded you how you imagined animals that leap from crag to crag must look. Llamas or mountain sheep. Fear of precipice. Strain of scurrying up rocky crags without daring to look back. Scramble of slipping feet.

And his pallor. It had somehow crept into his hair and into his eyes. Isadore was the color of something blanched. You could almost imagine that he had paled with fear one day and remained that way.

He was all tan. His face, his hair, and the little mustache that twitched in the bewildered, nervous way Charlie Chaplin's has of twitching.

"So this," said Birdie in her voice at its hoarsest, "is home!"

"Bird, you're sore at me now for not telling you how bad it was. I tried to, but you wouldn't listen. I tell you I've got the money to put us up at the hotel."

"Come here," said Birdie, drawing him to her with one big wrench of her arm. "You sweet, scared kid. I could live in a hayrick with you, Boy. That's the way I am. I don't fall often, but I do fall hard. Kiss me, darlink, and kiss me quick and again."

Isadore Slupsky was every inch as tall as Birdie, and yet when Birdie embraced her husband it was as if he had to lift his tired pale face to her, and literally she did overshadow his slimness in curves that all but obliterated him in the confusion of the caress.

"Boy of mine—of mine!" rather yammered Birdie, in the incredible fashion of seeming to talk along toothless gums.

"Toodles-oodles-Bird!" said Slupsky with equal strain upon the credulities and his light mustache nibbling to the saying of it, somewhere along Birdie's cheek.

"Take down those chairs off the sofa, darlingest," said Birdie, reaching for them herself and depositing them on the floor. "I want to talk. And open the windows," said Birdie, doing it herself and dragging the sofa over to it for air. "Never mind trying to clear up, Boy. I'll take care of all that later. There!" said Birdie, and threw off her hat and took his hand and tousled her hair with it.

"Oh, Bird," said Slupsky and let his pale head rest tiredly against the swell of her arm, "a fellow has got to get used to having you. I feel like somebody was kidding me. Honest, honey, you're too good to be true."

"You poor sweet kid. You don't know the half of it, dearie. If you think I'm too good to be true now, wait. You're just going to begin to live. You're like a canoe that somebody's thrown out in the middle of the ocean on a rough day. It's just as well, Boy, I spilled the beans at home tonight instead of waiting the way we planned. Waiting for what? Waiting for the gang to try and frame you another time?"

"I just felt, Bird, maybe it wasn't the best time—"

"I'd like to see anybody try to frame you from now on. If that crowd needs a goat, they got to go looking in somebody else's tin-can pasture. We're going to start new, Boy. Fresh. And let me tell you something else. This flat isn't bad. Five-room flats at twenty-eight dollars a month aren't lying around loose. We'll live out the lease here anyway, and by the time I'm finished with it, you won't know the place. I know this neighborhood. There's a fish market on the corner called Blatz's. When I was a kid down in Delancey Street, we used to be brought out here to visit our swell relations that had graduated from the Bowery to the Bronx. Very nice block from here."

"But, Birdie—Birdie, after what you're used to! I tell you I can afford—"

"After what I'm used to! What am I used to? Living in a swell ten-rooms and three baths that fits me like a yama-yama glove. Like pa always says, what's the use of three baths when you can only take one at a time anyway? You don't know what's what with me, Boy. We've been so busy falling in love we haven't had time to get acquainted."

"There's something in that, Bird."

"You can't realize without living through it yourself what it means to see a grand old pair like my folks being killed with prosperity. They have just given in, Boy, my old folks. And with a smile, God love 'em. But, Boy, come over here and let me tell you something. I'm a rough-neck, honey. A dyed-in-the-wool blown-in-the-glass one. I am what I am!"

"A darling."

"This is my speed, honey. Up here. Where you can hang out of your window and yell it if you're too tired to go down-stairs and say it. You watch me with this dinge of a flat. You give me seven days, fifteen yards of cretonne and a couple of those Mongolium rugs you read about in the backs of the magazines and I'll show you! This is my real speed up here, Boy. The Bronx, God love it."

"But—"

"Oh, Boy darling, I'm going to find you a steady Saturday night envelop job that will bring you home to some of the good old-fashioned grub I haven't tasted since we left Delancey. I'm going to give you a glimpse of a gefüldte heaven!"

There seemed to be no way that Slupsky could shake himself free of daze. He kept kissing her through the twitching of his mustache and brushing his eyes as if to rid them of web and letting himself seem to sink into the luxury of her presence.

"Bird, I'm going to work for you. And I'm going to set you up right too. I'm not broke, honey. I've had my ups and downs and you're right, I'm going to settle down. Somehow—I—I've been a fellow who has never been much for getting in with the right crowd. That's all has been wrong with me, Bird. That and getting somebody who cared if—if school kept for me or not."

"I know, Boy! That's what I told them at home tonight while the fur was flying. You've had your name linked with the wrong crowd. That can throw a shadow over any name. You're just one of those sweet boobs without any gumption to fight back. Well, I've got the gumption. I'd like to see any of that gang now! I love you for not having any gumption, Boy. It makes you sweet. It's what makes me want to take care of you and see that you get a new start. But just the same I've got it. Gumption. And I'm going to use it for you."

"And you've got everything else, Bird—that is good. If only I had some way of showing you that no matter what I am, you—where you are concerned, Bird, I'm there!"

"Boy, what will you give me if I tell you something? Something sweet about how happy you and me are going to be."

"Give you? Why, Bird—" said Slupsky with a sudden burn of flame along his eyes and his thumb and forefinger fiddling in his waistcoat pocket. "What'll I give you? Nothing I can give you is enough."

"I didn't mean it really—"

"But here. I hadn't meant to give it to you here—now—but—my girl is going to have it like the best of them. That's what I'll give you. There!"

"Why—what! Why, Boy! It's a square diamond. Darling, it's the slickest thing I ever saw. I could fool Morris with it. You running your blessed legs off to dig up a ring for me! Why, honest, Boy, if I didn't know I'd think it was real. It's the finest phony I ever saw. And say, how did you know I like them square! If this isn't the finest phony I ever saw!"

"Why, Bird! Birdie! You don't think I'd bring you a phony wedding present after you've gone and turned life into heaven for me! That's real, Bird. That's a genuine six carat. Six-and-an-eighth, and I wish it was seven."

"You—Boy—that piece of looking-glass—real—can't be—"

"It's real, Bird. Finest money could buy and I only wish it was finer."

"I don't believe it," cried Mrs. Slupsky, and got up and executed a pirouette. A dizzying one that shook the dishes in the basket. "My boy claps a six carat one on my finger just like that! Is that a real one in your scarf pin, honey? I always thought it was phony. I—I don't care, Boy. I like them and I'm not ashamed who knows it. I like 'em big and I like 'em white and I like 'em plenty. And, oh Boy, but I like them square!"

"And oh, Bird, how I like you happy!"

"What they set you back for this? Boy—you—you—what did this cost?" cried Birdie and wheeled him about toward her suddenly so that the forelock of light tan hair fell down over his eyes. "This ring cost a fortune. Thousands. Where did you get the money, Boy, to pay for this ring?"

For answer Slupsky kissed her, his lips level with hers, but seeming none the less to tiptoe.

"You've got it, darling, haven't you? You should worry how your hubby had to rustle around to do the paying."

"But I—do, Boy. I do."

"Take it while the going is good, girl. There's going to be no more in chunks when hubby settles down."

"Boy! Isadore! You! I know you, Boy. And when I know, I know! If they were to try and frame you for pulling wings off of butterflies and the arms off of babies, I'd know you for the come-clean sweet kid you are! But—but this ring—I'd never ask it out like this—but for the ring. Boy—there's nothing to this frame-up talk that you're under suspicion on all this crook stuff about the bonds? I wouldn't ask it except—the ring! Your hands are clean of—of any of it, I know that. But this ring. This ring cost thousands. Where did you get the money, Boy? Answer me!"

"For the love of God," said Slupsky, with something as canine as a cringe and a snarl to him, "that's a fine question to put up to me on what is practically our wedding night!"

"Oh Isadore!" said Birdie and folded him to her and kissed into his hair and his eyes. "I'm terrible. I am. The thought—just got me all of a sudden by the neck. By the heart. Seeing this ring. What if some of that bond money stuck to my boy—by mistake? Boy—the thought—I'm ashamed—kiss me, Isadore—I'm ashamed—"

"I'm going straight, Bird, from now on, so help me. With you. So help me, Bird, or I want to drop dead right here."

"What do you mean, Boy? From now on? You—Boy—wedding night or no wedding night. Look at me. Where did you get the money to buy this ring?"

"For heaven's sake, don't talk so loud!"

"Where? Isadore! Stop looking at me like that! I—you! All this time, whenever I took up for you—and you never denied it—I took you at your word—only now—as I remember it—there wasn't any word—it was all silence with me putting in the words. What did you mean just now, Isadore, by from now on? Where did you get this ring? Why—are you standing there looking at me like—like that? I can't stand it—Boy—"

"Why, you—Birdie—if a man cannot tell his own wife—"

"Then you—Isadore, you—"

"What has been is, Birdie. The point is, though, now I'm through. The man is not fit to live who couldn't come through clean for a woman like you. If I get out of this, Birdie, and I'm as good as out—may God strike me dead if I'm not through, Birdie—Bird—"

"Isadore," said Birdie and sat down on the bulge of sofa with her hand in a rather dreadful loose sort of drooling fashion along her face, "you mean all that talk in the newspapers—the mention of your name with the rest—that I couldn't even bring myself to mention to you, much less to—to—accuse—you mean you—Isadore, you, you aren't a—a—"

"Why, Birdie, you never thought, even though we never come right out and talked about it—you never thought I was worth so much as your little finger—"

"But—"

"I'm one of those fellows, Bird, easy-going, easy-make, easy-spend, that will follow the ways of whatever crowd he's caught up with. You know about me, Bird. I was born, it seems to me, and raised, it seems to me, on the streets. I'm what I am, because I guess, honey, I never had anyone cared enough. Why—why, Bird—I thought you knew what kind of a fellow I was. Told you often enough I wasn't fit to lay down and let you walk over me— much less marry you—but when you—you seemed to fall for me—I know I'm not fit to clean your shoes. Bird, I—"

"Then—this ring. Isadore—you're *wanted!* you're not just under suspicion on account of the company you keep. Isadore, you were in on that bond swipe! You're a thief!"

"Birdie—"

"Don't come near me! Don't touch me! I—let me think. I—I must be crazy. There's something going around—crazy, I tell you, in my head. The way I fought them. Ma. Pa. Morris. From the day I clapped eyes on you— from everything you said—your ways—I was so sure you were only the kind of a good schnookle kid was always getting himself framed. I was so sure. It made me want to take care of you. And now you—you're a thief! I'm mar- ried to a thief and this is my wedding celebration."

There was a tearing noise in Birdie's voice and a blanched foreboding look of hysteria smeared into the pallor of her face that made her eyes seem stretched and full of the anguish of one about to scream or remain a little terribly silent.

"Birdie, if I had known you—you—didn't know—I'd have cut off my right hand first."

"I don't believe it, this thing! You're not a thief. You didn't bring me a ring on our marriage night bought with stolen money. You didn't, Boy. Tell me you didn't."

It was no use. Isadore on his knees there beside her, and his lower jaw wagging up and down frantically for words that would not come and Birdie with her stretched imploring eyes looking at the mute and wagging jaw, and then Birdie, who was not given to the capacity for remaining a little terribly silent, began to sob. Great splashes of guttural guttering noises drawn up from the innards of her.

"Go away! I hate you. I'm not much. Never claimed to be. But I'm honest. I never did a crooked thing in my life. I would have banked my soul on you. Being my kind. A good schnookle that just naturally always got the short end of it, things—"

"Bird—"

"That's why—I've always been that way—when I met you—a sweet kid needing somebody. Why, if you'd been a sick kitten or a lame duck I—I would have loved you. I fell for you because you were a sweet boy and I lifted out my heart and gave it to you, even while the papers were full of the bond scandal, and I didn't care because I didn't believe it. And because I trusted you not to deceive me and now—the second night—what happens? I find myself married to a thief!"

"Birdie—oh—"

"A common ordinary thief. Me, that hates lying and deceit and pretense and low-down-ness with my very gizzard. Married to a thief! Don't you come near me—"

"Oh, oh—Bird!" said Isadore in a whisper and sat back very quietly on his heels and with the spaces between his features seeming to widen into moors. "Don't say that, Bird!"

"I do say it! I put you before my own flesh and blood. I'm going to take care of my boy, I kept saying, and get him on the right track, and show the world how a boy with the right stuff in him can't be kept down. Some day my folks will thank me, I kept saying to myself. My boy is of the stuff that will be good to my folks. It'll hurt them in the beginning, but in the end they'll thank me for bringing a sweet and gentle boy into the family. We'll show them some day, I kept saying. And now—and now—I wish I'd have died before I ever set eyes on you. I wish I had!"

"Birdie, don't say that—you're killing me—let me ex—"

"I will say it. I don't want to hear nothing out of you. I only know I never want to see you again. Something in me has busted. Busted flat. I wish I was dead."

And with that, as her stark face, fore-shortened from him, went back against the crazy walnut mill-work back of the couch, Isadore with the moan of a dog went forward with his face in his hands until they touched the floor. It might have been a faint because he remained there so long motionless, his pinch-back coat riding up over his enormously hunched back.

And Birdie, whose tears were big and round and wet and none too beautiful, sat there in her sprawl on the couch, her legs flung so that her heels dug into the floor and her toes pointed up and that stretched stark look in her eyes. It was curious to see them slowly lower toward the hump of Isadore, see them rest there. Fill. Scald. Overflow. Like dried pools with cracked clay bottoms that suddenly, miraculously, were filling.

Birdie flowing back into herself, warmly.

"Isadore," cried Mrs. Slupsky, stooping over to catch him by a handful of coat. "You get up! Isadore—Boy—you're not fainting or something? Wake up. Get up. Look, Boy. Look, Isadore. Look at me. Look at Birdie. Papa love mama? Huh—uh—uh stop that crying—you hear me! Mama'll spank—"

"Birdie."

"I knew you were needing me, Boy, but I never knew how much. You thought marriage would soften the law in case it should get you, didn't you?"

"No, Birdie, no. I never thought. I just felt. My love for you."

"You thought anyways, well, with marriage you had nothing to lose. Well, Boy, you didn't, only it's not going to protect you. You're going to pay. You hear. You've been a crook, Isadore, and you're going to pay, marriage or no marriage. You're going to pay up before we can come clean and start over."

"But—"

"Yes, I'm going to stick. And you knew I would! I'm going to stick. And fight back with you. You'll go up for a year or two, I guess, and I'm not going to lie for you to save you from paying up. Boy, you're going up. And I'm going too. And live next door to your little gray house on the hill. I never knew, Boy, my poor Boy, my darling Boy, how much you did need me. You've been framed all right, honey. But we're going to stage the greatest comeback this town ever saw. Me and you, Boy. Together."

"I could lay down my life for you this minute, Bird, and thank God for the chance, that's how I'm going to make good for you. I don't care how you manage it—how you punish me—just so—just so you—don't quit on me, Bird. That—would finish me. Don't quit on me, Bird."

"Don't, Boy," said Birdie with her hand clapped over his mouth and her cheek against that. "Don't. Don't. Don't be so meek to me. I can't stand your ever being meek to me. Just sweet. Not meek. I failed you a minute ago, Boy—"

"No, Bird, no."

"It was the shock did it. But I'll never stop making it up to you for that. You've got to go through with your punishment. I won't help to save you from that. But I'll never stop standing by, Boy."

"Nothing else matters then, Bird. Nothing—else—"

For the first time in a life consistently lacking in it, a certain dignity had come to old man Fish. It had come to him in what was to be his last illness.

He had passed out in such eclipse from the grotesque little jumping-jack man of the busy little beard of waggle due to haggle, into the little old Havana-scented figure of quiescent goatee, that had used to drowse the hours in the brace of sunny windows.

From his bed of final reckoning, Italian late seventeenth century, linen-fold design, Tewkington-Barr sale, there was something unexpectedly long in the lay of him under the coverings, sedate to the ridge of him; and the short pointy beard had a lay to it that was portentous. Even a little magnificent. Julius Goldfish was going grandly home.

It was a sedative sick-room of lowered shade, lowered lamp and noiseless placing of objects by a nurse who creaked slightly of starch.

It was a sedative sick-room, except for the thumping, stricken figure of Mrs. Fish in her chair beside the bed. Even in her silence the beating throat above the ceramic brooch of her husband seemed to make a throbbing note like the bleat of a dove. A hurt dove. With her poor little terrified eyes and the constant heaving of her small puffy bosom and her crouching into the Savonarola chair as if it were an eave, that was Mrs. Fish for you. A hurt dove.

"Papa, papa, darlink. Won't you please talk to me? To one of us? It's mama. Julius, it's your 'tilda. Papa, please—it's mama."

The hours of it. That word "papa." Whole hordes of the puffy little noun crowding up the room like so many of those softy pods that pop when you press them on the vine.

"Papa. Papa. Papa."

The nurse at her endless tiptoeing and noiseless placing of the objects. The endless days. The endless nights. The endless rigmarole of the sick-room.

"Papa, darlink. Papa, won't you even say hello to Morris? Look, he's brought you a silk-lined dressing-gown you should wear it always on the wrong side, when you get up. Papa, look! Here is Reenie. She's brought you some calves-foot jelly. Papa, here's Irma and the babies. Papa, papa, don't you got no more interest in any of us? Morris, how long these doctors sit there on their consultation! You don't think, son, papa has got something maybe more serious as we know about?"

"No, mother. Once we get his blood pressure down, I hope we'll have him up in no time."

"Reenie, ain't it terrible? Papa don't take no interest in us. It don't seem like papa he should lie there so—so tired of us all."

"Poor darling," said Mrs. Silk, who rouged her lips and whitened her cheeks and who also dripped finger nails like ruby cabochons and attended with her sister-in-law Irma Fish, fashionable Friday morning musicales, in tan duveteen, blue fox, trotteur hat with a brim that was kindly to profile, and impeccable curve of bobbed hair. "Poor darling. We'll know more after the doctors have consulted. I don't agree with Morris. It seems to me father's anemic. Low blood pressure or something like that."

"O God!" said Mrs. Fish and sat rocking herself in the straight-backed Savonarola. "Maybe it's a worse sickness than any of us realize. It's a week now since papa ain't spoke ten words to any of us. Just turned his back like it was on life. Why don't they hurry up from that room? Morris, you don't think papa's got anything—bad?"

"Listen, dear, that is why we have called in the best doctors that money can buy to determine for us. I doubt if there is anything more serious than just a general let-down with father."

"Let-down is right. It ain't natural such a busy man like papa should all of a sudden have been let down from business."

"I've been telling father for years he eats too much rich food," said Mrs. Silk.

"Yes, take away yet what little pleasure papa has got left. It's better, Reenie, papa should have a little pressure from his blood than have to put up with such empty looking clear soups like you send him and such jelly from calves' feet. Papa likes something what has got a stick to it to his ribs, like my lentil soup or a little spetzel with browned crumbs."

"Glue with browned crumbs you mean, mother. That's what coarse rich foods like that amount to."

"One thing I always must say for your sister Birdie, Reenie. Birdie with all her faults had so much sympathy for what papa liked. You think it was ever too much for her on his birthday to take herself down by Hester Street market for blintzes for him—you—"

"Now, mother . . ."

"If you muzzle me for it, I can mention my own child's name when her papa is sick. I don't say it ain't a disgrace to us. God knows I have suffered my share with the trouble she has brought on us, but when her papa is so sick—

suppose something should happen—with Birdie up there in Auburn living next door to the prison. Suppose without our letting her know it, something should happen to papa! I think we should send for Birdie!"

"That's fine sick-room psychology, mother. To confront a sick man with some one who will only call up a dreadful situation before him. Here come the doctors. Now, mother dear, we must all be brave."

It was a brief telling. Old man Fish was dying. Pernicious anemia was the professional saying of it. The rivers of his blood were running white. It was as if it was part of the fading out of old man Fish. The paling of the blood.

And with her eyes like two scars in her head and her lips scabs because her mouth and throat had gone dry, an old woman turned back to the bed and cried in dreadful sounds.

"Papa. Papa. Papa. My darlink. It's mama. Can't you wake up, papa, a minute? Morris is here and he wants maybe when you get well you should set yourself up in such a little furniture business again, only farther uptown. Morris—son—am I right?"

"Yes, mother. Father, I've had it in my mind for some time now. A little plan so the time won't hang quite so heavy, father. Won't you try to rouse yourself?"

"Papa, please! Morris is sorry. And Reenie. Look at Reenie. She wants you should get well and one night go over to her house for supper for the kind you like. No more such fanciness like shirt-fronts—Reenie wants you should come like it's comfortable for you. Not, Reenie?"

"Father. Father dear. Try, dear, and rouse yourself enough to look at us. I want to tell you about a little party, father, I'm planning for just us. Just you and mother, and the children aren't going to be put to bed before you arrive and mother is coming over and drive my cook out of the kitchen and prepare every single dish for you herself and there won't be a butler to serve, only mother—and—and me, and you can kiss the children all you want, father, no matter what their old *bonne* says, and father—father, can't you rouse yourself to look at us—all of us here—dear—"

And then old man Fish did open an eye. An old eye. A tired eye. A dreary eye, and lusterless.

"I want my Birdie," he said and a tear squeezed out of the crinkle that was a lid.

"Oh, my God, papa! You want your Birdie. Of course your Birdie. Right away, darlink, we will get Birdie. Morris—right away—where can we get Birdie?"

"Why, I—I don't know where exactly she's living. Somewhere in Auburn. I—"

"Then call up the prison. Right away quick. Long distance. You hear me?

Right away quick. Your papa wants Birdie. It's her place she should be home.
It ain't for two and a half weeks more he gets free. She is still there in
Auburn. Call up the jail . . ."

"Mother, not so loud."

"You hear me? Right away quick. Long distance. It is no time now you
should have time to think anything except your papa wants his Birdie. Yes,
papa—yes, darlink—Birdie is coming!"

At three o'clock that afternoon, by a miracle she was never quite clear
enough about to explain, that of accomplishing a five-hour journey in four,
Birdie, who must have been crying in splotches all over her face in the train,
just as Birdie would do it, burst into the room of the Heppelwhite that she
had not entered since the twelvemonth before when she had flounced herself out of it.

A paler Birdie and even a trifle wan Birdie, but in the same black satin
dress that climbed so and clung so about her legs. A breathless, gargly Birdie
who sobbed as she entered.

"Mama—mama—how is he? Don't tell me he—he—"

"No, no, Birdie. No, no, darlink—papa's awful sick but—but not—that—"

"Thank God!" said Birdie and began to cry in wet splashes. "I've been so
afraid. What if I hadn't got here—in time—to see him! My papa. My poor
little papa. Let me see him. Morris—Reenie—ain't it terrible? Our papa. He
wants to see me. Oh—he should ask to see me and I wasn't right here on the
spot when he wanted it!"

"Sh-h-h, Birdie. You must compose yourself before you go in. We dare not
excite him."

"Of course, Morris. I'll try. Give me your handkerchief. I wouldn't cry
before him—I wouldn't cry before him if it bursts my heart in two not to.
Give me some powder, Reenie. That's only the hem of my skirt dragging. I
had to jump off a platform for a going train. Cut it off with your penknife,
Morrie. Mama, tell me what did papa say when he asked for me? That's
nothing but a little bruise where I landed on that train. It'll stop bleeding. I
kept thinking on the train, mama, and it nearly killed me—you—you
remember that time, mama—he—papa—that time Morrie and me had the
chicken-pox and—and he—papa was so full of rheumatism that winter
and—he walked that night to—to get us lollypops six blocks in the rain for
the red ones we liked—and caught the lumbago so terrible—"

"Birdie—don't. I can't stand it. I can't stand it you should go back to those
days when papa was himself—"

"I didn't mean to. I'm ready now, mama, to—to go in. Stop crying now,
Reenie and Morrie. I'm going in now to papa. I want him to see us all smil-

ing. Now all of you!"

You never saw the like of the Birdie that entered that sick-room then. There was a swagger to that Birdie. Swagger and an old way she had of smiling with one eye screwed and an old funniness of hers of coming into the house with her neck and her knees doing an in-and-out turtle's motion.

"Hello, pops!" said Birdie and stood over the bed grinning down, kissing down, her voice at its huskiest and rustiest. "It's me, pops. Bird. How's every little thing? How are you feeling, pops? Rotten?"

Old man Fish opened his eyes then. "Birdie," he said and began to cry; not with tears; just with the motion his throat made; and he tried to fumble to get his hand out from the bed coverings and to feel for hers.

"Birdie. *Unbeshrien!* Baby-sha!"

"Look at him, mama. I thought you told me he wasn't feeling so well. Look at his color. If he looked any better, I'll bet he couldn't stand it. Papa, how do you get that way? You should have the nerve to lay there and say you're sick. In that Eyetalian bedstead I'll bet he feels like Julius Cæsar instead of Julius Goldfish."

"Ach, Birdie, you can laugh. I'm a sick man, Birdie. I got in my arms and my legs such a bearing-down pains, I don't wish it to a dog he should have them."

"Father, that's just weakness."

"Hush, Morris, don't you see papa wants to talk only with Birdie?"

Not once did old man Fish waver his glance from Birdie.

"I'm an old man, Birdie. They let me get into an old man before my time, from not having enough in my life to make it worth while I should want to live on. I got good children, Birdie, but I been lonesome for my business— Birdie—for you—"

"Say, papa, don't I know? Just you wait! I've got plans up my sleeve."

"I got pains, Birdie, when I so much as try even to lift my little finger."

"Say, papa, who should I meet on the street just now. You'll never guess. I give you three!"

"How should a sick man on his back know?"

"Shammas Gerstle! Shammas Gerstle and his Mannie. You remember the big-eared second boy—that stuttered?"

"Birdie, papa is too sick for such nonsense. Anyways, Shammas Gerstle died already two months ago."

"You don't say so, you met Shammas Gerstle!" said old man Fish, never wavering in his hazy effort to concentrate. "Shammas Gerstle. It's five years since I laid eyes on him—is he still in the Ludlow Street *Schule*?"

"I—papa, I—"

"Shammas Gerstle. He was a good friend I had to turn to, Birdie, while my family was growing up. He coached Morris for his *Bar Mitzvah*. It ain't nice how we got away from our old friends like the Shammas."

"You ought to see, papa, Mannie's ears. You remember how they used to wag. Well, now they flag trains. And, papa, I was thinking yesterday of something that made me laugh. Honest, I had to laugh right out loud. Remember old lady Gerstle, every time she smelt from next door we were having maybe a sauerkraut and boiled beef supper, like mama used to make, right away she used to send over Mannie who loved it so much, to waggle his ears for us children."

"Sauerkraut with boiled beef! I ain't had it in my mouth since—"

"You want some, Julius? It's only that we got restrictions in an apartment like this from noisy cooking that smells that we haven't had it. Right away when you get well and can eat again, we—"

The unswerving gaze of old man Fish. "So you talked with the Shammas, Birdie?"

"And, papa, I was thinking yesterday—just thinking back over things the way you do—remember—remember how one night when Reenie got her leg stuck in the fire-escape, you were so mad that while we had to send for the hook-and-ladder company to get her out, and were waiting, you started to spank her right there while she was caught in the rung and mama got mad and stood behind spanking you and by the time the hook-and-ladder came all Delancey was standing in the courtyard watching the Goldfishes spank each other."

It was as if the old lips of her father bent upwards then like a bit of rusty barrel hoop. And believe it or not, but old man Fish's beard was waggling, waggling so that the thin ridge of him under the covers shook and the tears, the tears of his laughter ran out of the corners of his eyes; and when between waggles old man Fish could find voice, the talk it danced on something like this:

"And remember, Birdie . . ."

"Do I! And remember, pops . . . when we moved up-town and mama cried so when we sold her old brass bed to old pirate Glauber . . ."

"Will you ever forget, Birdie, how Weintraub every *shabboth*—used to . . ."

"Don't make me laugh so, papa . . . and say, pop, will you ever forget the night you were all down on the front stoop to see me pass the house in my pink tissue paper dress, leading the East Side Girls' Papoose Club parade, and Meyer Weintraub turned the water plug on me and . . ."

And so on and so on to the waggling of old man Fish's beard and heaving laughter of him under the coverlets.

There never was so curious a death scene. It was a laughing death scene. Old man Fish laughing himself to death, surrounded by family laughing with him their tears of hysteria.

Literally, it can be said that when the old man finally breathed out he did it on a convulsion. Of merriment.

Not the heartsick laughter of those about him, but the deep inner merriment of one who, laughing last, laughed best.

The odor of funeral still lay. A warmish sweetishness with a humidity to it. A harp-shaped floral piece of roses and calla-lilies had somehow remained back and stood like an easel on the piano.

Poor Mrs. Fish. Dried out. Not a sniffle left. Lax in a chair there with her mouth and her eyes and her hands dry and open.

"Mother, won't you lie down? Morris, make your mother try to rest."

"Come, mother, Irma is right. You need sleep, dear."

"I got no rest—no more, children—with papa—gone."

"Mother dear, listen. Why don't you come right away now with Morris and me? Home. You don't ever need to come back to this apartment and its memories. Our car is at the door. Morris and I want you to come to us. Our home is yours."

"I can't realize it, children. Your papa gone—"

"Now, mother, don't sit brooding. Irma and Morris are right. You are going out of this apartment today for good. We aren't going to quarrel over who shall have you, mother. But my car is at the door too, and you don't need Irving and me to tell you that the best room our home has to offer is yours. Mother dear, you mustn't sit looking like that. So stricken. Isn't it something, dear, to have children with you?"

"My children. What would I do without my children? My boy. My Reenie. My Birdie. Where is Birdie? Birdie—come out from fooling in the back of the house. Bird-ie!"

"Yes, ma."

There entered Birdie then, with the red rims to her eyes making her look actually spectacled, and lugging a patent leather suitcase and a great clumsy something in newspaper under her arm and an old Paisley shawl over her elbow and her hat on the back of her head.

"Birdie, where are you going?"

"Home, ma."

"Home?" from Maurice Fish.

Mrs. Slupsky cocked the glance of surprise at her brother.

"Darlink, since when this interest in my movements? It is the first direct question I've been honored with. Sorry I haven't any calling cards with me. Try to remember the address. We're renewing the lease on the old family mansion, Brother Goldfish. Four-fifty-nine South Simpson Street, the Bronx!

Isadore, Brother Goldfish, has been away on an extended tour and is expected home this day week. He has learned during his extended sojourn of twelve months in Auburn-not-on-Hudson, the gentle art of automobile engineering and expects to enter his new profession shortly after his return!"

"You mean—"

"I mean," said Mrs. Slupsky, her words suddenly rapid-fire buckshot, "that Isadore is coming home with a trade and I have already landed him a job. We are asking nothing of anybody. You can take us or leave us. My year of work-ing in an Auburn tea room, waitressing—yes, Irma, don't get seasick—and living two blocks from the prison, has taught me this much. About the lone-somest road any man can travel is the road back. The road back from down and out. Well, me and Izzy have traveled it. And we're back, all right. No favors asked."

"Birdie—"

"Only remember if any member of this family is coming up to the South Simpson Street family mansion to call on mama, I want it understood that my husband is a member of that household as much as any of us, and I won't have him humiliated! Et cetera. Noblesse oblige; toot sweet. Or which every one of them means, put that in your pipe and smoke it! Come on, ma!"

"Why—what do you mean by—by come on, ma? Come on, ma, where?"

"Where? Why, Reenie darlink, to the aforementioned old family mansion. I'm going to give ma what we call the standing-room. It's only big enough for two things. You got to stand or lay. By the time Mr. Slupsky gets home next week, that little two by four is going to be transformed into the original cretonne and wicker-rocker bird nest of the back of the magazines. I—"

"Mother is coming to us. She is going to divide her time between Morris and me."

"You don't tell me so!" said Mrs. Slupsky. "You mean it's a choosing party? Mama, maybe I should have talked things over with you first."

"Maybe you should," said Mrs. Silk dryly. "Get your hat, mother dear. The car is at the door. Birdie can come down to the house sometime and then we will talk things over."

"Go get your hat, mother dear, nothing! Come get your shawl, mother dear, the subway is running. I've your old Paisley here over my arm for you. Hats make headaches on old ladies who weren't used to them from home. Don't bother about anything, mama. I'll come back here and get your things later."

"Mother, you—"

"After all," said Mrs. Maurice Fish, with the coolest and the clearest little tinkle to her words, "mother is entitled to make her choice, dears."

"You don't mind, do you, mama, to carry that newspaper package? It's not heavy. It's that nicked Della Robby placque Morrie gave me once from some wop sale. I found a place for it over a stove-pipe hole."

"Morrie—Reenie—my children—if you don't care—I—been so long a goldfish out of water, I—children—please?"

"That's all you got to carry, ma, the placque—and say, ma, could you tuck this up under your shawl? It's your hot-water bottle, that old red one you like for your sciatica. I can lug these all right. We could take a Bronx express up, but the local is better because I want to stop at Blatz's Fish Market and get a miltz so you can *gedaemfte* it for supper."

The face of old woman Goldfish. It came out from the wimple of her shawl as vivid as a moon. The atavistic look of a woman backed by whole centuries of women who have known how to tear the entrails from fish.

"Reenie and Morris—my children—you'll come often to see us—me—Birdie and Isadore—"

The clatter of them lugging out through the hallway. Birdie and her mother. Going home.

Song of Life

First Published: *Cosmopolitan*, September 1926
Reprinted: *Song of Life*, A.A. Knopf, 1927

In Doyer the smell of summer is the smell of Ohio sun on cowpatch and cornstalk dry enough to crackle when you plunge through. Hot clover. Hot rank weed. Stagnant ponds stewing under slime. Sweetish rank of cattle seated on folded knees in scraps of shade. The smell of long baking days that exude to the pull of heat.

There were too few souls in the township to invade the sun-and-earth stench of valley with the odours of humanity.

The little clutter of houses scarcely more than blistered the flow of meadow and farm and grazing land.

The smell of Doyer in summer was the smell of hot uninterrupted process of fructification and decay.

Sometimes the taint of gasoline followed the trail of a motor truck or threshing machine, but Doyer was five miles behind the state road and tucked into a fold of farming land as unostensibly as a penny into a little girl's pocket.

One motionless August morning a new smell lay on that somnolence. A sweet vertiginous one, as arresting to Doyer as the yell of a fire siren. The faint sickish sucking reek of ether.

In the woodshed behind the house, which was referred to as the hotel only on those semi-frequent occasions when it put up a lodger, Ida Hassebrock, with a white cloth tied over the lower half of her face, was chloroforming a sheep dog that had been born in that same barn sixteen years ago to the day.

Outside and down the rutted wagon road that wound toward a still more insular township called Deborah, Red Hassebrock, in the speck of shade thrown by a plane-tree, was leaning up against the bole of it with his face looking twisted and sick.

A great fellow, with eye- and mouth-slits cut upward, and loose-looking red hair, and more red hair that grew darkly on his white chest where the army shirt fell open.

A six-foot, two-hundred-pound fellow with not an inch or an ounce of overweight, white and faint there against the tree-trunk as the creeping sweetness came closer. And two hundred yards away in the hot, black mouth of the woodshed, his wife Ida, with a white towel across her mouth, held another to the muzzle of the dog, whose eyes, as she ceased to struggle, rolled backward and upward at her like two wounds that she could feel against the flesh of her breast.

All this should have been done the day, six years ago, that Lonnie awoke one morning with her hind legs two sticks of paralysis.

Ida had known that all along and had kept trying to muster the courage, only Red invariably turned that sick-looking white if you as much as mentioned it, and Missy, with her arms about Lonnie's shaggy neck as she lay helpless on her pallet behind the range, sobbed into the tangled old wool. And so one day marched into the next, until one morning the pan of warm food which Ida prepared daily for the dog would not go down.

Lonnie could no longer swallow.

It had to be done then. At once. The sooner the better. While Missy was still over at Katy's, and Red given time to get out of hearing and sight.

It was more terrible even than she had dreaded. The cling of those eyes to her, as, slipping away, Lonnie wanted to stay. The warm old tongue, licking out at her hand from under the cloth. If only she wouldn't do that. Licking her as she crushed her softly out of life with the towel to her nostrils. If only—if only she wouldn't do that! Lick and look up at her with those dying eyes that wanted to drag themselves back from the brink. . . .

It wasn't fair to have made her do it. Why should Red be the one to be spared, and Missy, too, the horror of putting old Lonnie out of her misery?

There was a warm lump in her lap and against her heart. Lonnie's head pressing against the sobbing wall of Ida as she held the cloth closer. Sweetish, sickish, black heat of that shed, and Lonnie's eyes that kept scrambling back from the brink to fawn over her face.

Lonnie was not afraid. In the six years of her almost total paralysis Ida had never failed her. Lonnie was not afraid. That was the heart-breaking part of it. The old eyes, as they felt themselves slipping, scrambled back to her face.

For a long time, while this strange thing kept happening and the sweetishness thickened, Lonnie was not afraid.

And then, suddenly, when her breath kept wanting to go one way and was all pouring out when she wanted to breathe in, fear smote the heart of Lonnie. Lonnie wanted back. Lonnie was going where she did not want to go. Lonnie wanted Ida. Lonnie began to struggle, to beat back, to whine back, in long terrified moans, that she had not the breath for. Moans that twenty yards down the road caused Red to turn his face and sob out loud against the tree-trunk.

Lonnie wanted back. Lonnie, with her great old shaggy body already half slipping in dead weight from Ida's lap to the black dirt floor of the shed, was fighting back with her eyes that would not leave Ida.

There was not a stitch on the great fleshy body of the woman that was not wringing wet with the sweat of this agony. Lonnie who trusted her was slipping off. Lonnie was being tricked into death, and Lonnie did not want to die. Lonnie wanted back! Lonnie who trusted her was licking her hand from under the death-fume. Suddenly, with a cry, Ida flung the cloth away from Lonnie's muzzle.

"Lonnie—come back!"

The eyes of Lonnie crawling over Ida. They wanted to come back. They were desperate to come back.

"Lonnie—you come back—"

The answer was a thump of a dead body and Ida fleeing from the shed with the crook of her arm up over her eyes as if someone was pursuing her.

The only street in Doyer was one block long. General Store. Gasoline station. Post Office. Hassebrock's.

Farmlands billowed all round it, with occasional houses and barns riding the acres like frail crafts at sea.

Hassebrock's stood on the corner. A great leaky piano-box of a house that had cost Red and Ida three hundred dollars, five acres and all, the day that they were married, eighteen years before.

The three hundred dollars had been Ida's, saved from fourteen years of hired-girl service to a farmer family named Idelweiss, three miles out of Doyer.

It was a gaunt house of eighteen rooms, seven unfinished and shut off. Winter hay was stored away in three of them, and in a fourth, the one nearest the living quarters, Missy or Ida was forever fostering a brood of new chicks or a sick ewe, and once, in Lonnie's palmy days, a litter of nine of her pups that had all died the first week in spite of ministerings of blankets and straw pallets.

It was a gaunt house except for the flock of ground-floor rooms that the Hassebrocks and the occasional lodger inhabited.

Ida had breathed some semblance of life into those, especially the kitchen, which had an enormous coal range at one end that roared all day of a plentifully stoked fire and was banked at night so that the embers shone through the cracks like grins.

There was a monster of a parlour too, with a stone kitten for door-prop, over which you stumbled on entering, and three red velvet chairs cram-full of springs and festooned with ball fringe that swept the floor, and calendars from the tobacco factory where Ida helped out in the busy season, hanging over almost every piece of furniture. A room that, all winter long, boasted the most superb window-panes. Brilliant, frost encrusted ones, etched in mountains, cañons, and cascades that leapt in glory.

The bedroom that Ida and Red shared was large enough to have an echo. A great iron bed in its centre, well away from the heat or the cold of the walls, sagged a little crazily from the heft of heavy bodies. There seemed no way to make this room look furnished. It had the makeshift appearance of a room over a barn, or in a box-car. Behind the washstand, a yellow oak horror of one, illustrated pages from motion-picture magazines were tacked on the wall against Red's splashings.

Ida put up new ones occasionally. She liked the gay faces of the cinema girls and imitated their postures sometimes as she dressed in the dawn, attiring her great hulk of figure in the kind of cotton, routine-coloured fabrics that lay in bolts along the shelves of general stores.

Not that all of Ida's clothes were drab in colour. Of a Saturday night, for instance, attired for barbecue, or a dance in the Lodge room up over the Post Office, or a Hot Corn Fest when the ears were ripest, or even for the weekly Motion Picture, or walk past the Post Office of an evening, Ida could blossom forth along with the best of them. And in daring schemes too, without fear of violent contrast, because Ida was all straw-coloured. Her hair, her sort of topaz-coloured eyes, and even the tinge of her flesh as relentlessly she grew stouter, one after another of the eighteen years after her marriage.

But Ida knew the delights of colour every bit as much as Missy, or the slim slabs of girls about the village. The girls who worked in the tobacco factory. The girls from the farms. The styles leaked in by way of the weekly motion picture, the illustrated magazines, the radio.

Missy, at seventeen, rolled her stockings, coarse ones of some sort of synthetic silk that glistened like a lead nickel. Missy's hair was bobbed, the boyish way, if you please, and in the cheap leather hand-bag that dangled from her wrist were such urban addenda as powder-compact in a round gilt box with mirror inset and a little cylindrical rouge-stick that dyed and belied the far lovelier tint of Missy's own lips.

Ida sometimes daubed on a bit of Missy's lipstick as they sauntered out together of a summer evening.

"The Big and the Little of it," guffawed the hardy perennial loiterers astride the empty cider-barrels in front of Grody's General Store.

Well, they were. Ida in her red cotton voile and white canvas shoes, billowing along like some great animated tent with a commotion going on inside it, and Missy dancing beside her as spry as one of those long lean iridescent dragonflies that skim along the surface of water without rippling it.

And yet she had rippled her way into the Hassebrock household. When she was only eleven, one lean winter when Red's lumbago made outdoor work as odd-job man on this and that farm a hardship, and Ida had gone to work in the tobacco factory, they had hired her from a family of squatters living in an abandoned shack near the state road.

There was old Katie, Red's aunt, who had reared him, to be cared for. She lived in a shanty, cat-a-corner from the rear of the Hassebrock's. Red had been born in there. At eighty, Katie Riggs was for all the world like an old wolf with a cap tied under her chin. Ida made these caps and fluted the ruffles with the tip end of her iron.

Much of Missy's task, at eleven, had been to tend the old woman, who was chair-ridden of an almost total paralysis, and then tear over to the big house to give Red his noonday dinner and brew the old woman's tea when Ida was at the tobacco factory.

Sometimes there was a lodger. A radio salesman. A brush-and-broom vendor. A crayon-photograph artist. Then Missy did for him too. Spry, nervous, quick, and pretty, in a flash-of-the-pan sort of way. The prettiness of her mother before her, who at fourteen had been a sprite too and at twenty had a sway back and gums almost as toothless as those of her babies.

Missy had seen the last of that mother, who, with fourteen other offspring, had little enough time to miss her, except to come scratching around from time to time for the gleanings from Missy's little wages.

In every way, except legally, the Hassebrocks had adopted Missy. They would have done it that way, but for the hold it would have released on Missy's wages. The squatters were not for that.

It did not really matter, though. Virtually, Missy was the Hassebrock's own. Ida sent her to township school, sewed for her, schemed for her, and Red never came home of an evening without stopping by Katy's to tweak at the old woman's wolf-shaped ear and then carry Missy across to the big house for supper by the outlandish device of holding her dangling by the neck of her dress like a kitten, his arm held out in a firm horizontal bar.

Red was so big. Missy could beat at him with all the strength in her small fists and Red laugh down and fleck her off like so much dust.

"Red, quit teasin' that there child," was a phrase that fell almost constantly and automatically from Ida's lips. "Drat it, Red, quit teasin'. Law me, look at her jump. That there child's half flea. Nothin's going to hurt you, honey. Red, you crazy nut, you, quit teasin' that child! Crazy nut, you!"

When Ida called Red "Crazy Nut," she usually took a pinch of his cheek between the thumb and forefinger and gritted her teeth, very much in the manner she did over a new chick or a ewe lamb. She treated him that way pretty generally, yelling abusive things at him in her great booming voice that her manner belied.

The house rang with the great contralto voice of Ida. In invective, in hilarity, in rolling thunders of laughter, in the hissing voice of gossip, and in the bellowing she used against Red's shiftlessness.

Her vitality was something as amazing as it was unquenchable. She did, for instance, the family washing, including bed sheets, Missy's finery, Red's denim overalls, wringing them free of water with one wrench of her powerful lower arms. She was up with the dawn, and it was her boast that never in all her life had she known a sick-abed day.

And eat! Nothing tickled Red more than Ida's unashamed appetite for the strong foods that men like.

"Eat 'em alive, girl. I'll bet on you."

"Only live once, boy, and you just know I'm going to eat 'em alive while the going's good. If you don't like me big, you know darn well honing myself down to the bone isn't going to help none. Look at Missy there. That child's made out of a slab of spare-rib. Can't fatten her up, neither. Only live once, I say."

"Thassa girl," roared Red, who loved to see her topaz eyes full of the glitter of her astonishing health. "Thassa girl. Give her some more of them beans on biscuit, Missy!"

Ida could outstrip Red, no mean eater himself, in helpings of white beans that had been baked for five hours in a great brown casserole with strips of salt pork across the top, pouring them, hot, bursting, and pork-saturated, over as many as three steaming biscuits split into halves, which she opened on her plate with the pry of a knife, as if they had been oysters.

"My honey don't mind me fat, do you, boy?"

"Wouldn't have her an inch lighter if she cost me her weight in gold!"

"Listen to that! Cost you! Heh—I've got a swell chance, haven't I, to cost you anything? Not a day's work has he turned in six months, and sits there talking about cost as if he had something in his pockets beside hands."

"Yaw—yaw—listen to her jaw."

"Yaw—yaw—if you did listen, there would be a hustler instead of a loafer sitting on my right." Stabbing up a great biscuit with the tip of her fork and opening it on her plate so that it steamed up. "Have another one of these biscuit, Missy. Hand one to her, Red. Honest, that child don't eat enough to keep a bird alive."

"Here you," roared Red, and reached over from where he sat at table, toward the oven for a fresh pan of them. "Eat one of them big biscuit, you little peewee, you, or I'll bite off your head!"

"Ida, make him quit!"

"Lay off teasing that child, Red. Come on, Missy, put a new needle in the victrola and put on 'Red Hot Mama.' I don't mind doing the dishes with something to tickle my feet while I'm doing them."

The kitchen, littered with sewing-machine, victrola, carpet-back rocking-chair, and the huge range that breathed like a dragon, clattered with the life of the household. Neighbours dripped gossip there. Lonnie in her lifetime had snored behind the door. Two tortoiseshell cats, great over-sized ones with distended hips, were for ever being shoved off tables and out of work baskets. The Hassebrocks, roaring with good humour and a coarse kind of excess vitality, spread their dining-table beside the monster stove. In a corner of the room in a child's rocking-chair that had been cut down to fit her size, Missy still snuggled of an evening, curling into the tiny cushion and sometimes falling asleep there while Red dozed in the carpet rocker with his head back and his hands lightly locked in his lap, and Ida puttered and did the hundred things a woman can find to do about her kitchen.

But usually in good weather, mild winter evenings and stifling summer ones, Ida and Missy, now that she was seventeen, rigged themselves up for the neighbourhood commotion of movie, barbecue-dance, or stroll along the Post Office front or sometimes into the woods beyond. Usually Red remained at home and snored beside the stove or bit of garden, or, if he went along to a motion picture, breathed with equal lust through that.

A truck garden, a precarious one at that, a flock of about fourteen scrubby sheep, the occasional lodger, Red's intermittent income from farmhand service, Ida's few weeks a year in the tobacco factory, kept them, including old Katie, body and soul together. With the occasional indulgence, too, of a homemade radio, a dollar watch for Red, a red celluloid bracelet for Missy.

Later, Ida also had to have a red bracelet. They were a curious pair of chums. Missy when she was seventeen, and Ida after she had been married to Red for eighteen years. Two children, with Ida far and away the younger in sophistication and greedily dependent upon Missy for much of the lurid and incredibly worldly wisdoms that crept into even this tucked-away, penny-in-a-pocket of a town.

They were as giggling a pair as any two out of boarding school. Full of secret little gossippings. Given to rushing off in corners to swap confidences and private remarks that were cryptic to the outsider but full of portent to these two. Exchanging looks in public that sent them off into gales of laughter for which they had secret reasons. An inseparable pair even to the point where they often danced together of an evening up above the Post Office.

But for all her weightiness, not a village lout but was glad to have a dance with Ida. With the not uncommon paradox of the cumbersome, she was light on her feet. And the joy of motion made her irresponsible in a gay contagious sort of way. She laughed as she danced. Her cheeks flamed. Moisture came out and made her face gleam. Irrepressible passion for life animated her.

The boys liked Ida. Chaffed her. Confided in her. Pleaded through her for Missy's favour. The women dreaded her quick tongue, but knew that her remorse could flow like milk and honey.

When Ida danced across the floor, Red, who had no flair for this sort of recreation, leaned up against the wall and touted her as she passed.

"Attagirl. Thassaway! Mow them down. Step easy there, Spud, that's my gal you're dancing with."

And then, when Missy, who was like the dragonfly on water, came skimming past, out went his foot to trip her. Sometimes he succeeded and there was a pell-mell of everybody's laughter. Ida's loudest of all. How she could laugh! Her great second scallop of chin, her high, strong bosom and heavy red cheeks rippling with it.

She was the terrific, the inevitable, the irresistible life of any party. Life of the community, because where Ida was there reigned jocundity, repartee, and gibe.

Red, who was actually only two months younger than Ida, but easily looked five years, that upstanding he was and knitted and firm-fleshed and personable, used to stand with the rest of the loiterers on the edge of these occasions and laugh at her antics.

She could hurl out a remark of local and blasting significance that would send the luckless victim toward whom it was directed scuttling from her presence. She bantered and aided and abetted lovers, she was quick and loud in her praise, and equally loud and declamatory in her disapprovals.

She was a person, Ida was. She delighted Red. In his big handsome indolent way, content to have her drudge for him, even to lug and do manual labour for him when she would without too much remonstrance, she fascinated him with her vitality.

He yowled with laughter at the spectacle of her dragging one of the young village giants across the floor by the ear as if he were so much meal in a sack and depositing the bashful bumpkin before Missy, whose grace he coveted.

He loved to sit by in the kitchen with his stockinged feet propped against the stove and listen to the powerful hilarity of her laughter mingling with Missy's little ringing bell of a giggle as the two of them swapped who knows what brand of secret lore in the bedroom adjoining.

She was so powerful. She was like the prow of a ship. And she was such a child. She ate, she played, she slept with the gusto of one. Sometimes, lying beside her on their rickety iron bed in the centre of the room they shared, the house, the night, the universe seemed filled with her. With the vitality of her. She was so strong, even in sleep. She was so everything in a more intense way than most people. So good-natured. So eager. So doting on those she loved. Even to old Katie, who still yapped at her like a wolf for marrying Red. Ida could lift her out of her chair and carry her across the house for Sunday dinner as if she were so much kindling-wood.

And Red: she babied him while she heaped him with abuses. She berated him for his shiftlessness and brushed out his red hair until she made it glisten. She yelled insolent commentaries after him for two hundred yards down the road, as she started off fishing, and the sizzle of the bacon-rind which he was fond of, and which she was already frying for his return, flew with little explosions up into her face.

And then sometimes, right on the heels of his departure, which she had riddled with invectives, let a neighbour so much as volunteer to tend old Katie, and down the very road that he had trod went Ida and Missy shortly after, swinging between them a basket containing picnic rations for three. Sometimes they crept upon him from behind so that, as he sat on a fallen tree dozing over his pole, he would all but fall in the water.

Sometimes they crept up from an opposite bank of the creek, stoning him.

Always they met in the unison of hilarity.

For half a mile around the quiet countryside, with the ribbon of water running through it, their laughter beat and scrambled the silence.

Sometimes, between them, Red and Ida made a basket of their hands and carried Missy all the way home.

She was like a puffball. So light. Her laughter went up like bubbles.

They loved the lightness of her, swinging her between them.

It is probable that, even before consciousness of it smote Red, Ida was aware of the thing that was happening.

Certainly long before there was as much tangible evidence as the batting of an eye, Ida, with an intuition that rammed into her like a dagger, knew! Knew, the year Missy turned a lovely seventeen, that Red was aware of the girl in a new, a sudden, a terrifying way.

There was almost an adolescence to his awakening to the beauty of the young maturity that was Missy's. Inexplicably, that year, Red, who had mauled her, and teased her, and pestered her for a period of seven years, became suddenly a gawk in her presence.

There was never a moment when consciousness smote Missy. She continued to try to shinny up his great flank like a squirrel for a place on his shoulder and to want him to carry her at the end of a rigid arm like the kitten, but now, if she as much as touched him, or importuned him to join hands with Ida to make the basket to carry her, he growled and shook her off and roared like a bull.

Ida continued to laugh just as loudly. Just as boisterously. To berate, to abuse, to condone, to slap, to play, to fondle, to threaten.

But suddenly, frighteningly, Ida's heart was a bonfire. Months of a raging conflagration that went on inside of her secretly, searingly, almost unendurably.

Red was in love with Missy.

There was no doubt of that. After all these years—Red was in love with Missy. That was a consciousness to carry about with you. To drive you mad! To cause your flesh to tingle as if every pore were an electric bell ringing. Of pain! Red was in love with Missy. Poor Ida. The thought became a hoop rolling through the days. Rolling and burning through the heart. Red was in love with Missy.

Sometimes at her work, Ida would call out suddenly as if a sharp pain had stabbed her and then clap her hand up against her mouth.

God. God. God. Red was in love with Missy. Ida's Red.

The senses would not seem to take it in, and yet there were the evidences. The evidences, infinitesimal to any except Ida's tortured naked eye, and yet as enormous in truth as the thunder that follows lightning, or the daylight that follows dark.

Red was in love with Missy.

He stumbled in to bed at night, always late now, to take his place beside Ida on their crazy old craft of a pallet; and lying there beside him, pretending to be asleep, the room was filled with the hoops that rolled through her eyeballs. Red was in love with Missy.

Sometimes after he slept, in a heavy, childlike manner he had, with his face in the crook of his arm, Ida would raise herself on an elbow to gaze at the troubled sprawl of him in the faint pallor of the clear nights that hung over the valley.

That was her Red lying there. Big handsome baby boy. Ida's Red, who was almost as much a part of her being as the breath that poured out of her, and the tears. A rope bound them. A rope of what to Ida amounted to ligament and fibre of her being—and a thread was leading him away. Silken thread of Missy.

Those were some of the fantastically hurting thoughts that twisted Ida's face almost beyond recognition as she leaned there in the dark. Over him. Her Red. And the tears that she cried were tears of pity for him as much as herself.

And the growing, the damning evidences that made her so sure were these: suddenly here was Red, who had romped through Missy's childhood with her, shying away now, from so much as the slightest contact with the little edges of her skirt, and reddening up and swearing if she plunged a hand in his pocket for the licorice drops she was apt to find there.

Poor little Missy, with all her astonishing knowledge of some of the vicious truths that found their way and practice into the town, she was as innocent as a babe where Red was concerned.

That made it heart-breaking, too. Missy, little innocent Missy against whom the tides were lashing. She fought back against these new and unaccountable brutalities of Red and often ran to Ida weeping with them.

And then, one night, there occurred the first bit of tangible evidence. After Ida had sat late over her lamp, sewing a little underthing for Missy, the sole garment, except frock, that she wore against the slim sheaf of her body, she tried it on the girl before she sent her over to her cot at the foot of Katie's bed in the shanty. Missy slept at the beck and call of the old invalid, awakened five and six times a night by her querulous call for water.

Red came in just as she was climbing back into her dress from having tried on the underslip, and so she took refuge behind the wide bulk of Ida, peeping around her like a saucy bird as she darted her arms back into the slip of calico dress.

Time had been when Missy would have stood out of her dress and without shame before Red. Now all that was changed. That was the frightening part, that was the part, those days as she laughed loudest, that lay like a clod at the terrified heart of Ida.

Late that night, when Red undressed in the kitchen before he came lumbering in to bed, he lifted the little underthing, a coarse one of percale, but already kissed with the print of Missy's body, out of Ida's work-basket on one end of the sewing-machine. From the bed, through the crack of the door where it stood open, Ida could see him standing there with that fribble of garment clutched in his hands as if he would wring it in two pieces. Clutched—clenched—

Red! Poor Red! Poor Ida! Poor, poor Red!

And the further heart-break of it to her was that with the sin of lust for Missy growing in his heart, Red, who had no logic, only an automatic code of social behaviour toward the enormously personable woman he called wife, began to soften in his manner toward her.

For instance, every time he sat between them in the little trumped-up barn of a motion-picture theatre, he let his hand steal clumsily toward Ida's because it lusted to be in Missy's.

In just such proportion as he yearned for the child he became demonstrative toward the woman. Suddenly and quite without precedent, since their courtship days at least, Red was tender, solicitous, amorous of manner toward Ida.

If he followed Missy across a field, just for the ecstasy of seeing her sprite of a body dance this way and that, he was sure to run a lumbering hand of caress across the hulk of Ida when he returned home. That almost killed her. She treasured his gruffnesses toward her. She cried inside of her if he stooped for an object she had dropped, or went off to do a day's farm-hand work when ordinarily he would have let her pick up the few needed dollars at the tobacco factory or do an odd day's housework for the family named Idleweiss with whom she had lived before her marriage.

It was as if the great hulk that Red had created with his indulgence was about to topple and crush him. Furtively, as she lumbered past him in the felt slippers she wore for housework, the tail of his eye was now newly conscious of the waddling hips, the high bosom usually spangled with the moisture of exertion, the great robust good-featured face, and the lips that at meal-time would be a little greasy from creature enjoyment.

Red had built this vastness with his boisterous endorsements of her vitality. Suddenly, as Missy became more and more a dancing sprite across his consciousness, the bulk of Ida grew in his disturbed brain even beyond her proportions, so that to touch her was to shudder. Secretly. Ashamedly. Heartachingly.

And Ida knew! That was the marvel of it. Every time she crossed a room or walked ahead of him at twilight with her hand in Missy's, Ida knew. The tent and the sprite walking along there ahead of him, and Red was tied to the tent with rope, and a little silk string was leading him.

When they were both in their thirty-sixth year and Red was still straight as an arrow and swift enough when his rheumatic knee and his indolence let him be, Ida was a hulk. They had let it happen in their coarse-grained, hilarious fashion, because there was that in her enormous vitality of spirit, of good humour, of appetite and desire, that had amused him.

And now what they had created was about to destroy them. And there was no rancour against Missy. Missy was a symbol. Missy was merely the sprightliness of youth dancing in Red's heart.

The devices of Ida against the pain and the terror were transitory and ineffectual. For a while she began secretly to cut down on her food, explaining at meal-time that she had already partaken of her share. Missy was at first concerned at any omission in Ida's appetite and prepared her special dishes to tempt her. But for two weeks Ida held out, nibbling scarcely enough to keep an ewe alive. Then, because of the years of over-indulgence, a black kind of faintness began to overtake her. Hunger-pangs. And Ida, who seldom knew fatigue, would drop into a chair in the middle of the morning, exhausted. That would never do! Red might notice, and besides, one of her chief weapons in the grim battle was the exuberance of her vitality. And so Ida, who had been naturally boisterous and of high spirits before, became now shockingly hilarious. Nervously, conscientiously hilarious.

All day and half the night her high laughter clattered through the house. There was never a moment that she would let herself run down.

There was never a moment, now that Red was awake to Missy, that desire for her was not burning through his spirit and his flesh.

The town began to notice. Let Missy so much as walk out of an evening with one of the hired hands from a near-by farm, or with a young lout of a fellow called Jo, whose father owned a considerable acreage up behind a cider-mill, and Red was like one possessed.

Restlessness made a bashing bull out of him. He could not remain seated for five minutes in a given spot. He listened to what the loiterers around the Post Office and the cider-barrels were saying with his eyes fixed and burning in the direction toward which Missy had disappeared. Often he followed, pretending to amble away aimlessly, but breaking into a run after he was out of sight of the villagers. One evening he missed the trail of Missy and Jo and ran hither and thither like one crazed, cursing and sobbing to himself.

He was nearly as frenzied as a man could be. Frenzied with desire. Frenzied with jealousy. With remorse. Frenzied with love for Missy and tenderness of Ida.

A dilemma that kept him in a fever. How did some men throw off the old so casually and then on with the new? Red was bound in such a manner that with every wrench to be free, ligaments of his heart seemed to twist.

The loiterers in front of Grody's began to openly laugh at him. And Missy, innocent as a babe of this sirocco she was causing in the heart of this man, began to twit him for following her about.

"Go 'long, you old Red, you. Go 'long," she said to him one evening before darting off for a walk with a youth from the town called Deborah. "What you always following me around for, Red? Go 'long, you!"

Ida knew! The loiterers around the General Store knew! Red knew, too, and yet he could not calm himself while she was out of sight. There was a bonfire in his heart.

One evening, while Missy was hanging over a picket gate talking to one of the rare lodgers who came their way, a young radio salesman from Cincinnati, Ida went out into the woodshed to get a bottle of chicken medicine to be administered by dropper, for a little brood she was nursing along in one of the unused rooms of the house. Lying stark on the black dirt floor of the shed, so that she almost stumbled over him, was Red, with his face pillowed in his arms, kicking with the toes of his shoes against the ground and sobbing. Audibly, but in the tearless fashion of a dry locked torment.

When Ida backed out of there noiselessly, she wanted the earth to open and swallow her up. She had looked upon something so terrifying, so private, so out of the innermost recesses of human passion that it was almost like—like daring to look squarely up at a fork of lightning for—for fear—

Red lying in there with the heart bleeding out of him for Missy.

Hours later, when Ida crept back there for the bottle and the dropper, she had to grope for them along a ledge in among a cobwebby bottle of horse-liniment, a can of axle-grease, the chloroform-bottle that had snuffed out poor Lonnie, and such obnoxious objects as a decaying chicken's foot, rusty hinge, and one of Red's discarded old pipes, rimmed in grease.

That was the evening of the day that the young radio salesman who travelled around the country in a little tin car decided to put up for the night at the Hassebrocks'.

He was a slim young fellow of no particular face, a belted-in coat, a blue-soft collar, and a polka-dot bow tie. Slicked-haired, a yellow right third finger, and the pert aggressive air of a salesman who has to talk rapidly and keep his foot between the door as the housewife holds it grudgingly open.

He was a bit more urban than most of the run of fellows who came through Doyer, and he smiled on Missy as all the youths who came to Doyer were beginning to smile, now that she had turned a lovely seventeen.

And Missy, who was saucy and full of the drolleries of a natural coquetry, smiled back. That was how, at the dusk of day, as she hung on the picket fence swapping incredible vapourings with the youth with the pinch-back coat and no-particular-face, she happened to start with him for a walk which led first through the village and then on across a meadow on the way to a wood.

Poor Red, stumbling after. Some of the dirt from the black floor of the shed still clung to his brow. He tried to loiter a bit at Grody's, his eyes roving pitiably after the pair as they plowed through the tall grasses of meadow toward the woods where the afterglow of a sunset still showed through the boles. He tried to loiter longer and to swap talk, but as never before his brain was on fire, and one of the country bumpkins, a day labourer who worked at road-building, openly derided, and gave courage to the others to follow quick suit. It was the first time they had ever dared to put it into words.

"Better hurry, Red. He's the best one that has come her way yet. He looked like he could eat her with a spoon. This one is going to get her! He's the best yet. . . ."

That was true. That was true. There never had been a fellow come to town who looked at Missy the way this one had all through supper.

His breathing from that thought became like the panting of an engine.

"Watch out, Red. She'll be stolen before your very eyes one of these days."

That was true. That was true. Just to behold Missy was to become mad with desire. . . .

"Lookie, Red! Look out there at them skittling towards Lover's Lane. That little fellow works fast, I'll say."

That was true. That was true. Only six hours in town, and almost every moment of them twitting around with Missy. That was true. . . . Them kind of fellows work fast.

"Watch out, Red! Them little devil kind are slippery."

"Damn you," shouted Red to the loiterers. "Damn you." And plunged his way after them, past shame now. Frantic. What if Missy were to slip away— through the meadow—through the woods—on through to—to some beyond that did not include him? That made a bonfire of him, all right. What if Missy were to slip away? Damn them for saying so. Damn that fellow in the blue collar. . . .

There were two specks now moving through the stripes of the trees with a sky like a blood-red curtain for background.

Here was a new sensation for Missy. This smarty Cincinnati fellow, obviously smitten. It brought out all her latent coquetry. A young fellow with slick quick urban ways. The enormous and plated-over assurance of a person with something to sell.

The cock-sure bravado of the man accustomed to have to talk fast, convincingly, and in the face of the housewife's impending slam of door, and Missy a little intoxicated with the quick tempo he brought to things.

It was summer and twilight, and there were birds twittering themselves to sleep in a great commotion all through the small woods, and when they walked they created quite a flurry among them of flying from bough to bough; and just out of sight and just within sound, there crept Red. Noiselessly, except for his breathing, which to himself seemed a gale, but to Missy and her companion was unheard.

How she played. Like a kitten. It made Red want to cry.

"You're a pretty little thing," said the fellow-with-no-particular face, and made a feint for her waistline.

"And you're a fresh little thing," cried Missy. She had a thin treble voice that had a tremolo in it. A tremolo that to Red was like the throb of a bird-throat when you hold a thrush in your hand and bend back its head.

"Kiddie—iddie," cried the youth-with-no-face, and tickled her little heart-shaped chin with the long nail of his third finger.

"Kiddie—iddie—" cried Missy and made a pretence of tickling back. If she had touched him, Red could not have stood it.

"Kiddie—iddie!"

The laughter of Missy. It cut Red in two as he stood there behind a tree, wilfully inflicting upon himself the pain of this scene.

"You're a card, Missy. You're a Red Hot Little Mama."

"Oh, oh, oh. I'm a Red Hot Little Mama."

"Kiss me!"

"No."

"Why?"

"Dassn't."

"Dast, too."

"Say, bossie, how do you get thataway?"

"Whataway?"

"Spoony."

"'Cause you're such a sweet little red hot mama."

"You're a little cutey, too, calling me a red hot mama," said Missy, and pursed up her nose until it crinkled and then waggled a nonsensical finger at him. It was coquetry out and out, and the youth-with-no-face-in-particular caught excitement from it and made a dive for her and grasped her by the edge of her skirt and jerked her to him, and for the moment his eyes focused of her nearness.

"I'll steal you."

"All right, who said you couldn't?"

"Mean it?"

"You said it."

"That big guy that's crazy after you. There'd be hell to pay with him if I did try it."

"Who?"

"That big guy that follows you around. The fellow you work for."

"Red?"

"Yeh."

"Him?"

"Yeh, him. Don't throw me those innocent eyes or I'll pick them up and make cuff links out of them."

"Red? He's just my—"

"He's just crazy, that's what he is. No guy with good sense is going to make up to you with that guy around. Not if he wants to keep his brains where they belong instead of leaving them along the roads of Doyer."

"You mean—"

"I mean he's jealous as hell of you. Aw no, you don't fool me with throwing innocent eyes again. That guy'll knock the head off of anyone who touches you, but himself. Come on, be a good girl and tell me just where you and him get off."

"Red? Him?" cried Missy, and went off into one of the freshets of her laughter. "Me and *Red*? Old hairy ape of a *Red*. Why he's Ida's. He's just like—like my pap would be if I had one. He's Ida's—he's just my pap—my old hairy-ape pap—"

"He's crazy for you. He's red-eyed for you."

Missy doubling up with laughter and hugging her arms across her frail little body with hilarity.

"Me and Red. Me and hairy old ape of a pap. Where do we get off? Say, you're crazy with the heat," cried Missy. "He's married to my big old, fat, sweet old fat Ida. Say, you're crazy, you are," cried Missy, throwing him the challenge of a tagging movement with her hand. "He'd give me the shivers and the jim-jams if he was anything but Ida's. Thank you, keep the change, no hairy old horrors for me! Dare you to steal me! Dare you to steal me. I want to be stole. Last tag!" sang Missy, and danced away. A sprite among trees. Wind-tossed. Youth-tossed. Beauty-tossed.

Hairy old ape. There behind the trees he was—his lower lip pursed out, hanging down, seeming to grow.

Hairy old ape! Youth had slapped him a ringing blow across the heart. There she was out there. Youth! A sprite among the trees answering back the call of youth to the fellow with no-face-in-particular. The song of life, it was there to be sung, and Missy was trying to sing it. Her way. Everyone had to sing it—his way—

Hairy old ape could not sing it to Youth! Hairy old ape, that's what he had been to Missy all the while that his old blood had been swinging in his veins for her. The swinging and the singing that should have been for Ida.

Ida! Ida! There was that in Red made him suddenly like a small boy wanting to race from a world of strangers home to the bosom that held the mystery of maternity for him.

Red wanted Ida! Red had been cut across the heart. Red had been lashed into a bitter stinging realization that made him, as he dashed homeward through the meadows, cry great isolated tears that ran down his face and splashed on to his bare chest where the army shirt fell open.

Red wanted Ida! He wanted to crawl up to her feet as old Lonnie might have done and lie there with his face against them.

There was that sweetish odour when he entered their room—where—before? There was something a little sickening to it that smote him at the pit of his being. Ida, great welt of her, was lying across the bed with a white cloth tied over her mouth and knotted at the back of her head. What? Toothache! She had it sometimes. Poor old darling Ida. It was blessed, like recovering from a great fever, to come home to her. Ida. Haven of Ida. He wanted to creep into the cove of her arms and lie there just silently to her heart-beat.

"Ida," cried Red, and went up to her almost with the whinny of a dog. There was a lamp burning on the table beside the bed, with its shade tilted back like a hat from a hot forehead. Behind the washstand all the photographs of the pretty picture girls, their arching necks and their bare shoulders, came out in the light. And in that same light, above the handkerchief tied about her mouth, there was something about the eyes of Ida! *There was something about the eyes of Ida!*

"Ida," called Red as if he were summoning her from a distance, and went up and shook her shoulder. What kind of toothache was this that made her seem receding that way?

And what kind of Red was this? was what Ida, who could no longer speak, was asking herself. Why—why—what was this look in his face? Why—Red had come back to her. Red was needing her. Red had been hurled out of somewhere—hurled out of the paradise of Missy. Red had come back and was needing her!

And Ida could not talk. Funny, too, while she was shouting so loudly down inside of herself. She was sliding off somewhere. She must crawl back. This was the way Lonnie must have felt that day in the shed when she wanted back. That had been the only way to do it. Lonnie's way. It was the only way she knew about. Once a man had hung himself from a rafter in a deserted barn down the road. But that was unthinkable. This way was easy, except now—suddenly, Red showing up this way. Ida wanted to come back. Ida wanted to crawl back, up the ledge. Red was standing there needing her. Life was suddenly so sweet—Ida must come back to him. Ida wanted to talk. To take his head between her hands. And she was locked into the silence that was sucking her under.

"Ida," screamed Red, and held the lamp high. "Ida!"

It was so black. The rushing sweetish sickish silence was like a black stream bearing her away.

Suddenly, terribly, to Red standing there with the lamp held up like a torch, she seemed gone, except for her eyes that he could feel against the flesh of his breast, like two wounds.

The Hossie-Frossie

First Published: *Cosmopolitan*, September 1928
Reprinted: *Procession*, Harper & Bros., 1929

The Hossefrosses populated their city well. Every family of them traced a relationship back to one Hesse Hossefrosse who had first set foot in St. Louis as body-servant to one of the earliest arrivals in America of the Schwimmer family of brewery fame.

There were seven Hossefrosses listed in the telephone directory, none of them more remotely related than second or third cousinship.

<pre>
Hossefrosse Charles, G.r. . . . . . . 3058 1/2 S. Grand Ave.
Hossefrosse Frank, r. . . . . .3486 a Hickory St.
Hossefrosse Frank, whl. poul. & pro.   486 S. Third St.
Hossefrosse Hesse, sadlery . . . . 8686 Gratiot Street
Hossefrosse Joseph, locksmith . . . . . . 346 Leffingwell Av.
Hossefrosse Leffert . . . . 5681 S. Seventh St.
Hossefrosse Oscar, Jr., surg. inst's. . . . 2367 Arsenal St.
Hossefrosse Rudolph, bootmaker . . 5708 S. Broadway
</pre>

A Hossefrosse might not so much as encounter a Hossefrosse year in and year out, but Joseph Hossefrosse, locksmith, for instance, who had clapped eyes only once on Rudolph Hossefrosse, and that once when they had been alphabetically thrown together while paying their water taxes at City Hall, knew exactly the degree of their cousinship, which in this instance was third.

Ella Hossefrosse (Mrs. Leffert) sometimes bought her poultry retail from the wholesale Frank Hossefrosse on the strength of the cousinship, but there was practically no intercourse between the families.

With the exception that on one occasion a Hossefrosse had married a Hossefrosse. Kate Hossefrosse, daughter of the sadlery Hossefrosse, whose great-grandfather had come over with a Schwimmer of Schwimmer's Pale Brew fame, had married Rudolph Hossefrosse, bootmaker and son of three generations of bootmaking Hossefrosses.

It had all been highly regular and within the pale of the Choteau Avenue

Lutheran Church. Kate and Rudolph were no less than third cousins.

Kate, in those days when a faint humor still hovered in crinkles along her eyelids, had railed good-humoredly at the fate which kept her, even to the outward manifestation of name, a Hossefrosse.

Hossefrosse. Hossefrosse. Later, it came to have a solemn lumbering sound to Kate. Written, the word looked to her like some great mammalian creature with a slow lope to it. A terrific gawk of a prehistoric horse, with slow heavy legs that were hard to raise and which dredged up mud.

When Kate's child was no more than six she once, with a fine disregard for prevalent theories of child psychology, manufactured out of this conceit, the story of the Hossie-Frossie—her unmodern device for frightening the little girl into obedience.

If you don't mind mamma, like a good girl, the Hossie-Frossie'll get you. M-m-m, great big gray ugly Hossie-Frossie, twice as big as this house, with a hook on his tail for dragging little girls around and around in a circle. 'Round and 'round in a circle with their noses rubbing the ground all their lifetime, till they get old and die, with their noses rubbed off from being dragged around and around by the tiresome old Hossic-Frossie.

At this, Paula's eyes would grow very round with a sort of uncomprehending fear.

Hossie-Frossie—that's almost my name, Mother.

Yes, that was almost Paula's name.

There was a set of neighborhood chimes on the old St. Mark's Church which used to seem to have to Kate, as they tilted out a clatter every hour over the neighborhood where the establishment of the Rudolph Hossefrosses had stood for well over half a century, a little sing-song all their own.

Hos-sie Fros-sie. Hossiefrossie. Hos-sie Fros-sie. Hossiefrossie. The rhythm of it was unmistakable. To Kate at least. Tra la la la. Hos-sie Fros-sie. La. La. La. La.

Rudolph, who never smiled, used to hammer away, on those semi-occasions when an order for a hand-made boot drifted into the store, with his mouth full of tacks, to what Kate suspected to be the rhythm: Hos-sie-fros-sie. Hos. Hos. Hossefrosse.

That was nonsense, of course. Rudolph probably knew less of rhythm than any man who ever lived. Kate would have been sure of that, had such a word as rhythm ever popped into her head.

And yet, three generations of Hossefrosses, grandfather and grandmother, then father and mother, and finally Rudolph and Kate, had had their beings as good husbands, wives; good eaters, sleepers; good shopkeepers, citizens, and conformers to an impeccable rhythm of routine in that tall lean house with the shoe-store on the ground floor and the living apartment rambling two and a half tall stories above.

Three generations of men had minded shop and morals on that strip of 40x100 lot. Three generations of women had minded both equally well, and kept immaculate house in the high-ceilinged narrow rooms, borne their children in the walnut bed of feathers, scrubbed little sags into the kitchen and side-porch floors, and kept white-washed the bricks that bisected the narrow side yard.

Kate, in those years before the crinkles of humor had flickered out along her eyelids, used to say that she knew every brick of that walk by heart. There was one down toward the middle that every spring sprouted a most insistent moss in its crack. You had to salt and salt it out. Rudolph hated a weedy walk. After a while, Kate came to hate a weedy walk.

She could ward off the impending moss with a squirt of lye or salt. Before she was nine, Paula, who was in the image of Kate, was already invaluable at the chores which made up the rhythm. She was a spick-and-span little girl with bright china-blue eyes and bound yellow plaits encircling her head, precisely as Kate's had been bound at that age.

The mills of the Hossefrosse gods ground slowly, the family managing to keep chinks closed to the invasion of the "high-falutin' idea"; the new fashion; the "shiftlessness" of modern ways.

A penny saved was a penny earned.

Of course, some change had forced in since the days when the boot-making Rudolph had wooed and won the bright-haired daughter of a saddle-making Hossefrosse.

To begin with, not only the boot-making and the saddle-making industries had changed, but the town had changed. The old South Side—the "solid south"—had disintegrated. The West End, becoming fashionable, had lured away many of the young generation from that section of their forefathers which had been known as "Little Berlin."

Many of the old residences still stood intact. Lafayette and Park Avenue and parts of the Tower Grove section maintained fairly brave fronts, there were still business men in Carondalet, and in extreme southern sections of town, whose grandfathers had been born on the sites where the businesses still stood, but since the marriage of Rudolph and Kate, a World War had cleft the old days from the new.

It took the stability of a Hossefrosse to withstand these slashing inroads of new times. Rudolph might be said to have withstood them like the great flesh-wall of an elephant quivers to an insect bite, is pestered, but not moved.

The house on South Broadway, with its narrow, high-shouldered look and the side yard that would not grow grass because the dirt was tired, remained practically immune, so far as its inner life was concerned, to the quick tides of change that washed around it.

It is true that the fine art of boot-making as practiced pridefully by the generations of Hossefrosses who had cobbled away on the old bench of glossy patine that was now crowded in the back of the shop, had now gone by the board, as the saying is.

The result was an out-and-out retail shoe store, with packing cases that had been stood on ends along the walls and transformed into shelves, and two bright yellow benches with brass tacks and perforated trimmings forming an aisle that was covered with a rubber strip and dotted with small foot-rests for the customers.

A far cry from the old workaday shop where senior Hossefrosses had cobbled by hand vici kid boots for the husky proletariat of the South Side. This was an aspect of it that Kate most hated, particularly as Paula began to grow up. The character of the business had changed. With the general evolution of footgear for women, the gentry trade had slipped away to the larger downtown emporiums of wider variety of stock.

The Hossefrosses now did a retail business—a thriving one, it is true, but the fitting of a shoe was no longer a prideful matter of sliding a handmade high shoe of vici kid on to the genteel foot of a local *hausfrau.*

The house of Hossefrosse now dealt in the fancy kids and shiny satins, too bright tans and blüchers, designed to meet the tastes of the servant girls, the chauffeurs, and street-car conductors of the post-war South Side.

Thursday was one of the evenings that Kate helped Rudolph in the store. Afterward, when they climbed to their old-fashioned rooms above, Kate's back ached from the strain of coaxing large cheaply made fancy slippers onto Polish, Finnish, and German girls, whose feet, due to vanity, ill-fitting high heels, and the hours they were obliged to spend on them, were overgrown and bulging.

If Rudolph regretted or resented this deterioration from his rôle of skilled boot-maker to retail merchant, he said precious little about it. The business was prospering well enough. One took things as they came.

Yes, you did that, if you were a Hossefrosse. Dear knows, Kate was an example of that congenital ability on the part of a Hossefrosse to fit into the pattern. Pretty Kate. There had been a moment in her prettiness when the gently moving history of the saddle-making and the boot-making Hossefrosses had seemed to tremble in the balance.

It was only natural. Any girl's, much less a pretty one's, head can be turned. Kate's had been, but it was turned promptly about again into its place. Square on her Hossefrosse shoulders.

She had sung in the Choteau Avenue Church choir and during the period that young Rudolph, who had a square shaved head and small eyes, was wooing her, the choir master had received a call to go from the South Side to the First Lutheran Church of Kansas City, and had offered to take Kate along, as a salaried member of his new choir.

For a day or two after that Kate's eyes had looked appealingly moist, particularly to the choir master, from the secret tears of her desire to go, and Rudolph had been told, when he called that week, that "Katey was not feeling so well." But later, at her father's dictation, Kate had written out, in her round immature chirography, a note which she transcribed slightly out of its dialect. It was a polite, if not particularly regretful refusal of the choir master's offer.

Yes, being a Hossefrosse, one took things as they came. Kate took Rudolph and the after years of fitting their lives into the mold of the house on South Broadway, with never so much as a backward glance.

After all, a backward glance at what? The saddle-making Hossefrosses had lived, procreated, sat in their *bierstuben,* paid their pew dues, accumulated their nest eggs, sent their children through seventh-grade public school; inculcated thrift, lived thrift, exemplified thrift, even as the boot-making Hossefrosses, and for that matter the Produce, the Locksmith and the Butcher, the Baker, the Candlestick-maker, Hossefrosses. No one of them had ever seen anything about him except the cardinal virtues that had their inception back in an idea that conservation was consummation.

Kate, whose voice had been pretty chiefly because it was a young voice, had let it peter out as her waist line began to go. There was a square piano in the upper front room, but as long as Father Hossefrosse, the boot-making father of Rudolph, had lived, it was never opened, and Kate came into the household the last six years of his life. After that, Mother Hossefrosse had sickened and died in those same rooms, and by that time Paula was already a tripper and a climber, and somehow there just was not ever the propitious moment for song.

No, it could scarcely be said that conformity was a trick for Kate. Old lady Hossefrosse lived to welcome into her home a daughter-in-law who promptly learned to swing the very tassels on the mantelpiece drape of plush-and-chenille, at precisely the angle to which they had been accustomed for two generations of Hossefrosses. Kate took over the whitewashing of the bricks, the helping in the store, the baking of the sour-rye bread, the making of her husband's nightshirts, the rendering of her own lard, the laying of her own fires, with never a jog in the machinery of daily life.

Not that there was anything remarkable in that. There was no other way for a Hossefrosse woman to be.

America was a land of opportunity. A land to which you gave the allegiance of good citizenship in return for its manifold benefits. But taking on the fidelities of citizenship to America was another matter from taking on its profligate ways.

Let the American live from hand to mouth. That was his concern. Triflers with life. Why, there were salaried men living on the South Side; men, mind you, without so much as a business to their names, wastrels, with not a penny ahead, yet who always showed the grin of ten-cent cigar points above their waistcoat pockets and whose wives kept "help"; whose children attended private schools and who themselves drove small sedans, when they owned not so much as a family lot in the cemetery.

Salaried men, mind you, salesmen, some of them insurance agents dependent on commissions, who bought their family coupés and their living-room "sets" on installments and whose children grew up without proper regard for the value of money.

Well, the Hossefrosses, who could buy and sell this type of South Sider over again, had no family sedan. Would not have had one at any price. Constant expense. Dangerous. Superfluous. Kate came to agree with Rudolph on that. Even if you could afford one, they certainly were a drain, what with the upkeep and all.

Lax, pellmell, improvident, ill-organized, this world of Americans that was tincturing more and more the Solid South of the city. Rudolph, magnificently insulated from it all, turned a stolid back and went his Hossefrosse way. So did Kate go his way, except for the vicarious influence of the public schools and the sidewalk life as it touched her child.

"No monkey business ways out of you," thundered Rudolph, on those beginning occasions when the world did begin to succeed in invading the tight sanctity of that gray brick homestead, and Paula perhaps begged for sateen bloomers like the small girls of the neighborhood were wearing to school, or for the tid-bit price of a visit to a near-by motion-picture theater.

There was not much "monkey business" of any sort in the carefully routined Hossefrosse household.

Of good food there was abundance; a form of indulgence that was characteristic. At forty-five, Rudolph bulged of well-being. His scrubbed pink skin shone; transparent and pink and polished were his bright ears. His neck, as it thickened and rolled down a bit over his decent white collar, was the same scrubbed pink.

Kate had not escaped the penalty of her full larders. Her jonquil, *fräulein* prettiness had overflowed its banks, so to speak. At forty she was any *hausfrau* who mixed a wickedly alluring batch of cinnamon rolls and whose pink cheeks asseverated to her ability to nibble as she cooked.

Where recreations and diversions were comparatively few, eating became a sort of righteous indulgence. Rudolph was entitled, after the long confining hours in the store, to tuck in his napkin with a will. Three times a day the Hossefrosses sat down to reap the gastronomic delights of Kate's skill at the large coal range in her large kitchen. Nourishing strong foods, perhaps even coarse, but under Kate's dash of paprika, bit of browned onion and flutter of bay leaves, a pot roast ran the most delicate juices and beneath the swirl of her powerful wooden spoon a cheese cake could be born a puff.

The Hossefrosses lived well. On rainy days of double-session at school, Paula's lunch box was sure to yield over and above the less stable delights of the other children. Kate's sour-rye bread sandwiches of half an inch of cream cheese sprinkled with finely minced *Schnittlauch* (the shredded tops of spring onions) made pretty pale affairs of the slabs of ham on store bread the American children brought. Paula used to share the great cold apple dumplings that Kate always crammed into one end of the lunch basket with them, too. The boys and girls fought for that sharing of apple dumpling.

There came a time, however, along about the period that Paula began asking for motion-picture money, when she crept off by herself to eat her bulky luncheon. A new and cruel awareness was upon her.

It might be said that when Paula was about thirteen, this awareness, rising off the heart of her daughter, began to creep like a fog into Kate. Suddenly it came, and yet there was in this secret stream of consciousness which seemed flowing through her in torment now, something of a recrudescence; something that should have died way back with the frustration of the choir position in Kansas City apparently had not died, but only gone off into a coma as long as the years. The thing that resuscitated, was lifting itself within her now, was akin to the brief yearnings back there, when Rudolph had been wooing her and the choir master had come with his opportunity. Only back there in her slim girlhood there had been only the briefest, if tormented, desire to seek new fields.

That torment, in choosing to return to her after its brief flash fifteen or sixteen years before, had come to her now in its component parts. A restless and detailed awareness of the "Hossie-Frossie" as she had used to describe it in baby lingo to Paula, which was about to drag her daughter around on its life-round treadmill, had Kate in its clutch.

Paula was just seventeen. An adorable seventeen in Kate's eyes, with crinkles of humor still along her eyelids. You could never seem to have done discovering new little cornices and corners to Paula's prettiness. Her chin was cleft, as if to prove definitely that it could not be marred, but on the contrary, became just that much more provocative. There was a small golden mole on the highest peak of her cheekbone that was just like the one Kate hid on the curve of her breast. Dear girl, with never much finery to deck it, Paula's young body, slimmer than Kate's had ever been, was pliant and full of the impulse for speed. Kate, beholding her young offspring turn eager face out toward the play and nonsense world which no Hossefrosse ever really entered, felt the stricture of torment at her heart.

Paula, much more than her mother before her, was laying back her young ears, so to speak, to the whinny of the youth which passed her in the streets, sat beside her in Bible class, lured her to the neighborhood theaters and beckoned her out to play.

And Kate, whose own rebellion sixteen years before had been only seven days long, began to dread.

There seemed something so incontestably foreordained about the destiny of a Hossefrosse. There was a gray procession of the women and a gray procession of the men. They were hay-foot, straw-foot, sort of people.

In some of the families which had grown up about Kate, even among the staid South Siders of rigid stabilities, the occasional cataclysm, irregularity or capricious thing had occurred.

One of the Deifenbach girls, for instance, had eloped with an artist, and was said to be living in Greenwich Village in New York.

Fred Whatmough, whose father had conducted one of the largest meat stalls in Union Market for over thirty years, fired with his reading of Stanley and Livingstone, had joined a motion-picture expedition and gone in quest of wild-game pictures in Central Africa.

Then there was the case of Lina Rinchoff, who had "gone away," as the discreet-mouthed South Siders put it, with her music-teacher, whose wronged wife and three children still resided on Shaw Place. Lina had since become quite a successful vaudeville actress and sang, "Great Grand-Opera Moments," to accompaniments arranged and played by her—er—lover.

From time to time there had been photographs in the Sunday rotogravure sections of Lina with "him" at the piano.

Kate had scarcely known her, although they had attended the same South Side grammar school. There had been little if anything in those days to indicate what power to spring must even then have lain crouched behind the rather solid prettiness of Lina.

What courage. What courage. Kate knew the Rinchoff family. The old man had amassed a fortune in sausage casings, but the family still lived in a rented, two-family house on Gratiot Street and Mrs. Rinchoff could still be seen of any Saturday morning on her back porch, squeezing pot cheese through a bag for Sunday morning's batch of cheese cake. What courage!

The way Kate, now that Paula was in her teens, found herself looking at it was, even if that brilliant smile of Lina's in the rotogravures was only looped over misery, it was a better kind of misery than the incalculably dull wretchedness of being a Hossefrosse or a Rinchoff.

That meant servitude to the relentless routines of respectability, repetition, and with the sole exception of indulgence of palate, frugality. That meant the relentless routine of carrying forward the rigid tenets of stability, morality, practicability.

Practicability, indeed! A Hossefrosse was taught to respect money with an austerity and reverence for its place in the scheme of life. You were meticulous to the penny about money. A penny saved was a penny gained. A Hossefrosse saved for that rainy day.

Once Kate had cut out a newspaper saying, "The rainy day comes to those who wait for it." That, of course, she knew was grossly untrue. But somehow—if one could only be a little gay about money. Money bought nonsenses. It seemed to Kate that nonsenses, bracelets, candies in silver wrappers, fancy dogs with ribbon bows, lingerie, nice table crystal, cigar-shaped roadsters, frail French sitting-room furniture, wrist watches, and bits of court plaster pasted on pretty cheek bones, could make life very gay.

But of course, rightly enough, too, the ideal of a Hossefrosse, over and above those things, was to be in a position where you need never borrow of your neighbor and you expected the same of him. A Hossefrosse never lent; but on the other hand it must be said for a Hossefrosse, that he never borrowed. Undeniably, that was fair enough.

Lina, Kate remembered, had always been careless about the tiny money matters of school life. A penny meant nothing to her. If it rolled beneath a desk, she would scarcely stoop for it. She borrowed freely. Slate sponges, lollipops, pencils. But she gave when she had it, even more freely. In the eyes of a Rinchoff that was as lax, both the giving and the receiving, as it was in the eyes of a Hossefrosse.

What a courage, what a courage Lina had displayed! Only a Hossefrosse, born and bred as a Rinchoff was born and bred, could adequately realize that.

So by the time Paula was sixteen and lovely and her young ears seemed to be laid back to the whinnying of youth to youth, strange, alien, and thoroughly terrifying thoughts were beginning to troop through the orderly brain of her mother.

Even if it should turn out to be a smile looped over misery, Kate wanted Paula in the end to have to conceal a less lowly unhappiness than the drab numbness of being a Hossefrosse.

What if Paula, who was a little snowdrop, should choose to—to go the wrong way of Lina. The bad way of Lina. Why, even as that thought popped for the first time into the appalled brain of Kate, she shooed it out with a literal stamp of her foot as she would a mouse nibbling on her immaculate pantry shelves.

Paula a bad girl? Not the kind of bad girl she had used to frighten out of childish insubordinations with the story of the Hossie-Frossie. Bad in the sense of—sin! No, no, Paula would be better dead than that. That was what they all said of Lina. Better dead. That was what you said of one who had sinned—that way.

And so in the beginning, when Paula started to come to her all agog in her lovely eager way for the denied pleasures she was only just growing up to, Kate was firm as her husband could have been under the pressure.

The idea! Movies on Thursday after school! What was the world coming to? There were plenty of movies to be done at home, helping, if she had so much free time on her hands. Movies on a week day! Who ever heard of such a thing? Such a thriftless American idea! In Kate's day, a girl came home after school and helped her mother or did her lessons. Movies! Fine come-off! Huh, who ever heard the like?

But, Mother, the girls are going to see Rod La Rocque this afternoon. It's only fifteen cents if you cut the coupon out of the *Post Dispatch*.

All the girls are going straight to the bad with their stage-struck ways and hand-to-mouth habits.

Mamma, you don't mean that. Just a movie.

No, Kate did not mean that either. She wanted to mean it. She aped the phrases that came so solidly from her husband's lips, but in her heart the shocking forbidden emotion was rolling about, refuting the words on her lips.

Ask Father to let me go, Mother. It's only fifteen cents.

"Only fifteen cents." Not much for girls whose fathers don't pay their bills. The sooner you learn the value of fifteen cents, the better.

Mother, you don't mean that.

No, Kate did not mean that, either. The mere thought of Paula learning the Hossefrosse value of fifteen cents was terrible to her. But like pebbles, the words that were in reality Rudolph's, kept clattering from her lips. "What-were-folks-coming-to? Wastrel. Hand-to-mouth-ways. Come to a bad end. Stage-struck."

It was not easy to maneuver with Rudolph, who was averse to motion pictures, except once in a while, if Kate went along with her daughter. Usually he came down hard on the suggestion of a matinée at the local stock company which revived old successes and was popular on the South Side.

It hurt Kate, on a Thursday afternoon, for instance, during the rush when the local servant girls, on their "day off," were in buying shoes, to see Paula's bright head bent over the task of trying to force a thick foot into a cheap satin slipper. Paula should have been at gay places, like a matinée, or a tea. There was something revolting in the spectacle of a heavy heel cupped in

Paula's hand, as she coaxed and prodded an unyielding slipper.

Kate in her time had coaxed many a hundred of those bulging feet into reluctant shoes. Every Thursday and Saturday evening for eighteen years, she had helped Rudolph in the store. But now, with Paula suddenly turned aware, so to speak, in the fretful chafing way of frustrated girlhood, not so much a rebellion, as a great fear, was opening up in the secret places of Kate's heart.

Already, on one or two occasions, Rudolph had mentioned as desirable, the Scheidig boy, Otto, who had come from Mannheim, Germany, three years before, to make his home with his uncle Scheidig, an old bachelor watchmaker who was quite a character on the South Side. Otto had not taken to watchmaking, but as foreman in a heel-and-counter factory was working his way toward a white-collar job.

Otto had wide-apart square teeth, a round, not ill-humored face, and a shaved blond head. He was rapidly becoming more and more Americanized in his speech and dress, and was known as a steady fellow.

The eye of Rudolph had swung solemnly upon him for the first time when Paula was sixteen and Otto had walked by the house one July Sunday afternoon with his uncle, as the Hossefrosses were sitting in the side yard for a breath of air.

There was no mistaking it. Otto had sidled up to Paula. It was the first time Kate had seen Paula boy-conscious. She giggled and batted her eyes and rolled them. Somehow Kate had been ashamed for her. Or perhaps only a little horrified. Or even more probably, it might have been the opening up, in the secret places of her heart, of her fear for her daughter.

Kate knew the workings of Rudolph's mind so well. Of late in particular, because a sciatic nerve was combining with overweight to render him less agile on his feet, he had alluded frequently to a hypothetical son-in-law, now that Paula was coming along. The business, while not exactly growing in scope, was growing in its demands.

Boot-making, in the good old sense of its practice by Rudolph's grandfather and father before him, was one thing, but the retail shoe-business was another. Competition was keen. The trade had to be catered to. Since hired help, such as servant girls, did their shopping, for the most part, after the last supper cup was hung on its hook, Rudolph was in favor of keeping the store open six evenings a week. That meant more help.

Rudolph was coveting a son-in-law.

Kate knew. Rudolph, in fact, so much as out and out said so. A steady fellow who could come into the family and take hold. No man, not even Rudolph, could expect to live forever. Kate was a good hefty woman, but for that matter, no longer what she used to be on her feet. Why, Rudolph could remember when Kate, on hands and knees, could scrub the whole of the woodshed floor before she served a six-o'clock breakfast, piping hot, of country sausages, fried potatoes, baking-powder biscuits, fried mush. Of course, there was no longer the woodshed, now that the bit of land back there had been sold to a gasoline station. Still, it is more than possible that even if there had been, Kate would no longer have been the woman she was. Sometimes, kneeling before a customer in the store, it was all she could do to get to her feet again. Rheumatic. Yes, Rudolph coveted a son-in-law, a steady conformative fellow, worthy the opportunity of walking into the chance of a lifetime and carrying on the tradition.

Otto was such a fellow. And Kate knew in her heart that it was a sin against God, against Rudolph, against her child, to harbor these secret places of rebellion within her. Rudolph, who was a hard, dull man, had at least never made her feel, by word or act, his disappointment that there had been no male issue of his marriage. It must, however, have rankled in him all these years. Once, sensing this bitterly, Kate had visited an obstetrician five or six years after the birth of Paula. Apparently there was no anatomical reason, but it was not to be that the house of Rudolph Hossefrosse be blessed with a son. And now, here in Otto was the opportunity for vicarious fulfillment. Kate bit down into her tongue with perplexity at the plight of her emotions.

Otto was amenable timber. Every Sunday he came walking home from church with Rudolph and Paula for midday dinner, and was visiting now, two and three evenings a week besides. And why not? Paula, at seventeen, was out and out pretty, without a threat of any impending deformities of the flesh or spirit. Small wonder Otto's eyes, even while he sat stolidly of a Sunday and talked "leather bellies" and shoe findings with her father, were all delight for her.

How maddeningly precious she seemed to become to Kate just about then, as, trembling on the verge of her adolescence, beauty flashed out over her, eradicating little-girl freckles and knobby places at elbow and knee, rounding her sweet young bosom and creeping along her eyelids in the same crinkles of merriment that had once winked along Kate's.

It was about then, just after Paula had finished the one year of high school which was one more year of schooling than her mother had had before her, that the sly something began to take definite shape in Kate's mind.

Lovely Paula, already too schooled in the meager ways of being a Hossefrosse, must somehow save herself from her destiny of taking up life in her parents' footsteps. Kate could see it all so clearly. Otto and Paula, after the passing of Rudolph and Kate, carrying on. Carrying on.

Pretty Paula, with the crinkles along her eyelids gone, and the lights out of her hair, stooping with Otto at sliding cheap shoes of the mode onto the great feet of the South Side servant girls; white-washing the brick walk that bisected the side yard; bearing her babes in the great ugly square bedroom that overlooked those whitewashed bricks, and hanging out their washings on a rope that was stretched across the upstairs porch outside the kitchen; sitting stiffly in church of Sunday mornings with her stiff Otto beside her, and worshipping before the stiff-eyed image that hung over the hand-crocheted altar cloth. Sunday, Monday, Tuesday, Wednesday, Thursday . . . nick after nick along the Hossefrosse hickory stick.

At thirty, Paula would know life with her eyes shut; at least, she would know that little edge of life which had not passed her by. So much of life would pass Paula. So terrifyingly much. Strange, strange, that in all the years, even including the brief moment of her own rebellion, Kate had not realized until now, with the pollen of youth so brilliantly out on her offspring, how appallingly little of life had ever found its way into that lean gray brick house with the shoe-store front.

The newspapers, the motion-picture screen, the customers' gossip, brought about the only hint of a life beyond that doorstep. Kate had been married for years before she even realized that romance had passed her by. Then Lina had taught her that. The Sunday magazine sections. The occasional visit to the stock-company or motion-picture theater. She began through them to realize that marriage was not the beginning and end of romance.

Paula, too, must be taught that. Take Mary Pickford. She was no more beautiful than Paula. There was that same blue sweetness to their eyes. Why, it was easy as anything to see the resemblance between them. Paula's hair, which Rudolph would not permit her to bob or curl, was lovely even in its tidy bound plaits. Gloria Swanson, whose hems were edged in romance, had no more dazzling smile than Paula's. It never troubled Kate to distinguish these favorites from the rôles they enacted.

As Otto's wooing became slightly more venturesome, the secret place in Kate's heart opened wider and wider. Otto was calling two or three evenings a week now, not excepting Sundays, and Rudolph, openly receptive, was offering him the highest tribute of his hospitality—one of the ten-cent Habanas he kept beside a wet sponge locked away in the top drawer of the ceiling-high wardrobe of their bedroom.

Kate wanted to shout out to Paula that she was walking into a pit with her lovely eyes open. She wanted to shake Paula out of her dangerous tendency to conform. She wanted to dart venomous words into Paula's placid ear, warning her. And yet, outwardly, so that she despised herself, to every stricture, every narrow formula, every rigid receipt of behavior to which Rudolph subscribed, Kate outwardly conformed.

No, Paula must not wear her stockings rolled below her knees in the vulgar vogue that had crept down to the South Side.

No, Paula could not walk South Broadway of a summer evening with the phalanx of South Side girls who twined arms for a stroll and an ice-cream soda.

No, Paula could not stay out late for an ice-cream cone after choir practice.

No, Paula, could not join the new Dutch Treat Club. Dutch Treat indeed! Boys nowadays had no sense of responsibility, letting the girls pay for themselves. A fine come-off! You notice Otto had not joined the Dutch Treat Club. As a matter of fact, he had not been asked, for no specific reason, it is true, but chiefly because he was not well acquainted with that particular group. He talked with an accent and that seemed to make a difference to the young folks. But when pinioned to the subject by Rudolph, Otto had submissively agreed that the right kind of a fellow did not begin life by dodging his responsibility. Dutch Treat? No, siree!

No, Paula could not join all those stage-struck girls who went every week to the Wednesday bargain matinées of the Mound City Stock Company. They were all "stuck on" a leading man named Laribee. He was a tall slim fellow, a perfect lover in his rôles, with a double wave in his rich dark hair and a beautiful sensitive profile. The girls cut his picture out of the newspapers and then sent them to him to autograph. Such nonsense! Thirty cents thrown away.

Once in a while, though, probably once a month, Kate and Paula attended a matinée together, usually on a rainy day when business was slack. There was no getting around it, there was something incontestably, incomparably exciting about Claude Laribee. Silly girls, of course, but what a lover he was in the rôles he played! Kate knew that Paula had an autographed newspaper photograph of him tucked under the very last handkerchief in her glove-and-handkerchief box on her dresser.

Then there began to awake in Paula herself resentments. Otto was all right one or two evenings a week and Sundays. Why, he was almost a beau, the first boy, in fact, she had ever been allowed to sit opposite long enough to elicit even his kind of blinking admiration. He liked her. He evidenced it in a half-dozen shy ways without ever putting it into broken English.

But now that Paula was out of school, the need for relaxation outside the long hours she spent at housework and in the store was greater than it had been.

It seemed to Kate that she could date the new restlessness from a matinée performance they had attended together, when both of them had sat forward in their balcony chairs, hands clasped and their breathing short.

Laura La Putte, the leading woman, was playing the rôle of a lovely, bad girl named Camille. Armand Duval, of course, was played by Laribee, love of whom was ultimately to save Camille from her evil life. There were moments in that play which Kate could not conjure before her without a combination of pain and ecstasy that was almost more than she could bear. It was not alone the death scene—there were numerous other scenes between Armand and Camille—that somehow were packed with the meaning of life. They were too precious to look upon. They were to become symbols, to Kate, not only of what she had missed, but of the things that Paula must not miss.

That night they lay in their adjoining rooms, Kate beside her soundly sleeping spouse, Paula on her bed of chastity, wide-eyed, with an excitement that kept them both strangely, luminously awake. A wakefulness that neither of them would ever have dreamed of admitting to the other.

From then on Paula began to connive actively. There began small white lies to her father as to her whereabouts. To Kate, too, when she asked, but gradually, with a finesse, Kate left off asking.

RUDOLPH: "Where haf you been so late, Paula?"

PAULA: "Just walking, father. It grew late before I noticed."

RUDOLPH: "Always exguses for laciness. Your mother or me got no help from you."

Kate knew that Paula lied about where she had been. She would have known it by her daughter's eyes and the little tormented way she had of rolling them under a lie, but it so happened that the tiny edge of the Mound City Stock Company program protruded slightly from Paula's pocket.

Kate was glad.

Half a dozen times a week it happened thus, while to her strange delight, and at the same time her horror, she beheld her daughter become adept at the subterfuge and the evasion.

Paula, where have you been? Paula, where are you going at this time of the afternoon? You got run-around ways all of a sudden that don't suit me. Where was it you said you stayed so long?

At the grocery.

Lies. Lies. Lies.

Why so long?

Oh, Father, can't a girl stop to look in a shop window or two? For goodness' sake, I've been to choir practice, too! . . . Well, I know, but there was an extra rehearsal this week . . . I'll do the dishes even if I am a little late, Mother.

Lies. Lies. Lies.

Paula was meeting Claude Laribee. Kate knew that privately, exultantly, and at the same time with horror. There were telltale notes beneath the last handkerchief in the glove-and-handkerchief box; there were telltale flushes along her daughter's lovely cheeks.

Claude Laribee, who walked in the beauty of romance, was wooing a Hossefrosse. The fact that it was surreptitious could not seem to matter as it should. In spite of herself, Kate found herself conniving to make subterfuge easier for her daughter; covering up her absences when she could, explaining to Rudolph the unexplainable; keeping Paula's things washed, starched, ironed, as they had never been washed, starched, ironed before.

Locking up nights, Kate failed to draw the bolt any longer on the side door, in order to save her daughter the heavy groaning sound that might waken her father as Paula took to stealing out evenings after she was supposed to have gone primly to her bedroom. Kate knew! It was to meet Claude after his performance. Then she lay, scarcely breathing beside the snoring Rudolph until long past one or two, when she heard her daughter creak in again. To save those creaks, Kate secretly rubbed the floor with lemon oil.

She was glad, triumphantly glad, that Paula made no confidante of her. Then it would have been impossible for her to aid and abet, because with her lips Kate still echoed Rudolph's sentiments. That seemed to give Kate a sort of shallow solace. She forbade her daughter this. She forbade her daughter that. Shiftless American habits. Hand-to-mouthers. What was the world coming to? The modern girl had neither sense of duty nor responsibility. Run-arounds.

If the suspicion ever smote Kate that between Paula and Laribee, whom she was now meeting with a regularity that took away the breath of her mother, all was not as it should be, even that could not down the private exultancy that was hers.

As the stock company's summer season advanced toward its conclusion, it seemed to Kate that the beauty that was Paula's fairly took fire. How tender her lips! As if they had been kissed as never in all her life had Kate's been kissed. She was doubly gracious in her new beauty, even to Otto, as one is under pricks of conscience. A new nervousness gave her sparkle, where before she had been phlegmatic after the manner of Hossefrosse resignation. Her father even remarked it.

"The more life she gets, the lacier."

And with a self-loathing that at times was almost more than she could bear, Kate slyly, skillfully, in a dozen ways, kept opening the cage. Motion-picture magazines found their way into the house to lie carelessly open, revealing the pretty, reckless faces of people who lived dangerously. At least they did in the opinion of Kate. Anything was better—even the unmention-able—than the dust-colored fate of a Hossefrosse that was hovering like a gray bat over the pretty Paula.

Every time that Otto came, Kate could see, with the exultancy in her heart, the dull eyes that Paula now turned upon this squat and stable fellow. His teeth were set so noticeably far apart, he cracked his finger joints, and for the first time Paula seemed to notice and complained hilariously to her mother. He had a square head and small eyes, and his touch was harsh and chapped.

All these little observations Paula vented merrily on her mother. That was as close as she ever approached to confidence. Kate saw to that.

Shame, Paula. Otto is a good, steady boy. He will make some girl a good husband. Your father says he already knows a great deal about the shoe business. He comes from good respectable stock. You shouldn't talk so.

It was all Paula could do to control her mirth. The crinkles were out in merriment along her eyelids. The wrinkles were out of her heart. Night after night, as Kate lay beside the dead-to-the-world Rudolph, stiff with the agony and ecstasy of what she was doing, the vicarious, dear delight of Paula's daring to live dangerously swept over her in wave after wave of emotion. Thrill. Dread. Guilt. Pride. Hope. Fear.

But the fear was mostly for the possibility of Paula's failure. If only Paula were sly enough. For weeks Kate had left a small leather purse containing a one-hundred-dollar bill she had inherited at the death of a brother, lying uppermost on her dresser. To tempt. Laribee must be the sort of a man to demand finery in a girl. For Paula to take from Kate, who was her identical flesh, would not be sin. If only Paula would realize that!

It seemed to Kate, sometimes, that the one-hundred-dollar bill was Paula's way out. And yet she dared not do more than place it there. She could only outwardly scold and contradict; forbid and corroborate Rudolph.

One day Kate heard that Laribee was married and had a wife and two children in Hollywood. She wondered if the neighbor who told it to her had done so innocently, or because gossip was abroad. To her terror it did not matter. To her supreme terror, even the wife and those two little children did not matter! Anything was better—sin—defeat—disappointment—despair—anything was better than that hovering gray bat of a Hossefrosse destiny.

Kate began to hate Otto. The way he masticated his beefsteak, when he came to suppers now on Thursdays, filled her with a kind of antagonism she could never recall having felt for anyone else in her life. He suggested to her the years and years of beefsteaks that a woman could prepare for a man who masticated slowly like that, for full flavor. Otto would grow meticulous about this foods, as Rudolph had. He would pare his square clean finger nails every evening after supper, as Rudolph did.

Life would be a very grave affair for the woman who married Otto, as it had been for the woman who married Rudolph. Respectability. Solidity. Stability. You paid your debts and you expected others to pay theirs. You gave upon occasion, and you expected to receive. You were industrious, pennywise and not pound foolish. Be thou likewise. Otto, like Rudolph, had no impulse. He was Hossefrosse timber, all right!

And so, finally, the last week of the summer stock company season came to hand and the light that hovered over Paula became more and more apparent, not only to her mother, but to the customers in the store, who commented on her new prettiness. But just the same, something tense and panic-stricken had crowded into the blue eyes.

What was going to happen? Would Laribee leave town alone after this season, or would Paula go with him?

To her unutterable shame, Kate found herself praying one night as she lay waiting for Paula. Send her away with him—no matter what—save her—

And the next morning, when Paula, on the pretense of wanting a half-day off for shopping, begged release from store duty, Kate, to salve her scorching conscience, corroborated roundly Rudolph's refusal.

Getting to be a perfect gad-about. What's the world coming to? Extravagant nonsense!

Nevertheless, under pretext of sending her on an errand for herself, Kate finally contrived to hurry her daughter out of the house by matinée time.

Even to the obtuse Rudolph, Paula was high-strung and not quite herself these days. Lovesick, most probably. The young Otto must be brought to understand that his advances were welcomed. Rudolph resolved to wait a week or so and then speak to him. He admired his reticence, but there was such a thing as a young man being too backward. When he confided this to Kate, terror rose high within her.

The stock company was disbanding in three days. Kate had seen Laribee and Paula walking in beautiful Shaw's Gardens twice that week, as she skulked along by-paths, knowing it to be their retreat. They were like a pair of young gods.

No matter what came, Paula must have something of life, even its pain, if need be. Any kind of life, good or bad or indifferent, was better than a Hossefrosse death, as Kate had come to phrase it to herself.

God, give her courage to force life a little—and forgive me for I *do* know what I do . . .

It was on a Sunday, the day after the closing of the Mound City Stock Company summer season, that Kate, walking into her bedroom from an early church service, noticed, as she crossed the threshold, that the little leather coin-purse containing the hundred-dollar bill was gone at last from her dresser! There was a note pinioned like a butterfly to the proverbial pin-cushion.

Paula had eloped! Or gone away—or whatever it was had been possible under the circumstances. Paula was free of the Hossie-Frossie. Tearing open the envelope, Kate's fingers were muddled and her eyes prayerful. It was a lit-tle note on ruled paper, with a tear splotch in its center.

> DEAREST MOTHER, forgive your Paula. No matter what I have done that is considered bad, I love you. Claude is my happi-ness. He loves me and will take me where I will be happy. And the way I figure it, you would want me to be happy for a while rather than never at all, but Claude will make me happy always. Tell Father and Otto at the same time at Sunday dinner, mother dear, as by that time we will be on the train and you will hear from your daughter who loves you soon.
>
> PAULA

> P.S. Mother dear, I borrowed your hundred-dollar bill. I had to have things. I will return it and more.

It had happened. It Had Happened. IT HAD HAPPENED. The words enlarged themselves one by one, until they rang out like chimes. It had happened! Paula, for better or for worse, and it could only be for better, was free of the Hossie-Frossie.

Thank you, God.

In the blue-and-black-shotted silk that Kate wore under a bungalow apron while she prepared Sunday dinner, she sat down on the bed edge to tremble. No one ever sat on a bed edge at the Hossefrosse's. Shiftless American habit.

Paula was free. Terror of the sin her child was committing washed over her and then receded again, leaving her thankful. God would understand. It was no sin for an innocent prisoner to work his way out.

Paula was too pure at heart to ever really sin. And yet—and yet—con-fronted with the appalling task of explaining to Rudolph and Otto that Paula had gone away with a married actor, of whom they in all probability had never even heard, the whole thing, now that it had actually happened, lacked reality. Paula free. She would not have to help pull off her father's heavy stiff shoes this morning when he came in from church. Or baste the roast. Or set the table for four, including Otto, who would walk home from church with

Rudolph, wondering why Paula failed to meet them after choir as usual.

Paula would not have to sit down to the heavy gorge of Sunday dinner, or clear away, while her father stretched out in his chair for a doze with a newspaper over his face, or sit in the side yard with Otto as he indulged in his favorite pastime of drawing human figures without lifting his pencil from paper.

Paula would not have to wash gray calico house dresses on Monday mornings, because Paula would never have gray calico house dresses.

Paula would never again have to coax unyielding slippers onto unyielding feet during those gay bright hours of the evening when supple women like Paula were at their loveliest.

Paula would win, even if she lost.

God, forgive Paula the wrong she is doing, if she is doing it, and make Claude a good man to her.

God forgive me . . .

That was what burned into her heart as she prepared dinner that frantic morning, fumbling among objects that were familiar to her, clattering pans to the floor, forgetting to baste the roast, twirling the summer squash around the great yellow mixing bowl to the consistency that Rudolph liked, and then, to her horror, letting the bowl and all, whirl from her hands to the floor. Rudolph liked his summer squash of a Sunday dinner. Somehow he seemed entitled to it after his six lumbering days. Sometimes Kate went as far as Soulard Market shopping for summer squash.

Whirlwind after whirlwind of emotion smote Kate as she rushed through that Sunday morning.

Presently Rudolph and Otto would appear at the top of the flight of back stairs that led into the kitchen from the back yard. Otto and Rudolph would wash their hands at the kitchen sink and dry them on the roller towel and then proceed to the dining-room to sit at one end of the already set table to wait for the dishing-up. Or, if the weather was fine, sometimes they sat on the ledge of the upper porch, while Kate and Paula hastened around indoors preparing dinner. Rudolph liked his seersucker in place of the heavy coat he wore to church. There was an extra one hung behind the door and sometimes he had Otto change into it. This Otto did good-naturedly, feeling too Americanized by now in his dress, to really desire to appear in a seersucker coat before Paula, yet relaxing gratefully to the comfort of the lighter weight garment.

Paula was free!

Any moment now, Rudolph and Otto, who was already half Hossefrosse, would come plodding up those back stairs. Rudolph, as he washed his hands with brown soap, would be querulous because Paula had failed to meet them after choir. Otto would be furtively eager. He had a way of moistening his lips when he looked at Paula. Well he might, because she would have been a choice morsel for such a dull fellow. And now, without intervention on the part of Kate, without ever having given voice to the traitorous thoughts that had burned within her, Paula was free.

There! They were coming up the stairs already. O God—help me to tell them—there they were!

There they were *not*. It was Paula's frenzied footsteps falling over each other as she dashed up the stairs.

Paula—Paula—no, not you!

I'm in time, Mother? Tell me I'm in time—they haven't come yet? Oh, thank God!— Oh, thank God!—I couldn't have stood it if I had been too late.

For what?

For Father and Otto—you haven't read them the note? Mother—quick—say you haven't.

Why, no! Why, no!

Thank God! Thank God! Mother, don't look at me like that!

Like what?

As if you didn't want me in the house. I was only crazy, Mother. I got my senses back at the station. I couldn't really do what wasn't right. He—Claude—kept making it sound all right, Mother, but when I got as far as the train, I knew, all of a sudden, I'm not the girl to live her life that way. I've come back to Otto, Mother, and to you and Father. Always—I'll be good—I'll try to be good—

You've come back . . .

Mother—Mother, don't look at me that way—as if you didn't want me! I've been terrible—but just promise that you'll never tell Father or Otto about the note. Here's your Paula back, Mother, just as she's always been. Never bad—only so near being bad. . . .

Standing there with a steaming apple pie held out before her, and feeling ridiculous as she had never felt ridiculous before, the words began to rattle mechanically off of Kate's lips.

Bad girl. Stage-struck. Come to no good end. Disgrace to parents. Scandal narrowly averted. What's the world coming to. Shiftless ways breed evil living. Wastrel.

Then tears. The bitterest tears that Kate had accumulated in a lifetime. Tears, tears, because of the return of the prodigal, and still the stiff, machine-made phrases keep coming. Bad girl. Evil ways.

As if grateful for the excoriations, Paula humbled herself before the avalanche, dropped to her knees before her mother, and let her face fall into her hands, as if inviting her mother's tears to scald her.

"Get up," said Kate, and jerked her to a standing posture. Her eyes were blazing in a kind of wrath. Kate was licked and Kate was mad with pain.

You fool! You fool! You fool!

Mother, forgive, Claude's gone for good. O God, he's gone—for good!

Cry, you fool! Well you may cry! You fool! You fool!

I won't cry for him, Mother, I promise you that. I'll settle down, dear, with Otto—just as you did with Father. You'll never tell on me, Mother—promise me you'll never tell. . . .

"Fool! Fool!" cried Kate, and turned her back on her daughter as if the sight of her prettiness were only further flagellation that she could not endure. And so in a way it was. Paula was in a new suit, a natty blue one, that struck her at the knees and had a little military row of silver buttons down one side. New blond kid slippers she wore, the kind that Hossefrosses' did not carry in stock, and there were clocks to her stockings, and on her wrist a large leather handbag to match them. There was even a boutonnière of little ruby crystal cherries on her lapel. Nonsenses. Claude must have pinned them there. Just nonsenses. Some of the nonsenses that Kate had craved so for Paula. And for what?

"Mother, if you don't forgive me, I'll kill myself."

"I forgive you."

"Not in that heavy voice, darling."

"Not in a heavy voice."

"And you won't tell—ever—"

"I won't. . . ."

"Give me the letter."

"No, no. Let me keep it."

"Give me the letter. I couldn't rest if you didn't."

"Here it is."

It made little sounds like little cries as Paula tore it to bits. There was nothing left now of Paula's rebellion as she crammed those bits into the stove. It had never been. It was a dream.

"Mother—That's Father and Otto now. Quick, let me climb out of these clothes."

It was the two of them arriving from the church, delayed, and Rudolph querulous because there had been no Paula on schedule.

Recriminations galore, as usual, and Paula quick with the ready-made little fib, throwing on the long-sleeved bungalow apron which her mother tore off and threw to her, until opportunity to change from the suit of the bright silver buttons into the uniform of a Hossefrosse Sunday afternoon.

Unreliable, these children of today. Loose American ways. Shiftless.

Irresponsible. Don't let it happen again.

No, Father.

Off with her father's heavy, square-toed shoes.

How usual! How like a dream! How like a squirrel cage spinning its way with impeccable velocity. The dishing-up, with Paula scurrying at the chores which were already second nature to her.

Could Kate be dreaming that she was dreaming?

Yet, no, there was Rudolph, trying to fit together the fragments of the yellow bowl and making talk about carelessness and waste. Then there was a heavy jest from him as Paula tugged at his boots. It was good to have one's boots dragged off by a pretty girl, eh, Otto? Well, never mind, one must wait his turn.

Otto, whose feet were burning in his shiny yellow shoes, was proud of their American nattiness, but he drew them under his chair as he reddened. Oh, but it would have felt good to have Paula draw them off, too. How pretty her hands. Little curves that one liked to watch doing things. She could do things, all right. Just like her mother. Just like Otto's mother in Mannheim.

Kate kept moving through the idea of dreaming that she must be dreaming.

The men were in the dining-room now, waiting.

Paula, the soup! Rudolph liked it in a tureen, steaming hot. There were creamed onions, great pearly hen's eggs of onions. Otto always half resisted these, ogling Paula, and then, tormented and tempted at the same time, invariably capitulated. There was a roast that ran red juices and made Paula sway-back as she carried it in on its platter. The flanges of the men's noses, sniffing it, widened.

Rudolph and Otto were talking now of a new shoe firm that had opened a Sunlight Factory on the South Side. It left the women bits of time to cover themselves more securely with composure.

What a little curtain of a person Paula was! All drawn before herself. Who could have dreamed, from the *mädchen* composure of her face, that tornadoes had blown through it that very morning. There was composure even to the way her braids were bound around her head. How Kate had longed to see her head shorn of them and bobbed.

It was only in her eyes that the death, a much bigger one than her mother had died eighteen years before, had taken place. It was doubtless the way the light was reflected, but it seemed to Kate, munching and munching from the meat to the potatoes and back again to the meat, that there was a small vertical dagger in each of them.

And yet Otto, even through the talk of the Sunlight Factory, try as he would to keep his respectful attention for Rudolph, could not keep his glance, excited, from sliding constantly around to Paula. His lips grew moister. He was ecstatically conscious of her. And she threw him her constant smile, with no pretense at subtlety.

Well, maybe it was for the best. The old pang of remorse at her incredible perfidy bit at Kate's breast. There was something to be said for the stability of these two stepping in to take hold where she and Rudolph must eventually leave off. Security was not to be winked at. Otto and Paula would procreate. They were strong young things. There was something about the flare of Paula's lovely thighs and the swell of her young breasts that made her fertility a foregone conclusion.

Paula would have children. Many of them. She would bear them in the black-walnut bedroom with the chocolate-ocher wall-paper. Their washings would hang on the short rope across the upper back porch. Yes, Paula would have children. The first should be a little girl. Girls were cozier. . . .

Funny Face

First Published: *Cosmopolitan*, July 1931
Reprinted: *We Are Ten*, Harper & Bros., 1937

In the very midst of selling a man a policy, some such thought as this would strike Harry:

What the hell! What's the big idea of standing here trying to sell life insurance to this fellow who is afraid even to talk of death. It's a goddam joke. Me, who loves death. Me, who has never wanted to live, anyway not with my very gizzard, the way this poor fish does.

That was true of Harry. Rather terribly true, although nobody knew it but himself, chiefly because his slightly oversized head, round as a toy balloon, was a comic mask that sat on the stem of a next-to-nothing neck close to his short and heavily squat body. A mask that creased into a thousand wrinkles in order to smile and that poured into its own crevasses to laugh.

It laughed readily, and, by the plastic trick of the wrinkles becoming crevasses, inspired the risibilities of the beholder.

Not only in that virtue, but in his early cognizance of it lay Harry's secret of success in business.

People—folks—the world—were so genuinely eager to smile. Something pathetic about it. Ever see a crowd of people trying desperately to laugh at some street scene that wasn't funny at all, or smiling over comic strips that were depicting some form of human discomfort?

Look at the way they jammed outside the moving-picture theaters if somebody like the Marx Brothers or even an old Chaplin picture happened to be the attraction. They stood in line, almost as if they had brought with them, under their overcoats or in their handbags, little bundles of laughter which they were pathetically eager to offer up. These people waited there with the desire for laughter trembling behind their straight lips. One little tickle from a backward kick of Charlie Chaplin, or a zany gyration from a Marx, and they would pour the precious fluid of laughter at the feet of their comedians.

There was a little backward kick somewhere in the facial expression of Harry. People smiled or wanted to smile as they passed him. Fellows in business slapped him on the back and told him he was good for what ailed them. Youngsters liked Harry, although with them he was shy, as if apologetic to them for the life to come.

Funny thing this youngster business. Toting them. Holding them up at zoos to feed peanuts to giraffes.

Watch the average young father show off his kid. Instinct, of course. You expected mothers to have it. But apparently so did fathers. Fatten a kid for life, just as you fatten a calf for slaughter. . . . Funny thing. Well, anyway, kids liked Harry, and one little one, son of a client to whom he had sold a large endowment policy, asked him once, in delighted treble, to make another face when Harry had not consciously been making a face at all.

He profited by all this. A sly knowledge crept in behind that humorous mask of his and gave him a selling technique.

Make 'em laugh!

It was not easy, because in selling life insurance your talking point was death. It was, ironically enough, if one were only permitted to cash in on it, the surest talking point with which a salesman could ever hope to be blessed.

You might talk with a fair degree of certainty to a man contemplating the purchase of a family sedan, an electric iron, or a bond, but the man who sold his product on the supposition of death, sold it on an absolute certainty!

"Ever think of that?" Harry used to ram home to the prospective owner of a policy, in the days before he had learned to reconcile himself to the fact that human nature would not reckon with this certainty. It was one thing for him to have chosen as his merchandise a product based on the one certainty in life: death. Not "Sir, *if* you die." But "Sir, *when* you die." It was another matter entirely to dare to introduce this perfect selling point to a prospective customer.

Men, if you so much as mentioned death, turned away with faces so drawn and apprehensive that one hesitated to behold this indecent exposure of fear.

And so, even if he had chosen the business of life insurance because it reckoned with the surefire, the sweetish, the tranquil reality of death, it took Harry just about two weeks to realize that the only way successfully to focus the buying attention of a man on the subject of death was to speak of it in terms of life.

"Old man, ever stop to think how you are some day going to enrich the life of that dear little wife of yours by protecting her with a life-insurance policy—endowment plan—against her future?"

Or, "My friend, life insurance today isn't merely a safeguard for your loved ones. It's a life line! Ever hear the story about the man who lives to be a hundred and ten. . . ."

Idiots! The way to fool them into cognizance of the sweet, invincibility of death was to sell them assurance of the walk in a vale called life.

One soon learned. You earned the living you lived. Harry, at an early age, was able to earn a fairly good one. Sometimes it seemed to him that this was perversely true because he cared so little. Not in the desperate and brooding sense of the neurotic. Rather, to Harry, ever since he could remember, death had seemed something in the nature of a grand going home.

In the main, however, the rather blasting periods of depression to which he had been periodically subject since his boyhood life with a widowed aunt in Utica, these strange almost irresistible yearnings, persisting through adolescence, for the lure of early death or the lethal waters of suicide, were not in the ascendant.

As a growing lad he had not dreaded these secret onslaughts into the normalcy of his days in Utica, of his strange etheric impulses toward death. They had seemed more normal than life itself.

Once the aunt with whom he dwelt, had routed out a drawerful of books which in her mind did not correlate beyond "truck," but which were unified by a common theme. Books accumulated by a lad on Death. *The Raven* (school edition). "Quoth the Raven, 'Nevermore.'" (Somewhere in that thought lay death.) *Twenty Amusing Ways of Committing Suicide.* (Ten cents, off a second-hand stall.) *Death of a Lady.* (Same stall.) The title, though, of that dime volume had been misleading. The lady had not died at all, except sort of socially because of bad morals, and that was entirely another matter. *Thanatopsis*, poetry that made sense, about death. *Life and Death of Abraham Lincoln.* Just think, the shot had entered him in the very midst of life, cutting him off almost immediately into death. And by now Abraham Lincoln, and most people in fact, had been dead so much longer than they had lived! Ten, twenty, fifty, a thousand times longer! Very dickens the way some thoughts were too big to clutch onto for more than a moment before they disintegrated in the mind and became mere confusion. So reasoned a boy.

But by the time one was twenty, twenty-five, then thirty, these secret contemplations riddled one less and less. Living life took every moment of time and every ounce of energy. To become a successful insurance agent meant to permit no grass to grow under your feet, but plenty of it across the idea of the grave. Sometimes months would pass without so much as a faint surging of the old desire to turn to the strange seclusion called death, an urge which was almost like a desire he had noted in babes, to turn face away from the approach of a stranger, into its mother's breast.

Whole months could pass now without the faint surgings. . . .

It was a mere trick of the face though, Harry decided, that had pulled him out by the boot straps.

How could a man with a round amused-looking face be other than just that? A man with a round amused face. And soul. Even with the now sporadic impulses to turn to the scarred breast of some motherlike earth and say "I hurt! Take me back," one could not, in business give in to such alien fancies. One certainly could not if the business was life insurance.

One had to buttonhole the man to whom one was attempting to sell life insurance, throw him, rope him, slay his sense of anathema to the proposition of a policy, with laughter.

Men smiled back at what they must have mistaken for Harry's smile. But for the most part Harry's smile finally became sufficiently authentic; a not too conscious lifting of the muscles to simulate love of life and zest for the job.

Before he was forty, Harry had plastered life-insurance policies across the futures of hundreds of men and women whose protection against tomorrow would ordinarily have been about the distance between hand and mouth.

Harry's a good egg. Might not think so to look at him, but that little fellow has advanced premiums on enough lapsing policies to pave his way from here to heaven. There's plenty of widows living snug as bugs in this town right now who would have been left penniless except for that good egg carrying some bad egg of a husband's policy.

That was true enough, although it was Harry's boast that in all the years of his coming to the rescue of jeopardized policies, in only two cases had his confidence in the ultimate integrity of the embarrassed policyholder been misplaced.

Indeed, in countless cases Harry had been known to carry along policies, collecting only after a demise.

But even more than in his Samaritanism, the secret of his success resided in his salesmanship.

"If anybody had told me I'd be sucker enough to tie myself up for life insurance at this low tide in my affairs!" more than one signer, placing his pen to the dotted line of one of Harry's policies, had remonstrated. "You're the darndest little fellow! What you grinning at? Don't blame too much. The laugh is on me."

As a matter of fact, the laugh was on Harry. Hung across his face as external as a mask.

The swoop of the so-called dove of love, this one a little battered, into his loveless life came with the suddenness of a visitation.

Into the boarding house and into the life of this little man of no sex history whatsoever, there entered, along about the same time he was forty-two, a woman who was even more of a ruin than she appeared to be.

And what a ruin! Great bandages of still-red hair wrapped her head as if the skull had been broken in a crash. Low-lidded eyes that should have been green and perhaps once were, swam behind mucus. A ruin of a neck splattered with pale liver blotches was hung with beads and chains into which powder lodged. A gaunt woman of great height. A dimming head which shone in the doused fashion of a lantern at dawn.

That was Mary, whom, from the moment his hitherto uncovetous eyes had clapped onto her, Harry, who had never lain with a woman, was to desire with all the aching of suddenly aroused flesh.

She was older than he, she was tireder than mountains are old, and what lay in her eyes was torpid.

What lay in her eyes when she first beheld Harry in Mrs. Paley's boarding house was even more torpid than their usual stale stillness. Lack of desire for this male, and a dead kind of pain of some sort, and high-toned disdain of the Paley environment that was like cotton toweling to a flesh that in its day had known fragrance and massage.

It was interesting and no little magnificent to observe her varying appetites for the foods which, if Mrs. Paley's boarders ate without any particular relish, they at least consumed with a certain respect for caloric nourishment and with that dogged principle of the will to live in order to carry on such occupations as those of public accountant, claim agent, stenographer, veterinarian, insurance agent, cashier, taxidermist, saleslady, and box-office clerk. The woman named Mary would turn over her helping of hip-steak or stir into the canary bathtub of succotash, and something in the mucous green of her eyes and in the flesh along her straight nose would seem to crawl up and nest in offended fastidiousness behind the bandage of reddish hair that lashed her brow.

At a board where plates were scraped empty or mopped up by permissible wads of white bread on the tips of forks, her untouched prunes or palid, rebuking slice of lamb, as it rode away on the palm of a rigidly unobservant landlady, gave her one more touch of preciousness in a whole string of them the like of which Harry had never known.

Sultry, tragic, thwarted grandeur suddenly set down here in the midst of the most unsultry, untragic, unthwarted atmosphere conceivable.

It made gossip fly, and through the hailstones of it there raged in Harry the first surging love-of-life he had ever known.

Love of life, and, long before he was knowing it, love of Mary.

Time became suddenly a grand mosaic of hitherto nonexistent, unobserved, or undreamed facts. The uplifted look to the breasts of women beneath their blouses was beautiful. Especially Mary's. How tender the lips of women could seem. Especially Mary's, since their contrast with her thwarted-looking eyes was so great. Perfume was an unsubtle invitation to the senses. . . .

There were changeable-silk pillows on Mary's bed. Mostly lavender and winking violet. He had had flashes of them in passing her open door. At sight of the small triangles, trimmed in cotton-stuffed grapes and tarnished gilt lace, and at the whiffing odor of her which had lain since her arrival like sifted body-powder through the hallways, a pain shot through the pit of Harry that might be said to have cleft the history of his entire experience in two.

The life before the advent of the burnished splendor named Mary. The life after.

He once tried to convey that to her shortly after their amazing, not to say incredible, marriage.

"Do you know, Mary, I have the feeling that all my life I haven't been really born until now."

She was in the ebullient spirits that one who feels himself slipping without hope of rescue down a steep mountain side must experience after he has been dragged back to the surface by a miraculously thrown lifeline.

Substantial, money-earning men, to whom women are potential wives, do not look into the human discard for them.

Harry had. On the down side of a life where men no longer even sought her body, this miracle on two stubby legs had walked first into her sense of the ridiculous and then into her desperate sense of her need for security.

One of those life-of-the-party boys that in one form or another grace every boarding-house table. Made her want to laugh, this little funny-face guy, even before he opened his mouth and caused the very particles of dreariness that made up her very being disintegrate into authentic impulse for laughter.

And God knows, God knows, God knows, at this time, on an abominable slope of her life, Mary needed to laugh.

And to think that on this slope there should appear on two stubby legs one not only willing to provide, but to husband her!

No great wonder that in his words to her, "Do you know, Mary, I have the feeling that all my life I haven't been born until now," there should seem an equal amount of miracle.

They were stricken, each of these two, with a sense of his own miracle come to pass.

How tired she was! It made him want to rest her with some of the buoyance which he felt that he could pour out of his bones into hers.

What a ninny he was! Comic valentine; and yet how indescribably precious to come actually bringing to her security, at a time when men in general, and one in particular, oh so terribly, terribly in particular, had done with her.

Harry knew that—at least the general aspect of it. She had told him of the one in particular in the soiled vocabulary that was usage to her. Somehow, on her lips, what in another might have sickened him, only quickened him.

She was like a summer storm that has spent itself and has only heat lightning left. To Harry she was all grandeur. For the first time life was sweeter than his congenital impulse to turn away from it, an impulse which died down completely when his body came awake to passion.

They lived in a good neighborhood in a good flat which she fitted up, between fits of almost overwhelming lassitude, in the key of the changeable-silk violet and orchid pillows which had first so inflamed his fancy.

"I'm a bitch and you're a prince, Funny-face, and don't ever think I'm not onto it," she told him once in one of the rare fits of tenderness for him that would overtake her.

"When they said at the boarding house that your little finger is worth more than my whole body, they were damn right and I know it."

"Don't, Mary," he said, and tried to enfold her gaunt splendor in his short arms. "When you talk like that it hurts me more than I can stand."

"I'm so tired, Harry. Tired and dirty with living. This deal you're giving me is like a warm bath."

But more usually she was just the rather burnished-looking sunset enfolded in the mists of a lassitude that made it possible for her to lounge hours on end among the ornate pillows, literally waiting for each day to pass and place itself on end against the beginning of the next.

Waiting.

But to Harry, in the home he had so miraculously been able to create for himself and this woman, was anything but the dreariness of fact.

She was a bloom on the window sill of his life all right, on the sill of a window which practically all his previous days had too often looked out over vales filled with doggerels and scraps of imagination. "Xerxes did die, and so must I." "Virgil and Dante walking on a plain that sloped downward into shade. . . ." The first was in a school book; the second, on a lithograph.

All that was changed now. No more, that recurring sense of an insanity of depression. No more, that almost overwhelming impulse to walk off a high place or press the little round cold gape of a revolver against the roof of a mouth under which imprisoned depression could no longer seem to contain itself.

Nowadays, when you sold a man life insurance, nothing popped out at you like an impish falsetto voice barking from your heart, "Well, what of it? What the hell! What does it all mean anyway? Why am I standing here trying to sell life insurance to a fellow whose life isn't worth insuring?"

The reason was jolly well apparent now. The reason was Mary. How the gal, bless her, could make the money fly! Not during the first year though. It was as if she had then been too tired.

It was as she began to brighten and regain what must have been some of her even more splendid splendor that this appealing naughtiness of her extravagance began to assert itself. It made a fellow jump all right, and on occasion dig down into a nest egg that had accumulated before her advent because of not enough zest for living, and for which he had never entertained great respect.

The zest flowing back into Mary was happy contagion. The flat looked less like a sample one that had been built and fitted out on the furniture floor of a department store. Flowers that cost like the dickens stood about in tall vases now. Curtains appeared before the windows in elaborate crisscrosses of laces and net. One shopped with Mary on Saturday afternoons, in and out of furniture and department stores, or waited around at glove counters while she delved into departments that had not to do with the ways of mere men.

Old friends of Mary's bobbed up. A man named Russel, a reddish lank fellow with a handsome lantern face. A woman named Gracie Darb. Such a "kidder." Good card, though, Gracie. Full of the Old Nick. Had lived all right, but then, God bless her soul, he wouldn't give a snap of a finger for the woman who hadn't. Another pair, named Elsie and Blackie, were in the offing too.

There had been dinner parties in the flat, and much gin and ginger beer, and at one of them Mary had sobbed something hoarse against the crumpled shirt-front of the man named Russel. A curt, snarlish fellow, this Russel, a man of no ostensible affairs, but a manner of seeming to have them. A fellow to whom you said as little as possible, chiefly with the hope of getting the same in return.

Well, Mary liked this crowd. No accounting for taste, but—it is possible that in the instant when Mary was pressing hot inarticulate lips against Russel's shirt-front, Harry must have looked the something that went through him as if someone had forced the ice-pick, with which either Mary or Gracie had been chopping ice all evening, right through his bowels.

There was something in the way Russel looked at Mary; in the way Mary looked at him. Something spilled from their eyes. Something old and crammed with memories. And passion. His fingers curved inward when he pawed her in a sham battle of the multitude of sofa pillows that strewed every scene that had to do with Mary. Their fingers seemed too magnetized to draw apart. Also, there was something in the forced noisy gayety of Gracie, whenever those two met in propinquity, which made it all seem for a moment to Harry, who sat with all the screwings of his face in their tightest grimace of laughter, as if she were trying to divert him from the spectacle of Mary and Russel, whose hands, when they touched on this pretext or that, could scarcely draw apart.

Was this the last lover who had discarded her, come back again now that a certain bloom had returned to Mary? Was this man's past linked with her just as—just as his body might have been?

The sensation of that red-hot ice pick darting through Harry was like cramp.

"I'm a skulking, suspicious low-down," he told himself, and began, with the sensation of cramp still cutting him, to try to partake of the gayety.

But at the point where Mary laid her lips to Russel's shirt-front and sobbed the something hoarse against his rumpled front, an explosion from Harry's lips and from the contact of a heavy bronze ornament which he lifted and brought down on the table brought the entire group of them up shortly.

Goddam—enough!

It was a clamp on the gayety of the party. It never happened again because there were no more parties. He loved her for that, because he knew to what extent he had played the ungenerous jealous fool and to what extent she, Mary, must have put a taboo on a brand of merriment and company that, try as he would to condone it, could never be congenial to him.

It had been one matter at these parties—always, mind you, with that sense of outsider—to expose himself to the "all-around-kidding," as they put it, and get the crowd laughing at his expense, but it was quite another to see a man like Russel, somehow in a devilish subtle way, lose no opportunity to put him in his place as jester to Mary's court.

These were friends of Mary's and, as such, entitled to all the consideration and hospitality he could give them; but when they ceased to be visitors after that episode of the bronze ornament, Harry did not comment. He sensed that Mary sensed how terribly he had been jarred, and gratitude increased his tenderness.

Darling gal. The days were her own to do with as she pleased, but the evenings were Harry's! The evenings and the nights.

Let her spend. Even if the afternoon bridge parties which she described as her pastime made inroads into the budget that sometimes startled even Harry, to whom money had so little, If any, of the value it can so often have to those like himself who have had to earn every penny of it along the way. Let her spend, even if it sometimes seemed that she poured too much into those mysterious coffers of the bridge table and too little spending seemed to show elsewhere. Sly economies. No more flowers. No more conspicuously thick and expensive cuts of steak for the Gracies and the Russels. Just Harry and Mary drawn up beside their own little table and served by a Negro maid who shuffled.

And after dinner, Mary, in the endearing fatigue that had her once more in its grip, stretched out on the living-room divan in something chiffon and the sultry color of heat lightning.

"Funny-face billikens, rub my wrists. I love so to have them rubbed. Buddie-billikens, massage my forehead. Just massage and massage it."

She could lie that way behind closed eyes for hours.

Once, as she lay beneath his stroking motion, relaxed, and with something beatific across her face which was not somehow characteristic of the way she took his caresses open-eyed, a thought struck him:

For all I know, she is lying there trying to imagine I am someone else.

She was.

He arraigned himself for such thoughts. They laid him low with a sense of treason. Here was a woman who had told him truths about herself which, even while they for the most part sickened, filled him on the one hand with an exultant realization of her dramatic bigness, and on the other with pity for the weakness and weeness of her in turning like a scourged child to the warmth of the security he provided her.

To hold doubts of such a woman, who had come frankly, showing her scars, into the tent of his bed and board, was to defile the very bigness of her courage in self-revelation, which from the first had given her grandeur.

What more could a woman do than Mary was doing? She bore with him, didn't she? And God knows nobody knew better than he, Harry, to what extent this woman, who was as tragic and as grand-looking as Bernhardt must have been tragic and grand-looking, must have stooped at the shoulders to enter the lowly tent of his life!

What right had he to question further than she chose to reveal? Suppose Russel was—suppose— What right had he to question further? He, the grimacing and allegedly comic little strip, who had dared to hold a life cheap— a life that would one day contain this woman.

My God, down on his hands and knees and belly would be more like it.

Wasn't she home every evening like clockwork, when he came from business? Why question what she did with her days if, as upon occasion, he unexpectedly returned of mere nostalgia for the aroma of her, never to find her there? Come supper time she was there all right. If she played away her days at the bridge tables of old cronies who, she knew, were not congenial to him, what was that but deference to his unspoken wish that she keep them out of sight?

As to the money itself, the steady stream of it which somehow seemed to flow into the bottomless pit of Mary's needs was his gladsome gift to her, wasn't it? If precious little of it seemed to go on her back in the gewgaws and finery with which it had amused her, following their marriage, to bedeck herself, who but a swine like himself would permit the malodorous suspicion to enter his mind that she might be diverting moneys to Russel! She avowedly liked playing cards for stakes—had confessed that to him early in their meeting and constantly since, in a way that did almost proclaim too loudly.

Was it—was it that the money was being diverted in some way to the man Russel, who had bobbed back into her life no sooner than marriage and security had resuscitated her beauty? Was he the man in particular, rather than the men in general, who had grown tired of her and then, on beholding the grandeur of her head lifting, had drifted back again to one whose love for him was stronger than her pride?

Curious that he, Harry, without a clue, should sense all this in Russel in those few gatherings in his home, and in the one occasion when the gesture of his disapproval had leaped beyond his control.

Pish, down on his hands and knees and belly in gratitude, rather than sniveling in suspicion, would be more like it.

Precisely so the day was saved, in realization that in suspicion lay ruin.

In the winter of Mary's existence resided spring for him. He knew that. He became content and even more content, as her pity, which was true, folded him into snug harbor.

And into that pity, and her desire not to hurt this little man, there poured the additional ingredient of desire to compensate. Sense of guilt made her more than kind toward him who had pulled her from the terror of those first lean months at the boarding house, when all men in general had done with her, and seemingly the one in particular!

The desire to compensate for what she could never be to Harry, either faithful or even decent, became almost as deeply rooted in her as her growing sense of panic at her dilemma.

To lie in the arms of Russel through days that she filched from Harry, to pour compensation moneys from the pockets of one man into the pockets of another in order that he would rescind his terrible ultimatum of having done with her, was, even in the tarnished eyes of Mary, anathema almost beyond endurance.

Despair made her tender.

"You're a good little ace, Harry. God never made better."

He grew, during their long evenings at home, to like to lie on the sofa with his head in her lap while she ran fingers, off which she had pulled their load of gold rings, in light, tickling sensation along his brow. In a way, it was his imitation of the something esoteric in her which was always demanding to be stroked.

"Rub my wrists, billikens—my head. . . ."

He loved to do it, as her eyes closed like slow fans. And yet it was all he could do, like someone who presses with all his weight against a door to shut out an intruder, to keep down that devil of a thought:

For all I know, she is lying here trying to imagine I am someone else.

To this man, whose adolescence had slipped in and out of his youth as innocuously as a plain woman passing through a ballroom, and who had lain with but one woman, and she his wife, the fact of impending parenthood slid about crazily in his mind for weeks.

Mary was going to have the child all right. Easy enough to grasp that. Women quite a few years her senior had their first successfully. The book *Plain Facts about Life* said that. The beautiful growing bulk of Mary, who almost from the first carried her child with great apparentness, proclaimed that.

It was where Harry himself was concerned that credulity failed him.

There are some people about whom certain situations are unthinkable. Parenthood for Harry was one. That weazened, laugh-provoking face of his, with the twisted look in the eyes and mouth that was meant to simulate merriment, did not harmonize with what was about to befall him.

"I can't imagine you, billikens," she said to him tenderly one night as she lay stretched on the sofa beneath his tireless strokings, a voluminous, badly mussed, lace dressing gown covering her bulbous body like surf whose spume is soiled. "You'll be good as hell to the child. There's no sin in bringing this one into this vale of tears, as the saying goes, with a daddy like you on its reception committee. But there are just some things one cannot imagine about other people. And yet why not! God knows you'll be ten times the parent I'll be."

He was deeply moved, because lying there with her eyes closed and the pallor of her impending travail already over her, she was about to yield from the mysterious tomb of her body an even greater miracle, if possible, than the miracle of herself.

My, my. He was no good at expressing the almost unbearable waves of ecstasy at the resurrection of the dead wastes of himself. No longer dust to dust. Life to life, now! His life into another! My, my.

Chirp, chirp. How he chirped. Sometimes, as she lay with her eyes closed, her finger nails bit into her palms and made deep half-moon indentations of nerve strain at these chirping sounds he made. "My, my. A little milk? Milk is nourishing. What's this here? Your cover slipping? My, my, that's just like me. It's your own Mother Hubbard I'm trying to tuck in around you."

Mother Hubbard! Wouldn't the ninny say Mother Hubbard! God, it would be a relief to tear that Mother Hubbard off her hurting body and wrap it around his neck, if that would stop his ceaseless chirpings and grimacing with that little walnut face of his. At least it was good for one thing, that face. It made you want to laugh. It made you want to laugh even while a pain the shape of a poker was stabbing through your vitals. It made you want to laugh, and if you ever got started laughing. . . .

"My, my, I've heard tell of hot whiskey. Or was it hot milk?"

Poor devil. Sit here and rub my wrists so I can close my eyes and—imagine—

At two o'clock on the morning following that evening the baby was born.

Out of all the to-do and frightening intimacies of a child born at home, even after a nurse had brought him out assurances and permitted him a glimpse of a bundle that held the small squirm of his son, the sense of let-down was terrible.

He stood beside a window he had flung open, fighting the ignominy of being sick and trying to attribute the sense of disappointment and chagrin or defeat that flowed over him, to reaction from strain.

There was a special kit of emotions supposed to be all set and ready, like tools in a box, for occasions such as this.

Well, there certainly was this much: the crying relief in his heart over the successful emergence of Mary from that endless night of her travail. Much of the sickness which was out in cold sweat over him and made his legs want to go down under him was relief from those hours of waiting. She had been so silent. Not a cry. Only the nurse on her endless, mysterious errands through the halls, and the sound of the doctor's voice and the clink of his instruments. "Thank God—thank God for Mary, and, of course—of course—for his son."

He asked to see him again, and this time the squirm in the bundle which the nurse held, slept, so for a while, quite unembarrassed before him, it was possible for Harry to observe his son.

"Goddam little brat!"

The phrase, shooting through him, shocked him so that for a moment the nurse thought he was going to faint, and, with her bundle hoisted on one arm, made him sit down and opened his collar, and forced some spirits of ammonia between his chilly lips.

"Now, now," she said in the professional tone she had applied to many a squeamish-feeling new father, "what you need is rest."

"Sure," he said, trying to fumble back among the wrappings of his ox-blood-colored child, and wanting to pour his restitution in caresses because of the terrible phrase that had come at him like a bolt out of the blue. "Nice little fellow, isn't he?"

"What a phiz," thought the nurse. "Right comic. That old girl in there must have known her onions when she married that map. She should know how nearly she didn't pull through!"

For that matter, not even Harry was to know that. By noon of the next day, Mary, strangely younger-looking and less the ruin with no pretense at rouge, was half-sitting among her pillows, her son, for whom she had not the yield of milk, lying in the immemorial nest of her arms that women shape for new infants.

"Big Funny-boy, look at little Funny-boy," she said to Harry.

Sly Mary. By no quirk of the imagination could Harry's son be termed Funny-boy.

Of all the solemn little codgers! Done up tight as a sausage in its casing, and, come to think of it, the same color as one of those little country sausages. That's the reason, thought Harry to himself, secretly sick with the yearning to open the kit-box of his locked emotions of parenthood, I feel so darned strange about the kid. I want to eat him with griddlecakes.

Strangely, even in her weakness, Mary was aware of the ragged peaks of inhibition that were towering between Harry and this small ox-blood-colored squirm of his son.

"He won't bite, Harry."

"What makes him so solemn? Hasn't laughed once."

"Silly, how can he? Such young babies don't laugh. Besides," said Mary, and through the wintry grandeur of her face that was old enough to be grandmother to her infant, there shot the crooked look she had worn when trying to smile through her labor pain, "besides, guess he's already onto the fact that there is precious little to laugh about in being born into this old madhouse called world."

That was terrible. It hurt Harry as if her playful words had been scissors nipping into his flesh. Not much to laugh about? He'd see to it that there was! Between him and Mary they would see to it that there was! Locked-away emotions in the kit-bag began to stir. Not much fun about being born? The son of Mary and Harry was going to find what Mary called this mad-house world packed with fun.

How could the son of Mary help it? Mary, who by her very being had taught Harry to love life enough to recreate it.

The cruelest thing happened to cut short this discourse. As if at the instigation of a knife shooting through her loins, the body of Mary suddenly raised itself on the bed to the arch of a bridge, a human, writhing bridge, the cry of her pain as chaotic as the sound of gale.

"Nurse!" shouted Harry, and began to do rapid inconsequential things with her flying arms, trying to press them and the rising ridge of her body back down against the bed.

That was the beginning of something harrowing and septic and unforeseen, even by the doctor, to whom her case from the beginning had been one to handle with caution and precaution.

Immediately, even though she called for it and shouted, the child was removed from the cave of her arm, and there began, before the terrorized eyes of Harry, the process of poison through this body that had just yielded a life.

It was as if suddenly the three of them, the wintry Mary, Harry, and even the wintry babe, had been swept away from moorings and were floundering in the deep sea of Mary's delirium.

"Bring him!" she moaned, sinking her teeth deeply into her bare arm as if to allay one pain with another.

To have placed back into her arms that mite would have been to incur the danger of Mary, in her sweating agony, crushing him beneath the weight of it, and yet, each time she came rearing out of the all-too-brief soporific of a hypodermic, there came surging back against her conscious lips that cry:

"Bring him!"

Finally, while the doctor held her arms against her casting them about in her pain, and it seemed to Harry that the agony of her being denied was not an instant longer to be borne, the nurse did bring the child, placing him beside the pain-racked body.

It was only then, after Mary, eyeing her son beside her, drew back her lips once more for the suddering reiteration "No, no! Bring him. Bring *him!*" that suddenly, terribly, as through a paralysis, Harry knew.

Mary was wanting Russel.

He came, and while the hours wheeled like slowing vultures lower and lower over the body of Mary, Russel and Harry stood beside the scene of her torment, sharing the bitter common tie of impotence before the immeasurable wrath of her pain.

No longer would she submit to hypodermic. "My time is too short," she panted, her bright eyes filled with fury of the agony that was happening to her, and alert and resentful of the wariest move of doctor or nurse. "No you don't! I want to look and see and feel and be. To the last. To the very last. Put my child there. Harry, are you there? Russel, you there? So. I want to look and see and be."

But it was constantly (and to Harry, God with what brilliancy!) that her eyes returned and returned again and again to Russel. It was as if the tall reddish Russel, with his somewhat evil, lanternlike face, and the frightfully tossed dishevelment that was Mary, could not let go of gazing. Their eyes clung, even as that night of a party their fingers had clung. Their eyes clung, and in the space between him, towering over the bed, and her, lying sweating on it, one could believe their souls clung.

Suddenly, with what clarity, finality, and resignation, Harry *knew*!

Those two, whose glances were joined by a web spun from her eyes to his, had begot the child!

A bat flying in the imprisoning tower of his bursting head beat this wordless knowledge against him as she died.

Old impulses, during these months with her when the will to live had become his resurrection, might have been lying lightly, as under a silk handkerchief, so easily did they stir.

Unimpeded, blackbirds out of the brief pastry of his happiness, they were back at him again. The will not to live. Old hungers that had not to do with living on. The need now, glory be, if glory there could be in the defunct glory of his castle, not to carry on.

The will to live, after that moment of standing at that death-bedside while the truth ran in a short wave from lovers crucified by the swiftness of their last darling moments, was something he could never again recapture.

Life, after this moment beside that bed, when the swift messenger had gone running from the eyes of Mary to the wanting eyes of Russel and back again to her, would be too crammed with fiercely hurting breast, anger, sense of soiled rôle in a soiled melodrama, anger at Mary, whose eyes were like two stains that you wanted to rub clean with the moistened end of a handkerchief, and always love of Mary and nostalgia for Mary.

Then there would be left to him to conjure with, in what could only be the butt-end of a life, the terror of a timid soul like himself living with the knowledge that Russel lived.

All the books and contemplations of the earlier years, *Twenty Amusing Ways to Commit Suicide, Studies in Hari-Kari, Nooses and Their Uses,* "Xerxes did die, and so must I," books and verses which were buried in an old tin trunk upon which Mary had never even clapped eyes, ragtags of old self-devised methods that lay moldering in his mind—all these, most of them elaborate, went into immediate discard.

There was a pearl-handled thirty-two. Dead Mary's, against fear of burglary. She had kept it buried beneath the fluff of a pile of handkerchiefs in a dresser drawer. Instantaneously, standing there beside the new corpse, the lantern-faced Russel, and the babe asleep on its pillow on a chair beside the bed, the resolve, full-baked like a cake in its pan, stood in Harry's mind.

A resolve that needed only the twenty-step excursion into the room that contained the drawer that contained the thirty-two. And so it might have been, beyond the shadow of a doubt, since doubt lay not in Harry's mind, except for what the sudden awakening and puckering up of what lay on the pillow beside the new mother from whom life had flown.

It opened up, that small ox-blood-colored face, eyes, mouth, riveted its glance upon the lantern face of Russel, hanging in its strange grief above the mother, stayed in glance, almost as if contemplating that mother who would never mother him more, and puckered.

"Boy, don't you cry!" said Harry, stepping forward as if to save the sacrilege of the splash of impending noise across the just-dead body.

"Don't cry!" And on that, diverted, the little weazened face of the child lying there beside dead Mary looked up at Harry and began to laugh.

Perhaps only a biological smile of a movement of muscles over which an infant has no control, but to Harry it was the old familiar smile of a tired world responding gratefully and eagerly to Funny-face.

How beyond the shadow of a doubt that sad-eyed kid would need a Funny-face.

Existence for dead Mary's child beneath the evil shade of that hanging lantern of Russel's face would be fetid. Terrible.

Well, once again, this time finally, no way out. Long sailing ahead. Before the age of six most of them got measles, whooping cough, chicken pox. Diapers. Toy balloons which stick to ceilings. Youngsters had to have college nowadays. Kiddie cars. Creosote was good for croup.

And on Sunday mornings when Harry so liked to bathe, shave, and pedicure, a kid to be toted to the zoo, hoisted high before iron bars so that a baby giraffe might be fed peanuts.

Home, James

First Published: *Cosmopolitan*, June 1936
Reprinted: *We Are Ten*, Harper & Bros., 1937;
*A Lady's Pleasure: The Modern Woman's Treasure of Good Reading with an
Introduction by Ilka Chasse*, Penn Publishing Company, 1946

There were yellow roses in discreet profusion on Eleanor's luncheon table.

Eleanor herself was seeing to it that all twenty-eight of them formed the perfect center. There were twenty-eight because Eleanor abhorred flowers that had obviously been ordered by the dozen. She counted roses or lilies in vases as automatically as she ran her forefinger across announcement or visiting cards.

There were the twenty-eight yellow roses in not too great profusion, Venice point doilies, Wedgwood bread-and-butters, Copenhagen flat silver, rock-crystal water and wine tumblers, and mammoth burnt almonds in tiny Dresden swans on Eleanor's luncheon table, and yet she kept hovering.

Caspar the butler and Nanine the waitress, conscious of having performed their last rites in the perfection of table accouterments, stood in unease at the continued unease of the mistress of the house.

"Very good, Caspar. That is a lovely idea, Nanine—white geranium for the finger bowls!"

And yet, obviously, Eleanor was not satisfied. The last word in this table perfection needed an epilogue. She pounced upon it, finally, by breaking up the two-gardenia corsage which she wore at the écru lace collar of the black velvet which became her, and placing one at the plate of each of her guests.

They were to be two men. Her husband, who made it a rule, before diving into his philatelist's den upstairs, to lunch at home on Saturdays, and Ralph Shoapes, who, thirty-one years before, had wooed and not won Eleanor Bates, erstwhile beauty and celebrated one, of Batesville, Pennsylvania.

Yes, the town had been named after her family. Lovely Bates girls had peopled the lovely Shenandoah Valley ever since the first Quakers had found settlement there. Grant Henchman had not found it uncompetitive going, even as a young railroad magnate, when he had finally captured the youngest of the five famed Bates beauties out of the famous hotbed of loveliness.

Thirty-one years had rolled over the Bates girls. Not without exacting toll of some of their beauty. Wives, all of them, and mothers, three of them grandmothers, dominant as Bates girls were sure to be, they were scattered from New Zealand to Chicago to New York to Paris to Budapest.

People still said of them, especially of Eleanor, "She must have been a beautiful young girl!"

Ralph Shoapes had last seen her in the full flower of that beauty. Never for a moment believing that he was taking her at her word, she had waved him an impudent *congé* one afternoon from under a blossoming apple tree in the splendor of a Shenandoah Valley spring day.

In the quarter-century since she had laid eyes on him, Shoapes had married, as he had threatened her that he would, a Wyoming ranch king's daughter, who had died three years later, and he had turned traveler, lecturer, explorer. And now, out of a clear sky, he had landed back into the experience of Mrs. Grant Henchman, née Eleanor Bates.

In the ebullient daily life of Eleanor Bates Henchman there was nothing epoch-making or breaking, in the turning up of an old, old beau. Men were constantly, if facetiously, declaring a lifelong and futile passion for Eleanor. But now, suddenly, revealingly, a little frighteningly, the coming of Shoapes seemed to be translating to Eleanor how tired and deprived she was.

She was an old woman in love with life. She was an old woman in love with life but married to a man more and more occupied in withdrawing from life.

The girl who, from under the blossoms of Shenandoah Valley had literally laughed Shoapes out of her existence, now felt suddenly that although her laughter still rang, she was laughing from the teeth out.

Extraordinary how the tiredness suddenly descended upon her. Her children married and out of the nest of the spacious home, her grandchildren isolated from her by all the devices of wealth and modernity, her husband more and more withdrawing from the industrial and social arenas into the strange solitude of philately, something in the high-strung gayety of Eleanor at fifty-eight seemed to collapse in a huddle of defeat.

It seemed desperately imperative to her that Ralph Shoapes, who, thirty-one years previous, had carried out his threat to pique her by marrying a ranch king's daughter, should not return to find her in the rôle of Eleanor Henchman who bore only faint traces of having been the beauty of Shenandoah Valley days.

The lovely face of Eleanor was all written over by now with the chirography of years. There were faint folds of dried flesh beneath the écru lace and black velvet, and the erstwhile swift figure was angular now, but still slim. Yet the famous Bates-girl lust for life still raged within those lively veins. Not even Grant's more and more hermitlike withdrawal from the marts and the more ordinary pastimes of men had succeeded in subduing that. Occupied as he was with his priceless stamps, his vast library, his Great Dane dogs, it had long been Eleanor's contention that her husband not only encouraged her to fill in her time with recreations, but was even ready to "hire a beau" for her in order that he might achieve his quiet evenings at home.

Her efforts to make life as gay as she wanted it to appear had managed to fill these latter years.

"I'm married to the darlingest old thing on earth," she did sometimes contend too loudly. "Grant not only has horse sense, he's got the human sense to withdraw to the things that matter. I haven't."

Perhaps. But to Grant his withdrawal was due principally to the simple fact of tiredness. Thirty-five years of maneuvering a vast railroad enterprise through two panics, a World War, a depression, and a growing and suspicious public psychology against private ownership, to say nothing of building up a name and a family into an edifice as vast as his ambitions, had left him broken neither in body nor in spirit, but with a nostalgia for a peace which he seemed never to have known in this life.

For almost his entire sixty-eight years the world had been too much with him. That Eleanor could not enter with him into the shaded places of the more twilit recesses of the spirit was not a matter for regret. The fact that she could not, seemed to him as natural as the sound of her laughter or the ebullience of her spirit.

As a matter of fact, he liked her zany kind of Bates lustiness, which for thirty-one years had filled his life and his household. It meant a ceaseless sort of pressure—five brothers-in-law married to five Bates sisters agreed to that—but it was perpetual adventure. What Grant needed was rest not from Eleanor, but from the world of which she was so vitally—almost, he might say, so terribly—a part.

Something within him sighed out of relief when her evenings were successfully disposed of; when their box at the opera had been successfully filled; when he could count on Eleanor being happily and excitingly provided for. She was his loan exhibit, to be cheerfully shared with the friends all too ready to clamor for the company of his high-spirited wife.

He liked his evenings to be devoid of her yet at the same time crammed with everything pertaining to her presence except her darling demanding self.

The coming of Shoapes was just the turning up of another of the old beaux with which the past of every one of the Bates sisters had been crowded.

Grant did wish, however, that he had not turned up for Saturday lunch, his one week day when he was at home for that occasion. But Shoapes was sailing on an afternoon boat, and his stop-over in New York was just long enough to admit of the luncheon with Eleanor.

Eleanor—how passionately, how silently—echoed that silent wish of her husband's. She did not know quite why. Dear knows, Grant was sure to disappear, like thin smoke, no sooner lunch was finished. There would be plenty of time alone with Shoapes up to his sailing hour. She wanted that time alone. For the life of her she knew not why—except—"Well," she cried to herself in a petulance not usual to her, "why does any woman with the natural impulse to charm and be charmed—want—well just—*want*—once in a while."

Yes, Eleanor would be in high nervous form, Grant could be sure of that. Apparently she had once been engaged to this fellow, or about to be. They turned up with less frequency nowadays, old beaux of Eleanor's.

There were seventeen roses in the alabaster vase in the entrance hall. It invariably meant an Eleanor in high and nervous expectancy when there were about seventeen roses in the alabaster urn in the entrance hall.

Then, too, when Grant entered the house for lunch he could smell over and above the spiced sweetness of roses, her most expensive perfume. Eleanor was doing herself proud for her old-beau explorer.

Eleanor and her guest were already in the drawing-room on the second floor, and the high laughter of Eleanor—not, by Jove, the laughter of a woman almost sixty, but the jerky young laughter of an adolescent—filled the halls.

Jove, it was extraordinary! She was more of a houseful than all of their grandchildren put together. She was gayer than a Maypole. Of all the Bates sisters she was the gayest!

"Grant, that you? Bring yourself right up here and meet my old beau, Ralph Shoapes."

Shoapes was big and gray, and, Grant thought, no little dull. He wished to heaven Eleanor would stop throwing her eyes. Throwing? Hurling was more like it. They were such sweet blue pools of eyes when quiet. But Shoapes seemed to find her amusing that way, and all through Eleanor's delicious, planned luncheon he matched his laughter to hers.

Lord, first chance he got, Grant must tell Eleanor to cut out being cute. He had never noticed it before, but her laughter rose to squeals. It became incessant. It became, well, if you had to admit it, high, excessive, constant. It became, to say the least, a little embarrassing.

Dear girl, he was too dull for her. He knew that. Let her spill over into fun. But why with a ponderous ass like Shoapes?

Ecuador—Ganges—ivory—apes—peacocks—Mongolian desert. Remember this. Recall that. "Remember, Ralph, the night we took the buggy ride to

Philadelphia? That was before I had even met Grant. . . . Oh, Shoapy, tell Grant about the afternoon you almost talked me into eloping with you to Germantown—make my husband jealous. . . . Let me pin your gardenia on you, Shoapy. Grant won't wear his. Never does. Hold still! There is your gardenia. For remembrance!"

"And adoration," said Shoapes. "I'm going to wear it and keep it fresh for every day of the voyage, and then press it so they can bury it with me."

"Hear that, Grant! There's romance in them thar Shoapes bones!"

"Idiot," Grant wanted to whisper to her, "save your ammunition for someone not so dull and so like an ass." But nevertheless it pleased even while in some inexplicable way it wounded him to see Eleanor so relentlessly gay.

Any husband, not only grave, square-faced, white-haired Grant, would have seemed a dull and heavy contraption in her blithe presence. If people said—and they did—"Dear Eleanor, so gay in spite of a husband turning peculiar and hermitlike in his old age," they would have said the equivalent of whomsoever she might have married.

No man married to a Bates girl was ever a match for her splendor.

The five brothers-in-law had formed an international correspondence club.

On the occasion of the birth, in New Zealand, of the Moapes twins, Sir John Moapes, the clever husband of Diana Bates, had written, and sent carbon copies to his brothers-in-law, a poem beginning,

We are the husbands of the five Miss Bates,

Thereupon becoming the Five Effaced.

Before the particular Miss Bates who was married to Grant Henchman, you could see the lines of delighted amusement begin to break out all over Shoapes' well-preserved face. Here was a man younger than Grant, but still well along in his sixties, with the complacency of one accustomed to the adulation of women, and yet whose delight in Eleanor's irrepressible spirits was obvious as a boy's.

What a woman!

Whatever Shoapes' status, or lack of it, with scientific and learned societies, his years of travel in Tibet, Indo-China, and Mongolia, and his guest membership in a financial and widely advertised Social-Register antarctic expedition had rated him high with women's clubs and study groups. If he had remained out of the urban centers, such as New York, Boston, Chicago, there were his own reasons for that. All of this, however, Eleanor had resolved to correct.

"Why have you been hiding yourself all these years in the small towns?"

"Oh, universities have been my specialty for so long, and the smaller towns surrounding them seem to clamor—"

"Well, I'm going to do something about all that. Us city girls have read a book, too. You hurry yourself back from running across those Siberian steppes or whatever it is Siberians run over, and I'm going to see that you lecture here before the Cosmopolite Club. I declare, I don't know how we've let this good-looking lecturer-explorer escape all these years, do you, Grant?"

If Grant did, he was not the man to say so.

That's the trouble with Grant, she told herself angrily, as her laughter rushed to cover up his silence. She was always rushing in to cover up his silences or see to it that he was properly amiable, considerate, or attentive to some purely social remark.

Why, oh, why had Ralph happened to be sailing on a Saturday, of all days! With Grant present, she could not hope to be at her best. Not that there was any reason—any particular reason why Grant should not be present. What did she hope for alone with Ralph?

In any event, something in Grant's very propinquity often made her feel ridiculous. Why, even thinking of him up there among his books, before his great Gothic fireplace, Great Danes at his feet, volumes at his elbows, made her, frittering downstairs over bridge or cocktails, feel a little absurd.

Well, he wasn't going to kill her joy today. Life was running. Life was fleeting. Unless she saw to it for herself, she would soon be an old woman. As a matter of fact, she was that already, unless she refused to see it that way. A mother of grown children. A mother of the mothers of children. A grandmother. An old wife of an old man. Not while Bates blood flowed in her veins! Bates girls simply did not grow old. There were five of them strewn over the face of the globe, all of them with vitality that shamed their husbands.

The brothers-in-law had once agreed to form a society for the protection of husbands from Bates wives. She told the story, at luncheon, of Sir John Moapes organizing his brothers-in-law. Too gayly.

Poor kid, thought Grant. I'm going to play with her more.

It pained him to see Shoapes bend to kiss the gardenia she had pinned to his lapel, and Eleanor's eyes flutter with a coquetry her face had somehow outgrown. Something akin to embarrassment mingled with his varied sensations during that lunch.

Nothing would do, when it became apparent that if Shoapes was to stop off at his hotel for luggage, he must leave at once, but that the family motor should be sent for and Eleanor herself escort him to the boat.

"Oh, but I daren't allow you to do all that, Eleanor! Of course, it would be gloriously fine for me, but—"

"Perhaps Shoapes has other plans, dear."

There went Grant again, being a ton of coal. Oh, oh, oh, when she had maneuvered so for this, what with it being a Saturday luncheon and Grant home! Oh, oh, oh, she wanted not to cry, but there was a tingling behind her eyes. She wanted that trip to the boat—alone with Ralph. That was asking little enough—of life—of fun—of she knew not what. What a pudgy thing to say—"Perhaps, dear, he has other plans"!

"Other plans! I dare him to have other plans when his old sweetheart wants to take him to the boat."

"Wish I did have, for the joy of chucking them."

If he lived to be a million, Grant could never deliver anything pat like that!

"You hear, Grant! You had better think yourself up a talent for pretty speeches, if you don't want competition."

Poor sweet, he must.

The car was announced and Eleanor appeared, wrapped in gray squirrel that matched her pale hair and became her blue eyes, and suddenly Grant announced that he was going too. Grant, who, like clockwork, could be counted on to disappear of a Saturday afternoon into his philatelic isolation from which not a crowbar could budge him! Grant, who had not ventured into a crowd for years!

"Why!" The soft gasp of Eleanor went up like a small explosion. "Why— why, Grant Henchman! Well of all things—why—"

She mustn't cry. She mustn't cry. She must not. She did not, blinking hard with her blue eyes.

Sweet foolish mother of the mothers of his grandchildren. He was going along.

"Ralph, isn't it just like a husband to spoil our nice little old-home week this way? Honestly, I think he's jealous. Are you jealous, honey? I think I feel a thrill. Grant's jealous!"

Sweet foolish mother of the mothers of his grandchildren.

"It hasn't been so bad, seeing me after all these years—now has it, Ralph. Or do you find me a croaking old woman?"

"Old woman! You're wonderful! You make me feel half my age!"

"Neither do I find you anything but what I wanted to find. Honestly, honey, if my darling old philatelist here hadn't taken it into his head to come along, we might have got young and foolish!"

God, he must play with her more!

It was on the drive home, after the goodbyes had been said, that the nervous hysteria pushing against the restraint of Eleanor suddenly got through.

"Grant, why did you come along!"

"Why not? Can't a man take an outing?"

"Not you. That's not why you came. Grant, *you're jealous!*"

Beneath her mounting hysteria, something like a sweet sort of anguish lit her eyes. "Are you jealous, Grant?"

"Maybe."

"No, I know you too well. You're too sure. Not too sure perhaps, but too complacent. Tell me Grant, why did you come along? Because you didn't trust me? Or in order to spoil what might have been just a wee moment of silly, harmless, romantic—"

"Eleanor!"

"Then why?"

"Must you know?"

"Yes, I must. I can't bear being made to feel so ridiculous—so second rate. Why did you come?"

"Don't make me—tell you."

"I will! I let you live your own life—up there among your books and stamps and silence. I try to eke out my gayety alone. I don't make you as ridiculous in your own eyes as you make me in mine. Why need you—why did you come—"

"Sweetheart, I don't want to—go into that—"

"Why did you come!"

"Eleanor, this fellow—he's a taker, not a giver. I didn't want you to be disappointed on this drive alone with him. Nothing was going to happen."

"You—"

"I wanted you always to think it was I who stood between you and anything happening. It would have made it easier. You see, I am so sure, sweetheart, that nothing was going to happen, and so I came along to spare your ever knowing and now you've spoiled it all."

"You—knew—that—nothing—was—going—to—happen—to—an—old—woman."

"Sweet, sweet, not exactly that, except that it wasn't even going to occur to Shoapes to flirt. It seemed sort of kinder for me to come."

She knew that if he touched her or put out a protective hand to match the protective something in his voice, she was going to cry terribly, right there in the car. She did not want to cry in the car. James, the chauffeur, was such a restrained chauffeur. The shape of his back was the most restrained shape-of-a-back conceivable. She dared not cry. Blessedly, Grant made not so much as a gesture toward matching the protective in his voice.

Suddenly, to lessen the strain of a moment too tender almost to be borne, they leaned forward as if to relieve it by the mundane gesture of reaching to pick something off the floor.

Idiotically, their heads met and bumped.

What they had reached for was a white gardenia, fallen from the lapel of the late Mr. Shoapes, lying there crushed and blackened in a corner of the car.

Bumping, their heads made a resounding whack. Laughing, they rocked in one another's arms, thus saving themselves before the restrained back of James, the chauffeur.

The Feminist Press at the City University of New York is a nonprofit literary and educational institution dedicated to publishing work by and about women. Our existence is grounded in the knowledge that women's writing has often been absent or underrepresented on bookstore and library shelves and in educational curricula—and that such absences contribute, in turn, to the exclusion of women from the literary canon, from the historical record, and from the public discourse.

The Feminist Press was founded in 1970. In its early decades, the Feminist Press launched the contemporary rediscovery of "lost" American women writers, and went on to diversify its list by publishing significant works by American women writers of color. More recently, the Press's publishing program has focused on international women writers, who remain far less likely to be translated than male writers, and on nonfiction works that explore issues affecting the lives of women around the world.

Founded in an activist spirit, the Feminist Press is currently undertaking initiatives that will bring its books and educational resources to under-served populations, including community colleges, public high schools and middle schools, literacy and ESL programs, and prison education programs. As we move forward into the twenty-first century, we continue to expand our work to respond to women's silences wherever they are found.

Many of our readers support the Press with their memberships, which are tax-deductible. Members receive numerous benefits, including complimentary publications, discounts on all purchases from our catalog or web site, pre-publication notification of new books and notice of special sales, invitations to special events, and a subscription to our email newsletter, *Women's Words: News from the Feminist Press*. For more information about membership and events, and for a complete catalog of the Press's 250 books, please refer to our web site: www.feministpress.org.